Beyond the Badge: Crew

Blue Avengers MC
Book 5

Jeanne St. James

Jeanne
ST. JAMES

————

Credits:
Photographer/Cover Artist: Golden Czermak at FuriousFotog
Cover Model: Lovett Taylor
Editor: Proofreading by the Page
Beta Readers: Alex Swab and Sharon Abrams
Logo: Jennifer Edwards

————

www.jeannestjames.com

Sign up for my newsletter for insider information, author news, and new releases:
www.jeannestjames.com/newslettersignup

————

————

————

Keep an eye on her website at http://www.jeannestjames.com/or sign up for her newsletter to learn about her upcoming releases: http://www.jeannestjames.com/newslettersignup

Blue Avengers MC Series

Beyond the Badge: Fletch (Book 1)
Beyond the Badge: Finn (Book 2)
Beyond the Badge: Decker (Book 3)
Beyond the Badge: Rez (Book 4)
Beyond the Badge Crew (Book 5)
Beyond the Badge: Nox (Book 6)

Glossary of Terms

LEO - Liquor Enforcement Officer and/or Law Enforcement Officer (used for both)

PSP - Pennsylvania State Police

The Plant - A place away from stations/barracks/etc. for law enforcement/a task force to conduct clandestine criminal investigations.

Plant Manager - Person in charge of wiretapping/transcribing calls

MC Chapter - The national club with a national exec committee (President, VP, etc.); Ex: Deadly Demons MC

MC Charter - Each charter is run independently, does not answer to a mother charter or a national chapter; Example: Blue Avengers MC

Sled - slang for motorcycle

TFO - Task Force Officer

UC/UCO - Undercover Agent/Officer

RICO - Racketeer Influenced and Corrupt Organizations Act

Re-upping - To refill one's drug stash

Trap house - A residence used in the illegal drug trade. Drug houses shelter drug users and provide a place for drug dealers to supply them.

Character List

Timothy Frasier - Liquor Enforcement Officer, PA State Police

Roland North - Lieutenant, Pittsburgh PD

Other Tri-State Drug Task Force Members:

Luke Rodgers - DEA Special Agent

Luis Torres - DEA Special Agent, Plant Manager

Ken Proctor - Officer, Uniontown PD

Carl Powers - Trooper, PA State Police

Sam Kruger - Corporal, Greensburg PD

Warren Reynolds - Corporal, PA State Police

Don Mullins - Narcotic Detective, Pittsburgh PD

Nova Wilder – FBI Special Agent, Organized Crime Division

Camila Cabrera - DEA special agent

Others:

Sapphire Loukanis- Current dancer/former hostess at The Peach Pit

Sloane Parrish - Legal assistant, Decker's woman

Melina Jensen (Mel) - Finn's fiancée, former manager at The Peach Pit

Bella - DAMC, Axel's wife

Valerie Decker (Val) - Decker's daughter aka Valee Girl

Viper - Deadly Demons president

Screw - Deadly Demons VP

Wolf - Head of the Demons Uniontown Chapter

Bulldog - Manager of Hawg Wild Saloon; Demons SoA

T-Bone - Deadly Demons prospect

Sadie Parrish - Sloane's younger sister
Saint - Deadly Demon in charge of The Peach Pit
Clark - Monty's boyfriend

Chapter One

His GIRL's throaty rumble filled his ears and got his pulse pounding.

It had been a while since she'd been between his legs. He'd missed straddling her. Riding her hard. Pushing her to her limits.

She had it all. Power, gorgeous lines and ball-tightening speed.

Some men his age went out and bought a Corvette. Some, like him, preferred a ride that would spike his blood pressure and make him feel alive. One that hugged curves taken at high speeds.

His ex, Sasha, might have won his prized Harley in the divorce, but he won his freedom.

The second the ink was dry on the divorce papers, he took the money he had left, rushed down to the local Harley-Davidson dealership and signed his name again. This time on a pink slip for something that would help him get over that painful mess.

A Harley-Davidson FXDR 114 with a custom black and

silver paint job to match his salt-and-pepper hair. He also added a custom seat so he could take one of the kids for a spin.

Not that they clamored to ride with dear old dad.

But if they ever did...

His girl, aptly named Silver Foxy, had a top speed of 160 mph and was capable of going zero-to-sixty in less than three seconds flat.

Not that he'd tested it.

At least not that often.

He'd lucked out. Today had been the perfect weather to take a long scenic ride to the DEA offices outside of Pittsburgh, since he'd been jonesing to get his girl out of the garage once winter decided to fuck off. He only hoped it stayed away, but in early April the weather could go either way.

Boiling hot one day, snowstorm the next.

Mother Nature was so unpredictable, she must've bought meth from the Demons.

Hopefully with spring arriving, Finn, as the BAMC road captain, would start scheduling monthly or bi-weekly runs. Crew was ready to take to the open road with his brothers.

It would also be good for Nox to get out on his bike, too. That was after they cornered him first for the intervention Axel Jamison had scheduled. Finding the time to get almost all the BAMC members together had been tough since everyone worked different hours and shifts.

But to Jamison—and the rest of them—doing the intervention was priority since Nox needed a little tough love right now and no one was better to do it than his fellow Blue Avengers who considered him family.

Crew found a parking spot occupied with another motorcycle and crab-walked Foxy in reverse next to it before shutting her down.

After sliding off his half-helmet, he hooked it over one side of the handlebars, scraped his fingers through his short hair and threw his leg over. Once his feet were on solid ground, he reached for the sky and arched his back in an attempt to loosen his tight muscles, all while groaning.

Even though he was only in his early forties, that ride alone left him sore and aching. An unnecessary reminder that getting old sucked.

Twenty years ago, he could've done backflips all the way into the DEA field office. Today, there might be a bit of a hitch in his step.

Damn, his bladder was also reminding him that it no longer liked to be full.

He hoofed it toward the building so he could take care of his personal business before heading to his superior's office to deal with official Tri-State Federal Drug Task Force business.

As he reached to pull open the reflective-glass door, it swung outward, and a whirlwind slammed right into him. Even though the woman was petite and about a foot shorter than him, the impact still knocked him back a step before he got his feet back under him and grabbed her by the elbow to set her straight, too.

"Jesus, watch where you're going!"

Her dark brown eyes narrowed on him and she pulled her elbow from his grip. "I could tell you the same."

She checked him out as he did the same.

Her well-fitted gray dress pants with a matching blazer emphasized her slender frame. Under the jacket was a lapel-collared white shirt that contrasted with her tawny complexion that reminded him of Rez's. That meant she was either really into tanning or her skin tone came naturally.

"You were running out of there like your ass is on fire. You need to pay attention."

"I could tell you the same."

Her dark brown, maybe even black, hair was pulled tight into a neat bun, and she wore just enough makeup to emphasize her natural beauty.

"The glass is reflective. I couldn't see you coming," he explained.

"I could tell you the same."

Holy fuck, was that the only response she knew?

"I accept your apology," he said dryly.

One of her dark eyebrows lifted. "I didn't give you one since you ran into me."

From what he could tell, she wasn't in her early twenties, but she also wasn't out of that decade, either. And for him, she was too young whether she was twenty-one or twenty-nine despite being dick-hardening hot.

"Clearly you're wrong."

Her lips curved the slightest bit and her eyes held a gleam he didn't like. "I could tell you the same."

Holy fuck. "I've got a meeting to get to." He raised his palm as her mouth opened. "Don't even." He noticed she wasn't wearing any ID, a requirement to be in the building. "Are you supposed to be here?"

That gleam turned into a sparkle that he *really* didn't like. "Are you?"

He set his jaw. "Do you even work for the agency?"

"Do you?"

He was done with this ridiculous conversation that wasn't even a conversation. He didn't know what the fuck it was. Annoying, that was what it was. And a waste of his time. "I actually have important business here."

She shrugged her narrow shoulders. "So do I."

He doubted that. "Then go do it."

Her eyebrows shot up and any amusement in her eyes disappeared. "I don't need your permission." As she pushed past him and booked it toward the parking lot, she called out over her shoulder, "It was not nice to meet you!"

"I could say the same to you!" he yelled back with a shake of his head.

He needed to get inside so he wasn't late but, damn, he couldn't resist watching her go.

He'd hit that.

If she wasn't so damn young.

And he had a roll of duct tape on hand to seal shut that smart mouth.

He wished good luck to the poor fucker who had to deal with her ass. They'd need it.

Thank fuck it wasn't him.

———

"Do I get to pick Butler's replacement? Is that why I'm here? To give me some options?"

For fuck's sake, say yes. Don't stick me with someone I don't want and knock my well-oiled team out of whack.

Unfortunately, PA State Police Corporal Ian Butler had to bow out from the task force. His wife was experiencing a difficult pregnancy and was bedridden until she delivered. That meant Butler was needed at home more than ever, both to tend to her, as well as their two other young children. The task force consumed more time than he could currently give.

It sucked but Crew understood that family came first. However, that left him a team member short. The whole reason he sat on the other side of the desk belonging to the supervising special agent in charge of group one's investigation.

And the man Crew reported to.

"No," Bob Williams answered.

"I picked the rest of the team."

"And I picked your newest member."

Crew stared across the desk, not liking Williams' tone. It made the fine hairs on the back of his neck rise. The SSA was normally an easy-going guy but something was up. "Do I know him?"

"No."

That meant this agent was most likely brought in from another field office. "Where's he from, or is he new to the organization?"

"She's newer but not quite wet behind the ears new."

She? He had to choke that down because it almost burst free from his lips and that would not go over well.

He had no problem with women in law enforcement.

None.

Not even a little bit.

He cleared his throat. "How new?"

"She graduated in the top one percent of her class."

"That means nothing." And didn't answer his question.

"To you, maybe, since you weren't in that top one percent."

Damn. "I did well in the academy." Graduating was all that mattered, not being an ass-kisser.

"'Well' is a subjective term."

Jesus. Williams was out for blood today. "When did she graduate?"

"A year ago. She has more grit and determination than a lot of our senior agents."

Had he walked into a massacre without a bullet-proof

vest? Crew had enough gaping wounds now that he was beginning to bleed out. "That's because she's fresh and determined to make the world a better place. Once she learns that's an almost impossible battle to win, she'll be as tarnished as the rest of us."

"How about letting her keep that enthusiasm for a while? You could take her under your wing. I see great things in her future and believe she'll be an asset to the agency, as well as your task force."

"How old is she?" If she graduated the academy only a year ago, she could be as young as twenty-one. A complete baby needing a whole lot of hand-holding. Right now, he didn't have to micro-manage his team.

He also didn't want to.

"She's young, so I think she would do well dealing with the Demons."

Dread filled his chest. "She can't go undercover. They're," he bit back an F-bomb, "bikers!"

Williams leaned back in his leather office chair. "They don't have women hanging around their organization?"

Organization? Williams made them sound like a legit business.

"Not without putting out. Hang-arounds and sweet butts don't get the pleasure of spending time with those lovely gentlemen without paying a price. I doubt she wants to bend over for a bunch of outlaw bikers. And I'm not talking only one." Crew shrugged. "Unless she tries to become an ol' lady. Even if she does that, do you want her having sex with even one of them?"

The reality was, no biker was taking an ol' lady who didn't put out. It wasn't romantic sex, either. Sometimes it was rough, degrading and bordered on abusive.

He'd seen plenty of it on the camera feeds. None of it was

hot and all of it was stomach-churning. Sex to the Deadly Demons wasn't an intimate connection, it was solely for busting a nut.

"No. Find something else for her to do, then. She'll be an asset to your team no matter what task she's assigned."

For fuck's sake. He'd preferred not to assign her anything at all. They were better off being one member short. "Why are you pushing this?"

"Because you're down a team member and she'd be perfect for it."

Perfect was a subjective term. "No."

Williams' eyebrows smashed together. "No what?"

"We're a cohesive team. We'll be fine with fourteen members."

"Are you refusing an order? Do I need to remind you that doing so is insubordination?"

Shit. "I haven't heard an order yet."

Williams got to his feet, picked up a paper off his desk and sailed it toward Crew. "Here's the official order."

It fluttered onto his lap.

Fuck! Crew grabbed the memo, folded it up and stuffed it into his back pocket without even reading it. "How soon does she start?"

Williams' rounded his desk, opened his office door and poked his head out, calling, "Cabrera."

Cabrera? Why did that last name sound familiar?

And Crew hadn't noticed anyone sitting outside Williams' office when he entered, except for the man's executive assistant.

Should he stay sitting? Stand? He had no fucking clue what was expected of him. With a grumble, he pushed to his feet and turned to see a woman entering the office, giving Williams a chin lift as she did so.

Not *a* woman, *the* woman.

Son of a fucking bitch.

Her heart-stopping dark eyes were laser-focused on him. Crew caught the slightest crinkle at the corners and a twitch of her lips before her expression turned blank.

No fucking way.

"Colin Crew is the group one leader of the Tri-State Federal Task Force that I told you about. You'll be reporting directly to him."

She stepped closer and jutted out her hand.

He stared at it for a second noticing what he hadn't earlier—her very subtle manicure and ringless fingers—before letting his gaze slide back up to her face. But on that trip, he noticed she now wore an ID badge around her neck.

She had probably forgot it in her car.

For fuck's sake.

"Camila Cabrera," she introduced herself, then tipped her head when he still hadn't shaken her hand. "Do you prefer Colin, Crew... or Sir?"

He blinked. *What?*

He opened his mouth, then shut it to clear his throat as he grabbed her hand, squeezing it more firmly than he normally would while shaking it. He might as well establish his dominance from the start because he had a feeling after their exchange outside, she'd be challenging his leadership.

At every fucking turn.

When she tried to pull her hand from his, he held it for a few seconds longer before finally releasing it. "Crew works. You? Camila or Cabrera?"

She shrugged. "No one calls me Camila except my grandparents. I respond to Cam, Cami or Cabrera. Or even C.C. That's what my daddy calls me."

"Good to know," he practically wheezed, having a hard time breathing after hearing that last part.

Not only did her last name sound familiar, so did the nickname C.C. Even so, his brain was having trouble placing her.

"Well, I look forward to working with you and your team," she said, a sparkle dancing in her dark eyes.

Jesus fuck, she was going to be trouble. She was going to overturn the fucking apple cart. He just knew it.

He opened his mouth to tell Williams that he wanted someone else to take Butler's place. Anyone but the woman in front of him.

But just as the words were starting to form, Cabrera turned to the supervising special agent to ask, "When do I start?"

"Today."

Today? He didn't even get a fucking minute to come to terms with this whole thing? To prepare his team?

"All right, I have another meeting in five minutes. I just wanted to introduce you two." He glanced at Cabrera. "Come to me with any problems."

Go to him with any problems? What the fuck did that mean?

"Will do, sir," was her answer. She turned to Crew. "Walk me out?"

Hell no. His eyes met Williams' and he swallowed that answer. "Sure." He waved a hand toward the open office door, and she stepped through it.

He followed her to the elevator. They said nothing while waiting for the car to arrive and once inside, both stared at the closed doors for the time it took them to reach the ground floor.

They said nothing as they stepped outside into the bright

sunlight. Wincing, he pulled the sunglasses from where he had them hooked in his shirt's neckline and slipped them over his eyes.

If there was a reason she wanted him to walk her out, she sure was keeping it close to the vest.

"Well…" he started, ready to get the fuck out of there.

"I bet you know my father. You seem to be about his age."

There was no fucking way he was her father's age. Unless she was conceived when her father wasn't a man yet but still a boy.

He snapped his gaping mouth shut. "Who's your father?"

"Williams didn't tell you?"

Like earlier, he didn't like the direction of this conversation, either. Not a fucking bit. "Should he have?"

"I figured that's why you don't look very happy about me joining your task force. Not because of our earlier run-in."

"I—" *didn't have a choice, that's why I'm not happy.* Crew shook his head. Telling her that he was forced to accept her as a team member wouldn't make things any easier for either of them. He didn't have any choice but to accept the inevitable. "No, apparently he didn't feel the need to share that information with me. Do you want to share it, instead?"

"My father knows you."

"He does?" He rubbed his forehead as if that would jumpstart his memory. "Is his last name Cabrera?"

"It is. Normally I'd use my mother's last name, but we decided to follow the American tradition of using my father's last name, instead."

He had plenty of questions about that little tidbit of info but right now he was more interested in who her father was, not why she was using his last name, a normal tradition for people living in the U.S.

For fuck's sake, should he even care why?

"I'm pretty sure you worked together."

"We did?" He wracked his brain trying to remember a fellow DEA agent with the same last name.

"I think it was about eighteen years ago. Luis Cabrera. Remember him?"

Oh fuck.

Crew almost swallowed his tongue and a sharp pain shot through his chest.

How the fuck could he forget? Not the part about working with him—because they did work a case together—but the most important part. Luis Cabrera was now the agency's principal deputy administrator.

And that was a huge fucking deal.

"You're right. I know your father. But you're also wrong. I'm not his age."

A small smile curved her lips. "*Hmm.*" She took her time taking in his salt-and-pepper hair and beard. "You look like it."

Jesus Christ. "I went through a rough divorce. Gotta go." He began hoofing it away from the building and out to the parking lot.

She followed him, somehow managing to stay close on his heels even with her much shorter legs. "I heard your divorce was ugly, but wasn't it years ago? You haven't recovered yet? Are you still pining away for your ex?"

"I'm already regretting this," he muttered, lengthening his strides, hoping to leave her in the dust. "I grayed early," he tossed over his shoulder.

"From the divorce?"

"From pain in the ass women in general." And she certainly qualified as one of those.

Luckily he had parked in a visitor spot near the building.

That meant he could escape more quickly. He stopped next to his girl and grabbed his helmet.

It hit him then. Who she really was. Like a two-by-four across his forehead.

His chest tightened painfully, and he spun on her. "I not only remember your father, I remember you." That might have sounded like an accusation, but he didn't give a shit.

Oh yeah, he remembered her now.

At the time he met her, she'd been an outgoing, mouthy ten-year-old. Also, at the time, she was cute. With pigtails.

The woman before him was no longer cute. And she no longer had pigtails.

He rubbed at the burn growing in his chest.

Her eyebrows rose when she asked, "We've actually met before?"

Her attempt at sounding clueless was a joke.

One he didn't find funny.

"*Mmm.*" And now, even though she was a damn adult, he felt like a dirty old man for checking her out earlier.

If she was ten at the time—he did a quick figuring in his head—she now had to be twenty-eight or close to it.

Old enough, but also *so very not*.

He hoped he had masked the panic from his face well enough. He slammed the brakes on his spinning brain. "How's your father?"

"Busy. But he always makes time for me and I'm sure he'll be interested in hearing that I'll be working with someone he knew and worked with personally."

Just fucking great.

One wrong move and she could run to her father. A man who led an agency consisting of thousands of special agents and intelligence analysts across both the United States and the world.

That man.

A man who could quickly put Crew's balls in a vice and crush them.

Williams fucked him and not in a way Crew normally enjoyed. And that asshole probably knew all of the info Crew only learned and decided to keep it to himself.

He swung a leg over his girl and settled on the seat.

"That's your ride?"

He glanced over to see Cabrera still standing a few feet away. "Yeah."

"Pretty risky. I'd expect someone in your age bracket to ride a trike instead. No problems with your balance?"

Christ. He was only forty-three! Just a distinguished forty-three. "No walker or cane needed yet."

"Impressive. Nothing like holding onto your youth by your fingernails."

"Definitely going to regret this," he grumbled under his breath.

"The day's only half over. What do you want me to do for the rest of it, boss?"

For fuck's sake. "Do you have the address for the plant?"

"I do. Williams gave it to me when he gave me my assignment."

"Report there at 0800 sharp tomorrow morning. Do you live close, or are you going to need to find a place nearby?"

"Since I just transferred from Virginia, the agency set me up at the SpringHill Suites temporarily."

"Where?"

"Near here."

Crew shook his head. "We're based out of Rockvale. I suggest finding a place closer."

"Have any suggestions?"

He strapped on his brain bucket and made sure it was

secure. "Nope. Your first assignment is to figure it out." He pushed the starter and somehow managed to avoid a sneer when he said, "Welcome to the team."

He revved the bike, causing Foxy's engine to roar loudly enough to drown out her answer. With a two-finger salute, he put it in gear and gunned it, leaving her standing in his dust.

Chapter Two

CAMI DOUBLE-CHECKED her GPS to make sure she was in the right spot. At first glance it appeared to be an abandoned building amongst many others in an industrial area of Rockvale. Or more accurately, an area that most industries had deserted years ago.

At this time in the morning, anywhere else would be considered rush hour with everyone heading to work. Here, she hadn't seen one vehicle on the streets yet. No cars were parked in front of the brick building, either.

She glanced at the time on the dashboard. 7:56. There was no way she was too early. Senior Special Agent Colin Crew had told her "0800 sharp."

The six-foot wood privacy fence jutting out from the left corner of the building looked on the newer side. Unlike the building itself. The boarded-up front entrance was tagged in graffiti. Neither the protective plywood nor the tagging appeared fresh. Even the windows on the second and third floor were covered.

"What the hell?" she murmured as she stared through her Audi's windshield.

This was the address Williams gave her for the task force's plant. She should've gotten Crew's phone number before he took off on his damn bike, leaving her in a cloud of exhaust fumes.

She had to admit, the silver fox looked damn good on that Harley. And the deep rumble of the bike had also done a thing or two to her.

However, just because the man was sex on a stick didn't mean she would go gaga over him. She was no longer bright-eyed and innocent, and easily swayed by appearances. She learned quickly that looks could be deceiving and the man could be rotten at his core.

Plus, he'd been pretty damn rude and condescending. To her, that was a huge turn-off.

Luckily, she was an expert at fighting fire with fire.

She sighed and turned her attention back to the building. If this was the correct address, it had to be a false front. A way to disguise that it housed a federal drug task force.

That would make sense. And was smart to boot.

Putting her RS Q8 into gear, she decided to check for an entrance at the rear of the building.

After turning the corner, she discovered an alley and as she drove down it, saw that the privacy fence continued along the side and the back of the building. But there was a gate wide enough for vehicles and since that gate was open, she pulled in.

And found where the task force parked.

In one of those parking spots was a tall man with short salt-and-pepper hair and a well-maintained matching beard. His ass was perched sideways on the seat of his bike as he leaned back and waited with his ankles and arms crossed, causing his shirt to pull tight over his broad shoulders. His stunning gray eyes, hidden behind mirrored sunglasses, were turned in her direction.

He'd been waiting for her.

No surprise.

He was most likely hoping she'd be late. It would give him one more excuse to be annoyed at her for being added without his approval to his task force.

As soon as she parked, he pushed to his feet and went to close and lock the gate.

She scanned the rear of the property. Another smaller fenced area was butted up against the back of the building, reminding her of an enclosed patio area. The windows on the second floor were uncovered but the ones on the third were boarded up like the front.

Interesting.

His long denim-covered legs easily ate up the distance between them as she exited her car.

"Daddy buy you this?"

Here we go...

He wasn't happy that he got stuck with her for whatever reason and was going to take that displeasure out on her, whether she deserved it or not.

Was the reason because she was a female? Young? Her father's daughter?

That was okay. She not only loved a challenge, she was good with de-cocking cocky. While fun for her, it wasn't always so fun for the one getting his ass handed to him. Doing some time in the Navy made her a pro.

"Why would you think that?"

"Most people in their twenties can't afford a ride like this."

That might be true, but in her case, it was not. "It's been a while since you've been in your twenties, so you might not be up to date on what twenty-somethings can and cannot afford."

With his hands on his hips, he slowly circled her car, taking his time to check it out. "Not an Audi fan."

"No? Then don't buy one. I bet it would blow the doors off of that." She jerked her chin toward his bike.

He lifted his gaze to her. "I have concerns with you being on my team if you think my Harley has doors to be blown off."

"It's a figure of speech."

He went back to circling her Audi. "What's the horsepower?"

He thought he would stump her. That she was simply a girl who liked pretty cars and didn't know what was under the hood.

He'd be wrong. She picked this vehicle for a reason.

"591."

His eyebrows rose just slightly above his sunglasses as he continued around her vehicle, acting as if her form of transportation needed to pass inspection and not her.

She decided to hit him with a couple more facts. "It has the capability of going zero-to-sixty in 3.2 seconds and tops out at 190 miles per hour."

His step stuttered. "Damn," he said under his breath.

"Like I said, it would blow your bike's doors off. *If* it had doors."

"Not off the line, it wouldn't. But when it came to distance, you'd be correct. My bike's top speed is 160. But anyone doing 160 while on two wheels on Pennsylvania roads has a death wish."

"They don't call it Pot Hole Pennsylvania for nothing."

His eyes would've locked with hers if he wasn't wearing

those mirrored sunglasses. Funny, most of the assholes she knew preferred mirrored sunglasses. They thought it gave them some sort of edge. All it did was make douchebags easily identifiable.

"Never heard it called that but even so, it's painfully true."

Oh, look at that. Did he just pull an inch of that long stick out of his ass?

She was used to having to prove herself, dealing with Crew and his task force would be no different.

He finished circling her car, stopped just inches away and tipped his face down to hers. "You figure out your living arrangements?"

"Not yet."

"What I'm hearing is, you failed your first assignment."

Apparently, he was going to do his best to make her miserable so she'd ask to be reassigned elsewhere.

He didn't know her. Because if he did, he'd know that trying to push her out would only make her dig her heels in deeper.

She was stubborn like that.

Don't tell me I can't do something because that will only make me work harder to prove you wrong.

But he didn't need to know that. He'd find out soon enough. "Since you didn't give me a deadline to complete it, I don't consider that a failure."

"You were almost late this morning."

"The word 'almost' means that I wasn't. And it had nothing to do with my commute, it was because you failed to tell me that the entrance to this place was hidden at the rear of the building."

"Since we deal in investigations, that was test number two."

Bullshit. "Really," she said dryly.

"Really," he echoed.

"What's my third test?"

"Now if I told you that ahead of time then it wouldn't be a test." He tipped his head toward the side of the building. "Let's go."

"No wonder your wife divorced you," she muttered under her breath.

His head twitched and his shoulders stiffened but he kept going without breaking his stride.

He led her around to a covered exterior stairway. On their climb up the steps, they passed a landing on the second floor, but he didn't stop.

"The feds only rented the third floor?"

"Yes."

"Are the other two floors abandoned?"

"No."

"Who occupies them, and do they know what we're doing on the top floor?"

"What *we're* doing?"

"Am I not part of the team?" she asked his broad back as they stopped in front of a metal door with a numeric keypad.

He spun on her, making her take a half-step back. "Not yet. This task force has been in place for a year now. We're a cohesive team. Everyone knows what they need to do, and they do it."

"And you think I'm going to screw that up."

"Don't screw that up," he warned and turned back to the door. He punched in a code she didn't catch because he was blocking it with his body.

"I'll need that code."

"Yep." He pulled the door open and walked inside.

The interior did not match the exterior at all. It was

surprisingly decent. Like a lot of work—and thought—had been put into the workspace.

The top floor was almost completely open. The exception was what looked like a bathroom and large closet along the back wall. In the center was a long conference table with chairs. Along the walls, desks were lined up with computers. Attached to another wall was a large whiteboard full of notes and scribblings. Next to it was a just as large cork board with pictures and mugshots pinned to it of who she figured were members of the Deadly Demons MC. File cabinets, a table full of snacks and a coffeemaker, along with a full-size refrigerator, filled the rest of the wall space.

She frowned at the cot tucked in the back corner by the bathroom. *Interesting.*

If late nights were going to be the norm with this assignment, getting a place in the vicinity would be a priority since she would not be spending one night on that cot. As soon as she was discharged from the Navy, she bought the most comfortable bed she could afford.

She valued her sleep, and she didn't see a cot anywhere in that equation. Tonight, she'd get serious about looking for an apartment or condo to rent nearby.

"Next time we have a meeting, you'll get to meet the rest of the team. For now, this is Mullins. He's a narcotics detective with the Pittsburgh PD."

The man rose from where he was working at the conference table and gave her extended hand a firm shake. He tried not to be obvious about sizing her up. He failed. "Don Mullins."

"Camila Cabrera. Narcotics detective, huh? This task force is right up your alley, then."

"Sure is. Welcome aboard."

That sounded like a genuine welcome. "Thanks. I'm looking forward to digging my teeth in."

While Mullins' smile had been warm, she didn't miss the exchange of looks between him and Crew.

Crew grabbed her upper arm and pulled her over to two men sitting in front of computers.

"This is Bradley Lennox, but he goes by Nox. He's going through some of the recorded footage from the two locations where we have cameras planted. We'll go over that another time."

Nox didn't get up, smile or shake her hand, he gave her a slight chin lift before turning back to the computer.

Friendly.

"Did you say Camila Cabrera?" asked the man two desks away. He got up from his seat and approached. Before Crew could introduce him, he did it himself. "Luis Torres."

He jutted out his hand first and Cami took it. His grip was warm and firm, and his eyes were inviting.

"My father's name is Luis, as well," she told him.

"*¿Hablas español?*"

Well, that was music to her ears.

"*Con fluidez.*" She spoke Spanish since she was born, so she definitely was fluent.

Torres grinned. "*Eso es genial. Conocerás a Antonio Alvarez. Crew aquí no habla nada de español, así que nos metemos con él. Mucho.*"

She tried not to laugh at the part where he stated that he and Alvarez messed with the task force leader by speaking Spanish.

"*Estaré feliz de ayudarte con eso.*" She looked forward to speaking Spanish with Alvarez and Torres. Especially if it annoyed Crew.

Torres' face lit up as he laughed. "Perfect."

"Do I need to enact a no Spanish policy here?" A frown marred Crew's annoyingly handsome face.

Torres ignored him. "Where's your family from?"

Cami took his cue and did the same. "My grandparents were from Columbia. Both sides."

"Alvarez's parents came from Venezuela. *Mi padre era de México; mi madre de Texas.* I consider myself Tex-Mex."

Cami laughed. "Love it. It'll be nice to have someone to speak Spanish with so I don't get rusty."

"Let's keep it to a minimum," Crew warned.

Torres grinned and tipped his head toward the task force leader. "Man's paranoid. He thinks whenever we're speaking Spanish, we're talking about him."

"Entonces nos aseguraremos de hablarlo mucho." She assured Torres that they'd make sure to speak it a lot to mess with Crew.

"Torres here is the plant manager. He's in charge of the wiretapping and transcriptions. And that redhead over there, fat-fingering the keyboard is Pippi Longstocking."

"Oh hey! I've heard of you before," Cami called out as they headed over to where the man with the red hair sat at a desk on the other side of the room. "You sure look different than I remember."

When the man stood and turned, Cami lost her train of thought. She had never been into redheads but then, she had never come across one as smoking hot as this one. She hoped she controlled her surprise well enough. "Do you go by Pippi?"

"Pippi works," Crew answered for him. "Or Heat Miser. Prince Harry. Conan O'Brien. Carrot Top. Ginger Snap. Little Orphan Annie. He answers to any and all of them. Or feel free to make up your own."

Cami's eyebrows rose as she waited for the man himself to answer.

"Stupid-ass nicknames are a requirement around here, but Finn works. The name's Daniel Finnegan."

They shook hands. "I'm assuming you don't speak Spanish, but maybe a bit of Irish Gaelic?"

Finn shook his head. "Not even close. But I can sing like a motherfucker."

"Lies!" burst from Mullins. "Cabrera, my first words of advice to you are to keep a pair of earplugs in your pocket in case he starts belting out a tune. That's if you want to save your hearing."

"I kind of like my hearing. It comes in handy, especially to hear Spanish," she joked, risking a glance at Crew.

"Hey, I smash it at karaoke!" Finn exclaimed.

"You mean they smash the karaoke machine as soon as they see you heading up to the stage," Crew added.

"Welcome to the team, Cabrera," Finn said before taking his seat.

Funny, he didn't seem bothered by her joining the task force, either. The only one so far was the leader himself. Though, she couldn't get a good read on the broody one with the steel-set jaws.

"All right," Crew started. "We've got two members undercover with the Dirty Angels. They've been undercover with that MC since the start. They attend team meetings via phone but you most likely won't see them unless they're pulled."

"Why the Dirty Angels since they don't have anything to do with the meth trafficking?"

"To make buys. Larger quantities for resale. Though, Fletch is working hard on getting patched over to the

Demons so we have someone on the inside," Finn answered, still pecking away at the keyboard.

"That was test number three. To see if you were up to speed on the investigation," Crew announced like it was some kind of "gotcha" moment.

"You just said this task force was formed a year ago. I was only told I was being assigned to this task force five days ago. And in that five days I had to move from Virginia to here. I know the basics, I didn't have time to get into all the nitty gritty details."

A snort came from the redheaded Finn.

"Then I guess you'll need to get up to speed. Since we have fifteen group members each with," Crew pursed his lips, "*mmm...* I don't know, probably three hundred and sixty-five daily reports or so, that might take you a while."

She almost choked on her own spit. "You want me to read *every* daily report?"

"Do you have something better to do?"

What a dick. "I would if you assigned me something better to do."

"Until I find the best way to use you, it can't hurt to begin reading through the reports."

Best way to use you.

She opened her mouth to ask what his own reports said. They were probably short and to the point. *"From eight to five, I was an asshole."*

Of course, she didn't ask. But, *damn*, did she want to. She had to remind herself that he was in charge and, no matter what, she answered to him.

She might've only been a special agent for a year, about the same length of time this task force existed, but she had a good reputation and wanted to keep it that way. She would not let the man cause her to get a black mark on her record.

Her father might be one of the top dogs in the DEA, but she got this job all on her own. Because of that, she wanted to be recognized for her hard work, not for riding on his coattails.

Most people in the organization most likely thought she'd have it easy.

She didn't want easy.

She wanted to be treated the same as everyone else.

Despite what anyone thought, he did not pull one damn string to get her into the agency. "Fine. I can get started today. Point me to the computer you want me to use. I'll make sure to take notes in case there's a quiz when I'm done."

The room was suddenly very quiet and as she glanced around, she noticed all eyes pointed in her direction.

The amusement was clear on Torres', Finn's and Mullins' mugs. Nox wore a blank mask and as for Crew...

It appeared that he was grinding his teeth.

"You'd be much prettier if you smiled," slipped out of her before she could stop it, resulting in a few howls of laughter.

Damn it.

Chapter Three

CREW'S GAZE automatically landed on Cabrera's Audi as he rode his Harley through the gate and into a parking spot.

Damn, she beat him here this morning. Most likely an attempt to earn some brownie points.

Since he had to assume she was already upstairs reading through the daily reports, after securing the back gate, he headed into the rear patio area of The Plant. He slipped his cell phone from his back pocket and dropped onto a lounge chair.

He needed his caffeine fix but that would have to wait until he made this call first. He found the number and pressed Send.

"Damn, brother, it's way too early to hear your voice in my ear. Unless you plan on whispering sweet nothings to me?"

"Did I interrupt you and Wilder getting wild? Put me on video chat so I can watch and score your performance."

"Fuck off."

Crew chuckled.

"So, what the fuck do you want?" Fletch asked.

"Got a proposal for you."

"I don't think Nova wants to share me. I don't swing that way, anyway. Try Monty. Maybe she'll feel sorry for you and toss you a bone."

"Monty's already getting some."

A long pause filled his ear. Finally Fletch asked, "Since when?"

"Don't know, but she brought him to the Christmas party... and Sadie's funeral."

"Why the fuck is this the first I'm hearing about it?" Fletch shouted.

"Why do you care?"

"Because she's one of our brothers... sister. Whatever. She's family. I hate being out of the loop. He's not an ex-con, is he? He didn't woo her with a bouquet of shanks while in a candlelit cell at SCI Greene?"

"We can't find out shit about him since she's being super sneaky. But we suspect he could be a serial killer."

"What the fuck?"

"Wears loafers, khakis and bowties."

Fletch must've had to digest that news since it took him forever to say, "Now I know you're fucking with me."

"I'm totally fucking serious. He's a complete nerd and even his name fits him. It's... get this... Clark."

Fletch released a low whistle. "That can't be all you have on him. Know where he works?"

"Nope. Just that he's an actuary."

"What the fuck is that?" Fletch asked.

"Exactly."

"You didn't run his plate?" Fletch asked next.

Crew scraped fingers through his hair. "Brother, they always use her vehicle so we can't grab it."

"Damn. Someone needs to pick his pocket and grab his license. Get Nox on it. He's good at picking locks, maybe he's good at picking wallets. Speaking of Fort Nox, when's the intervention?"

"Soon, I think. I need to touch base with Jamison. You know how hard it is to get the majority of us together at the same time."

"It can't wait too much longer. Hell, it's already been too long as it is. It doesn't need to be everybody, just enough to convince him that he needs help."

Crew agreed. "No shit. I told him that."

"So, you woke me up to tell me Monty's getting some nerd action?"

"No, but why aren't you already awake? Don't you need to go work at the gun shop?" Crew asked.

"Not until later."

"Any movement with patching over to the Demons?"

"Wolf's still resistant to presenting it to the prez."

He didn't want to lose out on his cut of the sales he made to Fletch. With as much as the feds were buying, that came out to a nice chunk of change. "Keep working him."

A loud yawn filled Crew's ear. "That it?" Fletch prodded.

"No."

"Jesus. Can you get to it, then?"

"I was thinking about your house."

"I've heard of some strange fetishes before but that might take the cake. I'm not sure I want you going over there to check on it anymore. Don't make me take a blacklight to the interior of my home."

"I make my deposits on the outside, so the rain washes away the evidence."

Fletch fake gagged.

"Are you interested in renting it out?"

"I thought Sapphire moved in permanently with Rezavoir Dog."

"She did," Crew responded. "It's not for her."

"Are you in financial straits and need to sell your place due to all that alimony and child support?"

"No," Crew answered. "But thanks for that painful reminder, jackass."

Fletch snorted. "You're reminded every month when your salary disappears from your bank account."

"Again, thanks for that. It's not for me."

"Then who? I don't want just anyone living in my home and sleeping in my bed."

Crew wouldn't, either. "If no one has told you yet, we got a replacement for Butler."

"Oh yeah? Where's he from?"

"The DEA. And he's a she. Her father is the principal deputy administrator."

"Don't know what the hell that is."

"Someone who could crush my stellar career if she runs to Daddy and complains about me."

Fletch whistled. "Then you're fucked because you're a complete asshole. So, Daddy gave her an in with the DEA," Fletch concluded. "What about the task force?"

"That's my guess because if I had a choice, it wouldn't be her."

"Why? Is she incompetent?"

No, she's a headstrong smart ass. "I don't know, I only met her yesterday." As an adult, anyway. "Today will be her first full day with the team."

"So, what's wrong with giving her a chance?"

"She's only twenty-eight."

"Okay? Nova was only thirty-one when she joined us. I know math is hard for you unless it comes to your alimony payments, but that's only a three year difference. And my woman's a great federal agent and task force member."

"What else is she good at?"

"Kicking ass. Do you want to test her? Okay... Why does... What's her name?"

"Camila Cabrera."

A chuckle came through the phone. "Please tell me she speaks fluent Spanish."

"Fuck off."

The chuckle became a full-blown roar of laughter. "Oh, man. The conversations between Torres, Rez and her should be interesting."

Crew sucked at his teeth. "If you can understand them."

"There's an app that'll help you learn so you don't feel left out," Fletch said, still laughing. "No wonder why your panties are in a twist. So, why does Cabrera need a place?"

"She just transferred from Virginia and has been staying at one of those extended stay hotels," Crew explained.

"Well, I guess if she stays in my place, then you guys won't have to keep going over there to check on it."

"The house would be safer with an occupant," Crew agreed. Cabrera staying at Fletch's would kill two birds with one stone.

"Yeah, especially when the house sitter would be a highly-trained federal agent. But just how long do you think we'll be on this assignment? I'd like to sleep in my own bed again sometime in this decade. Do you expect us to stay undercover all the way up to indictments?"

"No, but I don't expect her to stay in your place very long. It's only temporary."

"Because she'll get her own place?"

"No. My guess is she'll eventually cry mercy and ask to be transferred elsewhere."

"Damn, you're going to try to run her off? That's a dick move. What's wrong with her besides her being young and bilingual? Especially when neither are real problems. Actually, both can be assets. The whole father thing maybe not so much. For you, anyway."

"She's only been an agent for a year."

"Okay? That doesn't mean she can't do the job. Still not hearing the issue," Fletch said.

"They're *all* issues!" Crew yelled into the phone, then grimaced, hoping no one heard his outburst.

"The only real issue I hear is with you."

Crew sighed. "And I first met her when she was only ten."

"I assume that means you know her father personally."

"I worked a case with him eighteen years ago when she was a little kid."

"Yeah, only being ten means she was a little kid. What am I missing?"

"She's no longer a little kid."

"Yeah, you said she's twenty-eight now, so..."

Crew dropped his head back and gritted his teeth. He shouldn't have admitted that last part. Especially when he heard Fletch yell, "Oh fuck!" then laugh his ass off.

"Let me know when you're done," he said dryly.

Fletch's voice came muffled through the phone. "No, he didn't tell me a joke, baby. Crew's just a fucking idiot. That's why I'm laughing."

"Oh, for fuck's sake," Crew muttered. "Are you interested in renting out your place or not?"

"I guess—"

"What do you want for it?"

"I don't—"

"Five hundred?"

"A week?" Fletch asked.

"A month," Crew answered.

"A month? That's highway robbery."

"All right. I'll ask her if she's interested and let you know."

"I didn't agree to five—"

Crew hit the End button on his phone and hung up.

A text came through as he was heading upstairs and when he got to the top landing, he glanced at it. It was a picture of Fletch's hand flipping him the bird.

With a grin and a shake of his head, he punched in the code and stepped inside group one's headquarters.

He frowned when he saw Torres standing close behind Cabrera with one hand on the back of her chair as he leaned over her shoulder, speaking Spanish as they looked at the computer screen.

"How's the wife, Torres?"

Torres glanced over at him. "Spicy as always."

"Is that report you're reading in Spanish?"

Torres gave him a toothy grin and straightened. "I didn't know that was an option."

Crew's nostrils flared. Of course it had to be because he picked up the scent of coffee and not because of his annoyance. He spun on his boot heel and headed over to the coffeemaker, finding a half of a carafe on the warmer. He poured himself a cup and, on his way back to Cabrera, he stopped dead and stared at the conference table.

A box of donuts sat in the center.

"Who brought these?" He flipped open the top, searched what remained, found a glazed donut and clamped it between his teeth.

"She did," Torres said, tipping his head toward their newest task force member. Still wearing a shit-eating grin, the plant manager headed over to the desk used for transcribing wiretaps.

Cabrera glanced over her shoulder, trouble with a capital T filling her dark eyes. "Morning, sir."

His step stuttered and he caught the donut before he almost spewed it out. "Crew is fine."

She turned in her seat to face him. That was when he noticed she wore another suit today.

"You don't have to dress up. We're pretty casual around here."

"Sounds good, boss."

His jaws snapped shut on the donut causing a chunk of it to land at his feet.

"You never gave me the code. Someone had to let me in."

"Yep," he said around a mouthful of glazed donut.

"I let her in this morning and gave her the code, *sir*," came from Warren Reynolds, a corporal with the state police. This morning he was assigned to work with Torres and listen to "dirty talk."

"Hear anything interesting this morning?" Crew asked him.

"Fuck no. Too early for them to be up and about. I'm going over some of last night's chatter."

"And?"

"Not much," Reynolds answered.

"Got something for you," Torres called out. "Was listening in on Wolf's conversation last night with Viper. He brought up that Ghost has been riding his ass about patching over."

Ghost was Fletch's undercover road name. "Yeah? Are they considering it?"

"Wolf didn't sound so thrilled about it. Viper showed a bit of interest, but they ended up dropping that line of conversation to talk about... and I quote... bitches and cunts. Sorry, Cabrera."

She flung a hand over her shoulder. "No offense taken since I assume you don't call women that yourself."

"Hell no. My wife would slice my nuts off and shove them down the garbage disposal. She'd flip the start switch so fast, she'd break her damn hand."

Crew's stomach churned at that visual. "Jesus fuck, Torres, it's too early for that shit. At least let me finish my first cup of coffee."

He shrugged. "Ain't a lie, though."

"Okay, that might mean that Beavis and Butthead are at least considering it," Crew concluded. "Hopefully."

"It's certainly not one of their priorities, that's for damn sure," Torres said. "They're more interested in making money and treating women like shit."

"If they allow Fletch to patch over, they'll lose money. That's why they aren't giving it any serious thought," Nox mumbled from where he sat fast-forwarding through some recorded footage from the Wolf Den.

"Yeah," Crew said on a sigh. "I was hoping they'd go for it since we're out of options for getting anyone planted in their MC."

Torres spun around in his seat and caught Crew's gaze before letting it slide to Cabrera and back.

Crew shook his head.

Torres shrugged.

Crew went to stand next to him and said under his breath, "We've all seen and heard how they treat women. They only keep them around for their use and abuse. And even if it would be safe for her, you think they'd accept her?" He lifted his eyebrows, hoping Torres, out of anyone, would pick up what he was putting down.

"Yeah, maybe not. She's not their flavor. But you never know. Aren't bikers 'born to be wild?' I can't imagine anyone in their right mind would say no to her." Torres then mouthed, "She's hot," and bit his bottom lip.

Crew beat back the curl of his own lip. "They're not getting wild with her. Like I said, you know what they do to women. And I wouldn't allow her to do any of that, anyway. Neither would my superiors. Or her father."

Torres' head jerked back and his eyes went wide. "Fuck. We did have that conversation yesterday."

Crew pinned his lips together and nodded.

"Might as well get out a helmet and some bubble wrap. We need to make sure she doesn't even get a damn scratch. Do you think he's how she got her job?"

"That would be my guess," Crew murmured, glancing over his shoulder to make sure Cabrera didn't hear any of their conversation.

She seemed to be still engrossed in those exciting daily reports.

"My advice would be to give her the safest tasks you can," Torres suggested. "Like admin work."

"Why do you think I have her reading the dailies?" Crew tapped his temple.

"And here I thought it was to get up to speed with the rest of us."

"Also... keep your Spanish to a minimum during work hours."

"You're only paranoid that we're talking about you," Torres said on a laugh.

He was but he wasn't going to admit it. He simply shook his head and went back to Cabrera. On his way, he took a quick detour to the donuts again and snagged a cream-filled powdered donut.

He was going to have to add at least five miles to his ride tonight. His Peloton or his mountain bike, depending on the weather.

His ass was already starting to hurt thinking about it.

"You find a place?" he asked as he stepped behind her chair.

Without looking at him, she answered, "Last night I contacted a few complexes in the area and either they don't have anything available, or they will, but not right away. I might have to move into a short-term rental or a motel until I find something more long-term."

"I have another option for you."

She stopped reading and turned around in her seat with her eyebrows pulled high. "Your place?"

Yeah right. He'd like to keep his damn job since it helped support his kids. "I don't have any rooms for rent, but I do know of a house that's sitting empty right now and is available."

"Near here?"

"About twenty minutes away."

"How much is it?"

"Cheap."

"How cheap?"

"Five hundred a month."

She frowned. "Five? So, it's a tent?"

"Hardly."

"What kind of house can I get for only five hundred?"

He answered, "One that's sitting empty while the task force member is undercover."

"Fletcher's or Wilder's?" she asked next.

"Fletch's. Well, both, I guess." He assumed that once their undercover assignment was over, they'd move into his house together since they've already been living together in the apartment over Shadow Valley Pawn, owned by the Dirty Angels. And Wilder had to give up her condo once La Cosa Nostra discovered where she lived and ambushed her there.

Cabrera shook her head. "Both? Are they a couple?"

"They are now."

"Oh. Did they hook up before their undercover assignment or once they went under?"

"They didn't know each other before."

"*Ah*. A workplace romance, then."

Romance. Right. More like a surge of hormonal horniness. "Sure. If that's what you want to call it."

"What would you call it?"

"I don't really know what to call it since I don't analyze other people's love life." Only their sex life.

Her lips twitched at his answer. "Have you been to his house?"

"Many times."

"And it's nice?"

"Yes. We've all been taking turns checking on it. It's my turn to go over later, so how about after you're done with today's light reading, I take you over there?"

"I'm game." She grabbed her empty coffee mug and stood. When she turned, they were only inches apart.

His heart thudded in his chest when she reached out and brushed her hand over his shirt.

What was she doing?

"You had a bit of powdered sugar on you."

He glanced down, his pulse now racing at her unexpected touch.

What the actual fuck?

With a smirk, she went to get more coffee.

While he went outside to get some air because suddenly the walls on the third floor had begun to close in on him.

Chapter Four

CAMI FOLLOWED Crew into the paved driveway and parked next to his bike. She sat in her car as he dismounted and pulled off his helmet, exposing his sexy as hell salt-and-pepper hair. He brushed fingers through it to get rid of his helmet head before shrugging out of the light leather jacket he wore and tossing it over the seat.

Then he turned his mirrored sunglasses in her direction.

Shit.

Somebody had gotten distracted.

That somebody was her.

She pulled in a breath to cool off the warmth pooling in a place begging for attention.

She remembered him. From eighteen years ago.

When he and her father sat on their back patio having a beer together. They had been celebrating the completion of a successful investigation.

One they worked together.

It wasn't long after that they moved, since her father kept getting promoted. She wondered why Crew hadn't. Or maybe he loved being an agent. Some law enforcement enjoyed remaining in the ranks and getting their hands dirty. They didn't like being stuck in the office or didn't want to deal with the bullshit that came along with each link in the chain of command.

She opened her driver's door and climbed out, turning her attention to the house in front of her.

It wasn't a mansion but wasn't a hut, either. It was a sprawling modern ranch-style home with an oversized two-car garage. She wondered who was cutting the grass and maintaining the landscaping while Fletcher was undercover.

"Does that five hundred include utilities?"

Crew pursed his lips for a few seconds, then said, "Sure."

"Who will be responsible for maintenance? Like the yard and all that?"

Crew planted his hands on his hips and turned to stare at the house. "I guess you. Have you used a mower before?"

Since he wasn't facing her, she rolled her eyes and shook her head. "I've mowed grass before. I've also weeded. As well as vacuumed and cleaned toilets since I wasn't born in a palace with a full-time staff."

He glanced at her over his shoulder. "Your dad makes some decent money."

"Decent but he's nowhere near rich. We lived comfortably but normally. It's not like he's some CEO of a billion-dollar company. He works for the federal government. You should know better than most how the pay doesn't compare to the private sector."

He mumbled something she didn't catch.

"What was that?"

"Nothing. C'mon. Let's get this over with." His long legs quickly ate up the distance between his bike and the house.

"Is this cutting into your social hour?" she called out.

"Like I said earlier, it was my turn to come check on the house."

"It's nice that you guys are doing that."

"Well, he's a brother, so..."

She frowned. "He's your brother?"

"Not by blood, but by bond."

She shook her head. "Okay?"

When he reached the front door and dug into his pocket —she assumed for a key—she waited behind him.

"We work on the task force together but I've known him for a long time. We're in the same MC."

"I'm sorry, what? Did you say MC?"

He shoved a key into the deadbolt and turned it. Her ears picked up an alarm beeping. He quickly stepped inside, and she followed him into the cool, dark interior to see him punching a code into the security system panel.

"If I rent this place, don't forget to give me the code like you did for the plant."

"You assume I forgot." He turned and strode through the house. "We'll start at the back and work our way to the front."

His long stride had her scrambling to keep up with him. She barely got a good look at the two rooms off the small foyer before they quickly moved through what looked like a great room with a sprawling sectional sofa, a large screen TV and a gas fireplace.

He unlocked the door that led out back and stepped out onto a large deck.

She couldn't believe her luck. "A pool?" She somehow managed to bite back her squeal of excitement.

It was a pretty nice sized one, too. Perfect for doing laps. That was right up her alley.

"Yeah. He didn't uncover it last year so I have no idea what the water looks like."

"Do you think he'd mind me uncovering it and getting it ready for the season?" She hoped it was heated so she could use it sooner than later.

"I doubt he would if you're paying to have it opened."

"Deal!"

His brow furrowed. "You haven't seen the rest of the house yet."

Not only was the rent cheap, but to have access to a pool, too? She didn't need anything more. "I don't need to. I've seen everything I needed to see."

"You're that easy to please?" His spine snapped straight a second after those words tumbled from his lips.

His mind seemed to hang out in the gutter right next to hers.

Even so, she smothered her grin at how uncomfortable he looked. "I guess it doesn't take much."

He jerked his chin toward a shed. "He keeps all the pool equipment in there, along with the rest of the shit needed to lounge around the pool."

"Awesome."

The backyard wasn't large but it was fenced. It would be perfect for...

Shit.

"Uh... I forgot to mention something." A *big* and important something.

He turned and his gray eyes locked with hers. "What?"

"Another reason I was having problems finding a place was that I have a roommate."

His mouth parted. "Why would that matter?"

"My roommate has four legs."

"A cat?"

She shook her head and grimaced. "A dog. Do you think Fletcher will mind me having a dog here?"

"I can ask him. What kind of dog is it?"

"A hairy one."

Did he just suck on his teeth? Good.

"I meant size-wise."

"*Umm...*" *Shit.* She really didn't want to tell him.

His eyes narrowed on her. "What's the breed?"

She might have just fucked up her chances at renting this house. With a damn pool, too! "Have you ever heard of an Irish Wolfhound?"

"You forgot about owning an Irish Wolfhound? How the fuck do you forget a dog of that size? Its shit alone probably weighs five pounds."

That wasn't quite true. "Do you want to ask Fletcher if it's okay? He might not want a dog in his house."

"Is it house-trained?"

"Yes."

"Destructive?"

"No. He's out of the puppy stage and he mostly sleeps. He's actually pretty laid-back." Unless he sees a rabbit. A cat. Or a squirrel. Or anything that runs.

"Is he aggressive?"

"He's a lover, not a fighter. But his size alone scares people."

"Then fuck no, I'm not saying shit to Fletch. Just make sure he doesn't piss on the floor or destroy things. And pick up the yard."

Damn. That was too easy. Though, she wasn't sure if Crew should be making that decision for the homeowner. "Okay. Next question. Can I park in the garage?" She didn't like to leave her baby out in the weather.

"I'll ask him. I know he has his Harley and his truck in there but we can probably move his bike in front of his truck and out of the way to make room."

"Wait, you'll ask him about the garage but not the dog?" she asked.

He shrugged.

Something was up. Crew really *wanted* her to rent this house for some reason. Could it be he was simply tired of coming over to check on it? Maybe. But he seemed to have some sort of ulterior motive and she doubted it was to make her life easier.

"C'mon. Let's do a quick walk-through so I can get out of here."

"Got a hot date or something?"

"Don't you have a dog to walk?"

She grinned. "I pay a dog walker—actually, she's one of the front desk clerks—to walk him mid-day. I'll just have to find someone to do it around here if I end up working long hours."

She followed him back into the house. On the left side of the house was two smaller bedrooms sharing a Jack and Jill bathroom and another bedroom with its own bathroom. To the right of the great room was a nice sized kitchen with a breakfast nook. On the right side of the house was the primary bedroom with its own huge bathroom with a very inviting whirlpool tub, along with a laundry room right off the garage.

As they headed back out, the two rooms off the foyer ended up being a small dining room on one side and what looked like a cozy theater room with a small wet bar on the other.

She could picture herself in one of the comfy-looking recliners with the lights off, her feet kicked up and munching on popcorn while she watched the latest blockbuster movie.

The house was perfect and worth a hell of a lot more than five hundred a month.

After Crew set the alarm, they both stepped back outside onto the front porch, and he locked the door.

"Will that be my key?"

His fingers tightened around it before shoving his hand deep into the front pocket of his jeans. He acted as if he was afraid she would try to snag it from him. "No, I'm hanging on to this one. I'll grab one for you from one of the other guys."

"Why would you need to keep it?"

"In case of emergency."

Uh huh.

They headed back to their vehicles and once they stopped next to his bike, she asked, "So, what's with the MC thing? You never explained."

"The Plant isn't only the headquarters for the task force."

She shook her head. "I don't understand."

"I'm going to explain it, just give me a chance."

"You were the one in a rush to get out of here."

He slipped his mirrored sunglasses over his gorgeous eyes even though the sun was beginning to set. "The BAMC owns that building. They rent the top floor to the feds for our task force."

She pressed her lips together to keep from asking one hundred and one questions and did her best to let him explain first.

"The BAMC originally bought it as their clubhouse."

She pressed her lips tighter together because he wasn't talking fast enough. And she had no idea what the BAMC stood for.

"We redid the whole building."

Fighting impatience, her hands curled into fists, and she pressed them to her thighs to keep from bursting.

"We made the first floor our clubhouse. The second floor is Nox's apartment."

She pushed out a breath. "Can I talk now?"

"I'd prefer you didn't."

"Then I'm going to make a lot of assumptions that you may not want me to make."

He pulled in a breath. "Fine."

"Are you a member of this MC?"

"Yes."

"What does BAMC stand for?"

"Honor and loyalty."

"I meant the acronym."

"Blue Avengers Motorcycle Club."

She could've figured out the last part, but she let it go. "Is it all LEO?"

"Yes."

She nodded. "I've heard of that. MCs made up of only military, or members who are all firefighters. That's cool you're a part of one made up of law enforcement." Maybe that stick was only shoved up his ass when it came to her. "How many members are there?"

"A dozen. We used to be one large MC but we grew so much we voted to divide the club into six regional charters to make it more manageable. Nobody from Philly wants to ride all those hours to Pittsburgh for a meeting or a club run. And vice versa."

"That makes sense. So, if I buy a bike, can I join? Or do you not take women?"

His jaw shifted when he hesitated. "We don't discriminate. The main requirement to join is that you're a current or retired sworn officer or federal agent. Plus, you need to be able to pay your dues." His eyebrows pinned together. "Do you ride?"

"No, but I can learn."

He snorted.

"What? You don't think I can?"

"I didn't say that."

"That little snort sounded like you doubted my ability."

"You might want to make sure you'll be staying in this area first before investing time and money into buying a bike and learning how to ride."

Her eyes narrowed on him. "I don't plan on going anywhere for a while."

He *mmm*'d.

"What does that mean?"

"Nothing."

Did he not think she could hack being a part of the task force? She loved a challenge, and this was no different.

She stared at the biggest challenge of all. A man who doubted her. She couldn't wait to prove him wrong. "Thanks for the tour. How soon can I move in?"

"It's empty, so whenever you want."

"If I can get a key from you tomorrow, I'll start moving my stuff in tomorrow night. I might have to make a few trips since my car isn't big and Murphy takes up most of it. Unless you know anyone with a truck I can borrow?" He did mention that Fletcher had a truck.

"How much shit do you have?"

"Only necessities at this point. Most of my stuff is being stored at my parents' for now but I shipped some stuff out here already. Like clothes. But I don't have room for both that and Murph."

"You named your dog Murphy?"

"He came with the name since I got him from a rescue. His former owners didn't research the breed well enough and didn't realize how big he'd get. I benefitted from their mistake. He's the perfect companion." Unlike some men.

"All right. I'll get you a key tomorrow and I'll talk to the guys to see if anyone's willing to let you borrow their truck or SUV."

"You don't have one?"

"If no one volunteers, I'll ask Fletch if you can borrow his."

Nice deflection. "I appreciate it. Then I guess I'll see you tomorrow at the plant."

As she began to round his bike, he said, "Just so you know, we call the whole building The Plant, not just the third floor. So, if you meet any of the BAMC members not on the task force, I don't want you getting confused if you hear them calling our clubhouse that."

"That's not very original."

He shrugged on his black leather jacket that somehow made him look even hotter. *Damn it.* Nobody had the right to look that good. Especially a man who had worked with her dad.

"Yeah, well... I guess we're not very creative."

"Just the facts, ma'am," she quoted. She paused after opening her driver's door and stared at the interior for a second, debating whether she should address the elephant in the room.

Fuck it. She didn't want him to continue to spread rumors or make wrong assumptions. She might as well nip that shit in the bud.

She turned and called out, "Hey," causing him to stop securing the strap on his helmet and glance her way. "I heard you talking to Torres. If you aren't aware, your voice carries even when you're whispering. Despite what you think, I didn't get my job because of my father."

"You didn't, huh?" His disbelief was clear both on his face and in his tone.

"No. I earned my spot. I didn't squeak by in the academy, I was at the top of my class."

"I never said you weren't capable. But how did you snag that spot in the academy?"

"It could have had something to do with my 4.0 GPA from Northeastern University, my B.S. in criminal justice, being bilingual and my time in the Navy."

He stared at her with his lips slightly parted.

Had she rendered him speechless? Good.

"So yeah, my father didn't have to pull any strings. Not even a tiny one. I pulled those fuckers all on my own." She climbed into her car and slammed the door shut.

Before her satisfied smile grew too big, she started her car and backed out of the driveway, leaving him still standing next to his bike with his hands on his hips and watching her drive away.

Chapter Five

CREW'S EYES scanned the third floor as he stepped through the door. Cabrera was sitting in her spot reading through the endless daily reports. Her eyelids drooped heavily and her head was beginning to nod while a forgotten mug of coffee sat next to the computer.

She sat up straighter as soon as she saw him and quickly clicked on the mouse to look busy.

He shouldn't torture her by making her read through them all. But until he found her something to do, he'd let it continue and not feel bad about it.

Finn sat watching some of the live camera feeds on one monitor, as well as keeping an eye on recorded footage on another.

Torres, Proctor and Kruger, as well as Mullins, sat at computers working on either transcribing wiretaps, writing up reports or doing research.

Crew called out, "Finn, head downstairs."

Finn's eyes locked with his as he stood, giving him a chin lift.

"Where's Nox?" he asked his BAMC brother next.

Finn answered, "He headed down to his apartment about twenty minutes ago."

Crew nodded. "Okay, good. Torres, you're in charge."

"I'm leaving in about thirty. My oldest has a soccer game."

"Don't get thrown off the field this time."

Torres laughed. "Some kid tripped mine on purpose."

"It's a game," Crew reminded him.

"The little shit cheated," Torres exclaimed.

"Yeah? Letting your boy deal with it himself will prepare him for real life."

"Yeah, but as a father yourself, you know you want to protect them as long as possible."

"I let mine fight their own battles."

Finn snorted as he reached the door. "Sure you do. How many times were you banned from Dylan's baseball games?"

"Just once."

Finn coughed out a, "Bullshit." His smirk quickly disintegrated. "Meet you down there."

"Heading down now. I want to give Cabrera a quick tour before we do our thing."

"Is that the *thing* you guys have been talking about?" Mullins asked.

"Yeah."

"About time," Torres answered. "Every day I come in here, I keep expecting to hear bad news."

"Don't say that shit," Proctor growled. "I've been fucking worried about the guy."

"We all have," Crew assured him. "Let's just hope this helps."

"And if it doesn't?" Kruger asked.

"I don't know. None of us can force him to do anything.

We can only talk, hope he listens and takes our concerns to heart." Though, both him and Jamison had something up their sleeves to try to get Nox to cooperate. Hopefully it didn't blow up in their faces.

"That sucks, dude," Mullins murmured. "Good luck with that."

"Yeah, thanks. We're going to need it." Crew turned and called out, "Cabrera. You're done for the day. Come with me."

She twisted in her chair, with her eyebrows pinched together. "Come with you where?"

"Downstairs. Will give you a little tour before you leave."

"Let me log out." When she finished shutting down the work station, she stood.

His gaze slid over her from the top of her head to her toes. Her hair was pulled back in a simple ponytail, and she forewent the suit today. Instead, she wore dark gray cargo pants that emphasized the slight curve of her hips and a white button-down shirt with enough buttons undone to show a hint of cleavage. Her feet were covered with a pair of black, low-heeled boots.

"Did I pass *that* test?"

He lifted his eyes to her face to see a slight curve to her lips and a gleam in her eyes. "What test?"

"The test to see if I listened to you about dressing more casually."

"Yeah, you passed."

She slapped a hand to her chest, raising her eyes to the ceiling and mouthed, "Thank God." That emphasized her tits and the fact that her bra wasn't padded enough to hide her nipples standing at attention.

For fuck's sake. He dragged his eyes away against their will.

Unfortunately, too late. She caught him being a perv. Evident by the shake of her head. "How do we get downstairs?"

"The same way you came up."

"Really?" she asked. "I don't know if I've ever been in a building without a way to access the other floors from the inside."

"Well, now you have. Let's go."

"What's up your ass?" she asked under her breath.

He jerked to a stop at the door when he caught her words. His first instinct was to reprimand her. But then, he'd just visually assaulted her, so it was best to not pull rank right now. He'd have to remind her who was in charge when no one else was around.

"Nothing. I have shit to do." The first part was a lie, the second wasn't.

He'd had a dream last night of her swimming naked in Fletch's pool. Her slick body cutting cleanly through the water as she did laps.

Then he woke up.

And took care of the raging hard-on that little dream caused.

Then he beat himself up until his alarm went off over the fact he just jerked off to a woman fifteen years younger than him. One he met when she was only ten. And he knew her father.

A top dog in the DEA.

An organization where he worked.

From where he hoped to retire from with an honorable discharge. Because he needed that pension.

The medical benefits were kind of nice, too.

He'd also like to keep his good reputation and not have a stain marking his long career.

Christ, this whole thing could turn into a complete fucking disaster.

One thing he knew for sure was that Luis Cabrera would not be happy about Crew whacking off to his daughter.

Even though she was now an adult.

And tempting as fuck.

"Go!" burst from him.

For fuck's sake. He was losing his shit.

"Jesus," she murmured with a shake of her head and headed out the door and started down the steps.

He stood at the top landing watching her go.

He also checked out her hot as fuck ass as she did so.

He closed his eyes and growled.

"Are you coming?"

Fuck me.

She paused in front of Nox's apartment and pointed.

"No. Keep going."

She sighed and climbed down the rest of the way, then turned to stare up the stairs. "Is something wrong? Do you need assistance? Do you need one of those motorized stairlifts installed? Do I need to call a couple of the guys to carry you down?"

He sighed and jogged down the steps to prove her wrong. Only, halfway down he stumbled and almost tumbled the rest of the way.

"Holy shit!" she called out, starting to rush up the steps. "Did you break a hip?"

"Stay there! I don't need your help!" He took a breath and continued down at a more normal pace.

The only thing he proved was that he was a jackass.

When he reached her, he pulled out his keys, unlocked the side door and swept his hand out, indicating she should go inside.

"A conference table?" she asked as she moved through the BAMC's meeting room.

"It's where our executive committee meets." When she stopped suddenly, he almost ran right into her. "A little warning next time before you slam on the brakes."

"I figured you'd see me stopping. Or do you have cataracts?"

"Aren't you fucking hilarious," he muttered.

"Is it like a board meeting?"

"Exactly like that."

"How many sit on this board?"

"We have a president, VP, secretary, treasurer and sergeant at arms. Then Finn's the road captain, but he doesn't get a vote unless someone is missing."

"Wow. Do you have by-laws, too?"

"Yes."

"Will I need to be tested on those to join?"

"Are you always a smart ass?"

"Just with you."

"I feel honored, then. Head out." He jerked his chin toward the door.

He heard the voices before he saw everyone who had gathered downstairs. All in preparation for Nox's intervention.

She turned in a circle, taking it all in. "Couches, kitchenette, big screen TV. Pool table, darts, and a card table..."

"A patio out back with a fire pit and a grill," he added. He was proud about what he and his brothers had achieved in this former shit hole.

"Damn. This is like the ultimate man cave. I never would've expected any of this by looking at the exterior."

"We did that on purpose, and we also put a lot of work

into getting it to look this way. It's like night and day from when we first bought it."

"If it looked anything like the front, I'm sure," Cabrera murmured.

As he gave her a quick tour of the first floor, he introduced her to everyone available she hadn't met yet, including Aiden Cross, Roland North, Tim Frasier and Decker.

Then he took her out back and showed her the patio.

It shouldn't give him any kind of satisfaction that she was impressed with all the work they'd done on the place, but deep down it did.

And that was fucked up since he didn't need her approval.

Just as they were heading back inside, Rez opened the rear door and stepped out, his eyes immediately landing on Cabrera. As soon as Rez's dark eyes began to twinkle, Crew steeled himself for what was to come.

"Jamison's looking for you."

"We're heading back inside now," Crew told him.

"This her?"

Crew swallowed down his normal smart-ass comment and instead answered, "Cabrera, you haven't met Antonio Alvarez yet."

"*Llámame Rez. Torres me dijo que hablas español con fluidez.*"

"*Llámame Cami o Cabrera.*"

Of fucking course. "English!" Crew barked.

"Cami, huh?" Rez laughed. "Well, Cami, don't mind J. Crew. He gets paranoid because he thinks when we speak Spanish we're talking about him." Rez curved a hand around the side of his mouth and whispered, "We tell him we're not but we really are."

Crew sucked on his teeth.

Rez continued, "My parents came here from Venezuela. You?"

"Both sets of grandparents immigrated from Columbia," she answered with a huge smile.

"Damn. *Será agradable tener a alguien más con quien hablar español.*"

Rez mentioned something about speaking Spanish but that was all Crew could pick up.

"Same. With my parents back in Virginia, I was worried I'd get rusty."

He should get a language tutor and not tell any of them. Then, when they had conversations in Spanish, he'd know everything they said.

No more secrets.

"No worries around here. Frasier knows a little, too, but not enough to have a full-blown conversation."

"Maybe I can help teach him."

She could do what? No. "You'll be busy with the task force."

Rez barked out a laugh, hooked a thumb toward Crew and shook his head. "If you start learning now, Crewella, you might understand what we're saying in ten years or so."

"Probably a waste of time for him, because by then he'll have old timer's and will forget everything he learned."

Rez released a low whistle. "Damn. It'll be nice to have someone on the team who can give as good as she gets."

"Thick skin is one thing I developed in the Navy," she replied.

"Navy, huh?" Rez glanced at Crew. "Good choice."

He didn't have a damn choice. "We're lucky to have her." His response was as dry as burnt toast.

Rez laughed and whacked him on the back. "Jamison has

his panties in a twist. He's getting impatient to get this intervention started."

"Intervention?" Cabrera asked. "Like for drug addiction?"

"Depression and grief," Crew answered as he followed her and Rez inside.

"PTSD, basically," Rez added. "Nox is an Army vet but when his wife died, it really hit him harder than anything else did when he served."

"Oh shit. I noticed that he's really quiet and broody. Did his wife die recently?" she asked, moving down the back hallway.

"A little over a year and a half ago."

"So, what's the intervention for? Usually they're done to get someone into therapy or rehab. Oh... He needs professional help to get out of his funk. Got it."

"She's astute, too, Motley Crew. She'll be a great addition to the task force."

"*Mmm hmm,*" Crew murmured as they reached the common area of the BAMC church.

"*Podemos hablar más tarde,*" Rez said before peeling off from them and heading over to the couches where they planned on sitting Nox down to have a serious conversation with him.

Crew dipped his head close to her ear. "What did he say?"

"That we'd speak later."

"I bet."

She stopped in her tracks and spun on him. "Why would I lie?"

"To cover for him."

"I don't know him well enough to cover for him. Maybe I should teach you Spanish instead."

"I'm good."

"No, you're not," she said simply. "Should I go now and leave you all to do your thing? I'm sure you don't want me here."

"I have one more person for you to meet first." He reached out to put his hand on the small of her back to steer her toward Axel Jamison. When he realized that wouldn't be appropriate, he caught himself before he made contact and curled his fingers into a fist.

An important rule to remember: if he wouldn't do it to any of the male members of his team, he shouldn't do it to a female member.

A lot of men forgot that rule. Uninvited touching was usually unwelcomed.

"This way." He tipped his head toward the BAMC president where he stood at the front of the building, surveying everything.

Jamison looked a bit anxious.

Everyone did.

Crew only hoped this intervention didn't backfire on them and made more of a mess. "We waiting on anyone? Monty or Miller?"

"Neither can make it. And as you know, Fletch won't be here," Jamison answered.

He nodded and flipped a hand toward Cabrera. "Jamison, this is Camila Cabrera, DEA special agent and the newest member of the task force. She's taking Butler's spot. Cabrera, this is Axel Jamison, a sergeant at Shadow Valley PD and also our MC president."

They shook hands and exchanged the normal niceties.

"I might be interested in joining your little club," she announced next.

"Oh yeah?" Jamison's slate blue eyes cut over to Crew.

They locked gazes for a second before his went back to the woman standing next to Crew. "Do you ride?"

"Not yet, but I can learn. Unless you don't let women join?"

"We don't discriminate. The only requirement is that you have a badge. Or that you retired honorably."

Suddenly he was flanked by Rez and Finn. *Just fucking great.*

"We could use more members," Finn said.

"Have you ever ridden on a bike with someone else?" Rez asked.

Cabrera shook her head. "No."

"Don't you think that would be the first step?" Crew asked more sharply than he should've.

He didn't miss it when Finn and Rez exchanged looks.

"I don't know, would it?" she asked.

"Take her for a ride, Crewser," Finn encouraged him with a laugh and whacked the back of his hand into Crew's gut. "Or have her be your backpack on the next run."

For fuck's sake.

Cabrera's eyebrows pinched together. "What does that mean?"

"It means riding on the back of Crew's bike when we have our next organized club ride," Jamison explained.

"Oh, that sounds like fun. But after watching him almost eat it down the steps, I'm wondering if his balance is good enough to ride."

Oh, for fuck's sake!

"Do you think it would be safe for me to ride with him?" she asked next, trying to appear innocent.

It was all an act.

Both Rez and Finn snorted in stereo.

"I can take you for a spin," Rez volunteered.

"Sapphire won't mind, brother?" Crew asked him.

"Sapphire? What a unique name!" Cabrera exclaimed.

"She's unique all right," Crew muttered.

Rez scratched his cheek with his middle finger. "She's one of a kind. But no, she wouldn't mind. It'll be a quick spin on my bike. Now, if she was spinning on my—"

Crew clapped his hands loudly. "Okay! Time for you to go so we can get this intervention started."

"So, you'll take her for a ride, then?" Finn asked Crew, not hiding his amusement.

"Yeah, once I install my training wheels." He grabbed Cabrera's elbow and steered her toward Decker where he stood jawing with Cross near the kitchen area.

"Yo, Full Deck, throw me your key to Fletch's house."

Decker frowned. "Why?"

"We're done checking on it." For now, anyway.

"Why? Are you pulling him from the Dirty Angels?"

"No, she's going to be staying at his place and keeping an eye on it."

With his eyebrows hiked up his forehead, Decker's eyes landed on Cabrera. "Are you staying there by yourself?"

"Well, me and my—"

"Keys, Deck!" Crew shouted, making everyone stare at him in surprise. "Hurry up before Nox wanders down here."

"What the fuck's wrong with you?" Decker grumbled, digging deep into his front pocket.

"Nothing. The intervention's on my mind, that's all."

"Right," Decker murmured, pulling Fletch's house key off a ring and tossing it to Cabrera. "It'll be good not to have to run over there all the time."

"It sounds like a win-win situation for everyone involved," she answered.

He firmly grabbed her elbow again and guided her back

to the meeting room. "You can go out the side door. I'll make sure you get a key for our clubhouse, too."

"I'll start moving into his house tonight. It might take me a few days with my car."

"No, it won't. Fletch said you can borrow his truck. Just don't fuck it up. The key's hanging in the laundry room by the door to the garage. See you tomorrow." He gave her a little push. "I'd help, but as you see I'm busy."

She huffed, "No, you wouldn't."

They heard Jamison yell out, "Who wants to go up and get him?"

"I'll go," came from Cross.

"Okay, you gotta go," Crew said, opening up the side door and urging her to leave.

"Good luck," she said as she brushed past him.

They'd need that and more.

Chapter Six

CREW'S FINGERS dug painfully into his own thighs as Nox stepped out of the BAMC's meeting room.

The man stopped short and took them all in. "What the fuck is this?"

Cross moved to stand next to him and put a hand on his back, urging, "Go have a seat."

Even from where Crew sat in a folding chair set up behind one of the couches, he could see Nox's flared nostrils and his jaw sharp enough to cut glass. "No. We had no meeting scheduled, so I don't know what the fuck this is."

When he turned, Cross blocked him from going out the same way they came in.

Decker jumped out of his seat and rushed over to make sure Nox didn't leave out the back door, either.

"Have a seat," Jamison called out, pointing to the middle cushion on the center couch. A spot saved just for Nox.

Nox's dark eyes found Crew. "Is this task force business?" he asked sharply.

He knew it wasn't since most of the people there weren't

on the task force. The man was stalling. "No, but you still answer to me."

"Not off the clock."

"If you want to be that way," Jamison started, rising to a stand, "you do answer to me. I'm not only your sergeant at SVPD, I'm your prez." He jabbed a finger toward the couch. "Now, sit the fuck down."

Nox remained by the door to the meeting room with his spine stiff and his chin raised. "You can't force me to do shit." He turned and went toe to toe with Cross. "Get the fuck out of my way."

Cross shook his head. "No, brother, I'm not going to do that."

"Nox," Jamison called out. "Do us a favor and give us a few minutes of your time. That's all we're asking."

Nox glanced over at the BAMC prez. "You're not asking, you're telling. I don't like being ambushed."

Crew kept his voice low and steady. "And we don't like having to ambush you."

"But you did it anyway."

"Because we had no choice," Finn told him. "C'mon, man, just sit so we can get this over with."

"You're family and we all love you like a brother, and you have us all worried," North said.

Nox pulled at his chin and his gaze circled the group. "What's this about?"

"Sit and we'll explain," Jamison urged. When Nox still didn't move, he pulled out the card he was hoping he wouldn't have to play. "If you want to keep your job at SVPD and also stay on the task force," his eyes slid to Crew and Crew gave him a slight chin lift in approval, "you need to sit."

"What are you going to do, fire me?"

"I'll put you on administrative leave," Jamison stated,

"and if you're on that, you'll be automatically removed from the task force."

"For my own good, right?" Nox asked sharply.

"Yes, Nox, for your own good," Jamison answered. "Now, don't make me do shit I don't want to do."

"Then don't."

Crew pinched his nose and dropped his head. This was going just as he thought it would... Nox being too stubborn for his own good.

It was time to play hardball.

Crew surged to his feet. "You're off the task force!" Silence surrounded them as he met Nox's eyes across the room. "You made your choice, now you have to live with it. You can go back to SVPD and working patrol."

Jamison shook his head. "No, he won't. Like I said, with the way he is right now, I'll be talking to the captain. He won't be on patrol, either."

This tough love was killing Crew—and most likely everyone else—but it was necessary. The last thing any of them wanted was Nox to eat his own service weapon.

And every one of them in that room knew that was where it might be headed if they didn't do something. If they didn't take a stand and they lost him, none of them would be able to live with themselves because they didn't make an effort to stop it.

Nox stared at Crew for a few seconds, then at Jamison, before his gaze dropped to his boots. His chest expanded, stayed that way for a moment or two, then retracted when he released the held breath.

As they waited for him to decide, Crew swore no one else in the room breathed.

When Nox's head lifted with his mouth nothing but a

slash, his eyes appeared shadowed, and his expression had become a blank mask.

"We love you, brother," Rez said softly. "If you love us, then you'll hear us out."

Crew rubbed at the ache in his chest at Rez's words. He said what everyone else was thinking, but man...

He breathed a little easier when, with a single nod, Nox came over and sat in his assigned spot. He looked as stiff as the Tin Man from the Wizard of Oz, but at least he cooperated.

"Let's get this over with," Nox said with zero emotion, staring straight ahead at the dark TV screen on the wall.

"You've fallen down that deep, dark well again," Jamison started.

Nox's brow furrowed. "I'm fine."

"You were getting to that point," Rez agreed. "Until we found Sadie. Something triggered you when we did."

"We can guess what," Decker added, "so we don't need to discuss those details, but we do need to discuss you."

"I'm fine," Nox repeated, not looking at anyone.

Jesus. "I wish that was true," Crew said under his breath. He knew Nox heard it when the man tugged his baseball cap lower.

An attempt at hiding his eyes and his expression.

Hell, just hiding in general.

The whole reason the man rarely left The Plant. He didn't want to deal with life.

He felt hollow and alone. Despite the last being farthest from the truth.

They had all been shocked and surprised, even pleased, when he agreed to go undercover with Rez back in January. Of course, that didn't last long. And what happened during that period of time—finding Sadie dead in that Ohio motel room and in the condition she was—derailed Nox all over again.

Decker, Rez and Finn never should've taken him along. They should've known they'd find Sadie either dead or badly abused.

Though, they had no idea they'd find her corpse defiled. It was most likely seeing her in that condition that pushed him over the edge.

Crew pulled himself back to the present when Cross said, "We're here for you. No matter how bad it gets. But none of us have the skill or experience needed to truly help you."

"I'm fine."

"Christ almighty!" Crew bellowed. "You're not. Did you forget we knew you before..." He swallowed the next words and pivoted. "We knew you when you *were* fine. You are far from that now, brother. You can keep saying that, but it's all bullshit."

Jamison glared at him.

Crew closed his eyes and took a breath. His heart was no longer aching but burning.

When Jamison went over to Nox, he stared at what the BAMC prez was holding in his hand.

"Take them," Jamison demanded.

Nox did, but reluctantly.

Crew already knew what they were because everyone had a discussion about it beforehand. One was a business card to a cognitive behavioral therapist. The other was a pamphlet for a grief support group.

Not the same group he had attended right after Jackie's death, since he never shared the reason why he stopped going to that one. They had found another group specifically for spouses and loved ones of law enforcement and military, whether lost in the line of duty or not. Crew hoped it would be a better fit, even though his late wife had been neither.

Jamison had reached out to the person leading the group and they said he was welcome to attend since it was also open to law enforcement personnel experiencing loss, as well.

After a quick glance at the info, Nox asked, "I get to pick?"

"No," Jamison answered. "You're going to do both."

———

CREW TOOK a long ride after the "intervention" was over. He needed to clear his head and hoped it would help his heart-burn pass. He even hit the highway so he could open up Silver Foxy and feel all her power and speed.

He hated the fact that they had to ambush Nox like that. To Crew, it bordered on betrayal. As it did to Nox. But still...

If it meant saving their brother, it was necessary. Despite what Nox thought.

The man did not look happy when they finally let him go. It was also concerning that, instead of heading back up to his apartment, he walked out the door, straddled his bike and sped away.

Maybe he was doing the same as Crew. Blowing off some steam.

They considered having someone follow him, but both he and Jamison agreed to let him have time alone to process.

They did what they could do and only hoped in the end it would all work out.

He hoped to fuck it would all work out.

Just like the Cabrera situation.

Without planning it, he found himself at Fletch's house.

After parking Foxy in the driveway, he used his house key to go inside.

Since she hadn't returned yet, he figured he'd wait and help her unload the truck.

He went out to the pool, settled on a lounge chair, watched the setting sun turn the sky into various shades of color, released a long sigh and closed his eyes...

Something wet nudged his hand and it flopped up before it dropped.

What the fuck?

That same something snuffled his side, then a warm, wet washcloth licked his neck.

His eyes popped open and he sat straight up, pushing what was definitely not a washcloth away, and wiped at the dampness on his skin with his hand.

He was surprised to find that night had fallen, and he must have dozed off.

With a groan, he tried to stand but it took a few seconds for his body to catch up with his intention. It no longer worked like it did twenty years ago.

The dog's tail wagged back and forth slowly as the four-legged monster grinned up at him. "I assume you're Murphy."

Murphy's tail wagged a little faster and he released a little *woof*.

Once Crew managed to stand, the dog just about knocked him over when the moose leaned into him. "I bet she doesn't walk you. You walk her."

The rear spotlights came on and blinded him for a second, then Murphy's owner stepped out of the back door, calling out, "I thought I recognized that Harley."

"Jesus, is this a dog or a rough-coated pony?"

"Do you know any pony that eats dog food?"

"Do you know any ponies?" he countered.

"No, but I had one on my wish list every Christmas and birthday during my childhood."

"With the size of that animal, it looks like you got your wish." He headed toward the house with Murphy at his side. "What are you wearing?"

She was wearing worn jeans that fit her way better than they should, sneakers and... When she bent over to pat Murphy's side, he saw what was emblazoned on the back of her black T-shirt.

He shook his head at the huge yellow "DEA" block letters on the back and the agency's logo on the front. She might as well have a spotlight following her around as she sung, "Look at me! Can't you see? I'm a federal agent!"

With a frown, she glanced down. "Was I supposed to wear an evening gown, a tiara and stilettos to move?"

"Don't wear that shit again."

"Why?"

"Because... Just don't. We're in the middle of an investigation. And advertising you're DEA like that isn't smart."

She plucked at the shirt. "Anybody can buy this."

"But not anybody should."

She tipped her head in acquiescence. "I won't argue that point."

"As the task force leader, you shouldn't argue any points with me."

"Well, I *will* argue that." She sighed and planted her hands on her hips. "So, what are you doing here?"

"I needed to clear my head after that whole thing, so I went for a ride."

"And ended up here?"

He shrugged. "I figured you could use the help."

Her eyebrows rose at that.

"You don't believe I want to help you."

"No, sorry, I don't. I think you have some sort of ulterior motive for convincing Fletcher to rent me his house. You didn't want me to get anything long-term because you hope I won't be sticking around."

"I didn't say that."

"No, but it's obvious. And despite what you think, I'm good at my job."

That remained to be seen.

"How did the intervention go?"

"Like expected."

"I'm sure it was difficult."

He shook his head. He didn't want to talk about it. Not right now and not with her. "Did you get everything in one trip?"

"Yes, having a truck helped. Please thank Fletcher for me." Her eyes narrowed on him. "Or didn't he know I used it?"

"He knew."

"And he knows I'm renting his house?"

"Damn, woman."

"Well, you probably still haven't told him about Murphy."

He frowned. "Do you want to stay here or not? Your shit isn't unloaded yet. We can easily drop it off at a motel."

She rolled her lips inward. After a few seconds, she asked, "Are you always this cranky?"

No, he wasn't. But after last night's fantasy about her and then the intervention earlier with Nox, he was ready for this day to be over.

After he helped her move her shit inside.

Even though he shouldn't be here. She could handle it on her own.

But here he was.

Christ.

Maybe she'd put in a good word with her father.

He grimaced. He didn't need a good word. He was good at his damn job.

"Let's go," he barked, striding toward the back door. He would help her unload the boxes, then get the fuck out of dodge.

"You didn't answer my question," he heard behind him.

"No," he answered, not bothering to hold the door for her. He just plowed through the house.

Women's lib meant that she could hold her own damn door.

"No what? No, you're not always cranky, or no, you're not answering my question?"

"Where did you park the truck?"

"I backed into the garage. I figured it would be easier to unload it from there and if I didn't get it done tonight, at least my stuff would be protected from the elements."

He stopped in his tracks.

Well, damn. Proof she was smart and had common sense.

He shook his head and continued, heading through the laundry room and into the garage.

He dropped the tailgate on Fletch's truck and his head jerked back at the little that she had. It was about a half dozen large cardboard boxes, one large suitcase and two smaller ones.

He reached in and grabbed the nearest box. "These boxes aren't marked."

"No, because I don't have much. And I wasn't planning on moving into a house."

"Who doesn't label their boxes?"

"The person standing behind you."

He lifted the box and turned. "Where does this go?"

She shrugged. "It's not marked, so I have no idea what's in it."

"Are you fucking kidding me?" Maybe she wasn't so smart.

His head twitched when her laughter hit his ears and slid all the way down to his dick.

Jesus H. Christ. That was not good.

"Yes. I'm messing with you. It goes in the bedroom. All I have right now are clothes and personal items. Like I told you, the rest of my stuff is back at my parents'. I'll keep it there until I find something more permanent."

Good. She needed to keep it there in case this assignment didn't work out.

And if it was up to him, this assignment wouldn't work out.

He grunted and pushed past her, carrying the box inside. Fletch's bedroom was oversized, so he dumped the box in an empty corner. He'd stack the rest there, too. On his way back to the garage, he had to pause to let her through the bedroom door first as she dragged the large suitcase past him.

They continued to retrace their steps from the truck to the bedroom until the truck bed was empty. The last load ended up being a bunch of dog supplies, including food, bowls, a huge dog bed and everything else a massive canine needed.

Once they dumped all that in the living room, she wiped a bead of sweat off her forehead with the back of her hand, then scrubbed her palms down her jeans.

With a sigh and hands on her hips, she stared toward the kitchen. "I guess the next stop is the grocery store."

"Not tonight."

"No, not tonight. Though, that made me hungry."

"Go ahead and eat anything about to expire. Fletch said you can throw out anything already past its 'use by' date."

"I'll do that. But anything I eat, I'll replace."

"Here's a helpful tip. If it's furry, don't eat it."

With a soft cry, the big dog leaned into him and he had to adjust his stance so he wouldn't be knocked over. His fingers automatically dug into the fur at Murphy's neck to give it a good scratch.

"Aw, Murph, he wasn't talking about you."

"Jesus, he's heavy enough to knock me over."

"He weighs more than me."

He didn't doubt that.

She pulled in a deep breath. "Anyway, thanks for this."

He tipped his head.

"I'll put a good word in with my dad." The corners of her lips twitched.

"Great," he muttered.

It was time for him to go. This was officially her space and he was considered a guest now.

"See you at 0800 in the morning." He headed toward the door.

"Hey," she called out just as he reached it.

He paused and turned.

"I still need to find a local dog walker I can trust. Do you mind if I bring Murphy with me tomorrow?"

"It's a task force headquarters, not a stable."

"He sleeps most of the day."

His gaze dropped to the dog at her side, then returned to her face. Was she holding her breath?

That dog must mean a lot to her. Almost as much as his kids meant to him.

He pinned his lips together and nodded. "Fine. As long as he doesn't create chaos and a mess."

A smile lit up her face, making his heart thump wildly.

What the actual fuck?

"Murphy and I appreciate it. He'll be an angel, I promise."

"He better be," Crew muttered and pulled open the door. "Lock up and set the alarm."

"Yes, boss," was the last he heard right before it closed behind him.

For fuck's sake.

Chapter Seven

As soon as he opened the door to the third floor, he did a double-take. He had forgotten it was "bring your pony to work" day.

Cabrera's Irish Wolfhound took his time getting up from the dog bed next to her chair. Murphy stretched his huge body, yawned, then lumbered his way over to Crew.

When the dog got to him, the canine nudged his hand and gave him "poor me" eyes.

"He wants you to pet him," the dog's owner explained, as if Crew wasn't already aware of that.

"Thanks for clarifying. I thought he was panhandling," he said dryly.

"You know, that's a good idea. I should teach him to do that. I can hang a sign around his neck and have him guilt people into giving him a buck. He really needs to start chipping in toward his bills."

"I bet his dog food alone costs a fortune," Decker said from where he sat in front of one of the desks on the other side of the room.

Cabrera shrugged. "He's worth it."

Crew headed over to the coffeemaker, thanked the coffee gods for the full, fresh pot, grabbed his mug and filled it to the brim. After taking a long sip, he turned and almost tripped over the big galoot. "Can you keep him contained?"

"Murphy!" she called out and pointed to his fleece bed.

The big, fuzzy gray dog glanced around unbothered, then lumbered his way back over to her, before turning three times in place and settling with a loud groan.

Life must be really fucking tough for that dog.

Crew headed back over to her. "Are you still reading the daily reports?"

When she turned her deep brown eyes up to him, they held a gleam he wasn't sure he liked. "Since I want to be a team player and until the boss gives me another assignment, I'm doing what the boss told me to do."

"Stop calling me the boss," he growled and downed another mouthful of much-needed caffeine.

She leaned back in her chair, locking eyes with him. "Isn't that what you are?"

"Calling me Crew is fine."

"Crewella, J. Crew, Crewser, Motley Crew, any of those work, too," came from Finn, scrolling through some recorded footage. "Or come up with your own."

"I'm sensing a theme around here. Is it a competition to come up with the craziest nickname?"

"You could say that," Decker answered.

"I guess we need to come up with one or two for you," Finn told her. "Cami-sole is a good start."

"It's not a task force thing," Crew clarified, glaring at Finn, "it's a Blue Avengers thing."

"*Aaaah.* So, once I become a Blue Avenger, I'll qualify for the fun nicknames."

"Are you thinking about getting a bike?" Mullins asked.

"I'm thinking about it. Joining a law enforcement MC sounds like fun."

"It's not fun," Crew said quickly, hoping to discourage her from joining the BAMC.

She lifted an eyebrow. "Then, why would you belong to one?"

"It's a brotherhood," he explained.

"We have loads of fun," Decker countered. "How about Camshaft? Cam-omile."

"Or just Camo," Finn suggested.

Mullins decided to join in. "Cameo. BodyCam. Camelback. Camel toe!" burst from him on a laugh. "I could do this all day."

"But you won't," Crew told him, shooting him a scowl. "We have work to do."

"Yes, *boss*," Mullins teased.

Crew closed his eyes and shook his head. A few snorts made him open his eyes. He *knew* she would disrupt his team.

He needed to come up with a job for her that took her out of The Plant and put her elsewhere.

Like surveillance.

Nobody liked to do that job.

It would be perfect for her. It would keep her busy and keep her away from the rest of his team.

And him.

He went over to the coffeemaker, topped off his mug and settled in front of one of the available computers.

Decker dropped into the chair next to him, rolled it until it banged into his and whispered, "When did this turn into doggy daycare?"

"It's temporary."

"You mean the same as what you're hoping for with her? To be on the team only temporarily?"

Crew didn't answer him, but he did risk a glance over his shoulder to make sure Cabrera didn't overhear them. "I need to find something for her to do. She's distracting."

"For us? Or for you?"

Crew gritted his teeth. *Both.* "The team."

"She's not distracting me. Maybe the dog is, but we'll get used to the new task force mascot."

"He's not going to be the mascot!" he exclaimed a bit too loudly.

Decker chuckled, then turned in his chair and got to business. "Anybody see T-Bone lately on the cameras or the recorded footage?"

"Haven't seen hide nor hair of him," Finn answered. "Nox hasn't, either. Me thinks the Demon returned to his home in hell."

"We could only be so lucky," Decker muttered.

"How about Saint?" Crew asked. The manager of The Peach Pit had been down and out for a bit after Rez's woman tried to drive a platform heel into this brain, then beat him unconscious with the butt of his own gun.

Admittedly, it was the best thing Crew had seen in a while.

"Looks like he's back terrorizing the girls at The Peach Pit," Finn reported. "He looks uglier than ever since Sapphire did a number on him," he finished with a blinding grin. "Hey, *boss*, can I bring in Minx and Jinx?"

"No," Crew answered. "This isn't doggy daycare, despite what it looks like."

Cabrera spun her office chair around. "Who's Minx and Jinx?"

"Our Dobermans," Finn answered.

"Oh, cool. Fellow dog lover." She high-fived him in the air, even though they were on opposite sides of the room.

"They *are* cool."

When Finn returned the high-five, Crew rolled his eyes.

"What's up your ass?" the BAMC road captain asked him with a frown.

"A stick about four feet long is my guess," Cabrera answered, causing laughter from the guys.

For fuck's sake, she was fitting right in.

And that could be a problem.

"I didn't get much sleep last night," he lied.

Finn jerked his fist back and forth. "Too much porn last night?"

Cabrera's head twisted toward him as she waited for his answer.

No, too many fantasies about the woman he'd watched bending over and carrying in boxes last night. He almost got caught eye-balling her, like the perv he was, several times.

And maybe too much porn.

"Maybe not enough," Decker said. "You'd think jerking off to porn would make him fall asleep faster."

It was best to ignore them. If he argued, they'd only ride his ass harder. Instead, he turned to the computer and began to analyze all the businesses the Demons had purchased in the last couple of years since partnering with the Russos. They targeted businesses that could be used as a way to sell drugs, a way to launder their drug money, or both.

The task force already had plenty of evidence of drug sales out of Pizza Town. The team had cameras installed at The Peach Pit and their Uniontown church, so those locations were covered.

Where could he set her up to do surveillance? Where did

they still need to document the outlaw MC's activities? What would keep her out of his hair?

As well as his thoughts?

He scrolled down through the list of Demon-owned businesses.

The car wash...

The laundromat...

Wait...

Either of those would work, even though both had been purchased strictly for washing their dirty money. Realistically, there wouldn't be much activity there. One reason he didn't have anyone on his team staking out those locations.

Plus, forensic accountants would be utilized to prove money laundering for the upcoming indictments.

But then there was...

"Hey, did those fuckle-chucks actually buy the Hawg Wild Saloon?" he called out.

Decker's eyebrows pinned together. "You losing your memory, old man?"

Was he? "If they did, someone forgot to add it to the list. It's not my damn memory that's lacking."

Even so, he wasn't sure he wanted to put her in danger by putting her at that biker bar. If anything happened to her while on his watch...

He grimaced.

Yeah, it would be best to have her stake her ass out in front of something like the laundromat.

It would be boring, but boring was safe. Even better, it would get her out of The Plant.

His mouth curved into a smile.

"Brother," Decker murmured at the next desk. "I'm not sure I like that smile."

Cabrera probably wouldn't, either.

————

Sʜᴇ'ᴅ ʙᴇᴇɴ sɪᴛᴛɪɴɢ in this damn dark parking lot at a small strip mall for the past three nights. Of course, the only business open was Landry's Laundry. A business the Demons bought over a year ago.

She had no idea why Crew had her sitting on it. Her gut told her it was unnecessary, and only busy work. He wanted her out of his hair and to give her an assignment that wasn't risky.

When she got the order that she'd been assigned to the Pittsburgh field office and the task force, she'd been excited. She had driven the long hours ready to sink her teeth into an important investigation.

But here she sat. Twiddling her thumbs, yawning and drinking enough coffee to stay awake, but not enough that she'd have to empty her bladder every twenty minutes. Because at this hour, nothing nearby was open. She'd have to find a bush, a tree or an abandoned vehicle to squat behind.

Even so, it was obvious that the Demons weren't doing drug deals from this business. In fact, she had only seen one biker with a Deadly Demons cut go inside and even then, only at night. So far, it was usually around one in the morning when the 24/7 business was dead.

From where she sat in her nondescript sedan, she tracked the same young biker through the big glass windows every night go around and empty all the money from the coin-operated washers and dryers, remove cash from the coin changer, refill it with some of the loose change, then disappear into the back for a bit.

She had no doubt the assigned money collector was packing some heat. Most likely under that leather vest and not in a proper holster, either. Guaranteed, the dumbass had an unsecured gun shoved into his waistband.

A good way to get an extra hole in his ass. She guessed it would make it easier to shit.

After doing more research on both lawful and outlaw motorcycle clubs, she recognized that the colors he wore made him a fully-patched member of the Deadly Demons. It could be that the Demons didn't trust their prospects enough to handle large amounts of cash.

Either way, it didn't matter. What mattered was she was bored to death. And sitting in front of a laundromat night after night wouldn't be valuable for the investigation.

Her daily reports were just as boring as the surveillance. Basically, all she had to do was copy and paste every day and simply change the date.

Same location, same biker. Same old, same old.

If Crew was trying to get her to ask Williams to be reassigned to another investigation, it wasn't going to work.

He wouldn't win this fight.

Because she didn't like to lose. To her, and in this case, quitting was losing. She was more determined than ever to stick with this task force, even if her staying got under his skin.

Plus, this was only her first week. She had the next two days off and had a company coming out to open the pool at Fletcher's house while she drug all the necessary items out of the shed.

She couldn't wait until the water warmed up enough for her to do laps.

Hell, she might not even wait. She might attempt a polar bear plunge to get her heart pumping and her blood flowing.

What she also planned to do in the next two days was watch countless YouTube videos to learn how to make up her face so she looked like a drug addict. If she could get good at it and it looked convincing, she might be able to convince the task force leader she could go undercover to do buys.

As the sun peeked above the horizon, she checked the time. Normally, she'd be heading home right now, letting Murphy out to do his business before feeding him, then crawling into bed for an attempt at some shut-eye.

But instead, she decided when she stopped at The Plant to switch out the task force vehicle for her Audi, she'd stay long enough to log into one of the computers.

She was determined to make a plan. And plans needed research.

Twenty minutes later she was pulling the Toyota into the rear lot, then climbing the steps to the third floor. When she stepped inside the task force's headquarters, her gaze swept the room to only find Crew, Proctor and Powers working.

"What are you doing here?"

Why did Crew's question sound like an accusation?

"Dropping off the pool car and I figured since I'm here, I'd get my daily report off my plate since I have the next two nights off."

Without waiting for his response, she settled in front of an empty computer, and logged in. Instead of typing up her report, she opened the file for Landry's Laundromat and read the notes on the business. She wasn't surprised to find it already tagged by the task force as a business purchased for money laundering.

She shook her head. Of course, Crew knew that. He sent her there anyway to waste her time night after night. He had given her busy work, just like she suspected.

Did he feel threatened by her, or by who her father was?

It could very well be both.

That wasn't her problem. That was his.

With a quick glance over her shoulder to make sure he wasn't spying on her, she scrolled through files and notes on the rest of the Demon-owned businesses.

The Peach Pit, a gentleman's club. Money laundering and drug sales of methamphetamine and marijuana.

Lucky's Car Wash. Money laundering.

Pizza Town. Money laundering and drug sales of methamphetamine and marijuana.

She kept scrolling. It was more of the same.

When she hit the bottom of the list, she quickly scrolled back up a half inch to a business that caught her eye.

The Hawg Wild Saloon. It had been mentioned the other day, but she hadn't thought much about it.

Sinking her teeth into her bottom lip, she sat back and stared at the screen, letting her gray matter formulate a plan.

How could she utilize that business for undercover work?

Of course, the obvious would be that she could go in and buy drugs. However, a possible hiccup with that might be them having to warm up to her first before selling to her. Just to make sure she wasn't five-o. Unfortunately, that honeymoon period could take time.

She wanted to prove her capabilities quickly with Crew so she wasn't stuck with tedious and boring assignments.

She *could* go and hang out at Hawg Wild while not on the feds' clock and let her face become familiar to the Demons. Or to whoever was working the bar and selling.

If they were even dealing from that location. That hadn't been clear in the notes.

As she skimmed them, it stated it was solely a biker bar. That meant the general public most likely gave it a wide berth. So, some unknown Latina sitting in a corner by herself might catch some attention. And not the attention she wanted.

Or... She could go undercover there in another capacity.

During college, she had worked at a sports bar part-time during the semester and full-time during summer breaks. She had been mostly a server but occasionally filled in behind the bar when it was busy, or if they were short-handed. She learned to pour a draft beer properly. She knew how to carry a tray full of drinks and food without spilling any. She was good with customers. Even drunk ones.

The idea could work.

But convincing Crew to allow her to go undercover as a Hawg Wild employee might be more difficult than convincing the Demons to hire her.

She *could* hit the task force leader with a one-two punch. First, pretend she wanted to go undercover as a drug addict so she could go into Hawg Wild to do buys. When he balked at that, she could then suggest she go under as an employee.

And if, for some reason, he agreed from the start that she could do buys, then that was what she'd do.

She'd still get what she wanted. Which was action, of course.

It would also give her a purpose and make her an asset to the task force. If she was successful, it would look good on her employment record.

A win-win for everyone.

As she shut the computer down, a smile spread across her face.

Chapter Eight

SHE HID her car on the next block and wandered up to the back gate at The Plant. She wasn't scheduled to work today, so it was the perfect time to try out the skills she learned after spending hours upon hours on YouTube watching special effects makeup tutorials.

Luckily, making up her face to look gaunt, full of sores, along with dark circles under her eyes hadn't been too difficult after a few tries. As long as he didn't look too closely.

She made sure to arrive at the back gate super early. Once there, she squatted down and leaned back against the fence to wait for the task force leader to arrive.

Dressed in ripped, filthy jeans and a stained hoodie, she also wore an old baseball cap she dragged through the dirt and tucked her hair underneath before pulling the sweatshirt's hood over top of it to hide her face as much as possible.

She set a beat-up backpack on the ground next to her and staged an empty forty-ounce bottle of Busch beer nearby on the curb.

All she was missing was a stolen grocery cart overflowing

with clothes and household items. She wanted to appear like a homeless drug addict but she drew the line on actually committing a crime to do so.

She hoped like hell Crew would arrive at his normal time and didn't have to be anywhere else this morning. She didn't want to do this all over again tomorrow. She also wanted to avoid any other members of either the federal task force or the Blue Avengers.

Luckily, the man she planned on ambushing was a bit anal and normally arrived long before 0800 hours.

Hearing a Harley cruising down the alley, she blew out a relieved breath when she saw it was Crew riding at an unhurried pace.

His mirrored sunglasses immediately landed on her as he got closer, slowed down, then stopped in front of the gate. He would need to get off his bike to open it, but he remained straddling his motorcycle, with deep creases marring his brow.

She remained where she was, bobbing her head back and forth to appear drunk or high, but kept her eyes tipped up just enough to watch his every move without being too obvious.

This needed to be convincing. She needed to prove that she had the skill to go undercover.

To show him that she was damn good at her job.

That he needed to have faith in her so she could do that job.

She was not a piece of dust that could be swept under the rug and hidden away. She was a fucking Navy veteran who graduated top of her class from the DEA academy.

She was fucking capable.

He just needed to take those goddamn mirrored sunglasses off and see that.

She took another deep breath to calm her annoyance.

Now to test her ability with makeup and acting...

The second he dismounted from his bike, she rose shakily to her feet. She grabbed the fence behind her to steady her fake weaving.

He didn't move to open the gate, instead he continued to observe her. She could see his stance widen a little bit and his shoulders pull back in preparation of whatever was to come next.

He was on the defensive since he was unsure of the situation.

And rightly so.

He should be suspicious of anyone hanging around the gate of a building that housed a federal task force. Any DEA agent worth his weight in salt would.

She had heard good things about Colin Crew before joining the team. From both her father and Bob Williams.

The man before her was a good agent, had closed plenty of high-profile cases in his career and was well-respected throughout the agency.

Even though he came off as a bit of a jerk.

She took a few wobbly steps in his direction, keeping her face tipped down to hide her identity a little better. Since she needed to pull this off successfully, every step, every body movement, was calculated.

When she was only a few feet away, she disguised her voice by dropping it an octave and making it sound as rough as possible. She also added a slight slur for good measure. "Hey, *maaaaan*, got any spare change?"

He considered her carefully with his lips pursed and his head tilted to the side before answering, "No. Sorry."

"How 'bout a job? I can do *aaaaaaanything* you need."

"Don't have that for you, either."

She jerked her head toward the fence, then pretended to lose her balance. "Whoa! Almost fucking ate it there... What's behind the gate?"

"Nothing." His dark eyebrows peppered with a few grays pinned together. "How'd you get to this area? Did you drive here?"

She shook her head and rolled back and forth on her toes slightly, so she'd look wasted. "Got dropped off here."

"Who dropped you off?"

She jerked up her shoulders. "Dunno. Was hitchhiking and some rando picked me up. Didn't question it, just a... a... ppreciated the ride." She took a few steps closer so he could pick up the mix of alcohol and urine she had liberally sprinkled on her clothes.

She'd owe Fletch a new bottle of whiskey and Murphy an apology.

"Come *ooooon*. Just need a few bucks, man. Just to get me to tomorrow." She hacked a few times in his direction, not covering her mouth.

She struggled not to laugh at his expression. If she did, she'd blow it.

"For what?" he asked, the corners of his mouth pulled down.

"Food, man. Gotta eat. Haven't eaten since... Hell, don't even remember the last time."

"I can grab you food."

"Nah. I can get my own. Just need the money."

His eyebrows rose so high she could see them peeking over his sunglasses. "So, not for food."

"C'mon, man, I'll do *aaaaanything* for it." She moved even closer and when he stepped backwards, the backs of his legs hit his bike. She took advantage of that and grabbed him by the jacket, pushing herself against him from chest to hip. "Look... I'll do whatever you want. Whatever you're into."

His nose wrinkled as he picked up her scent. His hands came up, but he avoided touching her. "Back off."

She did the exact opposite and crowded him, instead. She was so close she could pick up his delicious scent over her gag-inducing one.

She grabbed his arms and pressed against him. "C'mon. Just a few bucks. Just some spare change. Just tell me what I need to do for it."

"You need to back off!" he shouted and shoved her.

Cami made a big production of falling back against the privacy fence, making sure to slam her back against the wood hard enough to make it rattle. "Damn," she groaned. "Have a fucking heart."

His nostrils flared and his beard-covered jaw was tight. "Wait here. My heart and I will go grab you a meal." He turned to get back on his Harley.

"Don't wanna meal, man," she called out. "Just need to earn a little dough. Like I said, I'll do anything. *Anything*."

He grimaced. "There's nothing I want from you."

"You sure?" With a huge grin, she threw her head back and stared him right in the eyes... or mirrored sunglasses.

His head twitched when he did a double take. "Cabrera," he growled and ripped off his shades.

She threw up her hands. "The one and only."

His narrowed gray eyes searched her face. "Holy shit."

"Was I convincing?"

His Adam's apple bounced and his jaw shifted. *For fuck's sake*, he didn't want to admit it.

Asshole.

"I had you going there, right?" she prodded.

"Did you lay in the grass and let your miniature horse piss on you?"

"Something like that. So, are you going to admit it or not?"

His expression went blank. "Admit what?"

"That I had you going."

"I knew something was off."

She rolled her eyes. "You can't even give me a little credit, can you? What do you have against me?"

"Nothing."

"You act like I'm some sort of burden, when I'm here to help. I was exc—" No, she wasn't admitting to him how excited she was to join this task force. *Fuck him.* "I want to do buys."

"I have you on surveillance."

"It's boring and unneeded."

"Are you questioning my authority?"

"You sound like Cartman from South Park. *Respect my authoritah!*" she mimicked. "Now it makes sense why Decker uses that ringtone for you."

His head jerked. "He does what?"

She dramatically slapped a hand over her mouth. "Oh, did I just fuck up?"

His eyes narrowed again. "He has Cartman as my assigned ringtone?"

"Maybe I'm wrong and just imagined it."

"Right."

"C'mon. Just let me do one buy and we'll see how it goes."

"What if it goes wrong?"

Then it goes wrong, she wanted to scream. Investigations and undercover work went wrong all the time. "Crew, I can think my way out of a jam and I can defend myself. I'm a goddamn federal agent just like you and want to be treated as such."

"You're not just like me," he said too calmly.

"If you say it's because I'm not a man..."

He pulled in a sharp breath. "I wasn't going to say that. You only have a year under your belt. That's my concern, not that you're a woman."

Bullshit. "I need something worthwhile to do. Let me prove myself to you."

He stared at her for far too long, then he slowly slid his sunglasses back over his eyes. "Let me think about it." He threw his leg over his bike and pushed the start button. "Open the gate, will you?"

She sighed but did it despite wanting to tell him to fuck off.

As he pulled past her, he yelled, "Close that behind me, then go home and enjoy your day off."

"Yes, boss," she muttered through gritted teeth as she shut the gate.

———

She had pulled off tricking him. Cabrera's acting had been decent, the makeup even more convincing.

But he still wasn't sure he wanted to approve of her making buys.

Why he was more cautious with her than the rest of the team members, he didn't know.

Well, there was the little fact of who her father was.

And the fact she was a newer agent.

But the truth was, how was she going to learn without him throwing her into the mix?

He sure as fuck hoped Williams wouldn't have added her

to his task force if he didn't believe she'd be able to handle it. Unless he'd been pressured to do so...

That was his worry.

If she couldn't do her job properly, it could be dangerous for her. And that, in turn, could be dangerous for him.

He'd feel better if she partnered up with someone on the team first. A partnership like Fletch and Wilder.

That had worked out well.

Too well, in their case.

As he hit the top landing, he pulled his cell phone from his back pocket and pulled up his contact list. He scrolled until he found Decker's number, then he punched in the code to the door and as soon as it unlocked, he pushed Send on his phone and pulled open the door.

He only hoped Big Deck didn't have his phone set to vibrate.

As he stepped inside, he heard it.

Cabrera was right. The asshole had Cartman from South Park screaming, *"Respect my authoritah!"* as Crew's ringtone.

Decker quickly hit a button to ignore the call and his eyes sliced over to him. "Did you just butt dial me?"

No, he didn't. "Is that your normal ringtone?"

"Yep."

"For everyone?"

"Uh huh."

Crew glanced over at Finn. "Call Deck's phone."

Finn's mouth gaped, then snapped shut. "I don't have his number."

Crew went over to where Rez was sitting and put out his hand. "Give me your task force phone."

Rez's head jerked back. "I forgot to bring it."

"Bullshit," he growled, then marched over to the phone in the middle of the conference table and punched in Decker's number. He heard nothing but a low buzz. "Take it off vibrate."

Decker's expression went blank. "I don't want to disturb anyone."

"Bullshit," he repeated as he shook his head. He glanced around. "Do all of you use that ringtone for me? You think I'm like Cartman?"

"Pretty much," Finn answered with a snort. "You don't think you are?"

"I—"

For fuck's sake.

Chapter Nine

AFTER CLIMBING OFF HIS BIKE, he peeked into the garage window to see her Audi parked inside.

She was home.

In a few long strides, he was at the door and ringing the bell.

No answer.

He pounded on the door next.

Still no answer.

He placed his ear to the door, hoping to hear footsteps or her calling out. Nothing.

She was most likely out back since the spring weather was perfect and the sun was out. Even the damn birds were chirping.

He really needed to get his ass home, grab his mountain bike and go for a long damn ride.

Riding—either his Harley, his Peloton or his Trek trail bike—always seemed to clear his head.

He needed that. Because someone was taking up a lot of his gray matter and needed to be evicted.

That someone happened to be renting the house he was about to enter.

He dug deep into his front pocket, pulled out his key ring and slipped the key into the deadbolt lock. He only hoped she hadn't changed the security code since he didn't want to have to explain to the local cops why he was entering a home without the renter's permission first.

Something he knew was wrong but was doing it anyway.

As soon as he stepped inside, he entered the code and it worked. *Thank fuck.*

He announced his arrival by yelling, "Cabrera!" so he wouldn't catch her in an embarrassing situation, especially since she had no idea he was stopping over.

Or letting himself in.

But the house was dead quiet.

No Cabrera. No Murphy.

No sounds at all.

Just like he thought, she was probably out back enjoying the day. He made quick work of heading to the backyard through the great room. Before he even opened the door, he could see a big gray hairy mass sprawled out flat on the concrete and sunning himself.

Great guard dog.

He shook his head, but a splash in the pool caught his attention next.

She had opened the pool already? The water had to be as frigid as a witch's tit.

When he stepped outside, the damn dog didn't even lift his head. *For fuck's sake,* what was the point of a huge dog if it didn't protect its owner?

As he approached the pool, Murphy finally lifted his head, opened his big yapper in a huge yawn and then flopped back down, closing his eyes.

"What's the point of feeding that thing if he doesn't warn you about or stop intruders?"

Her head popped up over the side of the pool with her eyes wide and her dark hair plastered to her skull. "What are you doing here?"

Good question. What the hell was he doing here? Why was he drawn to show up in person instead of using his damn cell phone? He didn't want to answer either of those questions.

"Wanted to talk to you about work." At least that was true.

"It couldn't wait until tomorrow?"

"I'm off tomorrow." Also true.

"You couldn't call?"

Of course he could. "I was driving by." Sort of true.

"Do bosses normally show up at their subordinates house unannounced?"

Of course they didn't. That would be fucking creepy. "It's not your house."

Oh, Christ on a cracker, he was such a dick.

"And then just let themselves inside like that?" she continued, with her eyes now narrowed on him.

"I have permission to be here."

With drops of water sliding down her face, one dark eyebrow raised. "Not from me, you don't."

"Again, it's not your house."

"*Umm...* I'm renting it, so technically it is. Do I need to find another place to live?" She shook her head, clearly annoyed. "I just opened the damn pool!"

"No one told you to spend money on opening the pool."

"Why are you such a dick?"

Another good question. "Because I can be." And another bullshit answer. He was batting a thousand here.

"That's not an answer."

Of course it wasn't. "Sounded like one to me."

"How's this? It's not an acceptable answer." She swam toward the steps at the end of the pool. Once there, she climbed out dripping wet, like a siren calling his name.

Luring him to his damn death.

He caught her shiver, even as slight as it was.

Goosebumps covered her body, including the two huge ones that were her rock-hard nipples.

Just like he thought, the water had to be frigid as fuck.

He grabbed a thick towel from a nearby lounge chair she must have dragged out of the shed and tossed it to her.

She caught it, mumbled, "Thanks," and began to dry herself off.

He was tempted to stand there and watch her like the fucking perv he was, but that might be worse than letting himself into the house she was renting.

To keep from doing that, he squatted at the edge of the pool and dragged his hand through the water to check the temperature. "Holy fuck. How can you stand swimming in that?" He stood and dried his hand off on his jeans.

"It's refreshing."

"It's cold enough to give you hypothermia."

"Thanks for your concern, but I'm old enough to decide that for myself. And, by the way, would you say that to a Navy SEAL in training?"

"Are you a SEAL?"

"No."

"Then how does that apply to you?"

She sighed. "Why are you here?"

With the towel now wrapped around her and knotted so it remained in place, it ended his view of her body in a wet one-piece bathing suit that hugged her curves and left nothing to the imagination. At least the little bit of curves she had. Which wasn't much.

She wasn't curvy and soft, but lean with an athletic build. He wasn't sure if her physique was from a regular swimming regimen or it came naturally.

He shouldn't care.

But for some reason he did.

Of course, he wasn't too picky when it came to women's bodies. He liked them all.

Even so, he preferred them to be baked a little longer. Twenty-eight was still too young whether curvy, lean or otherwise.

Not that he was looking for long-term. He wasn't.

Not that he was looking to hook up with the woman standing before him in a ray of sunlight—most likely to warm up. He shouldn't.

Camila Cabrera should be off limits.

For more than just her age. An age that was closer to his daughter's than his own.

But because they worked together.

And then there was her father.

He liked his career and he'd like to keep it. Especially since it paid the bills, including his alimony and child support.

And of course, it provided a roof over his head and utilities to make his life comfortable. Being unemployed would certainly be uncomfortable.

So, why the fuck was he drawn to her despite all the red flags? Why did he keep doing stupid shit like showing up at her house or being a dick to her for no good reason?

He was forty-three, not thirteen. He needed to stop acting like it.

Or he needed to find some other woman not named Camila

Cabrera and get laid. Push the thoughts of the woman he really wanted out of his brain, then slam it shut once that was achieved.

He cleared his throat. "Do you want to go change?"

"Do you want to explain why you're here? You said it was about work. So far, you haven't talked about the task force at all." She tipped her head to the side. "Or was that just an excuse to barge into my house and you really have no valid reason to be here?"

Damn. "Why would I show up here without a valid reason?"

"You tell me. Maybe it has nothing to do with work at all."

"Then what would it be?"

Her eyebrows rose and she took two steps closer, tipping her face up to him. She was close enough for him to see how her wet eyelashes clumped together.

She was close enough to see how a bead of water precariously balanced in the hollow of her throat, tempting him to put his lips there and drink it from her skin.

She was close enough to see her pulse pounding along her throat.

She was close enough to see something flash behind her eyes.

Surprise?

Or was she figuring out what he didn't want her to know?

The fact that he *wanted* her.

If it was anyone other than her, he already would've made his move.

But it was her.

It was Camila Cabrera.

And she was off limits.

Back off, you stupid fuck. Screwing her would screw you.

She took another step closer. With the way the sun was hitting her, he could see the gold flecks in her dark brown eyes. "Well?"

He swallowed. *Say something, dumbass.* "You're going to get what you wanted," he murmured.

"And what do I want?"

Why did her voice turn husky like that?

Did she want him, too? Did she have fantasies while lying in bed at night about him, just like he did about her?

Jesus, he needed to go.

Needed to get back on his bike and go the fuck home.

Because he was afraid this visit was going to take a turn. One he would regret later.

"You're scared of me, aren't you? And it has nothing to do with who my father is, does it?"

"I'm not scared of you."

The corners of her mouth curled up as she studied his face, which he purposely made blank.

"Yes, you're scared of me for some reason. Do you have a problem with women?"

"Only my ex. She's a nightmare." And that was a nice description.

"But you married her anyway."

"I was tricked."

"Or maybe you tricked her."

A valid point, but wrong. "I never pretend to be something I'm not."

Her eyes narrowed on him. "Aren't you pretending now?"

Fuck.

Fuck.

Fuck.

This woman was good. Too good for his comfort. "I have to go."

As he turned on his heel, she grabbed his arm to stop him. "Proof you're scared."

"Will you stop saying that?"

She shrugged. "Prove to me you're not."

"And how do I do that?"

He didn't like the smile that crossed her face. It puckered his asshole and tightened his chest.

What was she up to?

He sucked in a breath as she reached up slowly, curled her hand around the back of his neck and pulled his head down.

She stared into his eyes for a second before they slid closed, and her warm breath whispered over his lips.

He stared at her mouth. It wouldn't take much to close the gap between his and hers.

But that would be stupid and reckless.

Her eyes opened and she closed that gap.

He yanked free of the hold on his neck. "Not a good idea, Cabrera. In fact, it's a really stupid idea."

"What are you scared of?"

Tasting you. Touching you. And then wanting more.

"Chicken," she whispered.

"Fuck it." He grabbed her, slammed her chest into his and pressed his mouth to hers.

Her lips were still cold from the pool, but not for long. They turned soft, warm and pliant. They also fit too perfectly against his. He encouraged them open by drawing the tip of his tongue along the seam.

And when she did, he took her mouth like it was his.

At that moment, it was.

No one else could have it. It belonged only to him.

He swallowed her groan, and it encouraged him to take the kiss deeper, even though he should be doing the opposite.

He should be running, not walking, away.

Her slender fingers gripped his bearded jaw as she gave as good as she got.

Their tongues touched, tangled, and took turns exploring.

He curled his arm around her and tugged her even closer, if that was possible.

He wanted to prove to her that kissing her was nothing to him.

Nothing at fucking all.

He could kiss her and simply go on with his day.

Like nothing ever happened.

He wasn't afraid of her.

Or of this.

Or...

Her hard nipples pressed against his chest. Her hand not gripping his face and holding him in place as she kissed him deeper, more frantically, settled on his chest.

She had to feel his heart ready to beat out of his damn chest.

That wasn't fear. That was...

A man wanting a woman.

In all ways possible.

His erection was more proof.

Was she only testing him? Or was she grinding her hips against his because she wanted him as much as he wanted her?

Either way, it wasn't good.

This was very fucking bad.

If this continued, it could lead them on a path of no return.

A mistake they could not undo.

An action they would eventually regret.

Making working together uncomfortable and unbearable. It could disrupt the team.

This had to stop.

And it had to stop *now*.

He twisted his head, breaking the seal of their lips. He remained turned away with his eyes closed as he gathered his lost brain cells.

And his common sense.

Then he heard it. Her breathing.

Quick and shallow.

The kiss had affected her as much as him.

She *did* want him.

Fuck.

That was going to make it so much more difficult to keep things professional.

To keep things between them uncomplicated.

"Yeah, you're scared at where this will lead. You're struggling," she called him out. "You don't want to admit what you want. You don't want to give in to temptation."

Setting his jaw, he opened his eyes and met hers. "Shut up."

"See? You can't even deny it. And even if you did, that steel rod in your jeans would prove you're lying."

He released her and took a step back, putting space between them so he could think.

His only thought was to escape.

"I gotta go." He jerked into motion and strode quickly toward the back door.

"You never told me the reason for your visit," she called out, making him pause before going inside.

He should go to Williams and demand she be removed

from the task force. He needed to stay away from her. Because he wanted so much more than that damn kiss.

He wanted her underneath him, squirming and meeting him thrust for thrust. Crying out his name, encouraging him to fuck her harder.

He shoved that vision out of his head.

Focus, asshole.

He turned. "I'm approving for you to go undercover to make a buy. One. And if you do that successfully, I'll consider you to do more."

She smiled.

He scowled.

So much for getting Williams to remove her from his team.

Weak motherfucker.

He yanked the door open, strode through the house and back out of it as fast as he could.

Otherwise, he was going to turn around, grab her, throw her over his shoulder and toss her onto Fletch's bed, then fuck the hell out of her.

Until they couldn't think straight.

Until they were exhausted and sweaty.

Until they were both satisfied.

He didn't slow down. Not when he got to his bike, not when he threw his leg over it, or when he strapped on his half-helmet.

He rode the hell out of there like the devil himself was chasing him.

Chapter Ten

Of course he had left her no instructions.

Not where to do the buy. Not how much to buy.

He didn't even leave any federal money for her to do the buy.

Even though he was on days-off, she tried texting him.

A few times.

Enough times to be a menace.

But still... he ignored each and every one of her texts.

So, her first night back to work, she went and did surveillance again at Landry's Laundry.

By the end of the night, she was ready to give Crew what he wanted by quitting because it was so damn boring.

But fuck that, she'd never quit.

No way would she let him win.

He wanted her to leave, not because he didn't think she could do the job. Not because of who her father was.

Because he wanted her.

And he didn't want to want her.

Just like she didn't want to want him.

But, *Christ*, she did.

They were doomed.

Because that kiss between them by the pool had been fire.

His erection proof of how much he liked locking lips with her.

The soaked crotch of her bathing suit proof of what an expert kisser he was. So good that he caused a wetness that had nothing to do with pool water.

So yes, it was a problem.

Because he was a dick.

And she didn't do dicks. The people, not the appendages.

It was late when she pulled into the back lot of The Plant to pick up the sedan. She wasn't heading to the laundromat tonight. She had other plans, instead.

If Senior Special Agent Colin Crew didn't like it, too bad. He had plenty of opportunity to respond to her texts.

She might not have any money to make a buy, but she could at least scope out the Hawg Wild Saloon. She could rub elbows with some bikers. Make conversation. Drop some hints about her interest in buying meth.

Then she could write her daily report tomorrow morning and see how long it took him to notice where she had spent her night. When he returned to The Plant, she could confront him about teasing her with the idea of her doing a buy and then leaving her hanging like a flag without a breeze.

The rear lot behind The Plant was just as she expected—mostly empty—since no more than two team members worked overnight. One would monitor and transcribe wire-taps and sometimes someone would monitor the cameras.

But what she hadn't expected was a familiar Harley parked in one of the spots.

She couldn't be one-hundred percent sure it was their

dear leader since she wasn't a pro at identifying motorcycles. If it was, had something happened with the task force for him to come in on his day off? If so, she hoped it wasn't anything bad.

She needed to head upstairs to grab the key for the sedan anyway, so she might as well check to make sure everyone was all right before she headed out.

Just as she was turning the corner to take the covered exterior steps up to the third floor, the side door banged open and the man himself came barreling out, startling the shit out of her when he almost slammed into her.

She slapped a hand to her heart to press it back into her chest. *Holy shit.*

She did her best to sound unaffected when she asked, "What's going on?"

He stopped short and looked as surprised to see her as she was to see him. "What do you mean?"

She flipped a hand out, and explained, "You're here late."

His brow furrowed. "So are you."

"I'm working. You're supposed to be off."

"I wasn't working. This is the BAMC's clubhouse, remember? We were hanging out and..." He shook his head. "It doesn't matter what I was doing. Everyone else left and I figured I'd run upstairs and check on the guys before heading home."

Damn, maybe he wasn't such a dick. Maybe he had a caring and protective nature about him.

Oh hell, she'd rather continue to think of him as a dick. It was safer for her.

His brow dropped even lower. "What are you doing?"

"Going upstairs to pick up the key for the pool car."

"Where are you going?"

She blinked and stared at him. "Why didn't you respond to any of my texts?"

"You texted me?"

"Oh, for shit's sake. Are you serious? I have blisters on my fingers from as many times as I texted you. Check your phone."

"I was busy."

"So, you did get them."

She rolled her eyes when he said, "I didn't have time to respond."

She shouldn't have given him the benefit of the doubt. He *was* a dick.

Now he just needed to remain that way so he'd be easier to resist.

"I know taking thirty seconds out of your day to text me back will throw off your whole schedule."

"Funny."

"You hear me laughing?"

"You never answered me about where you're going."

Just like you never answered my texts. "I wanted to head to Hawg Wild to scope it out. Since you're only giving me one buy to prove myself, I figured I'd try there since you haven't documented any sales out of that location."

"We haven't tried to make buys there because they just bought it. Fletch and Wilder hung out there a bit but it was before it was in the Demons' hands. We don't know yet if they're selling out of there or not."

"Then, that's a perfect place for me to see if they are and what I can do."

He stared at her.

She closed her eyes and shook her head. "I'm going up to grab the key. Since you're heading up there, too, can you grab me a few federal bucks in case I get the opportunity to score?"

He grumbled something she didn't catch.

Whatever. Let him grouse. Tonight's plan was set and she was sticking to it, whether he liked it or not. She wasn't going to spend another night fighting off sleep in a dark strip mall to only watch a lanky biker collect coins out of washing machines.

As she began to head up the stairs, her heart did the two-step when he roared, "You're going dressed like that?"

He *just* noticed what she was wearing? The area wasn't really well lit, but still...

"Well, yeah." She soldiered on with hiking up the steps.

Earlier in the afternoon she had hit a consignment clothing store and bought what she thought biker women—like ol' ladies—would wear.

"No," he barked, following her up.

No? She rolled her eyes. "I want to fit in. I can't show up in a T-shirt and sweatpants."

She had found a perfect denim mini skirt, a black off-the-shoulder sweater that had an open weave so the black lacy bralette she wore underneath could be seen.

She had applied her makeup on thicker than normal. Her black eyeliner was over the top, as well as her dark eyeshadow.

Basically, she was dressed as if she was heading to a rock concert back in the nineties. She also lucked out when she found black, heeled knee-high boots to finish off the badass look.

"You need to go home and change."

Admittedly, the skirt was *extremely* short—like one wrong move and she'd be flashing her goodies—and the deep-V bralette showed a bit of cleavage—not that she had a lot—but it would attract attention and that was what she strived for.

"Jesus," he continued. "I can see your fucking ass cheeks. You're not wearing that around a crowd of bikers who have no fucking control. Who treat women like shit and think they can do whatever they want to them. You're not going into that hornets' nest dressed like that. Especially without backup."

He sounded like her goddamn father. When she was fifteen. She was now twenty-eight and Crew was *so* not her father. "I can take care of myself."

"Cami—"

Cami? Since when did he use her first name?

She stopped almost halfway up between the first and second floors and turned to find him only three steps down from her. "Crew..."

"Don't you dare fucking argue with me. I gave you a fucking order, so do it. If you want to go undercover, then do it my way or you won't be doing it at all."

His way. She gritted her teeth. "Fine. But if it's okay with you, *boss*, I want to grab the pool car first so I can head directly to the bar after I go change."

He sighed. Loudly. Dramatically. Impatiently. "Fine."

She turned around and continued up the steps, one side of her mouth pulled up. She made sure to emphasize each step up all the way up to the third floor, so he got a *really* good look at her ass.

Served him right.

When they reached the top landing, he crowded behind her. Before she could punch in the code, he reached past her to do it.

His arm brushing against her pulled a shiver from her and made her nipples tighten. She ignored her body's reaction to him being so close. To feeling his heat searing her back. To his breath moving her hair.

With her hand on the doorknob, his words stopped her from turning it. "I'm not sure I want you to go to Hawg Wild by yourself."

When she turned, they were almost chest to chest with barely inches separating them. "Would you say the same thing to the male members of your team?"

"Yes."

"No you wouldn't. Decker went to the Viper's Den down in West Virginia by himself a few times. As an undercover prospect, he went alone to the Wolf Den many times. Hell, he even drove all the way to the Mexican border with a Demon. He was states away without backup. And he's just one example. Do you want more?"

Even in the limited light of a single light bulb above the third-floor door, she could see his nostrils flare.

"Did you forget you made me read all of those reports?"

Karma. It was a bitch.

"You know, my father takes a supplement to help his memory. I'll ask him the name of it and let you know. You could probably use some in your advanced age."

"Funny," he muttered.

"You still don't hear me laughing."

As soon as they stepped inside, Carl Powers, a state trooper, released a low, long whistle. "Damn, woman. Someone's got an agenda with that outfit."

"I'd say," agreed Don Mullins, the Pittsburgh PD narcotics detective.

"Anything going on I need to know about?" Crew asked sharply.

"I thought you were off," Powers' gaze slid from Cami back to Crew. Curiosity filling his expression.

"I am. I was downstairs and figured I'd check on you guys before I head out."

"It's actually pretty quiet tonight," Powers answered, since he was on wiretaps.

"Same," Mullins agreed. "It's dead at The Peach Pit. And any Demons who are still vertical at the Wolf Den are only standing around playing pool, throwing darts, drinking and smoking. Pretty fucking boring, if I say so myself."

"Not your scene?" Cami asked with a grin.

"Fuck no. Now... If you asked if I want to head out to some club to go dancing with you wearing that outfit..." Mullins eyebrows rose. "That wouldn't be boring."

"She's heading out on an assignment," Crew told them.

Mullins' and Powers' heads spun toward her.

"What assignment?" Powers asked.

"She's going to do a buy," Crew answered him before she could.

Powers' brow furrowed. "Where?"

"Hawg Wild," Cami was faster than Crew this time with the answer.

A frown marred Mullins' face. "Alone?"

She sighed. More misogynist bullshit. Too common in law enforcement. Unfortunately, women had to get used to it, whether they liked it or not. Most of them had heard unwanted opinions on how women couldn't do what men could.

Women aren't as strong as men. Women shouldn't be in law enforcement. Women shouldn't be in the military. Women shouldn't be a DEA agent.

Blah blah blah.

Fuck off.

"We don't have cameras installed there. We don't have

anyone else in place to help if shit goes sideways," Mullins told her.

"I'm aware."

"You approved that?" Disbelief and disappointment colored Powers' question to Crew.

Oh fuck. They better not convince the task force leader to pull her from that assignment. She was afraid it wouldn't take much for him to squash her plans.

She also didn't need anyone fighting her battles. "Would you go in there by yourself?" she quickly asked Powers.

Powers swept his hand from head to lap. "With me being Black? Fuck no. Not even in a group. I've got more common sense than that."

Shit. She turned toward Mullins. "Would you?"

"I would, but I'd keep it low-key. That outfit makes you look hot as fuck. It's going to draw a shitload of attention. You'll be fresh meat."

"She's heading home to change first," Crew assured them. He turned toward her. "Wear something that will help you blend in more."

Like what? she wanted to ask. But she knew his answer would be something ridiculous, like a turtleneck and jeans. Maybe even a chastity belt. Besides the jeans, the rest he'd suggest wouldn't help her look like she belonged in a biker bar.

"You packing?" Powers asked, concern crossing his face.

"Of course." She had a compact Glock in a holster tucked at the small of her back. The whole reason she wore a sweater instead of a tight tank top was so the gun wouldn't print and give her away. Now, she only needed to avoid anyone at the bar from putting their hand there.

Not that she doubted any biker chicks didn't carry. Most

likely more than only guns. Cami was pretty damn sure some had a variety of weapons hidden on them. For good reason.

Even so, she needed to keep any of those bikers, Demons or not, from touching her. Since this would be her first time at Hawg Wild, she'd rather not chance having them become suspicious about her from the get-go.

She planned on making friends and influencing people...

She bit back her snort.

"Not sure if they installed a metal detector since buying the joint. I wouldn't put it past them since they kept the one at The Peach Pit. Being outlaws, I'm sure someone somewhere has a beef with them," Powers said.

"If they have one, I'll deal with it," she said simply. "I'm good at coming up with solutions for difficult problems." With that, she raised an eyebrow and tipped her head toward Crew.

Mullins and Powers both chuckled.

She headed over to the pegboard that held the keys for the task force's pool cars and Harleys, found the one she wanted—the boring sedan that wouldn't catch any attention —and snagged the key.

"You have my number, right?" Crew asked. "Call me immediately if you get in a bind. I can have the locals there as quickly as possible to get you out of it."

"Do I have your number?" Cami repeated in disbelief. "I don't know. Check your damn texts."

She heard more chuckles as she beelined toward the door. She needed to get out of there before he changed his mind.

He snagged her arm as she passed and forced her to face him. When he stared down at her, holding her eyes, he said low enough so the other two guys couldn't hear him, "You call

911 first if shit goes south, then you call me. Do you hear me?"

He pressed his lips together, drawing her attention there. She stared at them for a few seconds remembering the kiss by the pool in the afternoon sun.

It wasn't the memory of the sun that warmed her.

With a single nod, she said, "Understood," plucked the cash he was gripping from his fingers, pulled herself free, and headed out.

Of course, she didn't go home first, she got in the sedan and headed straight to the Hawg Wild Saloon.

Chapter Eleven

CAMI SAT in the sedan and stared at the lines of motorcycles filling the parking lot in front of the Hawg Wild Saloon. A few cars and SUVs were scattered among them, but not many. No one would drive by and question whether it was a biker bar or not.

It couldn't be more obvious.

Her heart thumped a little faster as she shut off the old Toyota's engine, slipped the key from the ignition and tucked it into the small cross-body bag she also bought at the consignment shop. It was big enough for her cell phone, a tube of lipstick, some cash, a small knife and the car key.

That was it.

She wasn't carrying any ID since one wasn't created for her undercover persona yet. She wanted to see how tonight went first before bugging Crew for a driver's license for her made-up identity.

She had decided to go with the name Rose Campbell. Simple and non-Hispanic sounding. If she could pass herself off as having a deep tan instead of the skin tone inherited from her parents, she'd do her damnedest since the Demons weren't into diversity and inclusion.

From what the other task force members had told her in the last week, the Demons were also far from Mensa candidates, so her plan of being a sun worshipper might work.

After climbing out of the car and wiggling her tight mini skirt back into place, she focused on the front door of the biker bar and, after taking a deep, bolstering breath, took determined strides toward it.

An important rule in her line of work: always appear confident, no matter what the situation. If she walked in like she owned the place, she'd probably get more respect than going in and looking like she was lost, out of place and extremely uncomfortable.

Was she that? A little bit but she was good at hiding it.

As she walked through the door, the noise slammed her right in the chest. Besides the rock music blaring from an unknown source, most likely a jukebox, the laughing, shouting, cursing, and even drunk singing, was deafening. It seemed to be a competition among the patrons to be heard over the racket.

Surprisingly, even though it was a Thursday night, it was more packed than expected. Did these people not have to get up early in the morning and go to work? Or did they all have alternative methods of putting cash in their pockets?

Running guns, distributing and dealing drugs, stripping stolen cars for parts, sex trafficking, prostitution... The outlaw biker business opportunities were probably endless. Only none of the above were legal.

Hence the reason she currently stood in a crowd of bikers of all sizes and shapes.

And smells.

Her nose twitched from it.

This is supposed to be your element, Rose. Act like it.

Cami pulled back her shoulders, straightened her spine and lifted her chin. Then proceeded to elbow her way toward the packed bar, dodging octopus hands and beer bellies pressing against her. None of it by accident.

As she worked the obstacle course of humans, tables and chairs, she felt brushes, squeezes and pinches, as well as heard obscene offers or whistles. At least it proved the outfit was working. While she received the attention she hoped, she could do without the bonus groping.

When she finally made it to the bar at the back of the room, not one stool was empty. She couldn't even see how many were working behind it because she was standing behind a wall of men, and even some women, the majority wearing various club colors. She scanned a few of the patches, not recognizing any of the MC names.

Despite that, she came here for only one. The Deadly Demons. Now the proud owners of this classy establishment.

A loud belch filled her right ear and when she glanced that way, a beer-bellied biker by the name of Torch, according to his name patch, gave her a six-toothed smile and licked his barely visible lips. With a yank on his long, disheveled beard, he greeted, "Hey, baby. You lookin' for me?"

She gave him a friendly smile and turned to face him. "Depends."

"On what?"

"On what you have to offer."

His thick brow furrowed. "Can offer you a beer. But don't expect to get it for nothin'."

It would be cheaper to buy her own beer. Getting a beer from this *gentleman* wouldn't be worth the price. "I'm worth a lot more than a Busch Light."

"Buy you a whiskey, then."

"And how much is that going to cost me?"

He pursed his lips and tilted his head as his gaze slid down from her head to her booted toes. That wasn't the only thing sliding down her. A shiver raced along her spine at the look in the man's eyes.

He reminded her of someone who took without asking.

"Depends how good that pretty little mouth of yours is."

"It's good at eating and drinking. Sometimes whistling and singing. But not much else."

A quizzical look filled his face. "What?"

She shook her head. "I'll buy my own whiskey, thank you."

"You one of those *eeeendeeependent* women? One of those who 'don't need a man?'"

"I got a man. And I'm not sure he'd like the offer you're making me."

Torch's head jerked back. "Who's your ol' man?"

"Throttle."

"Never heard of him. Whose colors does he wear?"

"Nobody's. He's only loyal to me."

"Lone wolf, then."

She shrugged. "He likes his freedom and doesn't want to answer to anyone."

"Except he's tied to a piece like you."

"Is that a compliment or an insult?"

"Could be either, depending on what a man's into."

"I guess he's into what I got."

Torch sucked on his teeth. "Bit too fuckin' skinny for my taste. Also, not my flavor. But in the dark, who the fuck cares, right? Long as both the pussy and mouth are tight and wet."

"Right." *What a gem.* "Funny how you just offered me a

whiskey in exchange for that mouth. I wasn't too skinny for you, or not your flavor, a few seconds ago."

"Like I said, in the dark, don't matter what you look like."

"You're a real peach, Torch."

A shift in the wall of bikers farther down the bar had her escaping Torch's top-notch company and shoving herself into the gap of bodies so she could make contact with someone who worked there.

She was ignored by the two guys behind the bar for about ten minutes. They served everyone wearing a damn cut, purposely skipping over her.

Assholes.

After she blew out a frustrated breath, "Who you belong to?" came from the old guy sitting on a stool to her right.

His cut appeared vintage and well-worn, his silver hair trimmed short but his gray beard long.

Bikers sure liked their facial hair. Either that or they hated shaving.

"Who do *you* belong to?" she countered.

The older biker chuckled. At least he had more teeth than Torch. "My ol' lady."

"Well, she's a lucky lady."

The man huffed, "Not sure she'd agree with you. What's your name?"

"Rose. Yours?"

He pointed a gnarled finger to his name patch. "Midas."

"Nice to meet you, Midas. What club do you ride with?"

"Ace's Wild."

She tipped her head to the side as she considered him. "Never heard of them. Where are they out of?"

"Virginia," he answered with pride.

Since she adopted Virginia as her home state, she understood that pride. "You're pretty far from home, aren't you?"

"Here for some business."

Cami's eyebrows rose. "What kind of business?"

He grinned. "The kind where you mind your own."

She returned his grin with a smile. He wasn't being a dick but trying to be funny.

"You'd have better luck gettin' one of the bartenders to serve you if you were wearin' your man's cut," Midas informed her.

"My man doesn't have one. I mean, he has one but not for an MC."

The biker's brow dropped low. "So, he rides but don't belong to any brotherhood?"

Shit. Did she fuck up? She had to simply own it. "You got it."

"Why?"

"You'd have to ask him."

"What are you doin' in a biker bar like this alone?"

She glanced around. "Am I alone?"

"Without your ol' man."

"You assume I'm not buying him a drink."

He cocked one of his gray, bushy eyebrows. "Are you?"

Her smile widened. "No. Looking to score."

He stared at her with narrowed eyes for a few seconds. "Plenty of assholes here to score with. Your ol' man don't mind sharin'?"

"Not that kind of scoring," she answered.

"What kinda scorin' you talkin' about?"

"The kind that will make my ol' man happy, not pissed off." She ran the pad of her thumb down the side of her nose.

Midas continued to stare at her, then without another word he leaned forward and whistled sharply. When he caught a bartender's attention, he crooked his finger, then pointed at Cami.

This could either be good… or it could go horribly wrong. She hoped it wasn't the latter.

The bartender, wearing a Demons cut, stopped in front of Midas. "What's up, brother? Need another beer?"

"Yeah. Gimme another one." He tipped his gray head toward Cami. "This 'lil lady's lookin' to try one of those specialty drinks you serve."

The biker bartender's eyes slid to her and he sized her up. "Who are you?"

"Rose," rolled right off her tongue like it had been her name since birth.

"Never saw you in here before."

"I guess there's a first time for everything, including coming to Hawg Wild." She made a show of glancing around. "Interesting place."

"Who told you 'bout our specialty drinks?"

The Demon's question pulled her attention back to him. "My ol' man is friends with a friend of a Demon. He got the word that you might have what he's looking for."

"Why ain't his ass standin' before me 'steada you?"

"Well, because of the obvious… I'm his ol' lady and do what he tells me. He told me to come to Hawg Wild and get what he's looking for. I don't question him, I just do it."

"Like any good ol' lady should," Midas said.

"Doesn't your ol' lady do what you tell her?" she asked the bartender with the name patch that identified him as Hook. "Or are you a pussy and let her boss you around?"

Next to her, a chuckle came from Midas.

The young biker frowned. "Ain't got an ol' lady. Don't need some bitch harpin' at me twenty-four-seven. And if I did have one, she better fuckin' listen to what I tell her."

Charming.

"Exactly. The whole reason I'm here, Hook. Now that we

got that out of the way... What size do those *special* drinks come in?"

For a few moments, she didn't think he would answer and when he did, he did so reluctantly. "A shot, small, medium and large."

Her best guess was a shot had to be a single dose, small a gram, medium an eight-ball and a large might be an ounce.

"How much for the medium?"

"A buck fifty."

"Damn. He didn't give me enough for that. What about the small?"

"Eighty."

The money Crew handed her before she left The Plant earlier was a marked hundred-dollar bill. "I'll take a small this time."

"Be back." Hook headed down the bar and through a swinging door behind it.

"Nice guy," she muttered to Midas.

The older man snorted loudly. "Gettin' what you came for, right? Who the fuck cares if he's nice or not?"

Cami shot him a grin. "True."

It wasn't long before Hook was on his way back to where she stood sandwiched between Midas and another biker. In the bartender's hand was one of those to-go coffee cups with a lid.

Maybe the Demons weren't so dumb after all. However, she wasn't ready to give them any credit yet for being ingenious since they were dealing out in the open in a crowded bar.

Any undercover cop could be in the crowd.

Or an undercover DEA agent.

He placed the cup on the bar top but didn't let it go. With a, "Thanks," she reached for it.

He quickly yanked it away. "Gotta pay for it first."

She dug into her bag, dug out the money and slid it across the bar.

He snatched it with one hand and pushed the cup toward her with the other. And instead of making change at the register, he dug into his cut and pulled out a wad of cash. He held it low as he peeled off a twenty and threw it on the bar top in front of her before moving away.

She shouldn't walk out of Hawg Wild with that coffee cup. She might as well put a target on her back. Instead, she might hit the head and hide the baggie of meth in her bralette or something. Or find some way to smuggle it out since she was sure Crew would want the cup as evidence.

But before she left, she had one more plan to set in motion first. "Hey, Hook," she called out, hoping he'd hear her over the din, "who's the manager here?"

He glanced at her from where he now poured a draft beer a few feet away. "Why you askin'?"

So she didn't have to yell, she waited until he dropped the beer off in front of Midas before answering, "I didn't only come here to try your specialty drink. I'm looking for a job, too."

He pursed his lips as he studied her. Without another word, he spun on his heels and walked away.

She sighed and turned to Midas. "Do you know who's in charge here?"

Midas looked past her and jerked up his chin. "The big man there following Hook."

She turned to see a huge dude with a lumbering gait following closely behind the bartender. Hook stopped in front of another customer but pointed in her direction.

The manager, also wearing a Demons cut, paused and

gave her a good once-over before coming over. "Asked for me?"

She quickly scanned his name patch. *Bulldog*. Well, that fit. Though bulldogs were usually cuter, and she always had the urge to *boop* their noses. Her gut instinct told her that this bulldog wouldn't appreciate that. "I need a job and I'm wondering if you have any openings."

"What kinda job?"

"I've worked in bars before. I can sling drinks or serve tables." She noticed that one patch on his cut declared him *Sgt. at Arms* and the other said *Uniontown*.

Shaking his head, Bulldog's belly bounced when he chuckled. "Table service? Here?"

"Someone has to collect the empties, right? Why not drop off full drinks while doing that? It might encourage the patrons to spend more since they won't have to fight the crowd at the bar to get service. I'll assume more money for this establishment means more money in your own pocket."

He pulled on his bearded chin as he considered her words. "Problem is, I don't wanna fuckin' pay someone to do that."

That was an easy fix. "I can work for tips to start. Then, if you're happy with my work, you can put me on the payroll."

One side of his mouth pulled up. "Ain't no payroll here. You'd be better off working at McDonald's for tips."

Say what? "No one tips at McDonald's."

"Exactly."

Was he trying to be funny? If so, his humor fell flat. "Look... My man's habit's fucking expensive. I got laid off from my last job and now I'm looking for anything you can give me to put money in my pocket."

He reached out and used his thumb to drag her bottom

lip down. "What can you do besides wrap that pretty little mouth 'round a big fat cock?"

She yanked her head away, breaking his hold.

Yuck. Not that she would ever do that, but if she did, she would have to rinse out her mouth with peroxide to avoid picking up any diseases. Because simply standing among them proved that these outlaw bikers weren't keen on good hygiene.

She fought a gag even thinking about giving head to any of them.

"Look... Just give me a shot. If it doesn't work out for you, then no loss, right? You won't be losing out on any money. Only my time will be wasted. That's a risk I'm willing to take."

His dark eyes raked over her. "You gonna dress like that when you're workin'?"

She glanced down. "You don't like my outfit?"

"Didn't say that. You wanna make good tips, might wanna show more fuckin' skin. Show more of your tits." His gaze honed in on her chest and he frowned. "Ain't got much to show off, though."

Ouch. "Got it. More tits and ass. I can do that." She'd stuff her damn bra if she had to.

Crew might blow a damn gasket, but, in reality, he didn't need to know what she'd be wearing or that she'd be enhancing her chest region.

"So, what do you think? It'll make my ol' man happy since I'll be bringing home the bacon and also something special for him." She lifted the disposable coffee cup. Bulldog's eyes stuck to that for a few seconds before returning to her face. "And again, it won't cost you a thing." *Except your freedom when your club goes down.*

"Who's your ol' man?"

"Throttle. And, before you ask, no, he's not in an MC."

"He got a sled?" Bulldog asked.

A sled? Wait... Wasn't that what these MC members called their bikes? "Yeah, he's got a badass sled."

"He wanna prospect with the Demons?"

"I'll ask him. But he prefers being independent and beholden to no one." She wondered if he knew what the word beholden meant.

Why the hell were they discussing a non-existent ol' man instead of the job she wanted?

She mentally sighed. Women were second class citizens to them, that was why. "So, how 'bout it? Will you give me a shot? It's not going to cost you a damn thing. It'll be risk free."

"Bitches are always a fuckin' risk." He shook his massive head. "But yeah, if you wanna work for free, ain't gonna stop you. You cause problems, though, and your ass is gonna be thrown outta here. Got it?"

She smothered her smile and nodded. "Got it! Thanks for the opportunity. You won't regret it."

Until you're trying desperately not to drop the soap, then you might.

"I can start tonight, if you want."

"I don't give a fuck what you do. Just stay the fuck outta my way."

Hot damn! "You got it."

And she got the job.

Now she only had to convince Crew to approve the assignment.

She was afraid that would be more difficult than convincing Bulldog.

Chapter Twelve

CREW STABBED THE DOORBELL. For the third time.

Murphy's deep *woof* answered him every time he jammed his finger against the button.

She had to be home. She didn't return the sedan this morning. Instead, it was currently parked at Fletch's. Outside, too.

Not smart.

She should've switched out the pool car for her Audi before heading home.

Bringing a task force vehicle home—worse, leaving it parked outside—was one of the reasons T-Bone discovered where Decker—aka Hatchet—lived.

That had been a bonehead move for a seasoned LEO. That mistake almost caused his daughter to be kidnapped. And it *did* cause his woman to be taken. Luckily, Sloane had escaped, but not without injuries.

A lesson hard learned.

Now Cabrera had done the same at Fletch's home. Totally fucking reckless.

He rang the doorbell one more time to give her a chance to answer it before he went ahead and used his key.

Just as he was slipping his hand into his pocket, the door was flung open and a sleepy Camila Cabrera blinked at him. "Jesus."

"No, it's Crew."

"Neither of you should be at my front door this early in the morning." She ended that with a yawn.

Her dark hair fell loose around her shoulders and looked like it hadn't been brushed in ages, pillow creases marked her cheek, and she wore a dark blue, oversized, baggy T-shirt that screamed NAVY in large yellow block letters across her chest, and... nothing else that he could see.

He allowed himself a quick glance, but made sure not to linger on her toned, bare legs since he shouldn't be eyeballing a subordinate like that. Especially one he had constant thoughts about. Thoughts that might get him in trouble if he shared.

Unfortunately, keeping his eyes where they belonged was a struggle.

"Then you should've switched out the pool car for your Audi before you came home."

She scrubbed a hand over her eyes, took a visible breath, then shook her head. "This was closer than Rockvale. I was nodding off as I drove, so I decided to come here, instead. I figured it was better than falling asleep at the wheel."

While he couldn't disagree with that assumption... "You had me fucking worried when I drove into the lot this morning and saw your Audi still parked behind The Plant. Especially after where you went last night."

That was true. His heart had stopped when he saw her car in the lot. He figured if she wasn't here at the house, he'd be making a trip to Hawg Wild next. With backup.

Murphy released a loud groan behind her as he lowered himself to the tile floor. She glanced over her shoulder. "Same, boy, same." She faced Crew again. "Sorry, working nights has been kicking my ass."

"Welcome to being on a task force." He tipped his head to the side. "Are you going to let me in?"

"I figured you're only here to give me shit and afterward, as the task force leader, you'd have more important things to go do. Like somewhere other than here. I didn't know you wanted to come in."

"I'm still standing here on the porch, aren't I?"

She frowned. "That means nothing."

"Maybe to you."

With a roll of her eyes, she stepped back. When she swept a hand toward the interior of the house, he smashed his lips together to stop his grin.

After shutting the door, she turned to face him. "Do you always make house-calls to your task force members? This is becoming a habit. At least you didn't let yourself in this time."

"I was about to when you finally answered the door."

"If you ever get the urge to let yourself in again... just don't."

"Just think of me as your landlord."

"You can simply crown yourself as my landlord like that? First of all, you're not. Second, there are laws about landlords barging in without permission or an appointment. But again, you're not my landlord. Do I need to speak to Fletch to see if he's okay with you being the keeper of his house?"

"Do I need to tell him you have that big, hairy monster living here?"

Her mouth gaped open and her brown eyes went wide. "You told me it was okay."

"Yeah. *I* okayed it."

Her eyes narrowed. "Why are you such an asshole?"

He shrugged. "It comes naturally."

"No shit." She spun on her bare heel and strode toward the kitchen.

"Where you going?"

"To get coffee, if you must know. Since someone rudely woke me up."

He quickly followed. "You have some made? It looks like you just rolled out of bed."

He flared his nostrils and sniffed the air.

There it was. The scent of black gold.

"I *did* just roll out of bed. But these new-fangled coffeemakers have this crazy feature called a timer. You'd know that if you weren't still brewing your coffee in a percolator over an open fire."

"I'm not a cowboy."

She slammed to a stop, spun, raked her gaze over him from head to toe and said, "No, you're not." She continued on into the kitchen, heading straight to the coffeemaker.

"Know a lot of cowboys?"

"I've seen enough westerns." She grabbed a mug from the cabinet over the coffeemaker and, of course, didn't offer him one.

"I'll take a cup."

She set the mug down and closed the cabinet, still not grabbing him one. And she called *him* an asshole...

"Speaking of cups..." she started.

He interrupted her by pushing past her to pull a mug from the cabinet. He poured some for himself as she headed to the fridge. With her mug only three-quarters full of coffee, she filled the rest with vanilla-flavored creamer.

"Jesus," he murmured against the rim of his as he

watched her also dump three heaping spoonfuls of sugar into it next.

She glanced up from stirring that mixture that could no longer be called coffee. "You said your name was Crew. Now you're my Lord and landlord, too?"

"That works," he said. "What's the point of making coffee if it no longer tastes like coffee?"

She took another sip. "*Aaah.* So good. Perfect, even." She lifted her eyes to his. "If you don't like something, don't drink it. Simple. I don't judge you for drinking it black."

He got thrown off the conversation when she leaned her ass back against the counter, holding her mug in one hand and pinning her other arm under her bra-free breasts. When she crossed her ankles, the hem of her T-shirt edged much higher, showing off her soft, supple and very young thighs.

For fuck's sake. It's nothing you didn't see when she was in her bathing suit, idiot. Focus.

He strong-armed his thoughts back to task force business. "You started to say something about a cup. Does it have to do with Hawg Wild and the Demons?"

She *mmm*'d as she took another sip of that mess in her mug. "So..."

"For fuck's sake," he muttered.

"I didn't even say anything yet."

"Coming from you, I'm sure whatever it is will give me heartburn."

"You should get your ticker checked then. You're at the age where heart attacks are common."

He closed his eyes and shook his head, trying to keep his patience.

"Are you okay? Do you need to sit down? I can help you to a chair. Or bring one over. Give me a heads up if you're going to keel over."

This woman knew how to push his fucking buttons. He could do the same all day, every day, with his brothers. Why did Cabrera busting on him bother him so fucking much?

He set his jaw and opened his eyes. "Just tell me whatever it is you're going to tell me."

"I got hired at Hawg Wild."

He blinked. And blinked again.

She did *what?*

"Did you hear me? Do you need to turn up your hearing aids?"

He ground his teeth and his fingers twitched with the urge to teach her a lesson. But if he did, he feared it would turn into something he needed to avoid like a flesh-eating virus. "I heard you. But what came out of your mouth shouldn't have. I didn't give you instructions or permission to get a job there. You were only supposed to make a fucking buy."

"Well, I saw an opportunity and jumped on it. I took the initiative to prove I'm an asset to the team."

"No."

Her eyebrows slammed together. "No what?"

"No, you're not working there."

They parted and rose up her forehead. "Too late. I started last night."

"You're not working there," he repeated. No fucking way was she going undercover at Hawg Wild without backup. It was bad enough sending her in once. But on the regular?

Too risky. Too dangerous. No.

"Oh... And I did a buy."

"Oh and you did *a buy?* Shouldn't you have led with that?"

"Depends." She set her mug down and pushed off the counter, heading over to the cabinet next to the fridge where she pulled out one of those cardboard coffee cups. She turned and held it out to him. "Here."

He stared at it. "What's that?"

"The meth I bought last night."

Within two strides he had his own coffee placed on the counter and was pulling the cup from her fingers. He popped off the plastic lid and stared down into the empty disposable cup.

No, not empty. At the bottom was a baggy full of white powder.

He glanced up. "Crystal?"

"I didn't test it, but I'd assume so."

"I'll get it tested, weighed and documented." He raised the open cup. "Is this how they gave it to you?"

"Yep, slid it right across the bar like that. Apparently if you order one of their specialty drinks, that's what you get." She air-quoted the word *specialty*. "I had to smuggle it out of the bar and hide it in the car before going back in to work the floor the rest of the night. I figured too many of those bikers in there would know what carrying around a disposable coffee cup meant since Hawg Wild isn't a Starbucks and it would put a target on my back."

Good thinking, but it also highlighted the fact that Hawg Wild was dangerous.

"Those assholes are dealing right out in the open," he murmured and shook his head.

"In that crowd? Do you think anyone in there gives a shit? You could probably drop a brick of coke on the bar and no one would blink an eye. Though, they might line up with rolled dollar bills."

She was probably right. "Did you have to ask for meth or did they just assume?"

Her forehead wrinkled. "I thought that's what they're dealing?"

"That's their main moneymaker, but they also sell pot."

"*Ah.* That's right, I did see that mentioned in the dailies. At that bar, I'm sure pot's a bigger seller than meth. Most of the upstanding, fine patrons look like they succumb to the munchies a lot."

He glanced into the cup again. "Looks like a gram. What did they charge you?"

"Eighty."

That was the same amount they were selling grams out of Pizza Town. Decker had gotten a list of prices while undercover there.

"The bartender named Hook told me one-fifty for what I assumed was an eight-ball."

That sounded about right. "And where's my change?"

"Yours or the feds?"

He sighed. "The feds. They do like to keep track of their money." Every damn dollar needed to be tracked and documented. For good reason.

"I have it for you. Don't worry, Grandpa."

"Stop it. My kids aren't even old enough to make me a grandfather yet."

Her mouth gaped. "You have kids? Will you need a walker by the time they graduate?"

He sighed again. If he didn't react to her smart-ass comments, maybe they would stop. He pushed on. "What job did they offer you?"

"Well, they didn't quite offer it to me, I kind of elbowed my way in."

"Doing what?"

"I'll be working behind the bar and also serving the customers on the floor."

"On the books?" If so, he would have to quickly get her documentation. *If* he allowed her to go back. Which he wasn't, so the point was moot.

"No, off them. I bet they cook the books." She made a face. "Actually... I only convinced them to let me work for tips."

"Tips? In that fucking place?" He couldn't imagine that the fine folks who drank in that place were big tippers.

"Have you been there?"

"No. But like I told you, Fletch and Wilder have spent quite a few nights hanging out there. Especially in the beginning of the investigation. I'm going to safely guess that crowd isn't generous tippers."

"Probably not. But I'm not in it for the money," she reminded him.

"You're not going to be in it at all. You're not working there."

Her voice rose an octave. "I have a solid in at one of their distribution hubs and you're going to pull me from it?"

"It's not fucking safe, Cami." *Damn it*, he slipped and used her first name again. It was the name he used in his head while his fantasies played out.

Late at night.

When he was alone.

"Being a DEA agent in general comes with risks. I signed up for this. I know how safe it is or isn't. Why don't you let me decide that?" A flush rose up her neck and into her cheeks.

What the hell, she was getting mad? Too fucking bad. "Because I'm the fucking task force leader, you're not. *I'm* responsible for your ass. You're the most junior member of the team and, even if you weren't, you still wouldn't get to make those types of decisions."

"My skills are being wasted by reading reports or watching a fucking Demon gather coins in a laundromat!" she yelled. "That's not why I joined the team."

His head snapped back. "Then quit."

"Of course, that's what you want. But news flash, that's also what you won't be getting. I'm not quitting since I'm not a quitter. You'll have to force me from the team. And you better have a good reason for that to fly. I *want* to do this. I *can* do this. Just because I'm a woman doesn't mean I'm fucking helpless, Crew."

He struggled to keep from shouting back. Somehow he managed it. "I never said you were."

"Bullshit. Since jump street, you've acted like I should be tucked in a corner and patted on the head. And if you deny that..."

"If I deny that, what? What are you going to do?"

She took a deep breath and slowly released it. "Time for you to leave."

He agreed because right now he wanted to shake the fuck out of her. "You shouldn't keep the task force vehicle outside."

"Fine," she bit off. "I'll park it in the garage."

"You shouldn't have it here at all."

"Fine. When I'm done with my shift at Hawg Wild tonight, I'll take it back to The Plant."

"That's not good enough."

Her chin rose defiantly. "It'll have to be."

"Don't make me write you up."

She laughed.

Actually fucking laughed.

"Go ahead. I'll help you."

What the actual fuck? "You're still considered a rookie with the DEA. You don't want a black mark on your record."

"I'll survive it. My prior assignments will speak for themselves. And then they'll see that *you* were the one to give me that black mark and it'll be ignored."

What? "What the hell does that mean?"

"Exactly what I said. Which part do you need explained?"

"I'm well-respected in the agency."

"You're delusional, too."

She was fucking with him. On purpose. To get his blood pressure up. For what good reason? Did she want him to snap? Because he was getting dangerously close to that point. "Why do you have to constantly push me?"

Her head tipped to the side. "Is that what I'm doing? Or am I just not taking any of your shit?" She shrugged. "It's called fighting fire with fire."

He jabbed a finger in her direction. "I'm your goddamn boss. You report to me, Cabrera. You seem to have forgotten that."

"And there we have it. You don't like me calling you 'boss' but you just said the quiet part out loud."

He gritted his teeth.

"If you didn't..." She shook her head. "You treat me differently from the guys. You need to stop doing that. I don't need you to babysit me. I'm here to work, so that's what I'm going to do."

He wanted to grab her and force her listen to him, to see reason. But he couldn't. It would only make her dig her heels in deeper.

She was determined to get what she wanted.

And he shouldn't stop her.

He was conflicted. What she wanted would be beneficial to the team and the investigation. If sending her alone into

Hawg Wild wasn't so damn dangerous, he'd have no problem with it.

Any task force leader in their right mind—which clearly he was not—would be lucky to have someone like her on his team. Her enthusiasm and her ability to think and work independently was an asset.

He just needed to get that through his own thick head.

He was overly protective of her without a good reason. It wasn't because she wasn't capable or because of who her father was.

That wasn't why he worried about her.

He didn't want to admit to himself why. And that thought spurred him to get the hell out of that house before he made a mistake that might affect his career.

"Make sure to document everything that happened last night in your report. And make sure that report isn't late. And park that fucking car inside." He turned and strode as fast as he fucking could to the front door before he did something he shouldn't. Something that would get him fired or, *hell*, maybe even arrested. "And make sure you document everything tonight when you go back to that fucking bar."

"Yes, Daddy." He heard from behind him.

First Grandpa and now Daddy? *For Crissake!*

He slammed on the brakes, did a one-eighty and strode right back to her until they were boot to bare toe. Until he towered over her.

Unable to stop himself, he fisted a handful of hair at the back of her head and yanked it back so her face was turned up to his.

He dropped his head and stared down into her deep brown eyes. He growled each word slowly and succinctly to make his point, "I'm not your grandpa. I'm not your fucking daddy. I'm not old enough to be either."

"No, you aren't," she admitted in a breathless whisper. Her pupils were so wide staring back at him, it made her eyes look black.

"Why do you frustrate the fuck out of me?" he ground out through clenched teeth.

Her chest rose and fell like she had just sprinted around the block. "Why do you frustrate the fuck out of *me?*"

"You constantly fight me."

"Because you don't treat me as an equal."

He didn't need this shit from her.

He didn't need this shit from anyone.

He got enough shit thrown at him from his ex.

Cabrera had been poking at him and poking at him to get a reaction.

He was done with being fucking poked.

Now it was time to react.

Chapter Thirteen

His lips were pulled tight. A muscle jumped in his cheek. A searing heat filled his gray eyes. His chest pumped almost as quickly as hers.

Almost, but she had him beat.

Her pussy pulsed and her nipples strained against her T-shirt, hoping for a touch, a brush. Anything.

Going head-to-head with him and fighting for herself got her blood rushing, her juices flowing.

He was so absolutely fucking frustrating.

So, why, why, *why* did Cami want to rip off his damn clothes and ride his cock until she was covered in sweat and left completely exhausted and satisfied?

It was official. She had lost her damn mind.

Yes, he was hot. However, it wasn't his looks that attracted her.

Her excuse had to be she never backed down from a challenge.

And Crew was a big one.

It was the only reason that made sense.

The man wanted to prevent her from doing her job. One she was fully capable of doing. One she was trained for and good at.

If he thought by challenging her and questioning her skills, he would make her walk away, he was so damn wrong.

Screw that. All it did was make her burrow deeper. Make her more determined to prove him wrong.

And she would. Not only with task force business but with how he was denying what he wanted from her. The real reason he wanted her to leave the task force. Not because she wasn't capable but so he would no longer be tempted.

She could see it plain as day in his face. In the way he held himself.

He was fighting it.

He was beating himself up over it.

Guilt.

He was full of guilt.

And besides that kiss by the pool, they hadn't even done a damn thing yet.

Neither had crossed that line. A very thin line that could easily be blurred. It would only take one of them making the next move.

Who would it be? Who would break first?

His grip tightened on her hair, causing her scalp to sting. His Adam's apple lodged at the top of his throat for a few seconds before dropping like a rock.

His eyes widened slightly when hers narrowed.

Neither said a word but so many things were being said between them.

They were either doing this or they weren't. Either he had to release her, or she had to break free of his hold.

He squeezed his eyes shut and whispered, "We can't do this."

His strained words didn't sound convincing.

"Then let me go." Hers didn't, either.

When his gray eyes flashed open, she saw his struggle, along with her own, reflected in his eyes.

"I don't want to."

Finally, some truth.

So, she gave some back to him. "I don't want you to."

"It's wrong." When his ragged breath swept over her lips, she licked them, drawing his eyes there.

"You're right," she breathed. "And I don't care."

"You should."

"Something needs to break."

His head dropped even lower, bringing his lips just a fraction from hers. "This is not how to break it."

"Then, let me go," she told him again.

"Make me."

"You don't want that."

FOR FUCK'S SAKE, she was right.

It was when her lips curved up into a wicked smile, he knew he lost this fight.

Right then. Right there.

She was going to win.

And he was going to let her.

"Fuck it," he murmured and took her mouth.

Their lips and tongues crashed against each other, fighting for control. He wouldn't give her the upper-hand and she wouldn't give it to him, either.

This kiss was just as hot as the one by the pool, but this time it wasn't going to end like it had that day.

He was done fighting it. He would embrace what he wanted and to hell with the consequences. He'd deal with those later. When his head wasn't filled with the woman whose lips moved against his. Whose groans filled his mouth. Whose tongue twisted with his.

He released her hair, reaching under her T-shirt and grabbing her ass with both hands. He expected her to be wearing panties. She wore none.

He squeezed the warm, bare flesh filling his palms, and pulled her even closer. They stood so tightly sandwiched together that she had to feel how hard he was. How hard she made him.

After all those nights he pictured doing this in his mind, today it would happen. He would finally be able to touch and taste her everywhere. He'd finally be able to fuck her hard and fast. For real this time.

No longer solely in his imagination. It would be so much safer for him to keep her there. But, *damn*, what man didn't want his fantasies to come true? What man didn't act on those fantasies if the opportunity presented itself?

It should be him. He shouldn't want it.

She was young. His subordinate. He'd worked with her father. A man who could crush his career. And he still remembered her as a kid.

Worse, she got off on butting heads with him.

She was all fucking wrong for him.

But what if wrong was right?

Because he had thought his ex was the perfect woman for him. Until she wasn't. Until her true personality was revealed. Until their relationship turned toxic.

And worse, that toxicity affected his kids.

For fuck's sake. Was he really trying to come up with a

valid reason for them to do this? To make this mistake and act like it wasn't one?

He was so fucking torn.

She was that piece of pie he shouldn't eat because he was already stuffed full from dinner. He knew he should say no, but ended up eating it anyway. Worse, regretting it later.

But, *damn*, it tasted good while eating it.

And, *damn*, she tasted good despite the fact she only recently woke up and didn't have time to brush her teeth. Or the fact she just drank some of that mess she considered coffee.

He didn't give a fuck. Neither did his cock.

Her groan shook him from his wandering thoughts, and he focused on the woman smashed against him.

The woman he rocked his hips against like a horny fucking dog.

Her nipples were so hard, he could feel them through both of their T-shirts. It was time to get rid of those two layers of cotton and go skin to skin. To feel her heat and softness without a barrier.

When he lifted her off the floor, her arms hooked around his neck and her legs circled his waist. He hoped like fuck that miniature horse wasn't in the way like a speed bump when he walked blindly toward the bedroom, their lips still locked because he couldn't get enough of her mouth.

Somehow he made it through the kitchen and into Fletch's bedroom without breaking any bones or causing any bruises.

The second his boots hit the carpet, he let her slide down his body and a groan of his own surrounded their clashing tongues.

When he finally ended their kiss, he pinned his forehead

to hers, gathering his breath and his scattered brain cells. "Jesus," he whispered.

In a husky voice, she said, "You said your name was Crew."

"Always have to be a goddamn smart ass."

"It takes one to know one," she countered.

He cursed himself and stepped back. That phrase alone reminded him of just how young she was. Only starting out in both her life and her career while he already had years behind him in both.

He was a divorced father of two teenagers.

She was single, childless and still thought she could change the world.

They couldn't be more different.

But why the fuck was he analyzing this? He never did this kind of thing when he was about to have sex with other women.

And that was all it was with the others. Sex. Plain and simple.

Why was this any different?

Goddamn it, it wasn't. Simply having known her in the past didn't change a fucking thing.

You want her and she obviously wants you. And here you are overthinking it, dumbass.

It would only be sex. He certainly wasn't looking for anything more.

After his divorce, his standard operating procedure was to only hook up with women and avoid any kind of relationship. His last one had burned him badly enough that he was reluctant to step into that fire again.

Not with anyone.

Those burns had taken a while to heal, and some scars still remained.

"Crew."

He had gotten so lost in his head that he didn't realize he'd closed his eyes. When he opened them, she stood facing him completely naked. Her T-shirt discarded on the floor.

Holy fuck.

Hoooooly fuck.

Was this actually happening? He wasn't still asleep in his bed and having another one of his dreams, was he? "Are you real?"

Her eyebrows pinched together. "What?"

He shook his head. "I'm awake, right?"

"Do you need to sit down? Since all the blood is in your cock, are you lightheaded? Do you feel dizzy? Should I call 911?"

He sighed. Of course, he was awake. Because in his dreams, she wouldn't have such a smart mouth. Actually, she wouldn't speak at all because her mouth would be full of his cock.

He grimaced.

"Are you having chest pains?"

"Cabrera," he growled in warning.

"Since I'm standing here naked, I think you can call me Cami. In this room you're not my boss or coworker."

"What am I?"

"About to get laid." That wicked smile was back. "Unless you're having second thoughts? Because only one of us is naked. You're not a voyeur, are you, expecting me to perform?"

That idea actually got his cock flexing in his now-snug jeans. He opened his mouth, then snapped it shut when he thought better of answering. He wasn't an actual voyeur but he wouldn't mind watching her do things to herself... Lots of things...

He let his gaze drift. He took in her loose hair falling around her shoulders, the sparkle in her deep brown eyes, the way her lips parted slightly, the delicate column of her neck, the hollow at the base, the indentations above each collar bone, the definition of her arms, the way her bronze-colored nipples puckered tightly, and the hard tips tempted him to suck them deep into his mouth.

He kept going even though he could stare at her breasts all day. Her ribcage was narrow and her stomach flat for the most part. His eyes followed the inward tuck of her waist and the outward flare of her hips.

Along his path, he discovered she was an outie.

Below her navel was a small black patch of hair decorating the top of her mound. Trimmed neatly but not shaved. His gaze hovered there for a moment before he forced it to continue. Down her thighs, both firm but inviting at the same time, over her knees, her slender calves and he finished at her toes, painted in a dark maroon color.

"I told you to call me Cami, do you want me to call you Colin while we're naked?"

He lifted his head to see a flush running up her chest and her throat, as well as it was blooming in her cheeks.

She was so fucking gorgeous. Absolutely breathtaking.

And he was about to make her his.

For the next hour, anyway.

"You can call me whatever you fucking want when you're coming."

That sparkle in her eye changed and he braced for whatever would come out of her mouth next. "Anything?"

He cut her off at the pass. "Anything except Grandpa or Daddy. If you call me either of those, don't expect to come because you'll kill my fucking erection."

"Not into that, are you?" One side of her mouth pulled up.

Not when I remember you at ten. Hell, I wouldn't want to be called that even if I'd never met you before. Instead of saying that out loud, he answered with a safe and simple, "No."

"Should I start a timer to make sure your erection doesn't last more than four hours?"

He closed his eyes, shook his head, pulled a deep breath in through his nostrils and when he opened them, he turned and strode toward the bedroom door.

He wasn't doing this. He was already regretting this whole thing and it hadn't even happened yet.

Doing this—doing her—would be a mistake. Someone might end up dead.

And he'd end up in jail.

"Rumor has it that you're the king of ball-busting. I guess the rumors are wrong, because if they were true, you wouldn't have such thin skin."

He stopped in the open doorway.

And stared straight ahead.

Keep going. Get the fuck out of here. Nothing good will come of this. Sex with her isn't worth the issues it will cause. For you or the task force.

Someone only needed to tell his dick that.

"I figured you'd be covered in Teflon and be able to easily shake off whatever I served you."

Normally, he was and he could. Why was he letting her get under his skin?

He spun around only to find her right behind him. Her bare feet on the carpet had been so damn quiet she had snuck up on him.

"Are you staying or going?"

Good fucking question. "Going... Fuck," his brain responded. "Staying... Fuck!" his dick said.

"Holy shit. Did you forget your meds this morning?"

"Christ, Cami. You don't know when to keep your fucking mouth shut, do you?"

"If I kept my mouth shut, I wouldn't be where I am today."

That statement went so much deeper than the words at the surface, but now was not the time to unpack it.

"I'll ask again. Are you leaving or staying? Can you handle my mouth or are you not up to the challenge?"

"It shouldn't even be a fucking challenge!" he yelled, then shook his head at his own irritation.

She smiled.

"Is this a fucking game for you?"

"Isn't sex supposed to be fun?" She shrugged, making her breasts bounce and draw his attention. "Leave, if you don't want this."

"I wish I could," he whispered.

"That means you're staying." With that, she dropped to her knees, catching him off guard and causing his head to jerk back.

"What are you—"

As she began unlacing his boots, he stood there and let her, like the stupid fuck he was.

He stared at the woman kneeling at his feet as she worked his boots free and peeled off his socks. While he did, his eyes followed the line of her spine, the outline of her heart-shaped ass.

He warred with himself. Stop her or let her keep going?

The moment his second foot was bare, he reached down and grabbed her hair, using it to pull her to her feet. Not caring one fucking iota how much it hurt. "How bad do you want me to fuck you?"

"How bad do you want me to fuck *you?*" she echoed, the challenge clear in her brown eyes.

This fucking woman...

She gasped when he jerked into motion, releasing the grip on her hair to grip her neck instead and swing her around. He pinned her against the nearest wall with both his chest and his hand on her throat. "You want it?"

"Fuck yes." The gleam in her eyes substantiated she wasn't lying. She wasn't scared. She was eating this up.

Of fucking course. "You're going to get it."

Her words came out on a ragged breath. "About fucking time."

Keeping their gazes locked, he reached into his back pocket and slipped out his wallet. After blindly finding the condom he kept tucked inside, he let the wallet fall to the floor, then tucked the wrapper between his teeth and reached for his belt.

The jingle of the buckle as he unfastened it could be heard over their rapid breathing. Using only one hand, he managed to unbutton and unzip his jeans, awkwardly pushing them, along with his boxer briefs, down far enough for his raging hard-on to spring free.

He didn't have to look at his cock to know precum clung precariously to the tip.

The pulse in her throat raced under one hand as he used the other, along with his teeth, to tear open the wrapper. He let it fall on the floor to join his wallet and reached between them to roll the condom down his throbbing cock.

With one knee, he nudged her thighs wider before bending both until he was in place. Without any more words or further preparation, he drove up and into her. Spearing her deep.

She'd been ready. Wet.

Proof she got off on messing with him.

Whatever.

He would give her what she wanted and then get the fuck out of there the second they were done. He wouldn't linger. This wouldn't turn into anything more than what it is. A quick way to get the both of them off.

Afterward, they would move on and hopefully forget it ever happened.

He could get back to concentrating on the task force. Sleep more soundly. Return to his regular dating life. Hang with his brothers.

Fuck.

Even he didn't believe any of his own bullshit.

Proving, once again, why none of this was a good idea.

He stilled deep inside her, giving her a moment to stretch around him since she was a snug fit.

It wasn't exactly as he fantasized.

It was so much fucking better.

"Crew..."

He focused on her face.

"I need you to move," she encouraged.

"Give me a second..."

If he had to admit it, he didn't only stay still to allow her to adjust. He needed to keep himself from losing his shit.

Luckily, she had no idea he had fantasized about doing this every fucking night since that day at the Pittsburgh field office.

She had no clue she haunted him in his dreams. Because if she did, she'd ride his ass about it.

Her short nails dug into the top of his bare ass, right above where his boxer briefs hung precariously.

Keeping his jeans on and remaining dressed was a good idea. It showed her that this was nothing more than a quick fuck.

Because that was all she was. All she could be.

Nothing more.

She was so damn wrong for him.

It would be stupid to think otherwise.

Chapter Fourteen

He wasn't moving.

He needed to move.

Her nails weren't long but she dug them deeper into his ass, anyway, to spur him to move. "Crew..."

He took a deep breath like he needed to steel himself, or maybe bring himself back from wherever he went.

Finally, he began to thrust up and into her.

Just what she had wanted, right?

Not exactly. She hadn't expected to get fucked against a wall. With him still dressed. After only a kiss and no other foreplay at all.

She kind of felt cheated.

To her, it was similar to getting the entree before the waiter even asked if she wanted a drink. Or before she was served her appetizer.

The man was in his early forties. She had hoped to experience some of the skills he surely learned along the way.

She'd been with older men before and they had never disappointed her. They seemed to care about making sure the woman was satisfied. In contrast, every time she'd been with a man under thirty, they tended to be a bit more self-centered.

It could have been just the luck of the draw.

Even so, she had a feeling Crew was holding back and still warring with himself.

For no good reason that she knew of.

Could being divorced make him more cautious with who he slept with? She had no idea since she'd never been in a relationship serious enough to have a bad breakup.

She got him to focus on her by calling out his name. "Crew." Once she had his undivided attention, she continued, "You might as well make this worth the guilt you think will eat at you afterward."

He stuttered to a stop. "Guilt for what?"

"You tell me. I expected for us to go at it hot and heavy. Instead, you're holding back. You're scared about something."

His jaw shifted. "I'm not fucking scared."

"Well then, fuck me like you aren't." She threw down the challenge glove. Would he pick it up?

"I *am* fucking you."

"No. You're going through the motions but—" She gasped when he slammed into her. "Yes, like that. Because if you don't want to do this..."

"Shut up, Cami. Just shut the fuck up. Stay out of my goddamn head."

"Forget my age. Forget who my father is. Concentrate on me. On what you're doing. Stay in this room and forget everything else."

"I..." Thrust. "Said..." Thrust. "Shut..." Thrust. "The..." Thrust. "Fuck..." Thrust. "Up."

She smothered a grin because she had goaded him into getting his head back into the game and back into her bedroom.

To concentrate on what they were doing.

To push past whatever guilt he had. Or the guilt he perceived he would have later.

The soft grunt he added onto the end of each stroke stoked the flames flicking at her core.

"This what you wanted?" he forced past his clenched teeth while continuing to power up and into her.

"Yes," came out of her on a breath.

"This what you wanted?" he asked again, louder.

"*Yessss*," she hissed.

"This what you wanted?" he yelled, her body jolting violently with each slam.

"Yes!" she yelled back. "Don't stop. Keep going."

And what did he do? Stop.

What the actual fuck?

"I can't do this."

Holy shit.

He was finally present and now he was going to stop and leave her hanging?

Son of a bitch!

"Not like this," he continued.

"Not like what?"

"This!" he barked.

Jeez, someone was a bit cranky. "Don't get your blood pressure up. I don't need you having a heart attack. I'm not great with CPR."

"Jesus," he muttered.

With a shake of his head, he pulled out, leaving her feeling empty.

"So, this is it? You're throwing in the towel?"

"No."

"Then what—"

Before she could finish her question, he picked her up

and tossed her over his shoulder like she weighed nothing. His Herculean effort was actually damn impressive.

"I'm not throwing in the fucking towel. I'm throwing you."

And he did just that when he tossed her on the bed.

After landing with a bounce, she quickly brushed away the hair that fell into her face so she could watch what he would do next.

This was definitely an interesting turn of events. One she wasn't going to bitch about since he was already pulling off his shirt.

And exposing a body that would make any woman look twice.

Holy shit.

Yep. Yep. Yep. This was worth the abrupt interruption.

Soooo damn worth it.

The man was in impressive shape. Even though she could tell he took care of his body with his clothes on, now that he was peeling his jeans and boxer briefs the rest of the way off, that superb physique was slapping her right across the face.

However, the way his latex-covered cock bobbed with each jerky movement proved he was still annoyed.

Most likely with himself. Maybe even with her.

Though, dealing with his crankiness wouldn't be a sacrifice at all, now that she was staring at him totally naked.

And prowling toward the bed.

Her pussy clenched hard.

Oh, yes, she'd suffer through his annoyance.

Especially if it meant orgasms. And hopefully more than one.

Using her elbows and heels, she pulled herself backwards toward the headboard, keeping her eyes locked on him as he climbed on the bed, stalking her on his hands and knees like a hungry tiger.

The look in his eyes made her feel like his prey... and was almost enough to make her come instantly.

As she opened her mouth, he narrowed those gray eyes on her. "Not another fucking word."

Fine. She'd comply. For now.

Pinning her lips together, she lifted an eyebrow and smiled at him, instead.

She spread her legs and bent her knees, giving him the access he'd need to continue with what they had started against the wall.

Hopefully this time without a hitch.

But he didn't immediately settle between her legs. Instead, he sat back on his heels and stared at her.

Not at her face.

Directly at her pussy.

Good thing she wasn't self-conscious.

While he did that, she visually explored his powerful, corded thighs and the healthy girth of his erection before her gaze drifted up his abdomen. He had the perfect blend of muscle definition and layer of flesh. Not too hard, not too soft. Just right.

Hell yeah, the man was hiding a drool-worthy body beneath his clothes.

He had small, tight nipples she was tempted to tweak, along with a small patch of hair on his chest that matched the hair on his face and head. She wanted to brush her fingers across it and feel the wiriness. Maybe even nuzzle her nose against it and let it tickle her cheek.

Since when did chest hair get her motor running?

Maybe Crew was the exception.

That hair skipped over his abs and picked up again at his

navel—without a hint of gray in it—and drew her eyes back down to the dark patch that nestled his pretty impressive cock.

Not too big, not too small. Just right.

A grumbled, "You done?" drew her eyes to his face.

"Are you?"

"Fuck no. I need to get a little closer." When he dropped between her thighs, he paused and lifted his head. "No commentary," he warned her.

She made a motion of zipping her mouth shut.

He rolled his eyes and dipped his head.

Then he dove in.

As it turned out, no commentary was needed. She'd been right about him.

He was old enough to know what he was doing, but not too old to do it.

Not too old. Not too young. Just right.

She was a regular Goldilocks.

Like his body, his actions were perfect.

He used his tongue the same way an artist used their paintbrush. Creating a painting she couldn't see but could definitely appreciate.

He shoved his face right in there like a contestant in a pie-eating contest. He didn't mind getting it messy while he ate.

His tongue stroked, licked and flicked, making her hips hop off the bed every time he concentrated on her sensitive clit.

She groaned when he sucked one swollen fold into his mouth, then the other.

But she truly lost her desire to say a word when he added two fingers into the mix, driving them deep, fucking her with them, before curling them and finding her G-spot.

More proof that over the years he had learned his way around a woman's body. He knew just how to draw gasps, cries and groans from her. How to get her body twitching and her clit pulsing.

He pinned her hips down with his arm as he continued to assail her with his skilled mouth, his long fingers and the wiry hair on his face.

Now, if he was as good with his cock as he was with his mouth...

All thoughts fled her active brain, leaving her squirming as he worked her into a frenzy.

Driving her to the brink.

And he didn't let up as an orgasm ripped through her, ripping every bone out of her body until all that was left of her was a sense of satisfaction.

And heaving lungs.

Holy shit.

This man knew how to eat pussy.

That made her doubt he was divorced because he sucked in bed. Though, it could be that he was a two-pump chump. She'd find out soon enough.

When she could muster the energy, she opened her eyes and lifted her head to see him kneeling between her still quivering thighs, his erection jutting out from his body.

The man had some staying power, she'd give him that. That gave her some hope he wouldn't be a minuteman.

"You're impressing me with how long you can hold an erection. I really thought you'd have to replace the condom before we got to the main event."

"I don't have another condom."

"Oh. Well... Then I'm glad you're still virile because I don't have any, either. I haven't stocked up on any yet since I wasn't expecting to do debauchery in Fletcher's bed so soon."

His forehead wrinkled. "Debauchery?"

"Do you need to google it? I can show you how on that fancy device you use to make calls."

He sighed. "Fletch will never know what we did in his bed."

"Unless he has security cams set up in his house."

He stared at her, doing his best to not look paranoid. "Have you noticed any?"

"I haven't looked. I figured if he wanted to watch me sleep, shower or do... other things—"

"What other things?" he asked before she could finish.

"Walk around naked."

"No. That's not what you meant."

"If you know what I meant, then why ask?"

"To hear you say it."

"Oh, you're into dirty talk?"

"Stating you masturbate is not dirty talk," he informed her.

"Maybe not to you it isn't, but I'm sure to some it is. Not that I said I masturbated. You did."

"Let's go back to the rule of you keeping your mouth shut."

"Was that a rule or a strongly worded suggestion?"

"A requirement."

"Do you get off on being a jerk?" she asked.

"Do you?"

Touché. "I match the energy I receive. So, take that as you will."

He dropped his head and his very attractive chest inflated, held for a few seconds, then deflated.

Jesus, Cami, keep your fucking trap shut. Otherwise, you're going to drive him away. That's not what you want. Just enjoy the sex and stop feeling the need to fight fire with fire.

You don't have to live with the man, you only want to fuck him. This isn't a commitment, it's a fluid exchange.

"I have one more thing to say..."

He lifted his head but his handsome face did not look happy.

"Carry on," she finished, then made a motion of zipping her lips shut before wiggling her eyebrows at him and dropping her head back onto the pillow.

Then she waited.

The bed shifted.

Was it too late? Did she drive him away?

If she did, it was no one's fault but her own.

Relief rushed through her when his hips settled between her thighs and his hands planted into the mattress on either side of her head.

Then he was practically nose to nose with her. "Cami..."

Instead of answering, she only lifted her eyebrows in response.

"Have you ever been in any kind of relationship that lasted more than a night or two? Or even longer than a week?"

She shook her head.

"No surprise." With that, he thrust inside of her.

Chapter Fifteen

HER SLICK PUSSY encompassed his cock as he thrust deep inside her, pulling a shudder from him with how fucking good it felt. Like hot velvet wrapped around him, despite wearing a condom.

Hell yes. His decision to move this to the bed was the right one since their size difference had made sex against the wall awkward. Plus, now he could feel her bare heated skin against his. It was soft and smooth and her tits bounced with each thrust.

With a last glance at her face to see her eyes closed, her mouth parted and a flush tinting her cheeks, he dropped his head and wrapped his lips around one of her nipples.

He wasn't gentle. But he was thorough.

He stopped banging her hard and switched to rolling his hips. He wanted to make sure to hit all the right spots as he sucked her breast into his mouth, flicking the tip with his tongue.

With the tip caught between his teeth, he gently scissored it. That had her slamming her hips up and into him.

He tipped his eyes up to see her almost about to burst.

He released her nipple and murmured against her skin, "Reactions or words of encouragement are allowed. Just no smart-ass commentary."

"Why do you get to make the rules?" Her question sounded a bit breathless.

Good.

Pressing a finger against her lips, he shook his head.

She rolled her eyes, but once he went back to her breasts, those eyes were rolling back in her head, instead.

Now *that* was the reaction he wanted to see.

A sigh.

A throaty groan.

His name cried out.

Those were the only sounds he wanted to hear coming from her mouth.

And he got that. Especially when he kept thrusting at a smooth, steady pace as he spent equal time between her breasts with his mouth and fingers. Squeezing and twisting. Plucking and sucking.

Her tits weren't heavy or large but they fit her frame perfectly. He'd always been a breast man, but had never been picky about the size. A mouthful, a palmful, or even large enough to need two hands.

Perky. Hanging heavy. Fake or real. Small or huge areolas that were pink, a deep red or even brown.

All unique and all worth worshipping.

But he was having a hard time concentrating on her breasts with the pull of her pussy. The way she squeezed him, the way she tipped and lifted her hips to meet him stroke for stroke.

He gave up trying and, using the flat of his tongue, dragged it up between her breasts to her throat, where he planted his mouth against her racing pulse. His lips vibrated from her groans.

Music to his ears.

Her not talking proved she could obey orders.

When she wanted to.

Which most likely wasn't often.

He had a crazy urge to tame her, but immediately realized he wouldn't want her any other way.

She was a challenge who got his blood pumping.

She was brave, outspoken and independent. If he had to admit it, she had all the characteristics perfect for a DEA agent and task force member.

Perfect for...

No.

This was only sex. A way to work out his frustration after dealing with her smart mouth. Especially after his last real relationship ended in a disaster. He was not stepping into that quicksand again.

He wouldn't even risk dipping in a toe.

Because next thing he knew, he might be pulled under, get bogged down and be unable to escape.

"Crew!"

He lifted his head to see her frowning. "What?"

"Get out of your fucking head and join me here in bed."

Shit.

He was holding her, not fucking her. Proving his point about the dangers of that goddamn quicksand.

He slipped his arms from around her and planted his hands on the bed, pushing his torso up to relieve some of his weight from her.

"I mean, if you're already worn out and need to take a breather..."

More jabs. *Of fucking course.* "I'm perfectly capable of

fucking you until you are worn out and begging for me to come..."

"Begging for *you* to come? You talk a big game."

He jabbed back. "You'll be begging me to hurry up and finish because *you're* worn out and need a nap."

"Oh, guaranteed I'm taking a nap after this. I have a busy night scheduled."

"Can we not talk work right now?"

"Sure. If you can finish what you started."

He went nose to nose with her. "Don't worry, I plan on finishing. But how badly do you want to finish before me?"

"You wouldn't."

"Try me."

"That's just wrong," she grumbled.

"Now... Are you going to keep your mouth shut? Because soon I'm going to lose my erection and my loss will be your loss."

"*Meh.* I have a pretty awesome vibrator that can take up your slack."

"Did you ever think the shit you say is why you haven't had any meaningful relationships?"

"How did yours work out?"

He pulled a breath in through his nostrils and squeezed his eyes shut to avoid losing his shit.

This woman.

He knew this would be a mistake.

He was right.

A touch to his face turned into a cupping of his jaw.

He pulled in another deep breath and opened his eyes to stare down into her face.

Her thumb brushed over his bottom lip. "That was a low blow. Sorry."

Chapter Sixteen

SHE WAS SORRY?

She should be after planting thoughts of the Wicked Witch of Western Pennsylvania into his head. Especially while his dick was inside her.

Forget talking about work, the last thing he wanted to think about was his ex while fucking the woman beneath him.

"Crew." His name being whispered pulled him out of his head. "Let's forget everything outside of this bedroom. Please."

First, she was sorry and now she was using niceties like *please*?

Should he be suspicious?

Of course he should. It could be a trap.

Why was he even doing this? This wasn't turning out to be anything like his fantasies.

He should demand to see the manager.

"I'm sure Fletch has duct tape around here somewhere," he muttered. Duct tape could fix just about anything.

"I think we both need it. Look... How about we keep our mouths busy in another way?" She dragged the pad of her thumb across his bottom lip again. "You're a really good kisser."

Now she was giving him a compliment? No damn way. Were pigs about to fly?

She hooked a leg over his hip. "Now... Kiss and fuck me like you mean it."

Instead of verbally responding, he figured it was safer to do just that.

When he took her mouth, she hooked her other leg around his hip and finally... *finally*, they fell into a rhythm that did what needed to be done... It evicted everyone else from that room and that bed, except for the two of them.

What started out to keep either of them from saying stupid shit, turned into a kiss that was purely electric. It drove all the blood from his brain back into his cock. He could finally concentrate on the movement of his hips, as well as the movement of hers and the way their lips and tongues connected. The way her hard nipples brushed against his chest as they bounced with each thrust.

He swallowed her gasps after digging his knees deeper into the mattress so he could power up and into her relentlessly. Her pussy pulsating around him made him worry that he really would finish before her.

He might have made that threat, but in reality, that wasn't what he wanted.

He wanted to give her an orgasm that would make her pussy clench later when she thought back on this time together in her bed.

He wanted to make her come so hard, she'd be inviting—if not begging—him to come over to do this again.

He wanted to make her climax so intensely, her thighs would turn to Jell-O for a full five minutes afterward.

He wanted to give her all that and more. But to achieve it, he needed to keep his head in the game and ignore everything and everyone else.

Her sucking on his tongue pulled his balls tight and he had to blank out his thoughts to keep from coming right then and there.

No surprise that the difference between them when they both kept their mouths shut was like night and day.

He twisted her nipple, capturing her cry within his mouth. Then he slid his hand along her jawline and drove it into her hair, fisting it. Using that grip, he forced her head to tilt back before breaking free of her mouth and pressing his face into her arched neck.

It was a risky move since doing so left her mouth free. He hoped he didn't regret it.

Thank fuck a few seconds later the only thing escaping her mouth was, "I'm going to come. *Oooooh* fuck, make me come. Keep doing that... with your hips... Like that. *Yesssss...*"

Holy fuck, that wasn't helping him last. Neither was her pussy squeezing his cock tightly, like she was trying to milk his come from him.

He continued to pump his hips, and every time he hit the end of her, he'd grind even deeper. By embedding her nails into his ass, it encouraged him to continue that pattern over and over. To get her to the finish line before him.

When a climax ripped through her, she cried out his name and convulsed against him, slamming her hips up one more time and holding there.

But he didn't stop. He kept going.

He needed to finish before she said something that would throw him off track. To prevent that, he lifted his head and slapped a hand over her mouth, her warm breath beating a tattoo against his palm.

Catching her eyes and holding them, he set his jaw and began to drive harder and faster.

He didn't have time to waste.

While focused on his own race to the finish line, she smashed her pussy against him again and shuddered, surprising him. Either she had another orgasm or an intense after-shock. But whatever it was, snapped the dangerously threadbare rope he was clinging to and sent him tumbling along with her.

When he landed hard at the bottom, he was panting just as quickly as she was. His cock continued to pulse as he emptied inside her.

It was the most intense orgasm he'd had in a long time.

She squirmed underneath him, pulling him back to reality. "Am I too heavy?"

"No, it was another mini-gasm."

Damn.

"You did it."

Of course he did. Had she doubted he could make her come?

He blinked in confusion when she raised her hand with her palm facing him. "What?"

"High-five me."

"*What?*"

"It's for a job well done." A smirk curled her lips.

Of course.

With a groan, he shook his head and secured the condom at the root of his cock before slipping from her and dropping to her side.

She rolled onto hers to face him, patted his chest and laughed. "You need to loosen up."

"I have no problem loosening up."

"Then what *is* your problem?"

You. "You won't like my answer."

"Do you have a problem with women in general? Or just me?"

"You won't like my answer," he repeated.

She sighed. "That's answer enough. So... Are you going to let what we just did eat away at you and destroy the rest of your day?"

He stared up at the ceiling. "Why do you have to be this way?"

"What way? Truthful?"

"You make it a sport to get under my skin."

She climbed on top of him and went face to face, making him scramble to pull off the full condom before it slipped off on its own and made a mess.

"You made yourself a target from the time Williams told you I was joining your team."

"Well, you're on my team now, so you can knock it off," he told her.

"I will when you treat me with respect."

"You have to earn respect."

She raised both eyebrows. "So do you."

He met her eyes.

This woman.

He thought he liked a challenge but now he wasn't so sure.

She continued, "As I said, I give back what I receive. For what it's worth, I'm never going to sit back and allow someone to judge me unfairly." His mouth opened, but she stopped him with a raised palm. And not for a high-five this time. "Don't say anything if you're going to lie. Look, all I'm asking is for you to give me a chance. That's it. It's not going to cost you a damn thing."

"That's where you're wrong. It could cost me. It could cost me a lot."

That list was too damn long.

She could cost him his job. The task force's investigation if she got into a situation where she was in over her head where they needed to go in and extract her.

Hell, she could cost him his sanity. He already had a woman in his life that drove him crazy.

"Do you want to explain that?"

He sure as fuck did not. "No."

"No problem. I'll just come up with some reasons in my own head."

Great.

She rolled off him and onto her back, tucking her arms beneath her head.

Why the fuck did he miss her weight on him?

He needed to get rid of the used condom and get the fuck out of there.

Why wasn't he doing that?

Did he really want the answer to that?

Fuck no.

She released a loud, long sigh. "Well, that was sort of fun. I'm glad I showered and brushed my teeth before falling into bed at around four this morning." She lifted her head and glanced at him. "You're welcome."

"I wouldn't have cared." Nothing was wrong with a woman who smelled like a woman and not a floral arrangement.

As long as they didn't smell like bloated roadkill, he was okay with it.

"Oh, yes you would. I couldn't even stand my own stink.

That bar is smoky and full of biker B.O. that clings to everything. I swear I came home smelling like barbecued roadkill."

Damn, could the woman read his thoughts? If so, he was in trouble.

He turned his head on the pillow and once again said something she wasn't going to like. "I don't want you going back there tonight."

Maybe, since she seemed to be in a more subdued mood after having a few orgasms, she'd actually be more compliant.

"Why? Because having your dick inside me changed everything? I hate to break it to you, but your dick isn't some magic wand."

Of course. He was a fool if he thought she'd be more agreeable. "Apparently. Because if it was, you'd actually listen to my orders."

She sat up with a look of determination and drive on her face. "This is getting old, Crew. I joined this task force to make a difference. I want to do my part. You treating me like I'm breakable is..." She closed her eyes and inhaled.

"Is what?"

"Frustrating," came out on her exhale.

"It's for your safety since you'd be without backup in a bar full of bikers who won't respect you."

"We had this discussion already. This is my fucking job. Just like it's yours. Let me do it. Crew, I need a task force leader who will support me, not treat me like I'm helpless."

"It won't be me knocking on your father's door if something happens to you," he warned.

"You're right, it won't. It'll be someone far above you."

Jesus Christ. Back to the jabs. "Damn," he whispered. That was a low blow, even if it was true.

"How about a compromise? If I feel like I'm in over my head, I'll let you know, and we'll change course. Deal?"

"But will you actually admit if you get in over your head? Or will you be too stubborn?" he asked.

Her head jerked back.

"That's what I thought."

"I said I'll let you know. I'll make that a promise." She spit in her palm and jutted her hand out toward him.

He stared at the wad of saliva in the center of her palm. "Are you serious?" He shook his head and sighed.

She jiggled her extended hand.

"Oh, you really want me to fucking shake it?"

"Of course. Gentleman's agreement."

"You're not a gentleman."

"Neither are you," she countered.

Well, they could agree on one thing, at least.

He grabbed her hand and instead of shaking it, he gave it a gentle squeeze. "I also need you to promise me that if shit goes sideways, you'll extract yourself from that situation as fast as you can without blowing your cover."

"I can do that."

"I don't want you doing something stupid that'll get you in more of a jam."

"Okay."

"Don't try to be a hero. The most important thing is you getting out of there in one piece," he added.

"Fine."

"And I want you checking in with me whenever you can while you're there."

He waited for her to roll her eyes or give him shit, and was floored when she only answered with, "I'll say I'm checking in with my ol' man if they question it."

Wait. What? "Your ol' man," he echoed.

"His name is Throttle. They called him a lone wolf since he's a biker without a club."

198

"He's a biker without a club?" he repeated.

"Are you sure your hearing isn't failing?"

"Are you saying you told them you're a biker's ol' lady?"

"That's what I'm saying," she answered.

Well, *shit*, that was a smart move. "That gives us some flexibility in case one of us needs to go in and check on you."

"I guess."

"And they might leave you alone if you're an ol' lady."

"It's possible."

He suddenly liked this plan a lot more. Though, he still didn't like the idea of her working in a biker bar by herself. Being an ol' lady might get her a touch more respect, but not enough to make him feel comfortable about it.

The only issue he saw with that was, since she wouldn't be wearing her man's colors, most patrons at Hawg Wild might not know she was an ol' lady. "You need to mention Throttle a lot while you work."

"Why?"

"Because it might give you a layer of protection. It might be a thin layer but it's better than none."

"I planned on it since I figured they'd trust me more knowing my man's a biker. Plus, that's who I was buying the meth for. He's my excuse to keep doing buys while I work there."

Damn it. He needed to give her more credit than he wanted to. "Whatever you do, don't describe Throttle at all. This way if I have to come up with someone to go undercover as him, it'll make it easier. Speaking of undercover, let's see how tonight goes and then I can get you an ID with whatever name you're using."

"Rose Campbell. But I'm going to be paid in tips. I doubt they'd ask me for my driver's license or social security number even if I wasn't."

He frowned. "Rose Campbell?"

"I picked a name that would pass as white. I figured they might believe I'm simply a sun worshipper and have a tan."

Once again her being quick-witted made him do a double take. "Good thinking," he murmured, if not a bit reluctantly.

She curled a hand around her ear and leaned closer. "What?"

"Are you mocking me?"

Her husky chuckle did something to him that made him wish he had another condom in his wallet. "Never."

He needed to get out of there before he decided to raw dog it. He'd been snipped years ago but that wasn't why he insisted on wearing condoms. "Okay, I need to get the fuck out of here and go back to The Plant. I'm supposed to be working not fucking." Though, technically they did talk about work, so there was that.

"But fucking is so much more fun."

"Depends on who it's with."

"*Ah.* So, you regret showing up here uninvited, do you?"

He rolled from the bed and to his feet. "Did I say that?"

"While you might not admit it, we both know why you showed up here."

"To check on one of my team members since she didn't check in with me," he said on his way to the bathroom, used condom in hand.

"I didn't know I had to."

"You wouldn't have had to if you hadn't brought home the pool car."

"Are you saying you wouldn't have been leaning on my doorbell this morning if I had switched out cars?"

He hesitated at the bathroom door.

"You were looking for any excuse to come over here."

He turned. "You're wrong."

For fuck's sake, she was sitting in that bed buck naked and looking freshly fucked. It took everything in his power not to climb back on the bed, flip her over, shove her face into the pillow so she couldn't say a fucking word and fuck her from behind.

"That's fine," she responded. "Don't admit it. But tell me... Was it everything you dreamed it would be?"

"Fuck no. In my dreams you don't have a mouth."

"I don't?"

"Nope. Just a pretty face and under your nose it's just blank. No lips. Nothing."

"Is that your perfect woman?"

"It is now." He shut the bathroom door, quickly cleaned up and disposed of the condom before going back into the bedroom where she now sat on the edge of the bed, once again wearing the NAVY T-shirt.

He stopped at his pile of clothes and as he was pulling on his jeans, he heard, "Tell me... what do you do to keep in shape?"

He paused after fastening his belt and twisted his head toward her. "My preferred method is to bike."

"Riding a motorcycle gives you that body?"

He tagged his shirt off the floor and while pulling it over his head, he answered, "No, but pedaling a bike does."

"Riding a bicycle gives you that body?"

After grabbing his boots and socks, he perched on the edge of the bed opposite her to pull them on. "I ride a lot of things. But I do more than cardio."

"What else do you do?"

"Resistance training."

"Like?"

"Medicine ball. Free weights. Squats. Pushups. Sit-ups. I also pick a fight with a heavy bag in my garage sometimes."

"Does it fight back?"

He finished lacing his boots. "You mean like you?" He stood and headed toward the door. "I gotta go. You don't need to walk me out."

"That's good because I wasn't planning on it. I'm going back to bed. Hey, can you let Murphy out back quick before you leave?"

He stared at her for a second, then glanced around for the dog. "Where is he?"

"He avoids the bedroom when I have sex," she said matter-of-factly.

"You trained him to stay out of the bedroom when you have sex?" Did his voice crack? *Oh, for fuck's sake.*

"Did you want him to join us?"

"That's not..." He sighed. "How often do you have sex that you had the opportunity to train him to do that?"

One eyebrow lifted. "Do you really want to discuss body counts?"

He opened his mouth, thought better of answering, then snapped it shut. "Take your own damn dog out. I've got shit to do."

"So does he," he heard yelled from the bedroom as he got the fuck out of there before she said something else that would get under his skin.

Unfortunately, he was worried that she had already achieved that.

Having sex with her didn't help shake her free, it only burrowed her even deeper.

Chapter Seventeen

IF SHE DIDN'T WAKE up tomorrow full of bruises, it would be a miracle. The bikers sure liked to be handsy and didn't have any concept of consent. She'd been pinched, squeezed, groped and pulled into so many laps, she'd lost count. And that wasn't even the worst of it.

If a woman was desiring some physical contact, all she had to do was go work at a biker bar. Cami learned quickly to spend the least amount of time on the floor and as much time behind the bar that she could. Having that two-foot-deep barrier between her and the customers helped somewhat.

Despite that, a few had reached across the bar and pinched her nipple or grabbed her breast. In any other establishment, they would be charged with assault.

If she wasn't undercover, she'd teach those handsy motherfuckers a lesson. But since she couldn't, she had to grin and bear it as best as possible. At least for now.

She only ventured out from behind the bar to take orders and deliver drinks but when she did, she darted like a rabbit escaping a hungry fox by weaving in and out of tables, chairs and bodies.

She tried not to stay in one spot too long unless she caught some interesting chatter the task force or even the DEA might be interested in. That was the only time she lingered. Other than that, she wanted to stay as close as possible to the Demons, her main focus for working there.

Both last night and again tonight, the bar was mostly full of bikers that, unfortunately, did *not* include Demons. She only saw maybe one or two playing pool and drinking, besides the so-called "employees."

Last night when she stayed after the buy, she had worked with Cap, the Demons road captain according to his patch, as well as Hook. One other guy came out from the back to grab dirty glasses, empty the trash and clean up any messes.

No surprise that plenty of messes needed to be mopped up. More than only spilled beer. If it could come out of an orifice, it could be found in a corner, on a table or the floor. She was glad she wasn't given that job or have to clean the restrooms. The women's room was disgusting as it was, she couldn't imagine how atrocious the men's room was.

She didn't want to imagine. She'd most likely be scarred for life.

Donnie, the poor guy assigned to those duties, was shy, lanky and young—maybe eighteen—and didn't wear a Demons cut. When she asked if he was a part of the MC, he stated he was considered a "hang-around" and hoped to be a member one day when he could afford to buy a "sled."

Having that as his future hopes and dreams depressed Cami. The kid should be getting an education, or learning a trade, and aspiring to be more than a Deadly Demon. Especially since that club might not even exist after the feds were done with it.

Tonight, she was working with the same crew. Bulldog was overseeing the joint, Cap was busy pouring beers and Hook was tasked with serving "specialty drinks" to customers or random people stopping in to get their fix.

A couple of those buyers looked no better than the walking dead. Meth addiction did quite a number on the human body.

She was doing her best to keep track of how many deals were made out in the open across the bar. If she didn't already know what was in those disposable coffee cups, she might not think much of it.

But she did and dealing out in the open like that was brazen.

While alcohol was still Hawg Wild's main moneymaker, their drug sales had to come a close second.

And of course, every sale of meth or pot was paid in cash. She had no doubt whoever the Demons had doing their accounting was cooking those books. The Demons were smart in the sense that they knew the right businesses to buy to easily wash their drug money.

They must have taken notes from La Cosa Nostra, the Sicilian Mafia running Pittsburgh. Though, she couldn't imagine that the Russos rubbed elbows with the Demons. Use them as mules to transport their product? Sure. Sit down to dinner with them to exchange ideas? Not a chance.

When she had read through the daily reports, some notes in particular had caught her attention. The task force, including all three groups, had heard some talk about the MC cutting out the Russos so they can deal directly with the Mexican supplier and then make all the damn profit.

Cami doubted the Russos would allow that to happen without any blowback. That blowback wouldn't be a little pop followed by a sizzle. It would be a *kaboom*, leaving behind nothing but scorched earth.

She had a feeling the Demons wouldn't even know what hit them until it was too late.

The MC might be making good money selling meth, but the Russos had a complete criminal enterprise making them more money than God. It wasn't difficult to figure out who would win if those two criminal organizations went head-to-head.

No matter who prevailed, devastation would be left behind and innocents might get caught in the crossfire. Cami was pretty damn sure that none of the federal agencies wanted to see a war between those two. If that happened, she could see the top brass snacking on Tums and guzzling Pepto Bismol to settle their stomachs and ward off heartburn.

A shouted, "Gimme a beer!" yanked Cami back to the bar from her wandering thoughts.

Damn. She shouldn't drift off like that in this crowd.

She glanced down the bar to the "gentleman" slamming his empty mug on the scarred wood bar top.

"Yo, woman, bring me a beer!"

For shit's sake. Though, being called "woman" was a step up from being called "bitch."

She headed down to the biker. "What are you drinking?"

"Beer."

"Figured that by the mug. What kind?"

"The cold, wet kind. Bet when you get wet, you ain't cold."

In Fletch's pool she was cold *and* wet.

This morning in bed with Crew she was wet and definitely the opposite of cold.

But that was not a conversation she was having with—she read the name patch on his cut—Vice.

Vice? *Whatever with these crazy names.*

"Will any draft do, Vice? Or are you particular?"

He stroked his beard. "I look particular?"

"So, Iron City Light, then?"

He just about shot like a rocket off his stool. "Hell no. Don't gimme any of that goddamn swill water. Get me a Bud."

She was learning quickly how to bring these guys to heel when they were being difficult. Which was practically all the time. By the time she was done with this undercover assignment, she should be an expert at herding cats. Alley cats at that.

Her eyebrows rose. "Please?"

He reached out and snagged her chin. "I'm fuckin' sure I can please you."

"By releasing me." She yanked her head back and freed herself.

Heading down the bar, she grabbed a clean mug from the stack as she went. As she filled it with the beer at the tap, she let her gaze roam over the crowd. Nothing appeared out of the ordinary.

She tracked Hook as he carried one of the disposable coffee cups from the back and passed it to someone she couldn't see because of the thick of bodies gathered around the bar.

That made at least a dozen deals already in the last few hours. That she witnessed. She needed to figure out where they were keeping their stash.

She steeled herself before returning to Vice and when she slid the mug across the bar to him, he jerked his chin toward her chest. "Need to show more of your tits."

Truthfully, she didn't have much more to show. What she wore tonight emphasized everything she had. She had pulled on a pair of black fake leather leggings, her second-hand black knee-high boots with a bit of a heel, and a semi-casual top that clung to her like a second skin and had a plunging neckline.

Maybe she needed to start stuffing those fake gel boob enhancers in her bra to give her more cleavage. But really... It wasn't like she needed the tip money. Anything she made she couldn't keep, anyway. So, did she really need to work at making more?

Basically, she only had to do enough during her shift to make sure Bulldog didn't kick her ass out the door. And since Bulldog wasn't paying her a damn dime, she doubted he was even paying attention to what she was doing.

"Girlie, whatcha doin' after you're done here tonight?"

Girlie? That was a new one. "Heading home."

"All alone?"

"To my ol' man. Just a little word of warning. He doesn't like to share, Vice."

Vice grinned, showing off teeth that were yellow from probably years of smoking or chewing tobacco. Or a lack of oral hygiene. "Didn't say I planned on sharin'."

Well, that was a relief. She mentally rolled her eyes. "I doubt he'd let someone steal me away, either."

"Borrow, not steal. Got no reason to keep you. Live my life loose and easy. Havin' an ol' lady ain't my idea of freedom."

"You just borrow other ol' ladies and give them back when you're done?" she asked, somewhat as a joke.

"Somethin' like that."

She shouldn't have been surprised by the somewhat serious answer. She didn't want to ask if the women were on board with being "borrowed." The answer might piss her off.

Before she could move down the bar and end that ridiculous—and sort of scary—conversation, another biker squeezed in between Vice and the guy warming the stool next to him.

"Ain't she a little too... baked for your taste, Vice?"

Baked? Like a fucking potato?

The yellow-toothed biker shrugged. "Bitches all look the same if you turn off the lights. All ya gotta do is find the wet spot."

That had to be a recurring theme for these guys. Don't like what the woman looks like? Just turn off the lights. A quick and easy solution.

In all honesty, the woman probably appreciated it, too. Who wanted to see some of these guys doing the ol' twisted sex face while sweating and panting as they hovered over them?

Not her.

Not any woman with two eyeballs and some dignity.

She also doubted any of these "borrowed" women got wet from Vice's romantic moves.

"Are you saying I look like a potato?" she asked the newcomer.

"Sayin' you look like your blood ain't pure."

"Pure of what?" she continued despite the fact she really shouldn't be pushing this, but it was annoying the hell out of her. "White and red blood cells?"

"Like you ain't born here."

She jabbed her finger into the bar top. "You mean, like *right* here? On this bar? You're right, I wasn't. That would've been a bit unsanitary."

"You got a smart mouth," the biker grumbled.

"I've been told that before." With a tip of her head, she decided it wasn't good to verbally spar with those fine folks and headed away from them.

As she did, she spotted the manager on the other side of

the bar. He was hard to miss since he was so damn big. While she was good at self-defense, she wouldn't want to take him on simply based on size alone.

As the next hour proceeded, she kept one eye on him as she mixed drinks and poured beers, delivering them to the customers both sitting at the bar and at the tables.

Once Bulldog was done making his rounds and socializing with various bikers, he joined her and Cap behind the bar. She sidled up to the big man. "Hey, boss."

He dropped his gaze down to her and grunted in response.

She took that grunt as a sign he was listening. "Just wondering if I can order one of those specialty drinks that Hook's making tonight to take home after work. My ol' man appreciated the one I got last night."

After running his gaze over her, he stared at her face for so long, she thought he wasn't going to answer.

Finally, he grumbled, "Gonna cost you."

Of course it would and she'd gladly pay with money. But nothing else. She drew the line at giving head or having sex in exchange for drugs. Just the thought of that caused bile to work its way up her throat.

Luckily, the agency frowned on that type of activity. As they should.

"Can you take it out of tonight's pay?"

"You're workin' for tips," he reminded her.

Damn. She was hoping he wouldn't remember that fact.

"You've been fuckin' hustlin' all night, makin' the bar more scratch than normal. Tell you what..."

Interesting. He'd been paying attention. That was news to her and she needed to keep that in mind for the future, especially if she started hunting around for their stash spot.

So far, she hadn't seen any cameras set up around the bar,

but that didn't mean they weren't there. Or it could be that the man was simply observant.

She had no doubt his ass would be hung out to dry by Viper, the club's president, if something happened to thousands of dollars' worth of methamphetamine.

Bulldog continued, "You keep hustlin' like that, not annoyin' our customers and makin' 'em happy, gonna give you a little bonus every night once you're done workin'.'"

Cami waited to hear the rest of this small windfall. Any amount of meth they could get off the street was better than nothing.

After a few moments and when he didn't continue, she asked, "What's the bonus?"

"Gonna give you a small special."

A small was a gram. They charged her eighty bucks last night for that amount.

"Well, damn, Bulldog, that's generous. But are you also saying I can work as many nights as I want? No limit? No forced nights off?"

"You work when you fuckin' want, but you gotta work a whole shift to get that bonus."

"That sounds like a great deal. And it's going to make my ol' man very happy. Better yet, when he's happy, he makes me happy." Bulldog showed zero reaction when she added a wink.

The bar manager leaned in closer and jabbed a finger at her chest. "But you make problems in this bar, the deal's off. No fuckin' bonus, not even any damn tips. You'll be done here. Don't need no bitch causin' problems in here. You got that?"

Oh yeah, she would not want to have to take down and cuff Bulldog. She would lose that battle. Most of her male counterparts would, too. "I do."

"Gonna go let Hook know you'll be seein' him at the end of the night."

She did a little bounce on her toes to appear excited by the news. "You're the best, Bulldog!" she practically squealed.

With a grunt, he turned and lumbered away.

Crew was going to be ecstatic.

Maybe.

She'd let him know about this news the next opportunity she had to check in with him. Just like he insisted.

Chapter Eighteen

SHE'D CHECKED in every couple hours throughout the night like he insisted.

Cabrera's last text said she was fine and would soon be on her way back to The Plant to drop off the pool car. Seeing her Audi still parked in the lot meant he managed to beat her there.

It was much earlier than he'd normally arrive at work, but he wanted to see her with his own two eyes.

Two bloodshot eyes because, between reading her texts and worrying about her, he hardly got any sleep. Since his ass was already dragging, what did it matter if he was out the door before four in the morning?

When he arrived, he left the back gate open, so he heard the sedan coming up the alley before he saw it turn in.

He fought the urge to rush over to the car before she even got out. Instead, he made sure to appear bored and unconcerned. Even though that was farthest from reality.

What the fuck was wrong with him?

Was he this worried when Decker went undercover as a

prospect with the Demons? No.

Cabrera could take care of herself. He was acting like a fucking idiot.

After climbing out of the car, she turned toward him and, even in the limited light, her eyes looked more shadowed than they should be.

Like him, she was probably running on exhaust fumes. Only she'd been on her feet all night, while he'd been on his back in his comfortable bed, waiting for his phone to light up with each text.

She approached him where he leaned against her Audi. "What are you doing here?"

"Making sure you return the pool car. Someone might need to use it today."

Her expression immediately told him she knew that was bullshit. Her words confirmed it. "You're a bad liar, you know that?"

"Why do you think I'm lying?"

"Because I told you I'd drop it off this morning before heading home." Her head tilted. "Unless you don't trust me?"

"I trust you until you give me a reason not to."

"Damn," she whispered. "You have issues."

He agreed, he did. His main issue right now was the woman standing before him. He shouldn't be more worried about her than any of his other team members.

But, *fuck him*, he was.

He pushed off her car and stepped directly in front of her with her eyes following his every move.

He studied her face carefully when he asked, "How'd it go?" because he had a feeling she was going to downplay any problems she had. She was determined to prove herself to him and that stubbornness could make the whole situation even more dangerous.

"It went as expected when you have a bunch of bikers drinking and partying." She lifted a finger. "I have something for you."

She dug into the V-neck of her top and for a brief second he thought she was about to pull out a tit right there in the parking lot. He was relieved when she pulled out a baggy from her bra, instead, and held it out to him.

Proof of how lack of sleep affected him. It made him stupid.

"Looks like a gram. Did they charge you eighty again?"

She shook her head. "No. Believe it or not, it was payment for a job well done."

She must have been making friends and influencing people last night.

It was good that the Demon in charge of the bar liked her. That could be beneficial to the investigation. The reason she was working at Hawg Wild in the first place, he reminded himself.

He took it from her and bounced the baggy in his palm. "I'll take it upstairs to weigh and document it if you want to go home and sleep."

"A shower and catching some shut-eye would be great about now."

He nodded even though he wasn't ready for them to part ways.

Not yet.

The next question out of his mouth surprised the hell out of them both. "What about breakfast?"

She tipped her head to the side and stared at him for far too long before she responded with, "I could use some of that, too. You buying?"

He took a deep inhale of the cool morning air. "I am."

"That sounds tempting. Unfortunately, I need to go home and let Murphy out."

"Already done." She had no idea just how close he lived to Fletch. Right now, he'd keep that to himself.

Her eyebrows jammed together. "What?"

"Now, aren't you glad I still have a key?"

"Debatable."

"You're welcome for me thinking ahead and letting out your pony. He takes a damn big shit, by the way."

"Did you pick it up?"

"Hell no, I left that for you. So... I know of a twenty-four-hour diner not far from here."

She smirked. "I'll follow you."

He smothered his own smirk. "Give me a few while I run your latest score upstairs and secure it."

———

"I'll TAKE the short stack, sausage links, scrambled eggs and coffee, please," Crew ordered, handing the menu to the waitress.

The server twisted toward Cabrera. "Your dad has quite the appetite this morning. And what will you have?"

Your dad? Jesus fucking Christ.

Cabrera turned wide eyes to him and bit her bottom lip. Most likely to keep from bursting out in laughter.

Before she could give her order, he said, "She'll have apple juice, served in a sippy cup, please, and an order of French toast sticks. You know the ones she can use her fingers to eat and dip in syrup. She's still learning to use utensils. And don't forget the bib."

"Thanks, Daddy, but I'm old enough to order for myself." She smiled up at the waitress. "I'll take the steak, medium rare, and two dippy eggs. Water and a small OJ. Please and thank you."

The waitress nodded and gathered the menus. "I'll grab your drinks and be right back."

As soon as the server disappeared, Crew returned his attention to the woman opposite the booth from him. "No coffee?"

"No. I want to sleep after this. I *need* to sleep after this. Especially since I'll be pulling an all-nighter again tonight."

"Do you feel safe enough there to go back?"

"You're just looking for a reason to pull me. I promised to let you know if I don't feel safe enough to continue."

But by then, it might be too late. It didn't take long for shit to go sideways when it came to outlaw bikers.

When the waitress came back with the coffee and water, he studied Cabrera's profile as she chatted with the woman. He had no idea what they discussed since he was once again distracted by the woman's natural beauty, still visible despite the heavy makeup she'd worn to work at Hawg Wild.

When her rich brown eyes turned back to him, he grabbed his cup of coffee and took a sip. It was strong and hot. Just how he liked his women...

Coffee. *Damn it.*

"Are we just going to ignore the elephant in the room?"

The elephant? Ah, fuck... "Yes."

She grinned. "I find it funny."

"I don't."

"Maybe you need to dig deep and find your sense of humor."

"I have a sense of humor. I just don't find someone thinking that the woman I," he leaned closer and whispered, "fucked is my damn daughter. That's disturbing."

"You could've just told her I work under you... literally."

She rolled her lips under. Despite that, she couldn't hide her amusement since the crinkles at the corners of her eyes gave her away.

"There is a Daddy kink, you know," she continued.

"It's not my kink."

"Would you rather be with someone shy and virginal?"

"Virginal? No."

"A doormat, then?"

Would he? One that didn't give him any shit?

In truth, no, that sounded boring.

He was fucked.

He dropped his head and rubbed his forehead. He needed more coffee.

"Do you have a kink?"

He answered that unexpected question with, "Apparently, women who like to be difficult."

Maybe it had been a bad idea to take her to breakfast.

Luckily, the great thing about diners was that the food came out lightning fast. So when the waitress returned, plunking down their plates, he hoped that was the end of that line of conversation.

He should've known better.

Cabrera held out her steak knife. "Daddy, will you cut my steak for me?"

"Don't start," he muttered with a shake of his head.

"Why, what are you going to do? Put me over your knee and spank me?"

"Stop."

"What part is bothering you? Me calling you Daddy, or the part about spanking me?"

"Cabrera," he growled.

"I actually prefer the second over the first."

He glanced up from drowning his pancakes with syrup.

"What?"

Using her knife, she was sawing at her steak and keeping her eyes on her plate, effectively avoiding his when she parroted, "What?"

"What did you say?"

"Nothing." She dragged a chunk of steak through runny egg yolk and then popped it into her mouth. She closed her eyes and *mmm*'d.

"You said..." He pulled in a breath. Between the spanking comment and her moaning over her meat, his dick twitched in his jeans.

What was wrong with him?

He needed to drop this conversation before he sat in this booth with a full-fledged hard-on, watching her lick her lips and close her eyes in ecstasy over her damn breakfast.

They were in a fucking diner, not a Ruth's Chris Steak-house. The steak couldn't be as good as she was making it out to be. It probably came from an old, dried-up milk cow and was tough as leather.

"Wow, that hits the spot." She took a sip of water, then grinned across the table at him. "Kind of like how your cock did."

"Cabrera," he growled. He was damn glad the tables and booths around them were empty at this time of morning.

She shrugged. "I'm just stating a fact. Here's another: My feet are killing me from being on them all night. If it wasn't too much effort to remove my boots, I'd put my poor sore feet in your lap and you could rub them for me."

"Maybe you shouldn't work in those boots," he suggested. Why did the thought of massaging her feet not turn him off?

He wasn't into feet.

Was he?

Why the fuck was she making him question his sexual

preferences?

"What do you want me to wear? Slippers? I need to fit in."

"You seem to be pulling it off with that outfit."

"You think? I was told I'm not showing enough of my tits."

Of course, that pulled his eyes down to her cleavage. "By who?"

"By anyone who had both a mouth hole and a dick. I heard it loud and often."

"You won't be showing more than that."

"Yes, Daddy."

"Stop."

Her husky chuckle floated across the table. "Why?"

"You know why."

"Because we had sex?"

"That's one reason. Can we not talk about sex while we eat?"

"Is it distracting?"

"It's not appropriate."

"Appropriate?" burst from her a little too loudly. "From what I heard, that word isn't even in your vocabulary."

"Apparently, what you heard is wrong since I just used it."

"And did it hurt for you to say it?"

He pointed his fork at her plate. "Eat."

"Yes, D—"

Before she could finish, his automatic response was to throw a sausage link at her. It bounced off her chest and disappeared below the table.

Her mouth dropped open and her eyes went wide. "Did you just start a food fight?"

Goddamnit. "No."

"So, your sausage just happened to launch itself across the table on its own?"

"It slipped off my fork."

She wiped the sausage grease off the shiny spot on her skin above her V-neck. "This is war."

"No it's not."

"It is." She dropped her napkin to the table. "I take that move as the declaration of your intent."

"Behave."

Her eyebrows jerked up her forehead. "Behave? You're telling *me* to behave? You just whipped a pork product at me."

"I didn't whip it."

She shook her head. "You're crazy—"

She was driving him to the edge of his sanity.

"—if you think I'm not going to retaliate."

As he opened his mouth, a "How's your breakfast?" had him snapping it back closed.

He reluctantly turned his attention from Cabrera to the waitress. "Delicious."

"Can I get you two anything else?"

"Just the check, please," he said quickly. They needed to get the hell out of there before things turned into a real battle.

"My father is struggling with arthritis. He accidentally dropped a sausage link on the floor. I'm so sorry for that."

"Oh, no bother. Food gets dropped all the time. We'll clean it up," the waitress said, pulling her pad out of her apron and tearing off the check before placing it next to Crew's plate. "I deal with a little arthritis myself. Try dipping them in warm paraffin wax. That helps me with the pain."

"He'd have to be supervised for that," Cabrera happily told her. "We had to unplug the stove so he didn't leave it on unattended."

The waitress *aww*'d in sympathy. "We all get to that point where we're forgetful."

"It's unfortunate." Cabrera shot a smirk across the table at him.

"Well, you can take the check up to the register when you're ready. And if you need anything else, just yell."

"Thank you," he muttered.

The waitress patted his shoulder. "Getting old stinks, doesn't it?" With that, she spun on her heels and left them alone.

"Make sure you don't choke on that steak," he warned.

She laughed. "You don't know the Heimlich?"

He shook his head. "I *forgot* how to do it. You know, since I'm old and forgetful."

They managed to finish their lukewarm breakfasts without any further food flying or verbal jabs since their mouths were busy eating.

After paying the bill, he followed her outside.

Since his Harley was parked near the entrance, he paused and watched her walk to the far end of the lot where she parked her Audi. Most likely to avoid door dings since the lot was now filling up with hungry early risers.

He watched her ass rock and roll in those skintight fake leather pants.

If he was smart, he'd let her go.

He sighed. Apparently, he wasn't.

He called out, "Hey, Cabrera!"

She stopped halfway to her car and glanced back over her shoulder at him.

"Just how tired are you?"

Because, yes, he was a fucking dumbass who hadn't gotten enough of her abuse yet.

But then, apparently that was his kink.

Chapter Nineteen

Since Fletch's house was on the way to his condo, they went there. Plus, he wasn't sure he wanted her to know just how close he lived. Yet.

His guarded, gated community was only about two blocks away. Fletch actually bought his house after driving by it on his way to Crew's place one night.

She pulled her Audi into the garage while he parked his Harley in the driveway and ducked into the garage before she shut the door.

"I need to let Murphy out. And I really should take a shower. These pants made me sweat and my hair absorbed every damn smell in that bar last night."

"Shower sounds good," he murmured, following her deeper into the house, since he planned on joining her.

They were greeted by the big gray galoot. The dog whined when he saw Cabrera and his tail wagged lazily as he lumbered over to her for a head scratch.

"C'mon, Murph," she called, heading toward the back door.

Crew waited in the kitchen while she went out back with the Irish Wolfhound. But it wasn't long before they came back into the house.

"All good?" he asked.

"Yes, I—"

He didn't even give her a chance to finish her thought before he tackled her.

"What—"

Once he got a good grip, he tossed her over his shoulder like a sack of flour.

"Crew!" she shrieked.

As he hoofed it through the kitchen, he ignored her complaints, as well as Murphy hopping around and releasing deep *woofs*, thinking it was playtime.

It was.

Just not with him.

As he carried her into the bedroom, it drilled home the fact of how petite the woman was.

And she was going head-to-head with big, burly bikers every night.

That did not relieve his worry.

Instead of tossing her on the bed, he set her on her feet. But before she could move, he snagged her wrist, sat on the edge of the mattress and yanked her so hard, she lost her balance.

He used that advantage to pull her across his lap face down, ass up.

"What are you doing?"

"Into spanking, are you?" She looked too fucking good across his lap.

"I was kidding," she insisted.

"I don't think you were."

"I swear! I've never been spanked before!"

And it showed.

"Always a first time," he said.

"I was kidding, Crew."

She might have been kidding but he wasn't holding her down and she wasn't trying to climb off his lap. She was simply lying over his thighs, occasionally squirming. He tried to read her expression, but her face was hidden by the fall of her long, dark hair.

"Oh, *now* it's Crew? You're not brave enough to call me Daddy right now?" He skimmed his palms over her perfect ass cheeks covered in the black, smooth fabric.

"That would be weird," she admitted.

"No fucking shit. I've been saying that. And, of course, you didn't listen. That's a bad habit, Cami."

"Oh, *now* it's Cami?"

"It feels weird calling you Cabrera when I'm about to spank your ass."

"You wouldn't." She squirmed again.

For fuck's sake, she actually needed to stop moving like that against his erection. "You're not the only one who likes a challenge. Now the question is, do I spank you with these tight pants on or do I do it against bare flesh?"

She lifted her head, but he still couldn't see her face. "Are you asking my opinion?"

"No. I'm considering my options."

"Can I suggest something?"

"No."

"Can I go take a shower first?"

"Also no." He pulled up the back of her shirt so he could see the waistline of the fake leather pants. "How do I get these off?"

"With my boots still on? You don't."

"I only need access to your ass."

He not only felt the rush of breath come from her, he heard it.

"Well?" he prodded.

"You expect me to help you pull my pants down so you can spank me like a naughty child?"

"I won't be spanking you like a naughty child, I promise you that."

"Well, now I'm *fully* on board with your plan."

"Your words don't match your tone."

"Of course they don't!" she yelled. "It was sarcasm."

He wedged his hand between her and his lap, checking for a button or zipper at her waist. He found none. "How the hell did you get these on?"

"They're made from Spandex. Ever hear of it? It's a space-aged fabric that stretches."

"You just added to your count." He grabbed the waistband of her pants and worked them down.

"Crew..."

"Careful with what you say next," he warned. "The more difficult you are, the more swats you're going to get.

"Swats," she echoed on a ragged breath.

"I want you to remember this moment later tonight when you're at Hawg Wild."

"You want me to remember what an asshole you are? That's hard to forget."

"I want you to remember the result of you having a smart mouth and not listening to orders."

"Do you spank your other team members?"

"I don't need to. They respect my authority." And he was damn sure if he tried that, he'd be on the receiving end of a bullet between the eyes. "Did you just snort at that?"

"No."

"You earned yourself another swat for lying." He worked

her pants down farther, slowly exposing her luscious ass cheeks.

No panties. Again. She'd been at that fucking bar without panties. *Jesus Christ.*

"Crew," she breathed and wiggled again.

"Worried?"

"No."

"Excited?"

He didn't get an answer and that was answer enough.

He pulled in a deep breath as he studied her bare ass displayed before him. It was as perfect as he remembered.

When he skimmed his palms over one bare ass cheek, then the other, he heard her shuddered breath.

Oh, *sure,* she'd been kidding. Her reactions proved otherwise.

He trailed a finger over the globes of her ass, then down her crease and didn't stop until he reached where she was hot and damp.

Her tremble shook his lap.

In truth, he hadn't planned on actually spanking her. It had only been an empty threat to mess with her. But now that he had her in position...

He was tempted.

His palm itched to make contact. And not in a gentle way. In a way that would make her want and ask for more.

And make him want to give her more.

He'd been with women who liked and preferred rough sex. He had spanked them, too. They encouraged him to strike them harder, to the point of turning their flesh red. To make it hot and swollen, or to even leave handprints behind.

Surprisingly, he discovered he liked it... To a point. Once it passed the point of pleasure and turned into pain, he only continued because that was what they wanted. What they demanded.

It wasn't what he wanted. For him, it went quickly from a turn-on to a turn-off.

Despite that, he'd had the best sex with some of those women because they had very few limits. However, would he want that type of sex every day? Hell no. While it could be a fun twist, he wasn't into that lifestyle.

"Crew."

Cami was completely quivering now. It had to be in anticipation because it was definitely not in fear. And, again, she made no move to get off his lap, even though she was free to do so.

She wanted this.

It just so happened that he wanted to give it to her.

One side of his mouth pulled up as he studied her flawless, creamy skin.

His target.

He lifted his hand so the only contact between them was her stomach on his thighs and rock-hard cock. When he hesitated with his hand in the air, she jerked.

Oh yes. Anticipation.

In a murmur, he reminded her of what she said. "You're not into this, remember?"

"I said—"

His palm made contact with her flesh, mixing the sharp crack with her gasp. He looked at the red spot left behind.

"Holy shit," she breathed, turning her face enough so he could finally see it. Her eyes were wide and her pupils expanded. Her mouth was gaped open and color tinged her cheeks.

Her eyes followed his hand as he slowly raised it again and when he paused, her nostrils flared. He dropped it hard and fast on her other cheek. Once again, a sharp crack filled the air as she twisted slightly and blew out a breath.

Two red spots now marred her normally golden skin.

His cock was so hard and aching so fucking bad, he swore it was about to explode.

She squirmed against him even more. "Crew..."

"Do I need to stop?"

Her eyes flicked up to his and their gazes held. He knew her answer before she said it. "No."

"Then put your head down and your ass up." He quickly wound strands of her hair around his right hand, tightening his grip when he made a fist. Then he shoved her head back down. He tapped her hip with his other hand. "Up."

"Oh God. Crew."

"Up, Cami. Unless you don't want me to continue."

She pushed her ass higher.

"Atta girl," he said under his breath. But she heard him because that praise had her quivering again.

This was so damn unexpected.

It was always the head-strong, pain-in-the-ass women that surprised him.

Cami was the last person he'd expect to want this. But then he hadn't expected to enjoy it so much, either.

He alternated smacking each cheek until her ass was so red, he began to worry. But she no longer flinched with each strike. She was grinding against him and groaning with pleasure, instead.

Jesus fuck.

She might not be at her limit, but he was.

He would have to tap out before she did.

He spanked her until his own hand stung painfully and his cock was dangerously at a tipping point. It was locked and loaded. If he didn't stop now, he was going to release that load in his boxer briefs and he hadn't had that happen since before he was eighteen.

He was far from eighteen now, so he'd prefer not to relive that experience. Plus, he didn't have a change of clothes with him. That ride home, even as short as it was, would not be fun.

A shower might help with his cock's hair trigger. Because if he fucked her now, he would be just as embarrassed as if he'd blown in his underwear.

She had to be close to her breaking point, too.

Should he risk continuing until she came?

No fucking way.

He pulled on her hair until her body bowed. "Get up. Time to shower."

When she went to stand, he gave her a hand since she was a bit wobbly from her head hanging over his legs.

"I stink from the bar."

"Actually, your pussy smells pretty damn good. But if you'd feel better showering first before I fuck you, I'm good with that."

"Are you joining me?"

"That's the plan."

Her lips curved upward and heat flared in her dark eyes. "Then, I guess, like you said, it's time to shower."

She turned away from him to unzip and pull off her boots and while she was bent over doing that, she made sure to show off his handiwork. Her cheeks had already turned a deep pink instead of bright red.

At that sight, he ran a hand down his erection.

Christ, that wasn't smart.

He got to his feet and stepped behind her, helping her pull off her top and unhook her bra. She peeled her leggings down the rest of the way and tugged them free from her feet before tossing them aside.

She turned, now completely naked.

His eyes skimmed over her from head to toe, then with a frown they rose again. At first, he thought he'd been seeing things. He hadn't.

She had a bruise on her arm near her wrist. And another on her left breast.

What the fuck?

"What happened?" he demanded. He circled her, making sure there weren't any more. Those bruises weren't fresh, so he didn't cause them from him throwing her over his shoulder or even the spanking.

She'd gotten them elsewhere. And he knew exactly where.

When she glanced down at where he was looking, her mouth twisted. "Murphy."

"No way. Not in those spots."

When she lifted her eyes again, she avoided his. "I'm clumsy. I bumped into a few things last night while working behind the bar."

"Bullshit. You don't want to tell me because you don't want me pulling you from the assignment."

"It's only a couple of bruises, Crew."

"Then tell me how you got them," he insisted.

"Only if you promise not to pull me."

He wasn't doing that.

Instead, he grabbed her arm and inspected the bruise right above her wrist. Of course he could make out the shape of fingers. Someone had grabbed her hard enough to leave a mark.

Clenching his teeth, he dropped her hand and studied

the bruise near her nipple. He beat back the growl bubbling up his throat.

"Crew... It's a hazard of the job. I handled it."

His nostrils flared as he pulled in a breath.

"Are you going to ruin our plans because of a couple of bruises?"

Was he?

"Can we finish what we started? I'm standing here naked. You need to be the same for us to share a shower."

Of course she wanted him to drop the subject.

But she was right, he needed to let it go. There'd been plenty of times he'd gotten bruises while on the job.

However, it was the way she obtained them that still bugged the shit out of him.

She distracted him by grabbing his shirt and tugging it up and over his head, skimming her fingers over his heated skin here and there. Drawing his thoughts from those damn bikers to the woman before him.

By some miracle he still had his erection.

As he worked on unfastening his belt and jeans, she went down on her knees to unlace and remove his boots.

Just like the other morning.

As soon as his socks and boots were gone, he dropped his jeans and boxer briefs to his feet, his erection bobbing as he straightened.

"Shower," he ordered. He didn't want any more delays.

Even so, he remained where he was and watched her head to the attached bathroom in all her naked glory, focusing on the marks he left behind on her ass. Not the ones left by others.

And holy shit. That sight just about took him to his knees right there and then.

She paused in the doorway and turned her head. "Coming?"

He planned on it.

———

HER DEEP GROAN caused by him massaging the shampoo into her scalp made his cock flex. As soon as he was done with that, he grabbed the hand-held shower head and rinsed out all the soap.

She grabbed a bottle of conditioner and held it over her shoulder. He took it and slathered it all over her hair. As it worked its magic, she turned and raised her eyes to him, her wet eyelashes clumped together. "Condom?"

Fuck. Since all the blood from his brain had pooled in his cock, he hadn't even thought about needing one for in the shower. That was fucking dumb.

He shook his head. "In my wallet." He had tucked two in there to replace the one he used with her the other day. Unfortunately, that wasn't doing him any good currently.

"I bought a box yesterday but it's in the nightstand."

She did? Had she planned on using them with him or with someone else?

He wasn't sure he wanted an answer to that question. "Then, we need to finish this shower."

She pursed her lips. "*Mmm.* Not yet. I still need some time to let this conditioner work."

Holding onto his waist for balance, she slowly lowered to her knees.

That might not be the best idea about now. He'd been dangling precariously from the edge since spanking her.

The time in the shower helped somewhat, but still...

After wrapping her hand around the root of his cock, she tipped her dark eyes up to him and opened her mouth.

He held his breath when she held the tip of his cock near her lips.

Jesus, the anticipation. Was she getting back at him for doing the same to her earlier?

He didn't have to wait long. His eyes automatically shut when her mouth surrounded him. He forced them open, because if he got lost in his head, he'd be done for.

When she swallowed him almost to the root, his head jerked back and he set his jaw and clenched his fingers into fists, hoping that would help keep him from losing his shit within seconds.

He inhaled each breath through his nose and exhaled out of his mouth. His pulse pounded so hard in his ears he had difficulty hearing past it. His cock throbbed dangerously as she swirled her tongue around his length. His balls pulled tight when she sucked the tip.

But it was when she took him deep into her mouth again, his hips began to twitch with the urge to thrust and he had to cry mercy.

"Cami," he whispered. "Unless you want me to come in your mouth, you need to stop."

Of course, she ignored his plea, the same as she did his orders. She considered them more as suggestions than directives.

"Cami," he started again, louder and much firmer this time. "You're playing with fire."

He needed to avoid whimpering. That just may happen if she continued to ignore him.

She smiled around his cock.

"If you want me to fuck you, now would be the time to stop." As much as he would like to, he couldn't spend the next few hours in bed with her. He had to get back to The Plant. And if he came now, he'd have to scrap his plans for sinking his cock deep inside her and making her come.

She released his cock with a wet pop.

Thank fuck.

"I guess I can live with that," she said as he grabbed her elbow and helped her to her feet.

Chapter Twenty

STRADDLING HIS LAP, she slowly rose and fell on his cock.

He wasn't sure where to keep his eyes trained. On the ecstasy covering her face? On her tits bouncing as she rode him?

On her throat working with each moan?

On his rock-hard cock as it disappeared inside her over and over?

Or all of the above?

Suddenly her eyes opened and locked with his. "Are you watching me?"

"Of course I am. What am I supposed to do, stare at the fucking ceiling?"

"You're going to make me self-conscious."

"Yeah, right. Is that even possible with you?"

She shrugged and shifted one of the hands she had planted on his chest over to his nipple.

He winced when she pinched it hard. "Ow! What the hell!"

She laughed and fell forward, smashing her tits into his chest and practically going nose to nose with him. "Don't be a wimp."

"Don't be a wimp?" he echoed, his voice rising an octave.

"Did you hear me whining when you lit my ass on fire?"

"That's because you liked it."

"You don't like me tweaking your nipples?" With another laugh, she did it again.

He slapped her hand away. "No."

"Your nipples are cute."

"That's a compliment I never thought I'd hear."

"You probably don't hear many, anyway." She planted her hands back on his chest and straightened until she was sitting again.

"You have to be a smart ass even while we're having sex?"

Her dark eyebrows rose. "Is that what we're doing? I thought I was having sex and you were just lying there so you don't overexert yourself."

"Did I not eat your pussy until you practically ripped my hair out while you were coming?" And screaming his name while she did it.

"I need to be careful with that since I'm sure you'll lose it soon enough." She sat still and ran her fingers through his hair. "You have more gray than my father."

He groaned. "Can we not talk about your father right now? I'll lose my erection."

"If you haven't heard, there's a pill for that, too."

"Cami," he growled in warning.

"So, it's Cami when we're having sex, Cabrera when we're not."

"It's weird calling you Cabrera when you're riding my cock. And to be clear, I'm not more gray than your father."

"Yes, you are." She added a little smirk onto that.

"Because he's fucking bald!" burst from him.

Her eyes went wide and she patted his chest. "Calm down. Getting overly excited isn't good for your ticker."

"Wrong. Cardio is great for my heart."

"If you were actually doing some..."

She released a shrill squeal-laugh combination as he rolled the both of them until he was on top and settled between her thighs. "Since you're complaining about doing all the work, I'll take over."

She twisted an invisible handlebar mustache. "*Ah*, my evil plan worked!"

"You're not right in the head."

"You're so fun to mess with."

"See? I told you I was fun."

She grabbed his ass and squeezed. "All right. Let's get down to business. I need to get some sleep and you need to go annoy everyone else on your team."

"I have to finish annoying you first."

"Yes, you do. So, get to it." She slapped him hard on the ass.

"You mean like this?" He thrust his cock deep.

"Very annoying."

"And this?" He shoved his hands under her ass and thrust again.

"I can't stand how horrible that is."

"How about this?" He stayed deep and ground his hips in a circle.

"Rude! But do it again."

He did. "Like this?"

Her face twisted. "The worst!"

He paused and dropped his head before shaking it, trying not to laugh.

This whole fucking thing was ridiculous.

When he lifted his head, he saw she was grinning.

But then, so was he.

As he studied her, out of the blue something foreign slammed into his chest and swirled around like a fast-moving tornado, causing his lips to turn the other direction.

Her grin disappeared, too. "You okay?"

No, he wasn't. "Yeah."

He needed to get the fuck out of there. This was a trap and he was not going to get caught in it.

He began to move in earnest, ignoring everything else. Only concentrating on what he was doing and the woman beneath him. Working toward the goal of making her come so he could leave.

It became a struggle to breathe and not because of the physical exertion.

With her moans filling his ears and her hot, slick pussy pulsating around his cock, he managed to push past whatever had come over him. He dug his knees deeper into the mattress and pounded her harder and faster, not giving it the time and space to take hold again.

He came over here to have sex with her. That was it.

Nothing more.

There could be nothing more.

"Crew..."

His name being moaned kept him grounded as he powered up and into her over and over.

Taking only what he came here for.

Nothing more.

Giving her only what she wanted.

Nothing more.

The second her short nails drove into his ass, her pussy slammed against him and her body bowed off the bed, he quickly chased her orgasm with his own.

That was all he came here for.

That was it.

Nothing fucking more.

The second his cock stopped pulsing, he wasted no time sliding out of her, rolling to the side and sitting up on the edge of the bed.

He ripped off the condom and stared at it.

He needed to get rid of it, get dressed and get the fuck out of there.

No cuddling, no conversation, no lingering.

Nothing more.

"So... what happened?"

"Nothing."

As he got to his feet, the fact that she didn't believe him was written all over her face .

Luckily, she didn't push.

Thank fuck she let it go.

Because he didn't have a good answer for her question.

Or at least one he wanted to admit.

————

WITH HIS JAW set and his cell phone pressed to his ear, he raked fingers through his hair. He was currently pacing out in the alley behind The Plant, away from any ears.

His rage burned hot, as it always did when he thought he might miss out on his court-appointed time with his kids.

Every damn time it had to be a fight. He was sick of it. He swore Sasha took pleasure in torturing him. He didn't know what the fuck he had done to deserve any of it.

"They want to spend time with me, Sasha."

"Do they? Have you asked them? They might disagree."

"If they don't, it's because of you lying and telling them

ignorant shit. You want them to push me away the same as you did."

"They get upset when I remind them that your weekend is coming up."

"Because you make them upset. Once they're with me, they're fine," he told her. And that wasn't a lie.

"They complain when they return, too."

"About what?"

"I don't want to tell you because you'll hold it against them."

More lies and manipulation. "When have I ever held anything against them? You're the one being difficult, Sasha, not them. What the fuck did I ever do to you to be like this?"

"You decided to be more faithful to your job than me."

She clung to that excuse to cover for her own transgressions. "Bullshit. Don't act like you didn't know what I did for a living on our first damn date."

"That was a date?"

He ignored that cut. It had been a great date and the reason they went on a second. And a third... And eventually got engaged, married and decided to have a family. "Unlike you, I never hid who I was or what I did for a living. My family has always come first. And speaking of faithful, have you looked in the mirror lately?"

"That's a low blow."

The truth hurt sometimes. "So is trying to keep me from my own children."

"You made me a widow when you weren't even dead!"

Wincing from her scream in his ear, he yanked his phone away.

Worse than her screeching was the fact she blamed him for her own fucking cheating. Talk about projection.

He took a deep breath before putting the phone back to his ear. "Sasha, we've hashed this over time and time again. It doesn't change anything, so let's move on. If we didn't have the kids, you'd never have to see me again. But we do, so we need to work together."

"You can sign away your rights."

Again with this shit? Every time she suggested that, a sharp shard of ice jammed him straight in the heart. "You know I'd never do that. And you keep forgetting that if I sign away my rights, you no longer get child support. You'd be one hundred percent financially responsible for them. Anyway, fuck you for even bringing it up again."

"Nice way to speak to the mother of your children."

He loved his children. The woman whose womb carried them, not so much.

Not anymore.

"Then act like their mother and stop the bullshit. I have every right to be in their life. I *want* to be in their life. Why do our discussions have to go down the fucking toilet every damn time? It's been seven years since we split, and you still aren't willing to work with me by co-parenting." He closed his eyes, pinched his nose and pulled in a breath to keep from totally unraveling. If that happened, he might say shit that he could never take back. "I'm done with this conversation. I'll pick them up Friday afternoon after school, so make sure they have their stuff with them. I'll text you once I pick them up."

"They have plans."

"Yeah, with me."

"They won't be happy to be away from their friends."

"When they have goddamn cell phones, they're in constant contact with their friends."

Originally, the cell phones were only supposed to be used

in an emergency but now they spent way too much time on social media. And he doubted Sasha monitored their online activity. That was another reoccurring fight he didn't want to start right now.

"Every goddamn month," he muttered under his breath. "Every fucking time it's my turn to have them. You'd think you'd get tired of being a fucking bitch. You know I am."

"That's fine. You can call me a bitch, even though I'm only looking out for my children," she stated.

"They're my children, too. No matter what you say, no matter what you do, that will never change. Make sure they're ready for the weekend. Don't make me have to get the lawyers involved."

"Nice threat."

"You're goddamn right it's a threat and you know I'll follow through." And, unfortunately, it would cost them both, but spending time with his kids was priceless and worth any legal expense incurred.

He would never give up on them no matter how difficult Sasha made it.

If it wouldn't turn his kids against him more, he'd file for full custody. Then she'd be the parent only getting them one weekend a month during the school year and one week a month during summer break.

It was never enough time.

It was bad enough that the divorce was painful, but not having twenty-four-seven access to his own children made the whole thing worse.

"You're an asshole."

Where had he heard that before? "If fighting for my kids makes me an asshole, I'll wear that badge proudly. Make sure they're aware I'm picking them up at school."

He ended the call at the same time a very familiar Audi slowly passed him and turned into The Plant's back lot.

Fuck.

He was in no mood to deal with Cabrera's smart mouth right now.

Hell, right now he was in no mood to deal with any fucking woman.

It had only taken one to taint his view of them all.

Painting them all with the same brush might not be fair. However, every time he was starting to believe differently and that he shouldn't lump them all together, a phone call to his ex-wife spiraled him right back to that belief.

Sasha was not only determined to destroy his relationship with his children, she also had effectively poisoned him against any real future relationship with women. Including the one climbing out of her sports car with her eyes on him as he walked through the open gate.

She remained next to her car as if waiting for him to approach. He didn't. He strode past her and toward the side of the building where the stairs to the third floor were located.

"Hey... you okay?" she called out.

"Yeah," he threw over his shoulder, not slowing down.

He heard her behind him scrambling to catch up. "Your expression says otherwise. Bad news?"

"No." For some reason he stopped short, turned and blurted out, "I'll have my kids this weekend."

Why the fuck did she need to know that?

Her face lit up. "Oh nice. Do you get them often?"

"Not often enough."

Her face fell. "Sorry. I'm sure the divorce was hard on them."

"Yeah. Just letting you know that I'll be unavailable this

weekend in case anything goes down with you at Hawg Wild."

"Okay."

"Torres will be in charge of the task force."

"Okay."

"I won't be over." *Oh for fuck's sake.*

"To be expected and I didn't invite you over, anyway."

Right.

"Do you think your dick is addictive like meth?"

He didn't answer that.

"And the way you left this morning made me think you had no interest in coming back."

He didn't respond to that, either. Because what the fuck could he say to that?

He had rushed out of there like his ass was on fire and not from being spanked.

Women. They were walking, talking traps.

All of them.

They sucked you in, gave you a false sense of happiness, then turned around and sliced your fucking throat.

"Hi."

He tipped his eyes down to the woman now standing only inches away. How did he miss her approaching?

The tension lessened from his chest making it a little bit easier for him to breathe. "Hi."

"I know we haven't known each other long but I can see how stressed you are."

"Pissed," he corrected.

A crease marred her normally smooth brow. "What?"

"Not stressed. Pissed."

"About?"

"About why one parent feels the need to use their children as a weapon against the other."

"Damn," she whispered. "I'm sorry."

He stared down at her. "If you ever have kids and you and the father go your separate ways, don't make your children suffer just to get back at him."

"What's she getting back at you for?"

"Simply breathing."

Chapter Twenty One

CAMI WASN'T sure how to react to what he said.

Some divorces were easy. Some, not so much.

Others left behind nothing but absolute scorched Earth.

She was lucky her parents were still happily married and even still madly in love. Even after thirty years.

They had given her relationship goals. Hopefully not an unrealistic one, since she wanted to have the same sort of solid partnership one day.

Her father sometimes serenaded her mother, despite being a horrible singer. And her mother loved every minute of it. They still flirted with each other. Touched and kissed. Whispered in each other's ears. And laughed together over the stupidest things. They even scheduled date nights. They shared household responsibilities.

They stood by each other's side through thick and thin. Through every move to a new state. Through two miscarriages and four more births after Cami was born.

They never gave up on each other. Not once. Any hard times they had only made them stronger.

So, yes, she wanted what they had, even though she wasn't sure she'd ever get it.

No matter what, she couldn't imagine falling in love with someone, being happy, building a family and a home and then watching it all get destroyed, leaving behind bitterness and anger.

When she reached out and put a hand on his gut, she could feel his body riddled with tension. "How long have you been divorced?"

"We separated seven years ago. The divorce took two years and a fuckload of money because Sasha fought me over everything. Every goddamn thing. My goal was to make sure my kids were taken care of. Her goal was to make sure she was taken care of."

Cami was surprised he told her that much. Maybe talking to someone about it would help. So she continued, "How old were you when you got married?"

"Twenty-seven."

"How old are your kids now?"

"Dylan is thirteen. Chloé will be fifteen in a few weeks."

"You got married when you were a year younger than I am. And you had your first child not long after. But you consider me young. Funny that."

"I look back now and realize we *were* too young. I now make better choices."

She tilted her head to the side. "But do you? We all make mistakes."

"Despite all my mistakes, my children aren't one of them."

"Of course they aren't. They're a piece of you. And your anger shows how much you love them and how much you want to spend time with them. If you didn't care, you wouldn't be so upset."

A muscle in his cheek jumped when she said "upset."

"What happened? Why did she divorce you?"

His jaw tightened. "Do you mean, why did I divorce her?"

Cami stared up at him. She couldn't read his eyes because he wore his signature mirrored sunglasses. "Is that what happened?"

He gave her a single nod. "That's what happened."

"She's still bitter about you kicking her to the curb? Is that why she's making your life difficult?"

"That's part of it."

Should she ask? Would he answer? "What's the rest?"

She really didn't have any right to know all the gritty details. Having sex with the man twice didn't give her that right. But she wasn't being nosy, she was truly interested in what made the man tick.

"She felt like I was married to my job more than to her. She used the excuse of being lonely to start a relationship with someone else."

"Damn," she whispered.

"Worse, when I was home, she turned into the Wicked Witch of Western Pennsylvania. Because of that, I stopped fucking her. Because I did, she began to accuse *me* of cheating whenever I was away on assignments."

"But you weren't."

"No. I wasn't," he said flatly.

"Basically, she was gaslighting you by projecting."

"She tried. It didn't work." He squeezed his forehead between his fingers and sighed. "I stayed for the kids as long as I could. Then it hit me one day, it was worse for them if we tried to stay together instead of separating. We were at each other's throats constantly. I didn't want them to see that anymore and I didn't want to damage them further. The hardest part wasn't leaving her, it was leaving them. I had hoped she'd be willing to let me see the kids whenever I wanted. I should've known she wouldn't be cooperative, to the point I had to pursue it legally. Everything was a fight with her. We butted heads constantly. If I said the sky was blue, she said it was green just to get under my skin." He glanced down at her. "Kind of reminds me of you."

She assumed he meant the butting heads part because she would never stop a father from seeing his own children. Unless he was abusing them. Then all bets were off.

"I started to stay away from the house more and more to avoid the confrontations until I figured it was better for their mental health for me to throw in the towel. Our relationship wasn't even close to being healthy. And at the time, I didn't even know about the cheating. I didn't find out about that until after I left and she rubbed it in my face trying to start another argument. It didn't make sense why she ended up being this way because she'd never been spiteful about anything early in our relationship."

"Was she jealous of your career?"

"She said I made her feel like a widow since I was gone so much. Maybe she was jealous of how dedicated I was to my job, even though my family always came first. A conversation about it, instead of finding reasons to pick fights, would've been nice. It could've avoided all the misery."

"Communication is key," she murmured. It was most likely why her parents' marriage was still so strong. Of course, every relationship had its ups and downs. How one dealt with the trouble spots determined if it survived. "And the kids? How did they take the divorce?"

"Not well."

"Because you left?"

"Because she began to poison them against me. I was the

252

bad parent. I had deserted them because of my job and with the divorce, I was deserting them permanently."

"Damn."

"Right. She told them I loved my work more than them."

"Was that true?"

"I love my kids more than anything. They can hate me, call me all kinds of shit, refuse to see me and I'll still love them until the day I die."

"I'm sorry," she whispered.

He pulled in a long breath, when he released it, he continued, sadness coloring his tone, "It's better now. I've been making some headway with them. But sometimes I feel like it's a losing battle. I get a few steps forward when they're with me. They get to see who I really am and how much I love them, but when they go back to Sasha, she works hard to take that progress away."

"Why is she like that?"

"I don't know. When I met her, I thought she was the woman of my dreams. She checked all the boxes and I thought we were perfect together. She ended up being a nightmare. I'm more pissed at myself for not seeing who she was at her very core."

"Have you tried to get custody?"

He pulled in another long breath. "I seriously considered it, but I don't want them hating me more than they already do by taking them away from their mother. I'm hoping the older they get, the more they'll see the truth with their own eyes instead of through Sasha's."

"Why do parents do that? Turn their kids against the other parent? It's self-centered."

"I could understand one parent keeping a kid away if the other parent is abusive or a bad influence. But to me, it's a crime to destroy a kid's relationship with a parent.

Especially one who wants to be actively involved in their lives."

She didn't know how to take away that pain, so she repeated, "I'm sorry."

"I deal with it."

"But not well."

"I deal with it," he repeated.

"So, you have your kids this weekend. Did you make plans?"

"I plan on taking them into the Burgh. I got us tickets to a Pirates game, then I'll take them to Primanti Brothers for dinner."

"They're both into sports?"

"Dylan loves baseball."

"And Chloé?"

He huffed out, "She'll be on her phone more than watching the game."

"But what's she into?"

"She loves to dance. She even takes classes with Finn's mom."

"Finn's mom teaches dance?"

"She's had her own studio for decades."

"What kind of dancing is your daughter into?"

She finally saw a slight upward curve of his mouth. Proof he loved his kids and was proud of them.

"All of it. She's constantly watching YouTube videos to learn new routines. She's really good."

"Aren't Rez and Finn's girlfriends dancers?" Maybe not ballerinas, but still...

"At fourteen, I'd prefer she not swing around a pole."

Cami clicked her tongue. "Since she's about to turn fifteen, she only has about three years before she can do it legally."

Crew pulled his sunglasses down his nose just enough to peer over them. "Perfect example on how you like to get under my skin."

She grinned and patted his very firm stomach. "I'm just lightening the mood. And there's nothing wrong with being a stripper."

"You're right, there's not. Unless you're talking about my teenage daughter."

At least it got him to stop thinking about his evil ex-wife. "When do you get them?"

He slid his sunglasses back into place. "Friday after school. Then I drop them back off Sunday night."

"That doesn't seem long enough."

"It's not," he agreed.

"Well, then I guess that means I can swim naked all weekend without worrying about someone barging in unannounced. Is that what you're telling me?"

His head jerked back, and his nostrils flared enough for her to catch it. "Sure. If that's what you heard. But just so you know, I'm not the only one with access to the house. There's a bunch of us."

"That may be true, but so far, you're the only one who has invaded my space."

"It won't happen again."

"I figured that after seeing you spooked this morning."

A crease appeared in his forehead over his sunglasses. "I wasn't spooked."

"Then what were you?"

It took him forever to answer. "Tired."

"I was the one who worked all night." She stepped back, putting space between them. "And I'm about to go do it again. I'll run up and grab the keys to the pool car. Are you heading up?"

He shook his head. "No, I'm going to head out."

Funny, since he had been headed upstairs before she stopped him.

She glanced at the time on her cell phone. "Shit. I need to get going, even though I doubt they'd notice if I'm late. Hell, they wouldn't notice if I didn't even show up. It's not like I have to clock in or anything."

"Being invisible might be a good thing. You can be more observant without your actions being noticed."

She nodded. "I try to stick close to the Demons so I can hear any chatter we can use against them. Plus, my goal is to find where they keep their stash as soon as I can. And on that note... I need to roll."

Without waiting for a response, she headed toward the stairs.

"Cabrera..."

She stopped and glanced over her shoulder.

With hands on his hips, he had his mirrored sunglasses pointed toward her. "Be safe."

She gave him an answering lift of her chin and continued on. She ended up waiting at the bottom of the stairs until she heard his Harley start.

That throaty rumble sent a little thrill through her.

Once she heard him ride away, she ran up and grabbed the car keys.

It was time to get to head to Hawg Wild for another fun and exciting night of dodging hands and hearing comments that were far from complimentary.

Chapter Twenty-Two

CREW BLEW out a relieved breath when he pulled Silver Foxy into the back lot and saw that the pool car had been returned. Once he parked his bike, he went over to the sedan and placed a hand on the hood.

Cold.

That meant she'd returned it a while ago and was now most likely home and asleep.

Hopefully she got out of Hawg Wild Saloon unscathed this time. Because if she had more bruises... Or worse...

He ground his teeth.

He hated her going undercover at that Demons-run bar without any safety net. He wasn't even sure if she was going in there with her weapon since the clothes she wore wouldn't hide shit.

As the group leader, he was responsible for her. He should pull her. It wasn't like they didn't have enough evidence already against the MC to ensure indictments on some of the major members.

Despite that, it would be better to put away as many as

possible. The more put behind bars meant the less out there roaming free to continue trafficking drugs. Or pimping out meth-addicted women.

After reading through Cabrera's daily reports carefully, he realized she had documented enough criminal activity in the first couple of nights working there to indict at least five more members of the Deadly Demons. Evidence he didn't have before.

If she remained on that assignment, that number could grow.

Her notes also indicated she was searching for where the meth supply was kept in Hawg Wild's supply room. Without getting caught, of course.

In truth, he had no good reason to pull her. By being there, she was doing her part to contribute to the investigation. If he pulled her, it wouldn't be because she wasn't doing the job, it would solely be because of him.

And his personal reasons wouldn't be valid.

But that didn't mean he couldn't keep the fact the bar patrons were manhandling her as an ace in his back pocket, in case he needed it.

No matter what, he had to trust that she knew what she was doing and that she could handle any shit she received on her own.

As he hit the foot of the stairs, he glanced up and saw Nox coming out of the third floor. Crew bet he was about to go hibernate in his apartment.

He rushed up the steps to make sure to catch him before that happened.

He got to the second-floor landing at the same time Nox did, only Crew was a bit more out of breath from sprinting up the steps.

"How you doing?" he asked, trying not to wheeze while

he did it. He made sure to stand in front of Nox's apartment door so his brother couldn't duck inside and get out of talking to him.

"I'm doing," came the flat answer.

"Yeah? How's the therapy going?"

"It's going."

"Nox, I don't want to pry..."

"But you will anyway."

"I just want to make sure you're staying on track."

"Whose track?"

"The right track. Is it helping at all?" Crew hoped to fuck it was.

Nox simply stared at him.

Crew raised his palms up. "I get it. You don't want to talk about it. I just wanted to make sure you're following the—"

"Ultimatum?"

"Plan," Crew finished. "Brother, you know we all love you like family. We all have your six. This—"

"Ultimatum."

"*Plan* was just another way of showing you how much we want you to be—"

"Sane?"

"Happy," Crew finished. "Jesus. We know you're not insane. But sometimes shit hits us harder than other times. Like my divorce."

"Sasha's still breathing."

It would be easier for him if the woman wasn't, but Crew kept that to himself. He really didn't wish his ex-wife dead, he only wished she didn't have it out for him, even all these years later.

"Still breathing fire, you mean. On that note, I have my kids this weekend. I might bring them by on Sunday, if anyone will be around downstairs. They'd probably like to see you."

When his face softened, it was proof the man did love children. And all the BAMC kids loved him back, including the moody teens. They thought he was cool because he used to tell them stories from when he was in the Army.

Some tales had been a bit embellished, but Nox managed to make military service sound much more exciting than it was in reality.

No matter what, Nox tried to spend time with them whenever one of their brothers brought their kids along to the BAMC church. Most likely because Nox and his wife had been about to start a family when Jackie died. He hadn't hidden his excitement about becoming a father.

All of that had been ripped away from him in a flash.

Right now, being around the kids was the only thing that brought him out of his funk.

"Hey, I was thinking about taking them for a ride on Sunday before I have to take them back. You interested in coming along and having Dylan as your backpack? I can take Chloé."

Nox dropped his head and stared at his boots for a few seconds. With his baseball cap pulled low, Crew couldn't read his expression.

But when the man nodded before lifting his head, Crew felt relieved.

"Yeah, I'm game. Maybe we can take them for ice cream or something."

Holy shit. That was a good sign. "I'm sure they'll be good with that. Maybe I'll get Deck to join us with Valee Girl. Do some sort of Daddy/daughter ride but not just with our girls."

There were others in the MC with kids who could go along, too. Cross and his twins. Jamison and his twins. Miller and his litter of children. The only problem with Miller would be picking which kid to go along. Probably the one most willing. And if some didn't want to be left out, Crew could recruit some of the other BAMC members to haul them around.

Or, even easier, he could let the BAMC road captain plan it. "I'll say something to Finn. Maybe he can throw together a club run on Sunday just for the kids. We should be able to get enough of us together to make sure they all have a seat if they want."

"Not sure Cross's boy will want to go."

"Then, he can bring Bri. And Jamison can bring Laney. Maybe it should be strictly a Daddy/daughter run. We could always leave the boys downstairs to play video games."

"Thought you wanted Dylan riding with me."

Oh fuck, that was right. Because if Nox didn't have a kid riding with him, he might not go at all. And going for a long ride in the fresh air would do him some good. Being around the kids might help, too. "Yeah. Brain glitched there for a second. I do. I don't get a bunch of time with them and this gives them a good reason to stay off their phones. Taking them to a Pirates game Saturday afternoon, too." Now he wished he had bought an extra ticket for Nox.

The man grunted.

"All right, I'll get with Finn and we can set that up. Unless you hear otherwise, assume it's a go."

"'Kay."

"You sure you're good?"

Nox set his dark eyes on him. "Will be once you stop blocking my door."

Crew shifted out of the way. "Got it. I'll be upstairs."

"Figured that." Nox pushed past him, unlocked his door and went inside.

Crew stood there long enough to hear the deadbolt click. He shook his head and sighed in frustration on his way up the steps.

Nox had been on the road to recovery before finding Sloane's sister Sadie dead in a motel room in Ohio.

Not only dead but with her corpse violated.

Crew heard it had been an ugly scene. He did his fucking best not to imagine it. It was bad enough to set Nox back by months, if not longer. The whole reason they had that intervention with him and gave him the "ultimatum."

Was the counseling and support group working? Seemed to be, but it was a damn slow process.

He punched in the code and the lock released. He went inside to see some of his team already hard at work.

Except for Rez, who was lounging on the couch hardly working. Of course.

He went over to the couch to see his brother's eyes shut. Crew thumped him in the chest with the heel of his palm.

"Hey!" Rez shot up, eyes wide, rubbing the impact point.

"Maybe you should stop fucking Sapphire all night and get some sleep. You're supposed to be working, not napping."

"Maybe you should find someone to fuck instead of your fist and you'd understand why I'm so damn tired." Rez got to his feet.

Crew went to the coffeemaker next. Priorities. "My fist doesn't talk back and is always nearby when I need it." He grabbed his mug from the stand next to the coffee and filled it to the brim. "Even better, my fist isn't high maintenance. It doesn't need money for clothes, purses and makeup and doesn't whine until it gets jewelry."

"Who hurt you?" Rez asked him.

Even though Rez was sort of teasing, he knew about all

the turmoil Crew went through during the divorce. He had witnessed a lot of it. So did the rest of his BAMC brothers.

Crew turned and found Finn sitting at the far end of the conference table working on a laptop. He had no fucking clue what Pippi Longstocking was working on since he didn't micromanage his team. He trusted them to get done what needed to be done.

All except for Rez.

"Yo, Little Orphan Annie!" he called out as he approached that end of the table.

Finn ignored him by keeping his head down and continuing to type away.

"Carrot Top," he tried next.

Still no response except for the snickers from the other guys sitting at various stations doing whatever they were assigned to do for the day.

"Heat Miser." When he still didn't get a response, he followed up with, "Prince Harry!"

Rez snorted behind him and pushed past him to drop into the office chair next to Finn. He leaned closer to their redheaded brother, stage-whispering, "Crewella Deville is calling you. Hide your puppies."

Finn glanced at Rez. "I thought I heard nails scratching down a chalkboard." He looked directly at Crew. "I was right."

"Hey, I was just talking to Nox…"

Everyone in the room stopped what they were doing and turned to listen. Well, now he knew how to get everyone's attention.

Finn sat back in his chair. "And?"

"Since I have the kids this weekend, I want to take them on a little club run on Sunday with everyone who has kids. I'll haul Chloé on my bike and Nox agreed to take Dylan.

Can you arrange something and get the word out? See if Cross wants to bring his twins and Jamison his twins and if they all want to go, we can have the childless members like you help out. I figured it would be fun. And, get this, Nox even suggested stopping for ice cream."

"No shit," Decker murmured from his spot at one of the computers.

"Yeah, no shit," Crew echoed. "You want to bring Val?"

"Yeah, she'd love it and she'll also be thrilled to hang out with the big kids."

"As long as they're not all pouting for being forced to go," Crew told him. He turned back to Finn. "See who wants to participate and make sure we have enough seats for them all."

Finn's brow dropped low. "How the fuck did I get stuck with doing this when it's your idea?"

"Last I checked, the damn patch on your cut states you're the road captain. You planning on tearing off that patch anytime soon?"

"For fuck's sake, I should," Finn grumbled and shook his head. "I'll send out a mass text and see who's available and how many want to go."

"Don't strain your fingers doing it."

"Finger," Rez corrected Crew. "He hunts and pecks when he types his texts."

"And you fat-finger yours," Finn countered. "Half the time I don't know if your text is in Spanish or English."

"It's Spanglish."

"What does 'typo' mean in Spanglish?" Finn asked.

Rez came back with, "It means yo momma."

Crew shook his head. "Hey, can we graduate from kindergarten to the first grade now?"

"Yeah, because you always act mature," Decker said from his desk. "Anyway, just do it, Finn. For Nox."

"I already have a run scheduled for two weekends from now."

"Like another one is going to hurt. Or can't you afford gas for that machine of yours since you're penny-pinching for Mel's new club?" Decker asked.

"I can afford gas just fine with all the wages the feds are paying me for this assignment," Finn answered.

Laughter filled the room.

"Yeah, I'm going to buy a Lamborghini with my federal paycheck," Reynolds said dryly from the far corner.

"Better buy a Hot Wheels track for it, too," Torres suggested.

"Anyway, get it done," Crew told the road captain.

"When did you get to be president? You don't even sit on the damn committee," Finn complained.

"Since Jamison isn't around right now and Fletch is buried deep within the DAMC, I'm acting president."

Finn huffed out, "Bullshit. It only works like that in your imagination. That's not what the bylaws say."

"Like you've read the bylaws," Crew scoffed. "Anyway, let's get back to the reason we're all on this task force. Let's start with the simple shit since it can't get any more simple than T-Bag. Has anyone heard any chatter about that prospect?"

"Nope. Nothing," Torres answered. "He just disappeared like a fart."

"Since we dropped hints about him skimming from their meth supply, the Demons probably stripped the prospect of his cut," Rez surmised.

Decker grinned. "Or made him magically disappear."

"Either way, no loss."

"Karma," Decker agreed with Rez.

"Couldn't have happened to a nicer guy."

Decker sniffled. "I need a tissue. I'm going to miss that motherfucker."

"Can we get them to do the same for Saint?" Rez asked.

"Saint's a patched member," Finn reminded Rez and Decker. "It would take a vote to get rid of him."

"And a good reason," Crew added. "Unfortunately, getting physical with the girlfriends of the federal task force members investigating their MC won't fly."

Rez shrugged. "Worth a shot."

"If anything, they'd give that fucker an award. Hail him as a hero," Reynolds chimed in.

"Don't worry," Torres began, "he'll get indicted along with the rest. He can make some new friends in the federal penitentiary."

"Him going to prison isn't enough for me," Finn said.

Rez agreed. "What he said. Prison will be too easy. It might be like a fucking vacation for that asshole."

Crew stared at the both of them. "Don't do anything stupid. Don't even *think* about doing anything stupid. That motherfucker isn't worth losing your damn jobs and ending up in the cell next to him."

"You're no fun," Rez grumbled.

"He used to have a sense of humor before..." Finn let that drift off.

"Before?" Reynolds prodded.

"Our latest task force member joined the team," Decker answered with a snort.

All eyes turned toward him. "I still have a sense of humor!"

Torres chuckled. "You've had a fucking stick up your ass since you went up to the agency's offices and spoke with Williams."

"And Cabrera joined our team," Reynolds added with wiggle of his eyebrows.

"Anyway... We have an investigation to run..."

A burst of laughter came from Finn. "Someone doesn't want to hear the truth."

Decker grinned. "The truth tends to hurt."

Since they were on the topic of their newest member... "Speaking of Cabrera, I don't like not having cameras set up at that bar. Maybe we should work on getting some in there."

"I'm not sure they'll approve that with the budget we have," Torres said. "Are you worried about her?"

"I worry about my whole team," Crew answered.

"But you worry about her a little more than the rest of us?"

"She's the principal deputy director's daughter." Since Torres was also a DEA agent, he knew what that meant.

"Is that the real reason?" Finn asked.

"What other reason would I have?"

Finn shrugged but had a gleam in his eye. "You tell me."

"I just told you the reason. But if you need to know another one... She has bruises from working there."

Decker spun around in his chair. "What are you talking about?"

"She got them from the fine patrons of that bar grabbing her... Maybe even worse. She wouldn't share the details."

"Wait. When I saw her dropping off the car this morning, I didn't see any," Finn exclaimed. "When and how did you see these bruises?"

"I stopped over at Fletch's yesterday and she was using the pool," he lied.

Rez's dark eyes narrowed on him. "Why would you stop over there? I thought we no longer needed to check on the house."

"We don't. I needed to get an update from her."

He didn't miss it when the guys all shared glances. And raised eyebrows. And grins began to pop up on their faces.

"Isn't that what the daily reports are for?" Reynolds asked, fighting a smile.

For fuck's sake. He might have just stepped in some shit that would be hard to scrape off.

Chapter Twenty-Three

"Maybe it has nothing to do with the fact that Cabrera joined the team and who her father is. Maybe what's up Crew's ass is Cabrera herself," Finn suggested, his grin bigger than the others.

Of fucking course.

"Could be." Decker stroked his chin and pretended like he was seriously considering what Finn said.

"She's a rookie agent and she's undercover in that bar by herself. A bar packed with outlaw bikers, if you need that reminder. Bikers who don't respect women and can be violent. Let's also not forget they think they can take whatever they want whenever they want it." *For fuck's sake*, why did he feel the need to explain himself?

"We're well aware of what motherfuckers they are, J. Crew. I'm sure she is, too. Did she say she was worried for her safety?" Rez asked.

Of fucking course not.

"I'll take your silence as a no. Isn't she the one who volunteered to go undercover there *after* she scoped out the joint?"

Rez waited about half a second before answering his own question. "I'll take your silence as a yes."

"You could always have Fletch and Wilder go in and observe. They haven't gone in there since hooking up with Wolf, right?"

Decker's suggestion might actually be a good one.

"I don't think they've been there recently." Crew didn't remember reading anything about it on their dailies. But then, he only skimmed theirs since Fletch and Wilder had their part of the investigation under control.

If anything major came up that he needed to know, Fletch called him.

"Well, there you go," Decker continued with a shrug, "they could go in and hang out. Even though it's now owned by the Demons, it's still open to anyone wearing colors, including the Dirty Angels."

"Maybe," Crew murmured as he considered this option.

"If you're so damn worried about her, they could be your eyes and ears," Torres agreed. "Even if we got approval to install cameras, it would be a while before that could be arranged."

"But they can't hang out there every night she works," Crew told them. "That would start to look suspicious. The Angels also have their own bar. Not only the Iron Horse Roadhouse but their own private bar in their clubhouse. There's really no reason for Ghost and Kitten to hang at Hawg Wild."

"There's a damn good reason," Decker told him. "Ghost has been trying to patch over to the Demons. Wouldn't he rather hang out with the club he wants to join rather than the club he wants to leave?"

That explanation could work.

"Oooooor... You could go in yourself, too. Just to observe

and settle your worry." Rez added a little smart-ass snort on the end of that.

"Not sure if I could pull it off. Plus, we don't have any club colors for me to wear besides our own. And of course, that shit won't fly."

"You'll go flying when they throw your ass out," Reynolds said.

"If I walk into that bar wearing BAMC colors, I doubt I'll only get tossed. I might not make it out alive."

But, *damn*, they were giving him some decent options. Cabrera told the Demons she had an ol' man named Throttle. A biker not affiliated with any club. Once again, he had to give her credit. That meant he could go there without wearing colors at all and it wouldn't look suspicious.

He could easily go undercover as Throttle and do a surprise visit at Hawg Wild with the excuse of checking on his ol' lady. That would establish his fake persona as possessive and protective of his woman. He could also have a little discussion with the manager and let the man know that he wasn't happy about his woman coming home with bruises.

He was liking this idea more and more by the second.

However, he knew Cabrera would hate it. She wouldn't be thrilled about him checking up on her.

"I mean... you could always pull her from the assignment if it's giving you heartburn," Decker suggested, watching him closely.

"He could," Finn said, "but if we can prove that they're dealing from that location, as well as using it to wash dirty money, the feds could add that business to the seizure list."

"The more businesses they lose and the more of their members who end up behind bars, the sooner the Deadly Demons MC will come to an end," Rez said. "*Adiós, pendejos.*"

"Let's fucking hope there won't be enough of them skating charges," Torres grumbled.

"Or getting short sentences so they can rebuild as soon as they're released," Reynolds added.

Decker put in his two cents next. "I have no doubt they'll rebuild. But when they do, they'll still be on the feds' radar. If they were smart, they'd stick to being asshole bikers and not mules or drug suppliers."

Crew responded with, "But they're far from smart and if they lose their drug connections, those dumbasses might get into running guns or sex-trafficking instead. A criminal organization like theirs will always find an easy way to make a lot of money."

"Easy money doesn't end up being so easy when you get caught," Finn stated.

"Right and if they get into that other shit, the feds might form another task force to crush them all over again," Crew said. "Whether it be the FBI or ATF."

Torres muttered, "It's an endless fucking cycle."

"A cycle that needs to be broken," Crew concluded on a sigh. "All right, I have some calls to make. If you need me, I'll be downstairs."

———

FLETCH'S VOICE filled Crew's ear. "Well, hell, I was just about to call you, Motley Crew. What's up?"

The more he thought about those bruises... What was up was his blood pressure. "Need a favor."

"Can it wait until I tell you my news first?"

"Is it good news?" He needed some about now.

"Good enough that you might bust a nut over it," Fletch warned.

"Hold on. Let me grab a sock to catch it in." With his cell phone to his ear, Crew sank onto one of the couches in the BAMC's church and propped his boots up on the center table. "Okay, I'm ready. Go."

"Brace yourself. When you come, it'll explode like a volcano."

"Just tell me."

Fletch chuckled and after a few seconds of silence, most likely to ramp up anticipation, he announced, "Viper's letting me patch over."

Crew shot up straight, plunking his boots back on the floor. "What?"

"Yeah. Surprised the hell out of me, too. I was at the point where I never thought it would happen."

"You and me both, brother. Holy shit!" This was damn good news. That meant they'd have someone planted inside the outlaw MC. Cameras and wire taps only went so far. "When?"

"He said as soon as possible. But as you know, it's not like they keep a schedule or anything. They do shit when they do shit."

"Did his offer seem suspicious?"

"No. My guess is he's thinking about numbers. Patching me over means one more member in his pocket and one less for the Angels, in case they get a hair up their ass and try to hone in on the DAMC's territory. Plus, I've been doing business with them long enough now that they trust me. Well, at least as much as they'd trust anyone."

"Well, Christ, they should since it's been over a fucking year."

"Yeah, no shit. I really didn't want to be in this assignment this long. The only reason I've lasted is because of

Nova. You better get down on your hands and knees and kiss her feet in gratitude."

"What we'll do for pussy, right?"

"Yo," Fletch growled.

"You know what I mean."

"So, now what?" Fletch sighed. "Patching over changes everything. That means Nova and I have to move out of the apartment over the DAMC's pawn shop. It also means we won't be working for them in their businesses anymore."

"Well, I'm guessing the Demons will have you dealing meth to make money but only for them instead of yourself."

"Yeah. They think I have connections on the street, even though in reality the drugs I buy from them get documented and destroyed."

Shit. Cabrera was living in Fletch's house. With Wilder and him patching over to the Demons, it could cause an unexpected ripple effect. "You don't want to move back into your house, right?"

"Fuck no. I don't want those fucknuts knowing where I live. I think we need to find a rental somewhere. Can you arrange that?"

"Where?"

"Since I'll be part of the Uniontown chapter, anywhere near there? Close enough to be heavily involved in that chapter but far enough that we'll have some privacy when we need it."

That made sense. "Okay, I'll get on that today and get it approved from the higher-ups. Shouldn't be an issue, though, since we ended up paying rent for your current apartment. I'm thinking they'll be thrilled you finally got your boot in the door with our targets."

"No doubt. Hey..."

"What?"

"I'm thinking Viper also approved me patching over because there's been increased talk of cutting out the Russos."

They knew it was headed in that direction. "Yeah, we're hearing whispers of that on our end, too. Those stupid fucks will be making a fatal mistake if they try to cut the Russos out of the equation."

"Agreed. The Russos aren't just going to give them a handshake and wish them good luck on their new venture."

"While them fucking with La Cosa Nostra might solve our problem with the Demons, we'll still need to monitor that situation closely."

"That's for damn sure," Fletch agreed. "Even if the Russos wipe that MC out, you know they'll just find new mules."

That they would.

Fletch continued, "They're not giving up all that meth money just because of some attempted coup by asshole bikers."

"No shit. That wouldn't be good business. Anyway, you definitely gave me a boner with this news. Though, you haven't finished me off yet. My sock is still empty. Start whispering sweet nothings into my ear."

"Sweet nothings," Fletch whispered, then laughed. "That do it?"

Crew shook his head. "You suck at phone sex."

"At least I don't suck in general, like you."

"Anyway... While I'm stoked that you're going to be my eyes and ears with the Demons, I'm not thrilled with the possibility of you and Wilder getting caught in the crossfire. If the MC tries to cut out the Russos, there *will* be crossfire."

"Hear you on that," Fletch murmured.

"Keep your eyes up and your heads down. You and

Wilder are fully capable of handling whatever shit's shoveled your way."

"We'll keep our fingers on the pulse as much as possible. One good thing about patching over is Nova will be able to rub shoulders with the other ol' ladies and maybe pick up on some gossip there."

"True. Women do like to run their fucking mouths," Crew said dryly.

"That's also one reason the members don't usually share club business with them."

"That's what they say. In reality, who fucking knows."

"True. I've seen firsthand the difference in how the DAMC women are treated and respected versus how the women of the Demons are. Night and fucking day."

"Yeah, Decker witnessed some of that shit while he was under with the Demons."

"I heard. He gave me the details of what went on down at the Viper's Den to prepare us in case we were invited down there for a party. I guess once I get my new set of patches, we'll have an open invitation for the party house in West Virginia."

"That's good. You'll have free rein to walk among them without them paying much attention."

"I'll just have to remind Nova not to go head-to-head with any of the established ol' ladies."

"Good luck with that." Wilder was another headstrong woman like Cabrera. But then, both women were federal agents and they couldn't be shy or wilting flowers. Most recruits without a steel spine were washed out during the academy. Both males and females.

Fletch chuckled. "All right. I'll let you know when they plan on handing me my patches. But definitely try to find us a place in the meantime. I doubt the Angels will tolerate us living in their apartment if we're wearing another club's colors."

"You're going to let the DAMC prez know you're bailing?"

"I can, if you want. Or we can have Jamison let his brother know."

"No," Crew said. "If you do it, I think Zak will consider it as a sign of respect, rather than him finding out second-hand."

"True. Respect is important to this club. It'll also be smart to stay on their good side."

"Agreed. They didn't have to help us out, but they did anyway. We need to make sure they know we appreciate it," Crew told him.

"All right. So, what's the favor you need? Besides the big one of being cut off from my brothers and my own home for over a year. Oh, yeah, and on that note, the favor of allowing the newest task force member to stay in my place for dirt cheap. Five hundred bucks," Fletch griped. "You can't even rent an empty refrigerator box for five hundred anymore."

"She appreciates it."

"Yeah, and how about her huge four-legged companion you kept a fucking secret, asshole?"

Shit. "Who ran their fucking mouth?"

"Not you, that's for damn sure. You tried to sneak that one past me."

"The dog's well behaved." The owner, not so much.

"I heard he's fucking huge."

"Just like my cock."

"Man, that's one thing I miss... Fucking with you all. When I finally get free of this assignment, I'm going to be rusty on my comebacks. Okay, still waiting to hear about the favor."

"Do you have time to go hang out at Hawg Wild tonight or in the next couple nights?"

"Why?"

"Cabrera is working undercover there."

Silence hit his ears for the longest time. In fact, long enough that Crew pulled his phone from his ear to make sure the call hadn't been dropped.

Finally he heard, "With no backup?"

"I hear your concern in your tone. I have the same." Actually, a hell of a lot more. "But she insisted and she's not afraid to be there."

"Crew..."

"Yeah, brother, I know."

"That's almost as bad as sending her on her own down to the Viper's Den to party with those assholes."

"Yeah, Fletch, I fucking *know*. That's why I'm asking you to head over there to check on her."

"I can't sit there for her whole damn shift, Crew-tons. Maybe once I'm patched over I won't stand out so much. But the Angels just don't hang at that bar. I got the side-eye every time I went in there wearing a DAMC cut."

"I know that, too."

Fletch sighed loudly. "I'll see if I can swing it."

"Let me know if you can't."

"Will do. What time does she start?"

"Whenever she gets there since she's not on any kind of official clock. She's only working for tips and meth."

"Damn. Okay, I'll work on getting down there. If not tonight, then maybe in the next few nights. You work on finding us a place. And when you do, find a place that isn't considered shitty chic. It doesn't have to be fancy, but at least make sure it's decent. I draw the line when it comes to bedbugs and roaches."

"Mice and rats are okay, though, right?" Crew asked.

"Only if they're big enough to eat."

"I heard that once you grill them, they taste like chicken."

Fletch made a retching sound. "You try it first and let me know."

"Hell, Rez's mom is such a damn good cook, she could make a dish that we wouldn't be able to tell it's rodent."

"Stop, man. Now I'm going to be suspect of anything she serves me." Crew's laughter didn't last long once Fletch asked, "How's Nox?"

"I want to say he's a little better, but honestly, I'm not sure if that's not just my wishful thinking."

"Fuck."

"Yeah. I figure as long as he keeps going to the therapist and that support group, he'll get back on track. Speaking of, I got the kids this weekend and we're going to do a little club run with them. Dylan will be Nox's backpack."

"Yeah? He volunteered?"

"I asked, he accepted. I think it'll be good for him. You know how much he enjoys being around all our rug-rats."

"Yeah. I know this might sound a little whacked, but I think if Jackie would've had the baby before she," Fletch blew out a breath, "died, then I think Nox would've made an effort not to sink into a deep depression. He would've worked hard to be there one hundred percent for his child. I mean, I'm not a therapist and maybe the result would have been the same, but that's my gut instinct."

"You could be right. But that's not how it happened, so we have to deal with what did."

"Man," Fletch started, "I fucking feel for the guy. And I'm probably stupid for telling your ass this, but... If something happened to Nova, I'd lose my fucking mind. So, I get what happened isn't easy for him to shake off."

"He'll never completely shake it off."

"Of course not. They were soulmates. They had that elusive once in a lifetime type of love. Not everyone is lucky enough to find that."

That was for damn sure. "All right. Now you're getting too goddamn mushy for me."

"With Sasha, you got saddled with a rotten one. Just wait. When the right woman comes along—"

Crew cut him off. "Gotta go. Let me know about Hawg Wild." He ended the call before Fletch could get in another word.

Chapter Twenty-Four

He decided he couldn't wait for Fletch and Wilder to go to Hawg Wild. Not if he wanted his heartburn to subside.

He had sent Cabrera a few texts but they had all gone ignored.

That made him even more itchy over the whole situation. And the only way he would be able to scratch that damn itch was if he went to the outlaw biker bar himself.

He found a pair of his oldest, threadbare jeans that luckily still fit and pulled on a Harley T-shirt given to him by the dealership where he purchased Silver Foxy. Since it was still a bit chilly at night, he donned a black leather jacket. A light one that would at least cut the wind while motoring down the road but not give him swamp ass.

He left his DEA badge and ID at home but strapped on his ankle holster.

To stay anonymous, he temporarily replaced Foxy's license plate with one assigned to the task force. He also grabbed a fake ID from the selection he kept at The Plant.

Before heading out, he tied a black bandana around the

bottom portion of his face and strapped on his half-helmet. Since it was only on the cusp of being dark, he slipped on his mirrored sunglasses.

What might help him fit in more would be one of those enormous leather wallets with a chain attached to a belt loop that bikers tended to use. And maybe a pack of cigarettes or a container of chew shoved into the back pocket of his jeans.

But he had neither.

He only hoped like fuck the moment he stepped through the door at the Hawg Wild Saloon, he didn't set off any alarm bells with either the Demons or their other fine cohorts. Because if he did, Cabrera would most likely have to break cover to help his ass out.

Or at least, he hoped she would.

When he finally pulled into the lot, he was greeted with lines and lines of bikes. For a weeknight, he was surprised to find the place packed.

Clearly the bar was doing damn good business. No surprise why the Demons wanted to buy it. Even without the drug sales, it had to be turning a healthy profit.

Unless they ended up running it into the ground like they did The Peach Pit. They did have the skill to take a diamond and crush it until it turned back into coal.

Truthfully, Crew didn't give a fuck about their business sense, he was only there for one reason and one reason only...

The dark-haired woman with the dark eyes hustling behind the bar. He got brief glimpses of her smiling and talking with customers as she dropped off draft beers or opened bottles. She actually looked like she belonged back there. A real fucking natural.

The bar's interior was deafening between the rock music and the talking and shouting in the attempt at being over-heard above it. The crowd was made up of mostly men, but he spotted a few women here and there. Some wearing "property of" cuts and others hanging all over the nearest biker. Most likely vying for one of those prized ol' lady cuts.

Crew didn't get it, but then he didn't live that kind of life. And that was what those types of MCs were, a whole damn lifestyle. He loved his brothers and he'd do anything for them since he considered them family. He'd also been part of the Blue Avengers long before the club split into separate charters. But his life did not revolve around his MC. He had a good career, as well as children he loved and wanted a better relationship with.

He couldn't think about his kids right now. Instead, he kept his head on a swivel as he weaved his way around bikers and tables, as well as stray knocked-over chairs here and there to get to the bar, which was standing room only since every stool had an ass planted on them. And every damn customer sitting there wore a cut from a one-percenter club. Some club names he recognized, some he didn't. He made a mental note to do some research on the ones unfamiliar to him.

He'd also tell Cabrera to keep a tally of which clubs hung out at Hawg Wild on a regular basis. It wouldn't hurt to keep those kinds of stats.

If the Demons tried to undercut the Russos and they retaliated, he wouldn't put it past La Cosa Nostra to find another outlaw MC to be their mules. They would need to use another criminal organization that was not the Mafia.

That was if Crew didn't pull her.

Tonight he'd watch her in action and decide. Only he wasn't going to let her know that. At least not yet. He didn't want her to change her behavior in any way as she interacted with the bikers, if he could avoid it.

She continued to pour beers, and mix drinks mostly made

up of whiskey or vodka. But the majority of what she served was bottled beer.

She kept an opener tucked in her cleavage, obviously enhanced somewhat from what he could only guess was a push-up bra. When needed, she'd grab the opener, pop the cap and then shove it back in its place for easy access.

His lip curled up in a sneer. How many guys tried to take it from her just so they could touch her tits?

Hopefully, if they did, they now had broken fingers. If she hadn't broken any, and he witnessed someone manhandling her, he'd be happy to assist.

Since he couldn't belly up directly to the bar, he stood behind a couple of guys wearing Pagans cuts. Crew couldn't hear a damn thing they were saying since they were talking low and the noise level around them was high.

He took the time to scan the bar patrons within his view to see if he could catch anything interesting. He saw nothing but drinking, smoking, joking, playing pool or darts. Typical biker bar activity.

"Brother, you need a beer or somethin'?" he heard to his right. When he looked toward the person asking, Crew was surprised to find the biker was talking to him.

Look at that, making friends wherever he went.

"Yeah, I do," Crew answered.

The man stood and jerked his chin toward the now empty stool. "All yours. Gotta get home to my ol' lady. I'm late one more fuckin' time, ain't gonna get none for a month."

"That would suck."

"No shit," the biker said on a chuckle.

"Appreciate you givin' me your spot." Who knew outlaw bikers could be courteous?

"Ain't a problem. And the view's fuckin' top notch. That new bartender gives me somethin' to think about when I'm railin' my ol' lady. You might consider doin' the same."

Crew forced a smile even though that was the complete opposite of how he wanted to respond. "Thanks for the tip, but she's actually my ol' lady. No imagination needed."

"Well, damn. Hope you don't mind me thinkin' about her when I'm bustin' a nut in my woman."

He kind of did. He wondered how one of these bikers would react if they were told the same thing. As entertaining as that might be, he wasn't there to get into a scrap. He had a much tighter handle on his temper than probably the majority of the bikers in that bar.

Or he did. That might get tested tonight.

"Long as you're only thinkin' 'bout it and ain't actually doin' it, don't give a fuck. Have at it." Crew shot him a cocky smirk. "I'm the only lucky bastard to get to fuck her for real."

The biker whacked him on the back. "Least I get to borrow her up here." He tapped his temple. "She's young and perky. Bet she can go all night." He took a step back and took a good look at Crew. "You, not so much, my man. Like 'em young, huh?" He added a grin so big that Crew could actually see the man's teeth, even with his mouth buried in long, unruly facial hair.

That had to be gross while eating. Food or pussy.

"You know how it is. Long as they're legal... And if they ain't, just lie." Did that actually just come out of his fucking mouth?

"Can you keep up with her?"

Jesus Christ. "Fuck yeah," Crew answered. "I let her do all the work."

"That's how you do it. Let 'em spin on your dick while you sit back and enjoy."

"You know it."

"Think I'm gonna see if I can talk my ol' lady into that tonight." With that he turned and headed out, giving Crew a better look at this patches. Tainted Souls MC.

He made a mental note to do a little research on that club, too.

"Rootin' for you, brother," Crew called out, not sure if he was even heard above the din.

He quickly claimed the stool before someone else pushed their way into that spot. Once he got his ass settled, he tried to keep one eye on Cabrera and one on the bikers near him. He also kept his ears open as best as possible in case of any interesting chatter.

But despite trying to keep aware of the activities around him, his attention kept getting pulled back to Cabrera.

She still had no idea he was there. Or watching her.

Her makeup was heavy tonight and she wore a tight red tank top blinged-out with rhinestones and had the neckline cut out in a deep V to showcase that bottle opener-holding cleavage. She also wore a very short denim mini-skirt and some kind of wedge-heel sandals that emphasized her toned, tawny legs.

Her almost-black hair was pulled back in a neat French braid, giving him a good view of her profile as she worked.

When she finally got a lull in the action, she paused to drink from a bottle of water she pulled from under the bar and wiped the back of her hand across her forehead. As she tipped the bottle to her lips again, her eyes scanned the customers and slid right past him.

On the return trip, she finally spotted him, causing her head to jerk and her eyes widen before she schooled her reaction.

He was probably the last person she expected to see in Hawg Wild tonight.

Or any night.

But then, he never thought he'd be sitting in the middle of enemy territory, either, getting ready to have a beer instead of hauling subjects off in handcuffs.

She tucked her water bottle back under the bar, skirted a Demon in the middle of pouring a draft beer into a pint glass and came to a stop directly in front of him.

"Hi, honey," he greeted her.

Her mouth gaped open. Well look at that, he finally left her speechless.

She leaned over the bar so no one else would hear her and hissed, "What the hell are you doing here?"

"You didn't answer any of my texts..." He frowned when he forgot what name was she using.

"Rose," she whispered, then increased the volume to say, "As you see, I've been busy..."

He leaned in until he was only an inch from her ear. "Well, Rose, nice to meet you, I'm your ol' man, Throttle."

She straightened and bugged her eyes out at him. For some reason, she didn't look amused at all.

"I don't need you checking up on me." Her expression was full of a whole bunch of unhappy.

Too bad.

Before he could answer her, a deep, thundering voice came out of nowhere. "Problem here?"

Fuck, where did that big dude come from? He needed to pay the fuck attention.

The massive guy came to a stop behind Cabrera and placed his big paws on her shoulders.

She kept her eyes locked on Crew when she answered, "Not at all, Bulldog. Just my ol' man coming in for a cold beer."

Crew scanned his front patches. *Bulldog. Sgt at Arms. Deadly Demons. Uniontown.*

His cut also had the diamond 1% patch. Along with a few others.

"And to check on my woman," he added.

"You gotta be Throttle, then."

"In the flesh." Crew's eyes dropped to his hands still gripping Cabrera's shoulders, waiting for the man to remove them.

He didn't.

"Your ol' lady kicks ass," Bulldog announced.

"Nothin' I don't know."

"She also said you got a sled."

At least she was making it known that she had an ol' man. "I do."

"Lookin' to join a club?"

"Not really. Don't plan on bein' someone else's bitch for a year. Why you ask?"

"Our prez is lookin' to expand our territory and grow our brotherhood. Wants us to be a force to be reckoned with."

No shit. "Against who?"

That got the man pursing his lips for a few seconds—and maybe even regretting letting that little bit of info fly—before answering, "Nobody specific."

Right.

That made him believe that, not only did they want to cut out the Russos, but they planned on expanding their territory into another MC's.

Like the Dirty Angels. Maybe dare to march even more north into the Dark Knights'.

If they were going to make that move—one that would be a mistake—it made sense to patch "Ghost" over from the Angels and continue to actively recruit more members.

None of it was a surprise and what they had expected to happen.

Bulldog gave Cabrera's shoulders a squeeze. "Table over in the far corner needs fresh beers. Go get 'em some."

Cabrera's eyes briefly met his and he gave the slightest chin lift. Luckily, she caught it. She pulled away from Bulldog and nodded. "I see that. I'll get right on it, boss."

Boss.

And here he thought she reserved that title strictly for him.

Once she was gone, the Demons' sergeant at arms turned back to him. "That one's a damn hard worker. Even better that we don't gotta pay her. You must got her trained well to get her bustin' her ass for your habit." His head tilted as he ran his gaze over what he could see of Crew sitting on the opposite side of the bar. "Though, don't look like you're drinkin' too many of those specialty drinks she's takin' home with her."

Ah shit. "Ain't for me."

"She said it was."

For fuck's sake, she never told him she used that cover story. Or if she did, he had missed or forgotten it. Unfortunately, he just stepped in some shit. It wasn't her fault, it was his for coming into Hawg Wild with no warning.

Even so, he needed to be careful with his story since he didn't want to blow her cover.

Or his.

He needed to come up with a valid story and fast. "It's actually for my brother. He lives with us and he's a miserable bastard when his sweet tooth is achin'. Those specialty drinks you all make here helps keep him on an even keel."

Not bad for a story made on the fly.

Bulldog's brow dropped low. "Why she say it was for you, then?"

Crew shrugged. "Why do women do anything? My guess is, it was easier that way since it ain't nobody's business who it's for. Ain't that right? Long as you're gettin' the scratch and we're gettin' the goods, does it really fuckin' matter who's appreciatin' the product? Or in this case, she's bustin' her ass in your bar in exchange for the goods."

"You're right. Ain't nobody's business... 'Less you're a pig."

"I look like a pig?"

Bulldog's eyes narrowed on him as he scratched at his beard. "Yeah, you kinda do."

"Then you need to get your fuckin' eyes checked. And why the fuck would you ask me to join your merry band of brothers if I smelled like pork?"

"Maybe I was testin' you."

Sure, buddy.

Crew needed to steer the conversation back to the meth and Cabrera. "Much better to send her out to work for it than use my own hard-earned cash. Am I right?"

"Ain't gonna complain that she's willin' to work for somethin' other than cash."

"About that work... When you had your hands on my ol' lady's shoulders, you looked like you were protectin' her. That right?" He had to handle this carefully. He didn't want to piss the big man off, but he needed to set some ground rules.

"Keep an eye on her 'cause she's a little thing. My customers ain't so little and can be a bit pushy when they see somethin' they want."

At least the man was aware of Cabrera's appeal. "And they want my ol' lady?"

"Who wouldn't? She ain't got no big ol' titties like they normally go for and she's a little darker than most 'round here prefer, but with everythin' else about her, it's damn easy to look past those two negatives."

Well, *hell*, that was a damn relief. The woman only had two negatives according to the critic standing before him.

Cabrera would probably be happy to hear that.

Now, if she asked Crew what her negatives were, his list would be a hell of a lot different than these outlaw bikers since they were all about "big ol' titties" and pale as fuck skin.

"So, Bulldog, the reason I'm bringin' this up is, I got a problem and maybe you can help with that."

"I'm listenin'."

"Saw some bruises on her this morning when she was ridin' my cock and to be honest with you, it twisted me up a bit. Means some of your customers are takin' advantage of her. That has me thinkin' you need to protect her better. And since that patch on your chest claims you're the Demons' enforcer, you should know how to do that, right?"

Bulldog's bearded cover jaw became as tight as an over-stretched piano wire. "Got shit under control here."

The man did not like being questioned about how he managed the bar.

To be expected. However, Crew wasn't finished yet.

"Those marks I saw on her ain't from me, if you get what I'm sayin'. That tells me you ain't protectin' her. So, that's why my ass is on this stool tonight. Either you're gonna have to do your job, or I will."

Chapter Twenty-Five

A MUSCLE JUMPED in Bulldog's cheek. He must not have liked Crew's threat.

Good.

However, he wasn't done yet. "If she keeps gettin' manhandled by your customers and marks that didn't come from my own hand, somethin's gonna have to be done."

"Like what?" Bulldog asked tightly.

"Well, first of all, I'm gonna have a little discussion with the asshole touchin' her. Warnin', it ain't gonna be with words. Then I'm gonna tell her she's done workin' here. That'll be your loss, not mine, as I can find other sources to buy those drinks my brother enjoys so much. You get what I'm sayin'?"

"You makin' threats?"

"Not to you. Only to the motherfuckers touchin' my ol' lady without my permission. Bet you wouldn't allow that with yours."

Bulldog pursed his lips as he considered Crew.

"You got an ol' lady, Bulldog?" Before he let the man

answer, Crew continued, "You okay with other men touchin' her? My woman had a bruise on her damn tit 'cause somebody pinched her there. Lucky I wasn't here when it happened. Otherwise, somebody woulda been leavin' this place in a fuckin' body bag and you would've had a big damn mess to clean up. And that ain't good for business, is it?"

"You can't come in here makin' your own rules," Bulldog growled.

"Ain't makin' rules for your place. Makin' rules for my Rosie. I'm just here to make sure those rules ain't gettin' broken. You feel me?"

"Yeah." The Demon leaned in really close. Close enough that Crew could smell his gag-worthy breath. "But lemme make somethin' clear. This is *my* fuckin' bar. You got a problem with somebody in it, you bring it to me. I'll fuckin' handle it."

Now they were getting somewhere. "I respect that. So, here's the deal... Make sure when she's ridin' my cock tomorrow mornin', I don't see any new bruises on her. I do, it ain't gonna be me and the asshole who touched her that'll have a problem. It'll be me and you." Crew said that with a hell of a lot more confidence than what he felt. The reality was he would not win against Bulldog but that didn't mean he couldn't bluff.

The bar manager straightened. It took a few pounding heartbeats before he said, "Gotta respect a man lookin' after his ol' lady."

"Glad you see it that way. That means we're on the same page, right?"

"Yeah, we're on the same fuckin' page."

Crew grinned. "Good. Now, I need a fuckin' beer."

Bulldog turned and, with a twist of his wrist, caught Hook's attention before tipping his head toward Crew. "Get this brother a beer." He turned back to Crew. "It's on the house."

"Appreciate that. Good talk."

Bulldog grunted and lumbered away.

Crew unpuckered his asshole and let his muscles loosen a fraction.

That motherfucker was at least twice his size. He wouldn't want to be on the man's bad side. And Crew had been close to stepping over that line.

But he also needed to look after Cabrera.

If that caused him to get thumped, then he'd have to take those knocks like a fucking man. He would simply regret it later. As in, a day, a week or maybe even a month later, depending on how long it took to recover. That was if he didn't end up dead, but then, if that happened, he'd have no regrets because he would no longer be breathing.

A few minutes later, Hook dropped off a pint glass of draft beer. Before the Demon turned back, the bartender spotted something down the bar. Crew glanced in that direction to see what he noticed.

A biker had elbowed his way up to the bar. The two shared chin lifts before Hook turned and disappeared into the back storage area.

Crew sipped his beer slowly, his eyes locked on the swinging door, and it remained there until Hook came out fisting a disposable cup with a plastic lid similar to the one Cabrera gave him after working there that first night.

Drug dealing right out in the goddamn open. It took some balls and Crew wondered how many other people in the bar knew what was in that cup. He wouldn't be surprised if there was a lot of them. If not most.

Damn Demons sure made it convenient for addicts to get their fix.

Looking for a drug drive-through? Shoot a text to one of the prospects at The Peach Pit and then pop on by. You don't even need to get out of your car.

Need it delivered? Order it from Pizza Town along with your dinner. Don't forget to tip!

Now this.

The newcomer didn't stick around long. Once he scored, he disappeared back into the crowd. Just like fucking take-out. Order at the counter and take it home to enjoy.

The Demons definitely had a system that worked with whatever business they were dealing from.

Cabrera came up behind him, placed a hand on his back and leaned into him. "Did you see that?"

"Sure did."

"Goes on all night. They're moving a lot of product." She pressed a kiss to his cheek like he truly was her ol' man before moving away and going back behind the bar to drop off empties and serve fresh beers.

———

It had been a damn surprise to see Crew's ass sitting at the bar. He was probably there looking for any excuse to pull her.

For the rest of the night, she was extra careful to skirt any grabby hands and if someone tried to tug her into their lap, their fingers got twisted in ways they weren't supposed to bend.

Hawg Wild's customers were quickly learning she wasn't taking their shit. If they pinched her nipple, she pinched theirs back even harder. If they smacked her on the ass, she smacked them right in the face. If they said nasty shit to her, her comebacks were even worse.

They were beginning to respect her. It might be slow, but it was something.

Crew ended up sitting in the bar for hours and nursing each beer dropped off in front of him for so long they ended up flat and warm.

Once the crowd thinned a little and the volume turned down a few notches, he actually left his stool a few times to either go to the restroom or play a couple games of pool.

From what she saw, he could hold his own with a cue stick.

He was even challenged to a dart game. A challenge he accepted and won.

Despite his neatly trimmed salt-and-pepper hair and beard—if anything, screamed law enforcement to her—he managed somehow to fit in. He had actually morphed into an ol' man named Throttle with his attitude, the way he dressed and how he spoke.

The man was damn good. A pain in her ass, but impressive.

She had to give credit where credit was due. She only hoped he did the same for her.

"Isn't it way past your bedtime, old man?" she asked him as she dropped off a fresh beer a little after midnight.

"That's *ol'* man to you."

She stretched over the bar like she was about to kiss him and whispered, "I didn't make you my ol' man, you did. I also didn't ask you to come in and babysit me tonight. What spurred this on, besides you not trusting me to do my job?"

Before she could pull away, he grabbed her and held her there. "Hey, you forgot to mention that you told the Demons you were getting the meth for me."

How convenient that he was changing the subject and ignoring her question. "I did. You must not have been paying attention. Or you forgot. It was a cover story I came up with on the fly."

"Yeah, well, I guess I look too damn good to be a meth addict." One side of his mouth hiked up.

Holy shit, the man could be cocky.

"Sure you do." She laid the sarcasm on thick.

"Weren't you impressed with my body only recently?"

"Was I? Like you, I must have short-term memory loss."

"You must. Anyway, your *boss* didn't believe your story when he saw me in the flesh. I had to come up with another reason."

"Maybe because he wasn't *supposed* to see Throttle in the flesh. What's the new story and why didn't you tell me it earlier?"

"Because there were too many ears around," he answered. "This place is busier than I imagined. Come around the bar and give your ol' man a squeeze."

When she pulled her head back to look at him, he cocked an eyebrow in an unspoken message.

She sighed but came out from behind the bar. He turned on the stool once she got to him so he could pull her between his thighs and wrap his arms around her to hold her close.

"So, what's the story?" she prodded. Despite him being an annoying jerk, him hugging her was kind of... nice.

She must be tired.

He nuzzled the hair near her ear, sending a shiver down her spine and making her nipples pop like two turkey timers. "The addict is my brother. He lives with us and to keep him on an even level we supply him with what he needs."

"Lame."

"The fucker believed it, so who cares how lame it is. Like you, I had to come up with a story on the fly."

"Speaking of fly, I feel something pressing against yours. And your hands are groping my ass."

"Yep."

Yep? "Everyone else in this bar who tries that is getting a lesson they won't soon forget."

"And you got one this morning. Remember that?"

"Should I remind you that afterward you got so damn spooked you ran out of there like a ghost was chasing your ass?"

"I had things to do."

He certainly was good at telling stories. "*Uh huh.* Anyway, I don't need a babysitter. You can go home and get your beauty rest."

"I'll leave when I'm ready."

"Then, I'll leave instead."

"Not without your pay first."

"Maybe I can get Bulldog to give me it early so you can take it with you," she emphasized, "when you leave."

"Why do you care if I stay?"

"Because you're only here to look for a reason to pull me."

"That's not why."

Bullshit. "Then why?"

When he pulled in a breath through his nose and released it out of his mouth, it tickled the strands of hairs that had escaped from her braid. "Those bruises concerned me, if you want to know the truth."

"I always want to know the truth. And I said I could handle it and I have. I just didn't want to take a stand the first couple of nights, so my ass wouldn't be kicked out before my foot was securely wedged in the door. Whether you believe it or not, I actually had a plan and it worked. Bulldog now sees my value, so if I hurt a few of his customers along the way for being handsy, he'll be more tolerant with my actions than pissed."

"I also had a discussion with him."

She frowned and pulled her head back to get a good read of his face. He might be annoying, but he was also too damn handsome for his own good. "What did you say?"

"Simple. I put my fucking foot down as any ol' man would do when his ol' lady is being touched—or even hurt— by another man."

"And how did Sasquatch take it?" Cami asked him.

"Surprisingly, better than expected."

"He must have since you're still planted on that stool and not being planted six feet under."

"Believe it or not, I have excellent interpersonal and negotiation skills. I can be very persuasive."

She snorted. "I'm glad I'm not drinking anything right now because you'd be wearing it."

His eyebrows rose. "Do you doubt my skills?"

"In bed, no." She'd at least give him that. "Your *interpersonal* skills, yes."

He grinned and his fingers flexed on her ass. Which was still slightly sore from this morning. "Oh, so you're saying I'm the best you've ever had in bed."

"That's not what I'm saying."

"That's what I heard."

"Then turn up your hearing aids, *old* man."

She fought her grin when his chuckle came deep from within his chest.

"You liked me spanking your ass and you *really* liked me fucking you afterward." His eyes flared. Most likely from the memory.

Her own memory of this morning made her clit quiver and her panties a little damp.

Damn him.

"It was all right," she lied. "Until you ran out of there with fear in your eyes. Like suddenly my pussy would magically make a ring appear on your finger."

"Again, you were seeing things."

"You're right, I saw the whites of your eyes with my own. You should know better than anyone, since you're a *senior* special agent, that to be good at our jobs we need to be observant."

"True. And because of that, I noticed when I mentioned spanking your ass, a flush filled your cheeks from the memory."

She automatically pressed her hands to her face and tried to pull away. He tightened his grip, keeping her there.

"Go home, *Throttle*," she hissed as she planted her palms on his chest and tried to push free. Her mission failed.

This man wouldn't let her go until he was good and ready.

"I'll leave when I decide to leave. How long are you staying?"

"Why?"

He shrugged. "I want to prove you don't scare me."

She would ask how he'd prove it, but since his erection pressed against her, she already knew the answer.

How the hell were they both getting hot and bothered in the middle of Hawg Wild?

"I was planning on staying until closing. I'm *working*, remember?" Not just for Bulldog but for the task force, the job that really mattered and also paid her in real money and not meth. "And anyway, I don't think my boss would approve of me having sex while on the clock."

"I thought you could leave at any time?"

"I wasn't talking about *that* boss."

"Then, as your *real* boss, you should obey me."

Again, so damn cocky. "Oh, aren't you funny? But the answer is no. I don't have to—"

He took her mouth while she was still speaking, taking advantage or her being mid-sentence to plunder it with his tongue. He kissed her long and hard in the middle of a damn outlaw biker bar, a place full of bikers who would turn on them if they knew their true identities.

But here they were, eating each other's faces like they were truly a couple.

Actually, no. Most couples she knew no longer kissed as intensely as the one Crew and her were sharing.

But, *fuck*, her panties would be soon soaked, and she really didn't want to work the next couple of hours like that.

She twisted her head to unlock their lips and she sucked in some oxygen to cool the heat pooling in her center.

When she turned back to him, she whispered, "Unfair."

"I never said I played fair," he whispered back.

"I need to get back to work."

"Since I've now successfully claimed my property in front of everyone in this bar, maybe now they'll treat you with more respect."

He might as well have thrown a bucket of ice water on her. "They already were since I told you I could handle it."

"A thank you would sound nice about now."

"If it was warranted, but it isn't." She jerked against him. "Let me go so I can finish this shift and go home to bed."

As soon as he loosened his grip, she broke free.

"Do you want me to let Murphy out?" she heard behind her as she escaped.

He was willing to go let out her dog? What the hell was up with that? "Up to you," she threw over her shoulder.

"Do you want me to wait for you to get home?"

Her feet stuttered to a stop, and she stared straight ahead, letting his question sink in.

This man confused the fuck out of her. She got whiplash dealing with him.

If she said yes, was he going to bolt again right after they had sex?

She turned. "Are you brave enough?"

She just threw down the gauntlet. Would he pick it up?

He stood, pulled out his wallet and threw some cash on top of the bar. He didn't look at her until he tucked his wallet away and approached her.

When he got there, he lifted her chin with his fingers, his gray eyes narrowed on hers. "Don't be late."

Her heart skipped a beat when he spun on his boot heel and made his way to the exit. Her feet seemed to be stuck to the floor as she watched him walk away and disappear through the door.

She stood there chewing on her bottom lip, wondering if having sex with him again would be a mistake.

For both of them.

She shook herself mentally. He was probably only fucking with her. Trying to throw her off balance.

When she ducked behind the bar, she came face to face with Bulldog. "Ain't he a little old for you?"

"I like them older, Bulldog. You know why?"

The big man grunted.

"Because when I'm not in the mood to fuck him, I can hide his little blue pills."

When she grabbed a rag to use to wipe down some tables and headed out onto the floor, a roar of laughter followed her.

At least someone was amused with the situation.

Because she sure wasn't.

Chapter Twenty-Six

AFTER PARKING her Audi in the garage, she glanced at the time. 3:15.

Exactly why her ass was dragging.

She stepped through the garage door and into the house, immediately deactivating the alarm.

She was actually surprised to see Crew's Harley parked in the driveway when she pulled in. The sight of it and knowing he was waiting for her got her heart racing. *If* she had to admit it.

But besides Murphy coming to greet her with a wagging tail and a few soft whines when she stepped through the interior garage door, she heard nothing else.

"C'mon, Murph. Let's take you out."

The Wolfhound's lumbering gait as he followed her out to the backyard kind of reminded her of Bulldog's. Though, she was pretty damn sure that Bulldog was a thousand times meaner than her Murphy.

She stood on the back deck, yawning three times in a row. After Murphy went and did his business in the dark yard, he came back and leaned against her for a few head scratches. She willingly obliged before going back inside.

She wasn't sure she could muster up the energy to have sex, so Crew might have been waiting for nothing.

It would serve him right.

On the way through the kitchen to her bedroom, she kicked off her wedge sandals, yanked the tank over her head and unzipped her denim skirt with a worn-out sigh.

She found the bedroom door closed, most likely so Murphy didn't crawl into bed to cuddle with him. Cracking the door open, she peeked in to see the room dark but not quiet.

Steady snoring greeted her.

She headed into the bathroom to rinse off the bar's stink, brush her teeth and toss her smelly clothes into the hamper. She decided she'd have to leave her hair unwashed because she didn't want to use a dryer, waking the man asleep in her bed.

She returned to the bedroom, naked and clean, and in the dark, she could barely make out Crew sprawled out and hogging the whole damn bed.

Of course.

He "claimed" her earlier with a kiss at the bar. Now he was claiming her bed, too.

With a shake of her head, she carefully made her way in the dark to the side of the bed, lifted the bedding and crawled in beside him.

The bed was like a damn oven. His body was not only hot to look at, it could put out some heat.

Within seconds of her head hitting the pillow, she was out.

CREW JERKED AWAKE, unsure of where he was.

Blinking a few times, it took him a good minute to clear the cobwebs from his brain and realize the woman he was spooning wasn't some chick he'd brought home after a late night at some hookup bar.

Not that he'd ever done that before.

Too often, anyway.

But it wasn't some random woman tucked in his arms, it was Cami. Completely fucking naked.

Did he actually just "sleep" with a woman without having sex? He hadn't done that since he was married.

His intention when he climbed into her bed was to rest his eyes only for a few moments while he waited for her. That ended up being a complete failure. It also proved he was well past his "go all night" partying days back in his twenties.

She even managed to sneak in without waking him. He must have been sleeping like the dead.

He wasn't the only one.

Her steady breathing and her relaxed state proved she was out cold.

He had come over here to fuck her. But he wasn't going to be a selfish shit and wake her up for that.

She had to be exhausted. So, he did what any decent human would do, let her sleep.

He disengaged and rolled out of bed, careful not to wake her. As he headed over to his pile of neatly folded clothes, he stopped midway, turned around and went back to the bed. He stared down at her for a few seconds, then leaned over and brushed his lips over the smooth, warm skin of her bare shoulder.

Before he could think too much of it, he quietly gathered his clothes in his arms and tip-toed from the room, pulling the door shut behind him, only to come face to face with her canine companion.

"I guess you need to go out?"

The dog's answering soft woof made him wince.

He pressed a finger to his lips. "*Shh.* Don't wake her."

For fuck's sake, was he having a fucking conversation with a dog?

Not only that, but while naked?

"Don't grab anything hanging within reach, dog," he warned as he pushed past Murphy, holding his clothes over his junk, and went into the guest bathroom to empty his own bladder and get dressed.

Maybe he didn't get what he'd come for. But at least he could go on about his day not worried that she got home safely.

However, this afternoon he picked up his kids and he wouldn't be able to head back to Hawg Wild this weekend to keep an eye on her.

Maybe another call to Fletch was in order.

If she wasn't happy about him sending someone else in his place, she'd just have to get over it.

———

"Hey, I handed in my DAMC cut to the prez. Also thanked him for letting us use their club as cover," Fletch told him while Crew sat in his car a half block from his kid's school.

He never got into the drop-off or pick-up line anymore since the mothers picking up their children ended up yelling at him and laying on the horn when he took too long. Sometimes even flipping him off.

They were vicious.

He guessed the whole system was supposed to be "stop, drop and roll."

He now had a designated spot where he met the kids without dealing with threats of violence.

"You didn't say anything to him about the Demons possibly trying to usurp their territory, right?" Crew asked.

"Fuck no," Fletch answered, "but something Z said made me think that they're aware of it."

"Well, that's just fucking great. We need to get indictments and shut down those motherfuckers before they try to take the Angels' territory around Shadow Valley."

"Agreed, brother. Hey, speaking of brothers... Now that I'm about to be a Demon, Decker asked me to keep an ear open to find out what happened with T-Bone."

"Be careful if you ask about him. We don't want it throwing up any red flags. My guess is that they already dealt with his ass and you won't hear a peep about him. It'll be like he never existed. But you can check to see if he still has his room at their church."

"Will do. Also got a call from both Finn and Rez about Saint. You on board with us handling him separately from the rest of those motherfuckers?"

What the hell? He needed to have to have a sit-down with those two. They couldn't be going all vigilante on the Demons. That could fuck everything up. "No. We're not risking this investigation for personal vendettas. He'll get dealt with. They only need some patience."

"I agree with that, too. Though, he does deserve some extra special handling."

"I won't argue that. When's the patch-over?"

"Tonight."

Fuck. That meant Fletch and Wilder wouldn't be able to head to Hawg Wild tonight. "Can you head to Hawg Wild tomorrow night and check in on Cabrera? She's going by the name Rose. I'll text you a pic of her so you know who you're looking for. Be aware that I already had a little discussion with the manager there last night about his customers being handsy with her. Bulldog is also the Demons' sergeant at arms."

"Yeah, I've heard of him. Big dude."

"Sure as fuck is."

"You don't think she can handle that shit herself?"

Whether she could or couldn't wasn't the point. "I'm the task force leader. It's my job to—"

Fletch's loud snort cut him off. "Don't even try feeding me that bullshit, brother. You certainly don't feel the need to visit me and Nova. Anyway, there's no way we can go to Hawg Wild tomorrow night. We're expected to go to a party at the Viper's Den this weekend."

"For the whole damn weekend?" *For fuck's sake!*

"That's what I said. We're supposed to head there once I get my new patches. On that note, I'll need another cut for those."

"Noted."

"We need a place to live, Crew."

"I'm working on that. I should have something for you after this weekend."

"What do we do until then?"

"Party all weekend at the Viper's Den?" he semi-joked. "Take a tent."

Fletch groaned. "We'll grab a motel until you get our living arrangements sorted. I'll save you the receipts."

"It's not easy finding a vacant apartment this quickly," he explained.

"Yeah, and we don't want a damn shit hole. Not if you expect us to live in it for a few months."

"Understood."

"I've turned my whole fucking life upside down by going undercover." Fletch sounded a bit annoyed and Crew didn't blame him.

"Yeah, I get that, and I appreciate your dedication. Wilder's, too. But remember, if it wasn't for the task force you never would've met her. And you'd still be a lonely fucker."

"Like you?" Fletch huffed. "There's more to life than free internet porn and your fist."

Crew spotted his kids walking down the sidewalk. Of course, taking their fucking time. Not like when they were little and used to be excited to see him. They'd run up to him and launch themselves into his arms.

How times have changed.

"Gotta go. Let me know how the whole patch-over goes."

"My guess? They'll hand me my rockers and colors and tell me to fuck off. It's not going to be any kind of ceremony like I'm getting a damn award or anything."

"I'm sure," he murmured. *Jesus.* Can his kids move any slower? They might as well be walking backwards. "All right, later, brother."

He ended the call before Fletch could even respond. He jumped out of the car and stepped onto the sidewalk just as they reached his vehicle.

"Hey, kiddos!" he greeted with a big smile, opening his arms for a hug.

They skirted around him and Chloé's face twisted when he turned to her with his arms still extended. "Can't I even get a hug hello?"

"I'm riding shotgun," Dylan yelled, shoving his sister out of the way.

When they began to tussle over sitting in the front passenger seat, he stepped between them and the car, using his Dad voice. "Hey, just for that, you're not. Get in the back, Dylan."

His son rolled his eyes as Crew grabbed their backpacks and went around the trunk of the car to throw them inside.

Once they were all settled, he pulled away from the curb with two moping teenagers. "How was school?"

Chloé, already playing on her cell phone, mumbled, "School," as an answer.

"Chloé, phone down. Talk to your old man, please."

She released a big dramatic sigh. "About?"

"Anything. School. Dancing. Clothes. Makeup. Boys. I don't care. I want to hear about what's happened since we last spoke."

"Dad..."

And that was all he got.

He sighed, but left out the drama, and glanced in the rearview mirror. "What about you, bud? How's baseball going?"

"Good."

"That's it?"

At a stoplight, he turned and glanced at his son. Dylan was the spitting image of himself at that age. Both of his children had his gray eyes, but Chloé took after her mother with both her facial features and her lighter brown hair. Hopefully, she didn't end up inheriting Sasha's personality.

"Mom gave me a copy of your schedule. So you know, I plan on attending as many games as possible."

"You don't have to," Dylan mumbled.

Crew's fingers choked the steering wheel tighter. "You're right, I don't have to. But here's the thing, I want to be there. You're my son and I love you. I want to see you do well in life. I want to be there for you and support you in all your endeavors. Even if it's something like baseball. I'm proud of you, bud."

He glanced over at Chloé. Her nose was still buried in her phone. "Same with you, Chlo. I'm proud of you and please make sure to tell me when you have dance recitals. I want to be there."

His daughter grumbled something.

That response meant he needed to call Finn's mother and get an updated schedule directly from her.

He pulled in a breath and focused on the road ahead when the light turned green. "What do you two want for dinner tonight?"

"Pizza," Chloé answered at the same time Dylan said, "Burgers."

"How about I swing by Bangin' Burgers on our way home? And then we can grab pizza tomorrow night. Will that work?"

Neither answered.

He sighed again. Otherwise, he was just going to get pissed. Not at them, but at Sasha. And he didn't want to risk taking out his frustration on them.

"Dad, can I sleep over at Megan's house tonight?" Chloé asked more nicely than normal.

"What? No. You're sleeping over at my house tonight."

"But she invited a bunch of our friends."

"You'll have to do it another night. I hardly get to see you. I don't want to miss out on even a minute."

"You should've thought about that before you divorced Mom," she said sharply.

Jesus fuck.

He opened his mouth to explain why he divorced her, but quickly slammed it shut again. They did not need to know their marital problems or that their mother cheated. He would never bad mouth his ex like that, even though Sasha said shitty, false things about him. And fed them all kinds of bullshit. He refused to stoop to her level. If she wanted to admit what she did to the kids, that was on her.

Children should not be used as pawns in a broken marriage. No matter how tempting it was.

"So... I have something really cool planned for Sunday. Do you want to hear it?" he asked.

He didn't get an answer. A quick glance in the rearview mirror showed Dylan staring out of the passenger side window at who knew what. And Chloé, of course, was texting up a storm, probably telling her friends what an asshole her father was for not letting her sleep over at Megan's house.

"No interest in seeing Uncle Nox and the rest of your uncles?"

Chloé's fingers stuttered to a stop and Dylan turned his head to ask, "Are we going to the clubhouse?"

Finally a spark of life. "Even better."

"What?" his daughter asked, actually looking interested. Miracle of all fucking miracles.

Like every weekend or week they spent with him, by the end of it, they were much more loving and talkative. But, *damn*, it was rough getting to that point. And by the time it got there, they were going back to Sasha's.

Then next visit, the cycle started all over again.

"We're doing a club run and all the kids are coming."

"Can I ride with Uncle Nox?" Chloé asked, her eyes actually a bit excited with the prospect of going on a ride.

"No, Dylan is."

In the back seat, Dylan did a fist pump and yelled, "Yes!"

She frowned. "Then can I ride with Monty?"

"I'm not sure she can make it, honey, she usually works Sundays. You're riding with your old man."

"Oh."

There went that tiny scrap of enthusiasm.

"Is Beck going?" Suddenly that enthusiasm was back, but in full force.

He glanced over at his daughter with a frown. Cross and Nash's adopted twins were about the same age as her. Chloé was only a few months older.

"Not sure if Beck will want to go. Hopefully Bri will."

Did his daughter have an interest in Beck? The boy had a shitload of issues. Most likely he'd end up taking after Nash. Crew had no doubt if he did, the kid would join the Dirty Angels MC, and not become a cop like Cross, a member of the Blue Avengers.

The kid was going to be trouble. Actually, he already was. He was constantly stealing and fighting and getting suspended from school.

He'd even run away for two weeks not long after the couple adopted him.

Cross and Nash had their damn hands full with those two. Brielle was a little easier to deal with. Beck had a chip on his damn shoulder that might as well be a boulder.

Crew wouldn't be surprised if the boy eventually ended up in prison.

"I'm going to text him and tell him to go."

Crew just about choked on his spit. She was going to *what*? "How do you have his number?"

Chloé shot him a look like he was an idiot. They probably exchanged numbers at one of the BAMC events or found each other through social media.

"How often do you talk to him?"

A curtain came down over her expression. "Not often."

The fuck if he believed that.

But that guaranteed one thing...He would be having a long fucking discussion with Beck's father, Cross.

Crew was determined to keep those two apart. He would do whatever he needed to do to protect his baby girl.

Whether Chloé wanted that or not.

Because Father always knew best.

Chapter Twenty-Seven

WHEN SHE DROVE down the alley behind the task force's plant, she was surprised to find the gate wide open. And when she went to pull in, even more surprised to find the parking lot jammed packed with bikes.

She had déjà vu for a second, since that was how the parking lot at Hawg Wild usually looked.

But this was not Hawg Wild and the people milling around were not outlaw bikers. They were all upstanding citizens.

For the most part.

She ended up putting her Audi in reverse and parking along the alley until she could find out what the hell was going on.

After walking through the gate, she saw a few Blue Avengers members—clearly identifiable because they were wearing their cuts—she'd been previously introduced to, even if briefly—as well as BAMC members also on the task force like Decker, Finn, Rez and Nox.

The last had a smaller girl child in his arms with her own

317

arms hanging around his neck. It shocked her to see how alive the man with the normally dead eyes looked.

The rest of the kids, mostly tweens or teens, were gathered in groups talking with each other.

She didn't spot Crew and wondered if his two kids were in attendance for whatever was happening.

As she worked her way around the line-up of Harleys and humans, she gave a few waves and nods to everyone she knew and headed toward the exterior stairs to the third floor.

But just as she was about to take the first step up, Crew came barreling out of the side door. He stopped dead and stared at her.

Funny, because she did the same.

"What are you doing here?" he demanded. It sounded more like an accusation than a question.

A frown twisted her lips. "What do you mean? I'm picking up the pool car." Did he hit his head or something? Maybe his memory *was* deteriorating.

"No."

Her head jerked back. "What do you mean *no*?"

"Did you work at Hawg Wild Friday and Saturday night?"

Did he not trust her to do her damn job? "Of course. Didn't you see my daily reports?"

"I've been busy with my kids and not task force shit."

She stated the obvious, "Well, you're here now."

He shook his annoyingly handsome head. "Not for work. I'm off today and so are you. In fact, take the next couple of nights off. You need to get some rest. You were dead to the fucking world when I left Friday morning."

"But—"

He stepped toe to toe with her and intently stared down

into her upturned face. "No arguing. That's an order. Sleep. Eat. Swim. But you better not go to Hawg Wild."

"Crew..."

He leaned in and growled her name in warning, "Cami..."

Her eyes widened for a split second before she quickly reined in her reaction.

Him growling her name did not scare her, it fucking turned her on. *What the hell?*

"You've worked more than enough hours this week. Take a fucking break." His gray eyes were heated as they quickly scanned the immediate area. When they landed back on her, they practically burned a hole right through her. "You go into Hawg Wild either tonight or tomorrow night, your ass will be purple instead of red."

Her breath hissed from between parted lips and her next words were breathless. *Damn it.* "Since when is it okay for a task force leader to spank one of their members?"

At his "threat," her heart began pounding in her chest and that wasn't the only thing pounding. Her pussy was pulsing and if she continued to stand there, she had no doubt her panties would soon be damp. Her own reaction annoyed her as much as he did.

She had tried to convince herself that she hadn't been disappointed when she finally woke up Friday afternoon and her bed had been empty.

Of course, she failed.

"When they deserve it."

"Oh, so that's not just reserved for me, then? You normally take Decker or Nox over your lap and give them a good paddle?"

He dropped his head until he was almost nose to nose

with her. "I don't fuck them until they soak my cock and scream my name when they come."

Her eyebrows lifted. "Did that happen?"

"I remember it quite clearly."

"I'm surprised, with your advanced age and all."

One side of his upper lip pulled up in a sneer. How did he even make that look sexy as fuck?

"Go home, Cami. Do whatever you normally do when you're not working," he ordered.

"Yes, *boss*." She clamped her bottom lip between her teeth, trying not to smirk when his nostrils flared.

"You're lucky there's a shitload of people around the corner."

"Lucky? It depends on how you look at it," she quipped, no longer fighting her grin.

"I have to get back to the group." He took a step back and scanned her from head to toe.

She was dressed in fake leather black leggings again, a see-through white sweater with a tight black V-neck camisole underneath and her black knee-high boots.

"You look..."

She raised her eyebrows.

"Good."

She raked her gaze down Crew, from the top of his neat salt-and-pepper hair down to his biker boots, pausing only on the leather cut he wore. He actually looked good in it.

Too damn good. Her pussy agreed. "You don't look so bad yourself."

He slipped on his mirrored sunglasses. "Didn't need you to tell me that."

"Same," she returned, and followed him around the corner, through the side lot full of vehicles and back to the rear lot where everyone else waited with their bikes.

"So... what's going on here?"

"A club run." His voice had instantly changed. It went from heated and growly to normal.

The man could give her whiplash.

"About time," Finn yelled across the lot when he spotted Crew. "We're waiting on you, Crewser, so we can get rolling."

Decker had the little girl Nox was holding earlier on his bike and she wore a kid-sized helmet. His Harley had some kind of special set-up with foot pegs for short legs and a back-rest so she wouldn't fall off.

She eyed the rest of the line-up before asking Crew, "Anyone have a spare seat and won't mind a passenger? I would *love* to go since my boss ordered me not to go into work tonight."

He frowned at her. "It's for the kids."

"Somebody has to have an empty spot for me."

"No, I don't think anyone does."

There was the asshole she knew and...

Tolerated.

"I would love to go along to see if I want to get my own *sled* and join your little exclusive club. I see Monty's here today." Cami had been told Monty was a federal prison guard and the sole female member of the Blue Avengers. That second part needed to change.

Before he could answer, a teenager ran up to Crew. She had light brown hair styled into two long braids and stunning gray eyes. She was absolutely beautiful. "Dad!"

Of course. The eyes should've given it away.

"Are you ready to go?" Crew asked his daughter.

"Monty said I can ride with her."

Cami watched Crew's jaw flex. "I already told you you're riding with me."

"I want to ride with her. She's cool."

Ouch.

"Oh... That's right. And your old man isn't."

"He's your old man, too?" Cami asked. When the girl turned to her, she realized she shouldn't have let that slip.

"Huh?"

Ignoring Crew's glare, Cami smiled at the girl and shook her head. "It was just a dumb joke."

"Oh."

His voice was tight when he said, "Chloé, this is our newest task force member, Camila Cabrera. She's a DEA agent like me."

"Hey," the girl greeted, her tone telling Cami that Chloé didn't give a shit.

"Hi, Chloé," Cami answered with enthusiasm, watching a curtain drop over the teenager's eyes. "You can call me Cami."

"Okay." She turned back to her father. "So, can I ride with Monty? *Pleeeeeeeease?*"

Cami watched Crew pull in such a deep breath his chest puffed out for a few seconds before it deflated and he insisted, "I wanted you to ride with me."

"Next time," she offered, a flicker of hope clearly in her gray eyes.

When his daughter said that, it caused Crew's body to visibly jerk.

Interesting.

Was Chloé just a typical teenager, or was there something more behind that reaction? He did tell her that their mother was a piece of work.

"She probably needs to take Beck," Crew said next.

Cami had no idea who Beck was, but it was obvious that

Crew really wanted his daughter to ride with him. He wanted that time with her.

Holy shit, was she really feeling sorry for him?

She'd probably feel the same for any parent if their child resisted spending time with them. It most likely had nothing to do with the fact she'd slept with the man.

"Beck's riding with Finn," Chloé informed him.

"Then she needs to take Bri," Crew stated.

"Bri is riding with her dad."

Despite being an accomplished senior special agent, despite being a task force leader, despite being a bossy shit, despite *everything*... this young girl was going to win this fight and Crew would lose and lose badly.

The man was going to be deeply wounded from that loss.

Oh yeah, she felt for him.

"Do all the rest of the kids have a ride?" he finally asked.

"Yes, I checked."

A resigned sigh filled the air. "Fine. Don't give her any problems."

"Thanks, Dad!" The excitement was back in her voice. She ran off and over to Monty, even though her eyes were focused on another boy about her age. One wearing a scowl.

She wondered if he was Nox's son because they sure had the same "I hate the world" expression.

Though, Nox wasn't wearing his today.

"Where's your son?" Cami asked, scanning the group again.

"He's going to ride with Nox."

"Oh, so the back of your bike is now empty? That means you'll be the odd man out. How about you just think of me as one of the kids... *Daddy*." She added on the biggest smile she could manage.

He practically bared his teeth at her.

"You can break my cherry by taking me on my first motor-cycle ride," she told him next.

"Jesus," he mumbled with a shake of his head. "You don't have a helmet."

He was going to find any little excuse for her not to go. "Do I need one?" She glanced around. "Not everyone's wearing one."

"Anyone under twenty-one needs to wear one," he advised her, walking stiffly toward his bike parked toward the back of the line-up.

She slapped her thigh and trailed him. "Oh, look, you actually told a joke!"

When they got to his Harley, he grabbed what looked like a plain black half-helmet off the seat and shoved it at her. "Wear this."

"Then, what will you wear? Or will your thick skull protect your pig-headed brain?"

Ignoring her, he threw one of his long, denim-encased legs over his bike. Once settled into place, he pushed the start button and his engine roared to life. The throaty rumble got her blood rushing the same as the man straddling it.

"You have two seconds to get on before I leave you standing there." He adjusted his sunglasses and pulled the bandana hanging around his neck up and over the bottom half of his face.

He revved the engine in warning as she scrambled to climb on behind him because she had no doubt that he'd follow through on that threat. She was strapping on the helmet as the rest of the pack circled them, every damn one of them motoring by very slowly and giving Crew a pointed look, a smirk or a cocked eyebrow.

He acted as if he didn't notice, but she was damn sure he was cursing her under his breath.

The fact was, law enforcement loved to gossip as much as high school girls and without uncertainty, plenty of it would be flying around after this.

He turned his head. "Make sure to hang the fuck on. You fall off, I'm not stopping to pick you up."

"Then you'll be down another task force member," she warned.

"I'm okay with that." After putting the bike in gear, he revved the engine one more time and it jerked forward.

She quickly wrapped her arms around his waist and held on for dear life.

———

HOLY SHIT. Once she found a more permanent residence, the first thing she was doing was heading down to the local Harley dealer, buying her own bike and signing up for a safety class.

She had loved everything about the ride. The wind in her face, the sense of freedom that filled her even though Crew controlled the bike, the way they hugged the winding curves of all the back roads. As well as the speed on the straight-aways and highways.

Add in the power between her thighs. Both from the Harley and Crew himself.

At the beginning of the run, Crew had been stiff as hell, most likely because he'd still been annoyed at both her and his daughter. He'd been bested by two females. But after a few miles in, she could feel the tension leave him, even through his leather cut. He leaned back just enough so they were pressed against each other. A few times he had even adjusted her arms to encourage her to tighten them around him.

She didn't resist because she was no fool.

Since they were riding at the back of the pack, when no one was paying attention, his long fingers would occasionally circle her calf and give it a squeeze.

She wasn't sure if he was just checking in with her, or if it was more of a possessive gesture.

Either way, she wished he'd done it more.

But his kids were on this ride and even though they were riding ahead of them and not once looked back at their father, it wouldn't take much for them to do so.

However, the BAMC members couldn't resist peering back at them whenever they had the chance.

Oh yeah. Crew's ass was going to be ridden hard by his MC brothers.

After the first two hours, they finally stopped for a break. Both to empty their bladders and fill their guts with ice cream.

Crew sat near his kids, so she gave them space. But it was hard to miss his mirrored sunglasses pointed toward the boy named Beck.

Was it young love? Or young trouble?

Cami sat at an angle where she could study the boy as she licked at her ice cream cone. Beck appeared to be the same age as Chloé but had trouble written all over him. In his expression, in the way he talked, even in the way he moved.

His father, Aiden Cross, also kept an eye on him more than his daughter Bri. Though Bri seemed a bit troubled, too, she didn't seem to have the same massive chip on her shoulder as her twin.

Also during the break, she introduced herself to the members of the Blue Avengers she didn't know yet, as well as the rest of the kids. As they chatted, every one of them watched her as closely as she had Beck.

It was to be expected.

She had a quick, but enlightening discussion with Monty about being the only female member of an MC and afterward, Cami was determined now more than ever to join. Women had to stick together.

But Chloé had been right about one thing. Monty *was* cool.

The whole time Cami talked to the federal corrections officer, Crew's gaze was glued on her instead of his daughter, like he was worried they were hatching some evil plan.

When they were finally getting back on the road and as Crew handed her his helmet, he asked under his breath, "What were you two discussing?"

"Hairstyles, purses and makeup."

His mouth gaped a second before he snorted. "Now, I know that's a fucking lie."

"Okay, we were discussing you." They hadn't discussed him at all. Cami wasn't the kind of woman who snuck through the rear to find out what she wanted. She had no problem pounding on the front door.

If there was something she wanted to know about the man she'd had sex with, she was going to ask him directly. Then she'd sit back and weigh his words, watch his expressions and evaluate his body language.

Her natural ability to do that made her good at her job.

"What did you find out?" he asked as she finished strapping on the helmet.

"Nothing I didn't already know," she answered.

"Monty's not one to gossip."

She planted her hand on his shoulder and climbed on behind him. "Then why did you ask?" When he didn't answer, she continued, "Why do you think I'd ask anyone anything about you? Why do you assume I'm interested in learning more than what I already know?"

"You're not?"

"Nope. Are you disappointed?"

When he started his Harley, his answering, "No," got lost in the rumble of his loud exhaust.

And he called *her* a liar.

She chuckled under her breath as the pack took off in formation, leaving the roadside ice cream stand behind as they headed back toward Rockvale.

During that last hour, his fingers circled her lower calf more often than not. It was as if he was staking his claim and didn't care if anyone knew. She was pretty damn sure if either of his kids had turned around, he would have dropped it as if he'd grabbed a hot coal.

She would've completely understood it if he had.

His kids would always be his top priority, as they should be. She also didn't want to add any more tension to their relationship. Even though his kids were old enough to understand he was not living the life of a monk, no one wanted to think about their parents having sex.

When they arrived back at the lot, she took her time unwrapping her arms from around his waist, making sure to drag her fingers slowly under his cut and over the small of his back.

She swore she heard a little bit of a growl slip from his lips when she leaned in close to his ear and whispered, "Thanks for the ride. I'm no longer a virgin."

When she handed him the helmet and began to walk away, his hand snaked out and he yanked her to a stop. Tugging her closer, he kept his deep voice low to say, "You think you bested me today, but you're wrong. I need to drop the kids off after this. Once I'm done doing that, I'll be over."

Her pussy clenched and her pulse sped up. "I don't remember inviting you."

"You invited me the second you went against my wishes."

"Chloé went against your wishes, too."

"She's my daughter. You're not."

She definitely was *not*.

Her voice caught and she cleared her throat so she could say, "I'll be waiting."

With that, she tugged her wrist free and took quick strides toward her car, not looking back at him once since all eyes had been on that exchange. They didn't have to hear the words to get a good read on what was said since, being all observant members of law enforcement, they were good at reading body language.

She kept her chin up and hoped her face wasn't flushed as those same eyes tracked her walking through the lot. While she did so, she did her best to hide the tremble of her thighs, not caused by riding on a motorcycle for the last three and a half hours.

But by the anticipation of riding the overbearing man with the gray eyes and salt-and-pepper hair.

Chapter 28

CREW SHUT off the engine and stared through his car's windshield to contemplate the house in front of him.

No, not the house.

The woman inside.

He shouldn't be here.

He hadn't walked through the door yet, which meant he could easily leave before doing so.

He drove straight over to Fletch's house after dropping off the kids. Since he wasn't on his bike, Cami might not even be aware he'd arrived.

You should go.

Getting involved with her was a mistake.

You don't need a woman like her in your life, complicating it. You already deal with more than enough conflict with Sasha.

Cami was headstrong. Independent. Highly intelligent.

And a damn challenge.

Unfortunately, one he couldn't resist.

If he walked through that door, she might no longer be a

331

fling, but become a *thing*. And that was not what he was looking for. It could make a mess of his life and screw up his career. *Hell*, fuck over the task force. Especially if this *thing*—whatever it was—turned sour.

Worse, if he hurt her, even without meaning to, it wasn't only her he'd have to deal with. It could be the HR department and maybe even her father.

His chest tightened. If that happened, would he ever be able to look the man he respected in the eyes again?

That alone was a reason going inside that house again wasn't a good idea.

He needed to fucking leave before it was too late.

As he reached for the start button to do just that, the front door opened and, for a second, he only saw her back-lit silhouette before it shut again.

"Fuck," he muttered.

His opportunity to escape just slipped through his fingers.

As she approached, he tracked her shadow through the dark and once she got within range, the motion light over the garage door lit up both the driveway and her.

Holy shit, the woman was so fucking beautiful. She had taken his breath away the very second he saw her and he never got it back.

Unfortunately, they were at different stages of their lives. She at the beginning, he in the middle. She was ready to tackle her career and life with energy and optimism, while his optimism and outlook had been tainted a few years ago.

More than that, he wasn't ready to start all over again.

For fuck's sake, he couldn't.

He knew now he couldn't save the world. Determination and grit were not enough.

He'd also done the love and marriage thing and learned a

lesson he wouldn't soon forget. He jumped in with two feet and ended up crawling back out on skinned hands and knees.

But he needed to consider one other thing... He couldn't have any more children.

Some divorcées took what they considered the "easy" route and started fresh by creating a whole new family and ruthlessly discarding the old.

He couldn't and wouldn't ever do that.

Despite the resistance from Dylan and Chloé, he would keep chipping away at them until they were back to loving him the same way he did them and the same way as when they were young. Before they'd been told lies. He wouldn't give up until they wanted to spend time with him by choice and not only when it was forced.

His children were the two most important humans in his life. Always would be. He *would* not and *could* not let them go. He would fight like hell for them both until nothing was left to fight for.

Any woman in his life would need to accept the fact his kids would always come first. Always.

He stared at Cami through the closed driver's side window as she waited only about a foot away.

That woman was also the type to never give up. She would fight for what she wanted. She would do whatever was needed to be done to protect the people she loved.

With that intense love and passion, she would make a great mother one day. If she wanted that. And if she did, he couldn't be the one to give it to her.

For that reason alone, he shouldn't be here. Because, while he denied that any kind of connection existed between them... one did.

He feared that every time he came over here, every time he ended up in her bed, it would only get stronger.

Only get more intense.

In the end, he did not want to do to her what Sasha did to him, even if unintentionally. To save her from that, he needed to make excuses and get the fuck out of there.

When he rolled down the window, she spoke before he could. "I could see the whites of your eyes all the way from the house. Why are you so damn scared?"

For fuck's sake. "You're seeing things. I'm not scared."

"Yes, you are. There's nothing to be afraid of, Crew."

She was so damn wrong.

"I don't bite," she teased.

Untrue. You've somehow sank your teeth so deeply into me, I can no longer escape without it tearing me apart.

He squeezed his eyes shut at that realization. *Jesus fucking Christ.* He couldn't escape. It might already be too late.

To prove her wrong about being afraid, he powered up his window and exited the car.

Before she could step back, he shot his hand out to grab her by the back of the neck. He swung her around and pinned her against the driver's door using his body from hips to chest.

When her head tipped up as his tipped down, he searched her shadowed eyes.

He couldn't see their color, but he knew what they were. He could picture every shade—from dark brown to light—the color of every fleck and the outer black ring around the iris. He knew this because he'd stared into them every time she challenged him. As well as every time they'd had sex.

"Why do you drive me so fucking crazy?" slipped from him. He hated to admit that, but it was true.

"Are you sure you didn't drive yourself there?"

His fingertips dug harder into her neck. "Fuck no. It's all you."

Since she was wearing a form-fitting camisole, her shoulders were bare even though the night breeze had a slight chill. She jerked one slightly in a half-shrug. "You could leave."

Like it was that simple.

"I could," he agreed, even though that was a damn lie.

"But you won't."

Goddamn it.

The confidence she exuded was nothing but a turn-on for him. It wasn't cockiness, it was pure strength.

He hoped she never lost that, or no one dared attempt to destroy it. But if someone tried, he knew she would fight tooth and nail to keep it.

Right then and there, the truth slammed him in the chest like a battering ram.

She was the woman he had hoped Sasha would be. One able to handle who he was. How he was. Even what he was.

At the time, he'd thought Sasha was "the one." He now knew he was so fucking wrong.

It wasn't Sasha.

Hell no.

It was Camila Cabrera.

He'd been so goddamn blind.

He'd been looking for a kitten when he should've been looking for a tigress.

Her, "Are we going to stand out here all night?" brought him back to the moment.

The moment.

This turning point.

But he needed to be truthful with her. To tell her they had no future if she wanted anything more than only him. Because that was all he could give her.

"Cami..." It pained him to admit, "I can't give you what you want."

Confusion crossed her face. "What do I want? Besides to go inside?"

"If you expect more from me—"

"Than sex?"

"Yes."

Silence filled the space between them for a few heartbeats. "Did I ask for anything more?"

"No." *Not yet.* "But..."

Hell, maybe he was overthinking this and, if he continued on this path, he would make a goddamn fool of himself.

"I thought this was casual," she said simply.

A valid assumption. "It is." *Or it was.*

"Then you have nothing to worry about. I want nothing more from you than you've already given me. And what you're about to give me. We're keeping it simple, right?"

Right. Keep it simple, stupid.

"Right?" she asked again. "Or am I missing something here?"

"You're not missing anything. I only wanted to make sure it was clear."

"Clear as a cloudless sky." She shifted against him. "Tell me... Is there a reason you still have me pinned against your car? I'd rather not have sex in the driveway under a spotlight. I'd venture to guess most of Fletch's neighbors would prefer not to watch that, either. Not to mention, I'd have to look them in the face whenever I take Murphy for a walk around the block. That could get a bit awkward."

His reason for coming over was to turn her ass cheeks a bright shade of red before fucking her. Realistically, he could still do that and leave right after.

For fuck's sake. Who was he kidding? If he went in that house, he wasn't leaving it again until morning.

After breakfast.

After another good fuck and a few shared orgasms.

He groaned at what a weak simp this woman made him.

There was nothing "simple" about their connection.

After Sasha, he had no problem keeping things only surface deep when he found a woman he wanted to spend some time with. And by "time" he meant hours at the most, not days or weeks. *Hell*, not even overnight.

After his divorce, he hadn't met a woman he wanted to wake up next to, roll over and greet with a "good morning."

This powerhouse of a woman made him want to, not only do that, but tell her goodnight as they both laid their heads down on the pillows in the dark.

His heart thumped heavily and an unbearable weight pressed on his chest.

When he released her neck and went to step back to give them both their freedom, she caught him off guard by clamping a hand around his neck in the same way he had hers and tugging him so hard, he crashed into her. Before he could catch his balance, she captured his mouth and kissed him until he no longer had one damn doubt about coming over.

Not one about going inside.

And definitely none about spending the night.

Driving his hands into her hair along both sides of her head, he curled them into tight fists so he could yank her head back even further and steal control of the kiss from her. Her fingers dug into his waist to hold him there, a sign he took as encouragement to continue the dick-hardening assault on her mouth.

At that moment, he didn't give a shit what the neighbors saw or even thought.

He could spread her wide on the hood and eat her pussy until she ripped the hair right out of his head.

He could open the rear driver's side door, make her sit sideways on the edge of the back seat and force feed her his cock.

He could drag her around to the rear of his vehicle to bend her over the trunk and pound her from behind until they both came.

He could do all of that and more.

But life was more than experiencing those moments he could easily get lost in.

All actions had consequences, whether bad, good or indifferent.

In reality, he liked his job and preferred not to get arrested for indecent exposure. Or have videos of them engaging in "lewd acts" on the car and under a bright spotlight go viral all over the internet.

That would be fun to explain to Bob Williams, especially since the other participant was also a DEA agent. Worse, it might not stop with him. It could climb the chain of command until it landed on Luis Cabrera's desk. And if it didn't officially, then the gossip could easily land in his ear.

So, *yeah...* They needed to take this inside before it went any further and while he still had a solid grip on his common sense.

However, his cock was jammed hard against his zipper, not only because of the intensity of the kiss, but due to her little groans, along with her grinding against his already throbbing erection.

While he appreciated her responses, they were not helping with his dilemma.

Slightly bending his knees, he hooked her under her ass and lifted her, managing not to break their lip lock. With her arms wrapped around his neck and her legs around his waist, he somehow managed to carry her to the porch without them both plummeting to the ground.

But when he almost stumbled up the single step, he reluctantly pulled his lips free so he could see where the fuck he was going. He managed to hang onto her as he turned the knob, pushed the door open with his boot and carried her inside.

"Make sure that monster stays out from under my feet," he warned. He wanted them both to end up in her bed, not the emergency room.

"He's more of a road block than a speed bump."

That was for damn sure, but that didn't lessen his concern.

Apparently, she wasn't worried about falling hard to the floor when she breathed, "Hurry," before tracing the outer shell of his ear with her tongue and nipping his earlobe.

"Jesus." That had sent a shock of lightning right into his balls.

Making him worry that his zipper might soon be embedded in his cock.

He walked faster. "Keep an eye out for Murphy."

"He's behind you."

"I know he is but that doesn't mean he won't dash in front of me and take us both down."

"Murphy doesn't *dash* anywhere."

"You know what I mean."

"You could put me down," she suggested with a smile curling those lips he wanted to taste again.

"I will when I'm ready."

Her short nails dug into the skin at the top of his spine. "You're stubborn."

He huffed. "You call *me* stubborn?"

He hooked a left into the bedroom suite and stopped in the middle of the room. He was proud of himself for not being out of breath.

"Get naked," he ordered as he placed her on her feet.

"Yes, boss."

He ground his teeth. "It's probably not smart to agitate a man about to spank your ass."

When her eyebrows rose, her deep brown eyes filled with mischief. "*Ooooor* is it?"

"Woman, you can push me all you want as long as you're able to deal with the consequences."

Her chin lifted. "It's a risk I'm willing to take."

He shook his head. "Always have to be a challenge."

"Life would be boring otherwise."

That was so damn true.

Just as he was turning to go sit on the edge of the bed, he spotted something new on the nightstand.

Every muscle and joint locked when he realized what it was.

What the ever-loving fuck?

Within three long strides, he swiped the framed picture off the nightstand and stared at it. "Where the fuck did this come from?"

"My parents shipped me more of my things."

For fuck's sake!

He slammed the academy graduation picture of her and her father smiling and hugging face-down.

Talk about a fucking cock-block. "I don't need your father watching what I'm about to do to you."

Holy shit, that could be enough to make him loose his erection.

"Oh, should I turn off the security cameras set up in the bedroom? He insists on keeping an eye on me. You know... to make sure I'm safe."

He spun. "What?"

She grinned. "I never saw that shade of pale before. Impressive. Are you feeling lightheaded? Do you need to lie down?"

"No." He headed back to the foot of the bed and sat on the edge. She was still fully clothed. Unacceptable. "Didn't I tell you to get naked?"

"Yes, but then you got distracted."

"Well, now I need to be distracted from what I just saw."

"A family photo?" A gleam filled in her eyes.

"You know it's not just any fucking family photo," he growled.

"Of course it isn't. It was an important milestone in my life. I was glad both my parents are still around to share it with me. They're proud of my accomplishments and my father would've discouraged me from entering the academy if he wasn't confident that I could handle the job. Not only do it, but do it well."

Crew pulled in a breath through his nose. "This is not the conversation I want to have right before you get naked."

With a shrug, she grabbed the bottom of her camisole and began to pull it up. "Well, it's the conversation you got because you couldn't ignore a simple photo."

It wasn't the photo itself. It was the reminder that he was fucking the daughter of a former colleague.

Not only fucking her, but spanking her goddamn ass.

Chapter Twenty-Eight

To be honest, Cami hadn't really thought much about the location of the photo before putting it there. Not that he needed to know that. When she unpacked it from one of the boxes her parents shipped, she wasn't sure that Crew would ever grace her bed with his presence again.

She could see how being "watched" by her father could be a little off-putting. She'd find a new location for it later. When she wasn't tied up with more important things.

Like the man sitting on the edge of her bed, waiting for her to finish getting undressed.

"You're not getting naked?" she asked him.

"Not if you don't want to be covered in my DNA while my hand leaves an imprint against your ass."

A shiver slipped down her spine at the anticipation of being across his lap, face down and ass up.

Her enjoying him spanking her was so damn unexpected.

Would she enjoy it with other men? Or was Crew the only one who could dole out that "punishment" and make her almost orgasm from that alone?

Either way, it was Crew sitting there waiting. No one else.

And she didn't want it to be anyone else.

Sure, he was older than her.

Sure, he could be somewhat cocky.

Sure, he could be frustratingly bossy.

But she was no wilting violet. She could meet him head-to-head and she liked that challenge. It kept them both on their toes.

She needed a man who could handle her personality, her sense of humor, and what she did for a living.

The man watching her peel off her leggings could do that.

Plus, he was sexy as all get out.

Not only was he a natural leader, he could handle a bunch of shit thrown at him. It came from all sides, too. From the job, his ex, his own children and even his brothers.

The first being stressful, the second aggravating, the third heartbreaking and the rest? All in good fun.

Did she add to it? Of course.

"Why the hell are you grinning?" Suspicion laced his voice.

"Am I?"

His gray eyes narrowed on her. "Do you have something up your sleeve?"

She flung her arms out as she turned in front of him. "How can I when I'm not even wearing sleeves? Do you need glasses? If you haven't noticed, I'm naked."

"My eyesight is perfect."

"But yet, you still sit there despite that."

He patted his lap. "That's because you need to come to me."

"*Aaah*, I missed the memo."

"That memo only has two words..."

She cocked an eyebrow. "And they are?"

"Come here."

His gaze scorched her bare skin as she traveled the short distance separating them. As she did so, her pussy pulsed, her nipples beaded tightly and her lips parted as her breath quickened.

She could already feel the impact on her ass.

"You're lucky you're good in bed because your personality has a lot to be desired," she teased as she draped herself over his lap. Very willingly, of course.

"Ditto."

His cock was so hard beneath her stomach, she might as well be lying on a steel pipe. The discomfort had to be worse for him. "Do you prefer women who do as they're told? Women who are dependent and soft spoken? The total opposite of me?"

When she wiggled to find a more comfortable position, a sharp intake of air made her still.

"You're playing with fire, woman."

"What's a few blisters?"

"On my hand or your ass?"

It was her turn to suck in a breath. "I want to get wet, but not from tears."

"I doubt you would cry."

She actually considered that a compliment. "Can you please remember that I'm not a naughty child. I'm a horny woman."

"I never once spanked my children."

"Only women?"

When he didn't answer, she twisted her head enough to glance up at him. He was studying her ass while his fingers skimmed lightly over both cheeks.

He met her eyes. "Only ones who asked."

Huh. "I didn't ask, so why me?"

"Because you deserve it."

With a grin, she rolled her eyes. "Okay, boss man."

"Just for that..."

His palm struck her so hard, she jolted against him. "Damn!" Once she breathed through the sting, she urged him to, "Do it again."

"Are you in a position to make demands?"

Actually, she was since she was sure he'd comply with anything she asked. However, this wasn't serious, it was all play to her.

Foreplay they both got off on.

"I'd say yes."

"Wrong."

His serious, even slightly dangerous, tone made her laugh, but she choked on it as he swatted her ass again. This time on the other cheek.

Holy shit. It hurt so damn good.

She might have a bruise after this. Not on her ass, but on her lower stomach where his cock pressed. If possible, he was now even harder.

She wiggled against him just enough to cause him to groan. "Now I see why you couldn't do this naked."

As she waited for the next strike, it didn't come.

She figured he was holding off so she wouldn't anticipate the next one. But as the seconds ticked off, she didn't feel the movement of his body as he lifted his arm or the rush of air as he let it drop.

"Crew..." As she tried to flip over to see what the problem was, he pressed a hand against her back to keep her in place.

Could she get free? Of course. It wouldn't take much.

But something was up...

Was he having second thoughts? A panic attack? Was he frozen in fear?

Holy shit...

"I knew it," she whispered, then repeated it a lot louder. "I knew it!"

"Shut up, Cami."

She'd been right. He was scared to death about where this was headed.

If she had to admit it, she was, too.

But unlike him, her reason didn't have anything to do with an evil ex making her life miserable. Wasn't the saying... Once burned, twice shy?

She might not have escaped a bad relationship—though, he'd never really escape since he shared two children with his ex—the point of her coming to Pittsburgh was to catch bad guys.

Not feelings.

That was exactly what happened. And blazing quick, too.

They were supposed to be keeping things simple, but once emotions became involved... Shit could get complicated.

Fast.

"Crew..." she tried again.

"Cami, no."

Oh yeah, the Teflon armor he most likely donned whenever he had any kind of intimacy with a woman must have dislodged and left a gap just large enough for those feelings to slip through.

It was why he left unexpectedly that morning, looking spooked.

It was why he sat in the car in the driveway, white-knuckling the steering wheel.

It was why he wanted to ignore talk of it now.

Could she see herself having an actual relationship with this man?

Would he even want that? Or would he push any potential of that aside using any excuse in the book? Starting with her age, of course.

Because that was an easy one for him.

Add in who her father was, and that Crew was her "boss" in a way...

That was just some of the many excuses he could come up with. Valid or not.

In some ways they couldn't be more different, in others they were too much alike.

It could work perfectly. Or it could be a disaster.

They could either complement each other or would they one day throw the white towel when their relationship became too exhausting from constantly butting heads and busting balls.

Either way, they'd keep each other on their toes. Guaranteed, life wouldn't be boring.

Holy shit, was she seriously considering this?

She had wanted to concentrate on her career and hadn't been looking for any kind of relationship. At least, not yet. She had plenty of time for that. But if anyone would know how important her career was with the DEA, it would be another DEA agent.

However, would he want to interfere with her assignments like he tried with her going undercover at Hawg Wild? Using the excuse it was for her safety?

Fuck.

Lying naked across Crew's lap wasn't the most opportune time to consider her future, both personally and professionally. It definitely wasn't the smartest time to make life decisions, either.

If the man knew where her thoughts had wandered, he'd be sprinting for the door after dumping her onto the floor, leaving her naked and unsatisfied.

She rolled her lips under so she didn't laugh at that image.

But it only took him dragging a finger through her slick lips to bring her back to the situation at hand.

What happened to his urge to spank her? Had he been having the same conversation with himself? Had he been contemplating his future, with or without her?

"Crew..."

"We can either talk or we can fuck. But what we won't do is have the conversation weighing on both our minds while having sex. Choose wisely."

So, he *had* been considering their future together.

"We can fuck," she answered, "but we can't ignore the rest."

"You're right, we can't. But we can put it off until later."

"Are you going to run before we can address the elephant in the room?"

With a sigh, he turned her over until her back was braced by his strong, thick thighs.

He didn't avoid her eyes when he asked, "Do I want to have that conversation? No. Do I have a choice? Maybe. Can I ignore it completely?"

Something crossed his face but before she could figure out what it was, it was gone.

"I wish I could," he finished on a whisper. "This was totally fucking unexpected."

"Agreed," she whispered back.

"This never should've happened."

"I didn't trap you."

"No, you captured me. You hold me hostage just the same."

"If it bothers you so much, break free."

He jerked against her. "That's the fucking problem. I can't. I cannot break free of you."

Holy shit. "And you hate that."

"I didn't say that."

"You might as well have," she countered.

"I didn't want to talk about this now."

"I didn't, either, but *Crewwwwww... Ooo,* damn," she moaned when he dragged a finger back through her folds.

That wasn't fair. Even so, she was back on board for skipping the conversation for now and going back to the foreplay and what happened afterward.

He dipped a finger inside of her, driving it all the way to the last knuckle.

Yep, her vote was for less words, more action.

And that action was gentle, a stark contrast to the spanking.

He dropped his head to wrap his lips around her nipple.

Pressing her head into his thigh, she arched her back to make it easier for him to reach her breast and pressed it deeper into his mouth, so he could give it the attention she desired. She spread her thighs enough to give him unfettered access and he took advantage of that by adding a second finger.

Her eyelids slid closed as he drove them in and out of her, no longer being gentle but being thorough.

When a whimper escaped her, her eyes opened in surprise and she noticed him watching her closely as he continued to suck her nipples, one and the other. Again, no longer gentle. Now with intensity and determination.

But it was when his thumb began to manipulate her clit

that she lost all control of her own body and handed it over to him.

She was literally putty in his hands. Soft and pliable as he worked her.

And, *fuck*, he knew how to work her.

Grabbing her hair, he used it to pull her head up, crashing their mouths together in a deep kiss as he continued to relentlessly fuck her with his long fingers, curling and uncurling. Teasing that spot deep inside her as well as her clit.

They shared her moan as the tension built and a fire roared at her center. Growing and burning hotter by the second.

Then like sparks caught in a breeze, her orgasm blew through her. Searing her skin and melting her bones. Turning her to liquid.

It took her breath away as well as any doubts or concerns. Right now, the future did not exist.

She was only in the moment, twitching with every tiny aftershock as his fingers continued to glide in and out of her slowly. His lips moved across hers a couple more times before disappearing.

The man was a master manipulator. But in a good way.

A few moments later, she inhaled deeply to slow her pounding heart, to bring herself fully back to awareness. Lifting her heavy eyelids, she met his steel-gray eyes.

Her heart skipped a beat at what she saw in them.

He wasn't hiding shit right now. Was he even aware of that?

Instantly, it was gone. Tucked away. Maybe never to be seen again.

That caused a twinge in her heart... But she understood it.

He was a man with a past that would always affect his future. It tainted his outlook on life and relationships.

She almost fell off his lap when he scrambled for his wallet and a few seconds later held out a wrapped condom.

The second she took it, he wedged his hands between them to unfasten his belt and pull it free from the loops. He folded it in half and held it in front of her face. "Luckily you haven't pushed me to the point of using this yet. If you think it stings when I use my hand..."

"Don't threaten me with a good time," she warned him with a wink.

With a shake of his head, he tossed the belt aside before unbuttoning and unzipping his jeans.

"Would it be easier if I got up?" She had no idea what exactly he had planned but she could guess what it involved in general.

"Sit up and straddle my thighs."

His intent was becoming clearer.

He offered his hand to assist her and she took it. His fingers were warm and strong for the few seconds it took for her to get in the position he wanted her.

Even though she was straddling his lap, she hadn't dropped her weight yet. Instead, she hovered by standing on her own two feet as he worked his jeans down his thighs only far enough so his cock sprung free.

The tip was shiny because it had to have been leaking precum like a damn fountain during his efforts of bringing her to orgasm.

She'd only seen a handful of cocks in her life, but if she had to rate them, Crew's was toward the top of the list. He could be a cock model, if they existed the same as hand and foot models.

His sharp, "Condom," had her pinning her lips together to keep from grinning like an idiot.

After ripping open the wrapper, she rolled the latex down his twitching length that made her think he was probably teetering on the edge.

If she wanted to climax a second time, she might have to do it with haste.

Setting his spread feet securely on the floor, he grabbed his cock, held it up and waited.

She continued to hover for a second. Until their eyes locked.

Both of them took one united breath. Then one more.

Their gazes continued to hold as she lowered herself, slowly sinking until his cock completely filled her. Until he couldn't go any deeper.

Then she lifted her feet and dropped all her weight, drawing a gasp from her because he was so damn deep, it was almost uncomfortable.

His jaw was tight, his lips pressed into a thin line and a vein protruded at his temple. His fingers dug into her hips to the point of pain.

He was battling the urge to come. His cock was a stick of dynamite about to explode.

"Do you need me to wait?"

"Give me a sec," he forced through his tight lips.

She would do her best to give him that, but he wasn't the only one fighting a battle. The urge to ride him relentlessly and recklessly until she came again was strong.

She took his fingers loosening their grip as a sign she could finally move.

Chapter Twenty-Nine

WITH ONE HAND wrapped around his neck and the other gripping his bearded jaw, Cami tipped his head back and took his mouth.

It was hers.

He was hers.

And, *fuck*, she was his.

She began to move, using her toes on the floor to lift herself before dropping her heels along with her weight. With his hands clamped on her ass, she settled into a steady rhythm of rising and falling.

Down until he completely filled her. Up until only the crown of his cock remained inside.

With their lips remained smashed together, their tongues twisted and tangled, tasting and teasing.

She couldn't get enough of him. His cock. His mouth. All of him.

He confessed that she drove him crazy. It was only fair since he did the same to her.

Could she deal with his overbearing bossiness for more

than a few hours at a time? Could they work *and* live a life together without killing each other?

She was getting ahead of herself by already building a future with him before they even discussed it. *Hell,* they hadn't even gone on one damn date.

Okay, eating together at the diner could be considered one. Sort of.

Not really.

Crissakes, she *had* lost her mind.

All it took was some verbal sparring, some hot, satisfying sex, and here she was, ready to become permanent partners with this man?

Snagging her nipple between his thumb and forefinger, he pulled and twisted, causing her back to arch and for her to swallow down her moment of panic just as a groan slid up her throat.

Every time he pinched and rolled, shocks of lightning radiated through her, starting at her nipples and shooting up to the top of her head as well as down to her toes. After a soft spank to her ass, he drove his hand between them and found her clit.

Him knowing where that was, along with her G-spot, made any panic wash away. Crew might be considered a unicorn. And who the hell let go of a unicorn?

Fools, that was who.

Cami, stop overthinking this! Enjoy the moment. You're not becoming the next Mrs. Crew tonight, tomorrow, or even next week.

Her brain glitched.

Mrs. Crew?

What the fuck! Did she even actually have that thought? Being a Mrs. Anyone wasn't even on her bucket list. Not even all the way at the bottom.

She ripped her mouth free and dropped to his lap, spearing herself on his cock. "I need a damn drink."

His eyebrows knitted together. "Now?"

"Yes and it's your fault."

"How the fuck is it my fault?"

Because you make me picture myself as Camila Crew.

She frowned. That was a horrible name. "I'm never taking your name."

"What the fuck are you talking about?"

"I like my last name. It fits," she explained.

"Cami, have you lost your goddamn mind?" he bellowed.

She squeezed her eyes shut and pulled in a breath. He was right. She was sounding crazy.

Absolutely one-hundred percent certifiable.

"I think I have." *I've gone crazy over you.*

"Can we finish before I'm forced to order you a straitjacket?"

"Yes. But so you know, I take a size small."

A laugh burst from him. He grabbed her face and kissed her hard, still laughing.

She smiled against his lips.

Now... Back to business.

She removed one of his hands from her face, shoving it between them and back to her clit.

Thankfully, he obliged.

She blurted out, "I want to come," as if that wasn't obvious.

"That makes two of us."

"How long can you last?" she asked.

"The fuck if I'm putting that kind of pressure on myself."

Oh, he had jokes. "Long enough for me to come?"

"That I can guarantee."

"A written guarantee?"

"You'll have to take my word on that," he answered.

"Can I trust you?"

His amusement fled and he said with all seriousness, "You can absolutely trust me, Cami. I will never hurt you... On purpose, anyway."

"Except for when you spank me. Please put that in the fine print."

"Whatever you want."

Well, if he was taking requests... "I want you."

"I'm pretty sure my cock is inside you."

"Is that what that is?"

"Last I checked."

She rose up and peeked. "Yep. That's what it looks like." She sank back down, once again taking his full length.

"Now, are you done?"

She purposely misinterpreted his question. "Absolutely not." She began to rock back and forth, on his cock and against his hand. She wrapped both arms around his neck and pressed her smooth cheek to his wiry one.

In turn, he wrapped his arm around her, too, holding her close, but leaving enough space to continue to work her clit with his fingers. Pushing, pinching, circling, flicking.

"Crew," she whimpered, now riding him a bit more frantically.

Up and down. Back and forth. Hitting all the right spots.

Her movements became even more frantic as she chased her orgasm.

"Baby, you need to slow down unless you're ready to come," his gruff voice warned in her ear.

"I'm so fucking ready," she told him in his, not slowing down even the slightest. She ground harder against him because she *was* ready.

Sex didn't have to be a marathon; sometimes it could be a fast and furious sprint and still be more than satisfying.

"Cami..."

"I'm ready," she insisted.

"Warning you now... The second you come, I'm done."

He said that as if it was a bad thing. "I'm okay with that." If he stayed tonight, they had until morning.

"I doubt you'll have a choice."

"Then, we'll just have to do it again." She said that as if it was *not* a bad thing.

"I'm okay with that," he echoed her.

"I doubt you'll have a choice," she echoed him.

His chuckle shook her, but not for long. As soon as she began to move again, she was determined to get to the finish line this time without any more interruptions.

She evicted all unnecessary thoughts from her head and concentrated on the man whose cock she was riding.

The man who hadn't lied about coming a second after her.

———

CREW KEPT HIS HEAD DOWN, but still managed to keep one eye on his phone and one eye on Cami as she stood over by the key rack talking to Rez.

In Spanish.

She had stopped upstairs to grab the keys to the pool car since she was heading to work a shift at Hawg Wild.

He still didn't like it but, at this point, was smart enough to keep his mouth shut. About her being undercover at the biker bar, as well as speaking Spanish to Rez or Torres. Both of his original team members knew it got under his skin, so they did it as much as possible.

That wasn't the only thing he was smart about. Last week he found an app that translated someone speaking one language into another.

Was it perfect? No, but it gave him the gist of what was being said.

They knew enough not to use his name, but that didn't mean they weren't talking about him.

And if they weren't, he still wanted to know if she was telling either of them any trouble she was having with the Demons. Something she might not want to share with Crew to avoid him pulling her from the job.

Confidence was great but it wouldn't get her out of a jam. And even though she was proving herself as time went on, he still worried about her being around all those outlaw bikers without any kind of backup.

And if anyone asked, he'd tell them he'd never stop worrying.

Not until she was done with that assignment.

Plus, the late nights put a kink in them spending time together. And that kink wasn't the good kind.

In the past few weeks, he found himself heading over to Fletch's empty house most nights, letting Murphy out to do his business, watching some late night TV, then falling asleep in Cami's bed. On his request, she'd check in with him throughout the night via text when she could.

In the early morning hours, after dragging herself home, taking a quick shower, she'd climb in beside him, wake him up in a variety of ways he couldn't complain about, then they'd have a quickie that still more than satisfied them both.

Afterward, she'd roll over and crash while he'd stare at her sleeping in the dark. Like a fucking creeper.

Once it was time for him to head out, he'd press a soft kiss to her bare shoulder before rolling out of bed quietly and carefully so he wouldn't wake her. Before leaving, he'd set up her coffeemaker so she had a fresh pot when she woke, then let Murphy out again and feed him.

Some nights, he'd don his Throttle persona and head down to the outlaw biker bar himself to keep an eye on her for a few hours, ignoring her assurance that he didn't need to do that.

Yes, he certainly fucking did.

He had no idea how long this routine would last. But for now, this was his life.

He caught himself thinking about her just as much as his kids. That was how important she had become to him.

When Cami walked through the door of The Plant a little while ago, she had hardly acknowledged him except for a chin lift and a, "Hey, boss. How's it hanging?"

They still acted like they weren't fucking like rabbits just about every night when she didn't head into Hawg Wild or early morning when she did. If they could find the time, sometimes both.

What they did in private was their business, not the rest of the team's. Or his brothers'. Or even her father's.

He didn't need to be served a rash of shit.

But now she stood with the pool car's keyring hooked over one finger, wearing a black leather mini-shirt—too short for his liking—her black knee-high boots with a heel, and a very snug camisole with Harley-Davidson emblem that pushed her tits up enough to make them look bigger than they were.

She'd probably be tucking that bottle opener in her cleavage again and those motherfuckers would be tempted to touch her there.

He closed his eyes and sucked in a breath, then realized

he was missing out on eavesdropping on her and Rez's conversation.

He tipped his cell phone up and visually scanned the app. Some words were missing but he got the basics of the conversation. They were talking about the differences of culinary dishes between their two cultures. His being Venezuelan and hers being Columbian.

Rez promised to bring her some of his mother's cooking. Excited about his offer, she began speaking so fast, the app couldn't pick up on most of it.

Crew had to admit, Carmen Alvarez's cooking was some of the best. Any time he could snag an invite to sit at her table, he took it.

Suddenly a hand flashed in front of his face and snagged his phone.

"What the fuck?" Finn yelled and hooted behind him.

Crew surged to his feet and tried to grab it back, but Finn danced out of the way, twisting and turning to avoid him.

There went his goddamn secret. And his advantage.

"Hey, this asshole is listening in on your conversation by using a translation app," Finn announced loudly, lifting Crew's cell phone in the air over his head.

"Give me my phone back," Crew hissed.

Finn wagged a finger at him and clicked his tongue. "You shouldn't listen in on someone's conversation without them knowing, you sneaky fucker."

Cami stared at the phone in Finn's hand with her eyebrows pinned together. "You were using your phone to translate our conversation?"

Fuck. "I'm—"

"Of course he is! I also caught him using Duolingo," Torres snitched loudly from the other side of the room.

For fuck's sake! Did no one have any loyalty to their leader around here?

Cami's eyes swung from Torres to him. "You're learning Spanish? I know you don't like us speaking it around you because you feel left out, but isn't that a bit drastic?"

"Are you that fucking paranoid, J. Crew?" Decker asked on a laugh.

"Fuck off. I'm not paranoid! It can't hurt to learn."

"Can an old dog learn new tricks?" Cami teased. "Let's see..." She spoke very slowly, "*¡Hola!¿Cómo estás? Me llamo Cami. ¿Y tú?*"

"Even I know that much," Crew grumbled.

"Then tell me... what did I say?"

"Hello. How are you? My name is Cami. And you?" he translated, finally getting a chance to grab back his phone from Finn. He locked it and shoved it in his back pocket.

"Hey, your name is Cami, too?" she asked with a laugh. "What are the odds?"

"No. *Mi nombre es Crew.*"

Torres yelled out, "Look at you, now fluent! Better watch out, the agency might put you undercover with a cartel."

"I'm no expert. I remember that much from high school," Crew announced.

Decker smirked. "They taught Spanish in school in the early 1900s?"

"Why are you learning Spanish now, Crewella?" A grin curled Rez's lips as he cocked an eyebrow toward Cami.

"It's the second most spoken language in this country. That's why."

He ignored the laughter and hoots.

"Are you sure you don't have another reason?" Torres tilted his head and also raised his eyebrows.

"I don't need another fucking reason."

"We've known each other for years and you've never bothered to learn it for me," Rez said, then pouted and gave him sad puppy dog eyes.

Crew needed to change the subject. And quickly. "Anyway..." He turned to Cami to see her lips pinned together and the corners of her eyes crinkled. He was sure he'd hear about this later. "Can you stick around before heading to Hawg Wild?"

Chapter Thirty

Cami's amusement quickly fled. "Is something up?"

"We're about to have a quick task force meeting. I figured it would be good for you to join in."

She glanced at her cell phone. "Since they don't have a time clock, I'm sure no one will miss me being a little late."

"The Demons don't know the word punctual," came from out of thin air.

"Ladies and... *ladies*... Ghost and Kitten have joined us." Crew called out, wearing a smirk.

Finn *pspspsps*'d, then meowed.

A groan could be heard through the speaker phone sitting in the center of the conference table. "Yeah. We're here and we've been listening in to Crew's downfall." Fletch chuckled.

"How's the new apartment?" Crew rushed to ask to steer the conversation away from his so-called downfall.

"Compared to my house? It sucks. Can we wrap up this fucking investigation soon? I miss my pool and my own bed."

"Hey, it's not easy finding rentals right now. Especially

with the budget the agency gave me. Just be glad you're not living in a camper down by the river."

Decker burst out in laughter.

"Does that mean something?" Cami asked.

"She's probably too young to know that SNL skit," Torres said.

"SNL as in Saturday Night Live?" she asked him.

"Yeah," the plant manager answered. "Do a search on YouTube for SNL and Chris Farley. You'll get sucked down a rabbit hole and you won't regret it."

Rez did the sign of the cross. "Gone too soon."

"Amen," Torres murmured.

"Can we get this meeting started?" Nox asked impatiently.

"You in a rush?" Finn asked him.

"Got somewhere I need to be soon."

He either had a therapy appointment or a grief support group meeting to attend. Either way, Crew didn't care if he went in the middle of a workday as long as he went. And kept going.

"Before we get started on the official business... Any signs of T-Bone, Ghost?" Decker asked Fletch.

"None. I haven't seen him or even heard his name mentioned once. I saw another prospect coming in and out of that first room in their quarters. I just want to confirm that was T-Bone's, right?"

"Yeah." Decker turned to Cami. "Have you seen or heard about the prospect at Hawg Wild?"

"Not a word." She slid into a seat at the conference table while tugging her skirt down to prevent flashing the whole team.

Crew sure as fuck hoped she was wearing underwear. Iron underwear. With a lock.

"At this point, my guess is they eighty-sixed him," Fletch said, pulling Crew out from under Cami's skirt and back to the conversation at hand.

"Good," Decker said.

"Couldn't happen to a nicer asshole," Finn said next.

"That'll be one less burden on the taxpayers," Nox said from his office chair over at one of the desks.

"If the Demons got rid of him, I really hope they got *rid* of him. The Earth will be a little bit safer for women," Decker said.

"Losing one asshole doesn't make much of a dent in that department," Wilder told them through the conference phone.

"True," Cami agreed. "Plenty of other entitled men out there who think we can't survive without them. Or don't understand the word no."

"Or 'fuck off,'" Wilder added. "I swear these Demons are the worst, too. I can be standing right next to Fletch and they still try to pull shit with me."

"How many fingers have you broken?" Finn asked.

"Apparently not enough for them to get the message," Wilder answered. "But most of them are pretty fucking dense."

"Aren't you protecting your ol' lady, Ghost?" Crew asked.

"Excuse me?" Wilder's shout filled the room. "I certainly don't need Fletch protecting me. I'm capable of doing that on my own, fuck you very much."

"We're not simpering females who collapse with the vapors when we're challenged," Cami stated.

Finn snorted. "The vapors?"

"Try Google," Cami suggested. "It's a search engine found on the internet. It's like a Magic 8 Ball. You ask it a question and it gives you an answer."

"Damn." Wilder laughed. "I'll have to remember that one."

"Okay," Crew started, "do you have anything to share, Fletch, on your end, now that you've been with the Demons for a few weeks? Wilder, feel free to add anything since I know you've been working on getting the ol' ladies to trust you."

"Working is right," Wilder answered before her partner could. "They are tight-lipped. Either because they're protective of their club or they truly don't know shit."

"Technically, the members aren't supposed to share club business with their women," Decker said. "So, it would be no surprise if they were truly clueless on what those fuckwads are doing."

"It's pretty easy to figure it out," Fletch began. "What they're doing is expanding their drug business. That said, they haven't completely cut out the Russos yet, but they're heading in that direction. From what I've overheard, they've made a deal with the cartel to buy extra kilos every time they head down to the border for the Russos. Of course, they're keeping that from La Cosa Nostra. I think they want to build their enterprise as much as possible before they completely cut them out. They believe the more money they make and the more they expand their territory, it'll make them invincible."

Wilder picked up from there. "They couldn't be more wrong. First of all, I doubt the Russos give a shit about them expanding their territory as long as the Demons don't step on their toes by moving into Pittsburgh itself. However, the other MCs in that surrounding area, like the Angels and the Knights, will. But the Russos *will* care that they're buying extra kilos because that could mean less sales to their own street dealers."

"If the Demons keep going the direction they are, they're going to have more than one enemy," Nox murmured.

"They'll have a minimum of three, depending on how far they try to push it," Crew surmised. "Only out of those three, who will crush those assholes first?"

"Don't forget us," Finn reminded him. "You're only considering the MCs and the Mafia. We're also breathing down their neck."

"Right," Crew agreed, "we're the only ones who know every damn thing they're up to. Of course, the Dirty Angels have an idea—which is why they let Fletch and Wilder go under with them—but they don't know all the details. And we don't want them to."

Fletch spoke next. "Right now the Russos have no clue that they're being cut out, but they'll discover it before long. How soon can we get indictments rolling and at least take the biggest players into custody before the shit hits the fan?"

"Depends how fast the Russos find out they're getting fucked." That might not be a good answer but it was the only one Crew had. "And you know what it takes to get indictments."

It wasn't like filling out a simple form. It was a complex legal process.

"That's what I figured. Then we need to prepare and do what we can to minimize the mess. Because when it happens, my gut instinct is screaming that no one will be safe from the splatter."

Fletch's gut instinct was solid in that respect. Crew feared the same results.

"Another problem is, once the indictments come down, we need to round up everyone in one shot and when they're least expecting it. But we also need the charges to stick so our evidence has to be rock solid," Crew reminded them. That evidence also needed to be rock solid for the grand jury to indict in the first place. But all of them in that room and on the other end of that phone already knew that.

"Brother, we have transcripts and video. Plus, first-hand knowledge," Decker told him. "We have enough right now to put away their major players."

"And that's all well and good, but I'd like to cast a wider net. And I'm not the only one, if you catch my meaning." His higher-ups wanted to put away as many as possible. They wanted to make a major dent in the meth trafficking business. "We don't want many, if any, of the Demons left free. They'll only need a handful to continue doing what they're doing and to start rebuilding their club again. It's like cutting off a weed at the ground. It'll grow back. Dig out the fucking root, and it's gone forever."

"Or spray it with goddamn Round-Up," Nox suggested.

Wilder's voice could be heard through the phone. "We have our own version of Round-Up. It's called an early morning sweep like the FBI did with New York's five biggest crime families back in 2011. Not sure if any of you remember that, but they used eight hundred agents and law enforcement officers to haul in a shitload of members from the Bonanno, Colombo, Gambino, Genovese and Luchese families. In one shot, they snagged the small fish to the big whales in one hell of a net. It was a huge and impressive coordinated effort."

"You actually remember that, Wilder?" Torres asked, surprised.

"No, but I studied that case and some others to prepare me for going undercover with the Russos."

"My woman's a badass," Fletch bragged.

"So is mine," Decker said.

"And mine," added Rez.

"Don't forget mine," Finn said next.

Decker smirked at Crew. "Crew? Got anything to say on that point?"

Crew set his jaw and scraped a hand through his hair. "Yeah. Let me schedule a meeting with Williams and let him take this info up the ladder. I'll press the fact that the Demons cutting out La Cosa Nostra will cause an explosion. That alone should be enough for the higher-ups to swallow a whole bottle of heartburn preventative. Last thing they want is to let three MCs and the Pittsburgh Mafia get into messy war. It won't be good optics for the feds if we were capable of heading that off. As it always happens, shit like this is never neatly contained. The casualties won't be limited to the criminals we don't want to see the light of day ever again. Some innocent bystanders could get caught in the crossfire."

If Decker expected another response, he wasn't getting it.

"Fletch and Wilder," he called out, "make sure you email me everything you have on this shit show. Don't leave out even the smallest detail. While I want to take these fuckers down, I also want to make sure our asses are covered." He turned to Torres. Since he was the plant manager, the man was in charge of the wiretaps and transcripts. "Make sure we aren't missing anything. Again, the smallest detail might not seem like anything but sometimes it's the most important. Anything you think I need to see in those transcripts, make sure you point them out to me."

Torres gave him a single nod. "Got it. It can't hurt to put extra people on listening in and transcribing."

A few groans circled the room.

"Yeah, I know transcribing sucks, but it's important work," Torres told them.

"Agreed," Crew said. "I'm also going to set up a meeting with the leaders of both group one and three to compare notes and make sure we're not missing anything."

"If the Demons keep growing as fast as they are, we'll be getting out of this rat hole and back into my house sooner than later," Fletch announced.

Crew glanced over at Cami at that news. She met his eyes and slightly lifted one eyebrow in response.

She should start looking for another place. It had been hard enough for him to find Fletch and Wilder a crappy apartment, so finding something nice would be even more difficult. Decent rentals were getting snapped up almost immediately.

At worst, she could swap places with Fletch and move into that apartment temporarily until she found something better.

Or...

He considered Rez across the table. His brother frowned back at him, probably wondering why Crew was staring at him.

Another option might be that she could rent a room in Carmen Alvarez's house for a short stint. Rez's mom would probably love the company and they could speak Spanish with each other until their throats were sore.

Plus, Cami definitely wouldn't starve. She'd be eating damn good.

But that would be a last resort, as he definitely didn't want Rez riding his fucking ass right now. He had enough on his plate with this latest task force news.

"All right, anything else?" he asked.

His question was greeted with silence and a few head shakes.

He clapped his hands together. "Then let's get back to being the Demons' worst nightmare."

"Fuck yeah," fellow DEA agent, Luke Rodgers shouted.

"We'll do our part. Later, brothers," Fletch called out before hanging up.

When everyone in attendance got up from the table or turned back to their desks, Cami carefully rose from her seat, once again tugging at her skirt.

If she had to keep doing that, maybe she shouldn't fucking wear something so goddamn short.

Crew swallowed all of that down and instead, pulled in a calming breath.

Torres released a low whistle. "Damn, woman, you're probably beating those Neanderthals off with their own clubs."

Crew scowled at him. "How's the wife and kids, Torres?" The man hadn't made a comment about her outfit earlier when she first came upstairs. He was only trying to get Crew to react. And of course, Crew did like an idiot.

Torres shot him a grin. "Just because I'm married and a father, doesn't make me blind."

"Your wife might blind you if she finds out you're eyeing up other woman," Crew warned.

"I'm appreciating, not ogling."

"Your better half might not agree."

"Anyway..." Cami said loudly. "*Gracias por el cumplido,* Torres."

"*De nada. Cualquier cosa para molestar al jefe.*"

Crew knew that *jefe* meant boss so they were clearly talking about him. He'd repeat what Torres said into his translator app later when no one was watching. Or listening.

"Be safe out there," Nox said to her.

"Always," Cami replied, giving him a smile. Her eyes

flicked to Crew in an unspoken message before heading out the door.

As soon as, "Make sure to check in with me whenever you can," slipped out of him, every muscled locked and his asshole pinched shut from his obvious fuck-up.

Nox's gaze slid from the closed door to Crew.

Was the man actually smirking?

"Shut up," Crew grumbled.

Nox threw up his hands. "I didn't say shit."

Oh yeah, he was smirking. A quick glance around the room proved that everyone else was, too. "Your thoughts are loud enough that I can hear them."

Rez hooted loudly and fell forward laughing. "Nox might not say shit, but the rest of us won't hold the fuck back."

Crew jabbed a finger in his direction and warned, "You don't need to say shit, either."

"How the mighty have fallen." Decker snickered.

"Fuck off. All of you. I didn't say anything to her that I wouldn't say to you all."

Rodgers barked out a laugh.

"I thought you wore some kind of herb or garlic concoction around your neck to ward off women?" Finn asked.

"He sure as fuck does and only removes it when he wants to get laid," Decker answered.

"Did you lose it?" Finn asked. "I figured you would have it padlocked around your neck."

Crew got to his feet. "I didn't lose shit. I wouldn't be a good leader if I didn't worry about my team."

"Damn, brother." Finn's smirk was now a full-blown smile. "You know what's so great about him falling for her?"

Though, he wasn't the one being asked, Crew interjected, anyway. "I didn't fall for anyone."

"Is that she won't take any of his shit," Finn finished.

"She's his karma," Nox announced, not hiding his amusement with this whole thing. "Karma Cabrera."

"Oh yeah, he deserves someone like her. Someone who can serve him the same shit he dishes out. I'm fucking *loving* this," Decker crowed.

At least someone was.

Chapter Thirty One

AFTER HAVING a meeting with both the leaders of the other task force groups as well as Bob Williams, what happened next was now officially out of his hands.

Unfortunately, the wheels of bureaucracy, as well as justice, moved slowly.

All he could do was report his group's findings and hope for the best. Luckily, Williams had a good head on his shoulders and also recognized what a mess it could be if the Russos got a wild hair up their ass and decided to take out the Deadly Demons MC.

Crew could guarantee the Russos would get a wild hair up their ass. No way would they sit on their hands after finding out the Demons were about to screw them out of money. And possibly their cartel connection.

Hell no, they would burn the Earth down in retaliation and the Demons were too fucking stupid to realize that they weren't playing with fire. They were playing with C4 explosives.

The Demons might think they were irreplaceable, but they were dead wrong. Plenty of other organizations were okay with hauling their asses down to the border to make a shitload of money simply by being a powerful Mafia's bitch.

And those dumbasses might soon find that out the hard way.

If the carnage would only be contained to their MC, Crew, and most likely his superiors, wouldn't give a shit.

It would be a case of "too bad, so sad."

But anyone who'd dealt with this kind of criminal organization in the past knew better.

Stray shrapnel could be just as damaging and deadly as the explosion itself.

Either way, whether the Russos took out the Demons or the feds did, the investigation would soon be coming to an end.

He looked forward to it on one hand and didn't on the other.

Once the investigation concluded, he had no idea what, or even where, he'd be assigned next.

He liked his team. He liked the fact a bunch of his BAMC brothers worked with him on that team.

He also really liked the team member he just finished fucking. The woman not afraid to go toe to toe with outlaw bikers and, despite his original doubts, ended up being an asset to the investigation.

In reality, Cami, as a newer agent, could end up being assigned somewhere else, too. Like far away from him.

Could he do something about that?

He wasn't sure. But what he did know was he wasn't ready to let her go anywhere.

And if she was assigned anywhere other than the Pittsburgh office, he couldn't follow. He needed to stay close to his kids. He also had his BAMC brotherhood.

His life was here.

If the agency ever insisted he move, he would retire and get a damn job at a fast food restaurant first. Luckily, Williams knew that Crew's family came first.

"Hello."

He blinked and stared down at her very relaxed face. "Hey."

"You know you're still inside me, right?"

He wouldn't be for long.

With a groan, he held the condom securely around the root of his cock and pulled out. Before he could roll it off and dispose of it, she stopped him by cupping his cheek. "You are too damn handsome for your own good."

Where the hell did that come from? "I can't help it, it comes naturally. On that note, how did you get to be so damn gorgeous?"

"It comes naturally." She added, "Just ignore the big makeup bag in the bathroom."

He searched her face. "You're not wearing any makeup now and you're still beautiful as fuck."

"Wait... Are you being a smart ass?" With her bottom lip tucked between her teeth, she stared up at him.

"No, I'm being serious."

His heart thumped heavily in his chest. Since leaving Sasha, he'd done everything to prevent getting involved with another woman long-term.

He had failed spectacularly.

He hadn't lied when he said she was gorgeous, but she was so much more than her looks. She was the complete fucking package.

She grinned up at him. "Then I'll take the compliment.

Do we need to come up with some sort of signal between us for when we're being serious?"

"What would be the fun in that? I think we need to keep each other guessing." He rolled off both her and the bed, removing the condom before it slipped off from his quickly deflating cock and landed on Fletch's carpet, leaking his DNA everywhere.

A few minutes later, after heading to the bathroom to dispose of the full condom and clean himself up, he climbed back in bed with her.

When he sat against the headboard, she shifted until her head was in his lap and her silky dark hair spread over his bare thighs. He combed his fingers through it while contemplating how to start the conversation they needed to have.

And he could no longer avoid.

"The investigation is winding down. You gave us plenty of good shit from Hawg Wild. Names, evidence and even the location of where they keep their stash. I couldn't ask for anything more. Because of that, the team will be storming that location and arresting any Demon on site when the sweep happens."

Her fingers trailed lazily up and down his arm. "Good. I'm glad I could make a difference."

"You no longer have to go in there. Your undercover assignment is finished."

"I figured you were leading up to that. It'll be nice to go back to a normal sleep pattern."

"You did good, Cami. Despite my worry."

"You didn't need to worry about me," she reminded him.

"Easier said than done."

"Are you bringing this up now because you're preparing me for the fact I'll soon be evicted from this beautiful house with the very awesome pool?" she asked.

"That'll be one of the changes."

"That's a major one. What's the rest? Besides learning that I never want to be some outlaw biker's ol' lady. Or a sweet butt. Or work in a bar full of smoke again. It's going to take my lungs a while to recover."

The rest of the changes had to do with them. As in *them*. The two of them. And a possible future with each other.

But before he could talk about a *them*, he needed to be honest with her and lay it all out on the table so she could make the best decision for herself.

He'd had a vasectomy when Dylan was about two and he realized his marriage was doomed. He didn't tell Sasha, he only said he had to go out of town for an assignment and he got it done. He didn't want to risk bringing another child into, what was by then, their irrevocably broken marriage. It was bad enough their two children were already affected by their tumultuous relationship.

He also couldn't pretend he loved Sasha or was attracted to her anymore. Her ugliness on the inside marred her beauty on the outside. That was when he stopped having sex with her, as well. Of course, that led to the accusations of him cheating when in truth, it was her.

Gaslighting at its fucking finest.

After the shit he went through with Sasha, and was still going through, he never expected to get into any serious relationship again.

Even with a woman like Cami.

Especially with a woman like Cami.

Even if they were perfect for each other, he could never give her children, if that was something she wanted.

He needed to tell her now before things went any further. Because if she was dead set on becoming a mother in the future, it would not be with his children.

Could he have his vasectomy reversed? Maybe. Sometimes it worked, sometimes it didn't. It was a crapshoot.

But the real question was... Did he want more children?

Would it be fair to the two he already had? Would it be fair to any future children? While technically he wasn't too old to have them, that didn't mean he should.

If she really wanted children, they plausibly could adopt. Cross and his husband Nash had done that. Decker also adopted Valee Girl. And Crew was damn sure it wouldn't be long before Sloane adopted her, too.

Axel Jamison's kids were his by blood but born from a surrogate. His wife Bella couldn't have children of her own due to tragic circumstances. They found a creative way to make it work with the cooperation of family.

No matter what, Crew's children would be his children whether born from his sperm or not. Once he claimed them as his, they would be his forever.

But still...

Was that what he wanted?

It was a discussion they needed to have. Especially since he was going to broach the subject of him spending the rest of his life with her.

And find out if she wanted to do the same with him.

They might not be quite at that point yet, but he could see they were traveling in that direction and how she took the news might determine if they continued on that path.

Or if they slammed on the brakes.

He worried that even if she said she was fine with not having a family of her own now, she still had a good fifteen years to change her mind. What would happen ten years from now if she decided to find someone able to give her what she wanted?

Was he willing to take that risk?

Or would she stay with him and slowly become bitter because he couldn't give her everything she wanted?

He did not want a repeat of his relationship with Sasha.

They'd only known each other for about three months. Rushing into a relationship wasn't a good basis to start a future together.

He wasn't young and easily swayed. He was seasoned. He'd been there, done that, had the divorce, alimony and child support papers to prove it. If he was going to get into any kind of serious relationship again, he wanted to be one-hundred percent sure about it first.

And that led him back to letting her know, if things kept moving forward with the two of them, he could never give her children. That could be her deciding factor. She'd have time to walk away before things between them got any deeper.

While he didn't want her to walk away, he also didn't want to hold her back.

Even so, he had to be careful on how he brought it up, since she might not be on the same page. He could be making more of this than he needed to if she didn't want anything more from him than what she was already getting.

His cock.

And a few orgasms.

"I had a vasectomy," he blurted out.

Oh, for fuck's sake!

He groaned, dropped his head and pinched his forehead.

Silence met his admission. For one pounding heartbeat, then a second.

"Okay? Are you saying we can forego the condoms? I mean, there are other reasons to use them."

He lifted his head to see her eyes on him. "Yes. I know..."

"And I'm on birth control, of course."

That he didn't know but assumed.

She continued with, "I'm not one to let a man go bareback without taking other precautions."

Jesus fucking Christ. "I just wanted you to know because—"

"I mean, if this is going to continue between us, I guess we both can get tested. Is that why you brought it up?"

No. "Yes." He grimaced. *Christ almighty.* "No."

"Then, why?"

"Because you need to know I had a fucking vasectomy years ago, Cami."

"You said that."

"I can't have any more children."

She blinked at him, and her dark eyebrows pulled together. "Okay? Are you regretting that decision? Why are you telling me this?"

"Children might be important to you."

She blinked again. Then her eyebrows shot up her forehead and her mouth turned into an O. "Wait..." She jackknifed up from his lap and sat cross-legged, facing him.

He stared up at the ceiling. "I can't give you kids."

"Crew..."

"That's not fair to you," he continued.

"Colin..."

"You have your whole life ahead of you."

"So do you. I only joke about you being old to get under your skin."

"You succeeded. But in a way I never expected." He pulled in a breath and finally met her confusion-filled eyes. "I want you, Cami. I want to be with you. But here's the thing... I don't want you to be with me and then regret it later. I don't want you to hold it against me that you can't have everything you've ever wanted. I admit I can be a dick but despite that, I don't want to be selfish and ever hold you back. Or make you regret choices you made on a whim."

Her head jerked back. "A *whim?* Do you think I'm a flighty, sex-crazed teenager unable to make good decisions?" Her voice raising an octave was not a good sign.

"No, that's not—"

"Do you have this mistaken notion that you'd be holding me back because you can't knock me up?"

Wouldn't he, though? "Don't most women want children?"

Her mouth opened and hung there for a second before snapping shut again. "I don't know, Crew. I haven't taken a poll. Apparently, you haven't, either. Instead of worrying about 'most' women, how about asking the woman here in bed with you? The one you're apparently considering a future with if you're bringing this up. That's why you're bringing it up, right?"

"It's crossed my mind."

He grimaced as she rolled her eyes and sighed.

Shit. He was blowing this already. He needed to be straight with her since he'd want that from her. "Do you want kids?"

"Before I answer that, aren't vasectomies reversible?"

"Some are. There's no guarantee. And even if mine was, I'm forty-three, Cami. I don't want to start over with babies in my mid-forties. I have my eye on retirement, not diapers. More importantly, I have two kids I'm already fighting for. I never want them to feel like they've been replaced."

"You would never do that."

"You're right, I wouldn't. But despite that, they might think I would. It wouldn't matter what I said or did, Sasha would tell them otherwise. I can't risk that. I cannot lose my kids." The thought of alienating his kids caused an ache deep within his chest. He rubbed at it.

She grabbed his hand, stopping him. "I'm sorry she did that to you. To them. That's not fair to any of you."

"I will never give up."

"I know."

"So, I need an answer... Do you want children, or have you ever considered having them down the road?"

Chapter Thirty Two

"Do you want children, or have you ever considered having them down the road?"

Cami interlaced her fingers with his and squeezed.

She was not expecting this topic tonight. This was *heading-into-a-serious-relationship* type of talk.

Did she want that with him?

She carefully considered the man before her. The one she had not expected to want that kind of relationship with in the first place.

But her answer was quite clear. Yes. Yes, she did.

She appreciated him being honest with her before they actually made it official. She understood that he was trying to prevent giving her future heartbreak. But in reality, if they went their separate ways now, she'd still suffer from it. And suffer badly.

This man had no idea that he owned her heart already.

But despite her feelings for him, she had to be careful with her answer. "Of course I've considered it." When he tried to extract his hand, she held on tighter. "I'm not finished. As a child, I was never one to carry around a doll and pretend it was my baby. In fact, I never was into dolls, or dressing up, or any kind of what could be considered 'girly' things. Instead, I looked up to my father and envied both him and his career. By the time you met me at ten, I already knew I wanted to follow in his footsteps and not my mother's. Is there anything wrong with being a wife and mother? Absolutely not. I love and respect her. I also recognize that being a good mother is damn hard work. Thankless, too. But truthfully, I never had that instinct."

"Never," he murmured.

"No."

"But that could change."

"But that could change," she agreed. She wasn't going to lie about it. That would do neither of them any good. "I come from a big family. I'm not sure if you know this, but I have four younger siblings. Growing up with seven people in your household can be chaotic and overwhelming. Some people love it and want to repeat that with their own family. Some," she shrugged, "do not. I prefer my chaos limited to my career, not my home life."

"When I met you back then, I sympathized with your father, thinking he would have his hands full with you alone and then he mentioned you weren't an only child. But I do remember him saying you were the oldest of four, not five."

"I'm sure he would accept your sympathies. I think there were some nights he regretted not having a vasectomy, too." She laughed softly. "Especially after the fifth, Gabriel, who was an *oops* baby."

"The exact reason I got a vasectomy. But my *oops* was marrying Sasha."

"Crew, you need to take some of the blame. You either ignored the red flags or didn't look closely enough."

He nodded. "You're right. I rushed into a decision when I shouldn't have. I don't want to make that mistake again."

"I understand that's the reason for this discussion. You want to make sure all your T's are crossed and your I's dotted."

"Basically. I don't want to travel a path that may lead to a dead end. I slammed into that wall before. It's painful."

"And if I want children, that's your wall." She continued before giving him a chance to respond, "Look, I'm at the start of my career. Maybe when I'm well established, I could decide I also want a family, but as of now, I don't."

His chest rose and fell as disappointment filled his face. "I can't risk you changing your mind."

"Because you're being upfront with me, I'll be completely upfront with you. If I choose you, Crew, it's because I choose you as you are. Despite not wanting more children of your own, you have two who might give you grandchildren."

"But would grandchildren be enough for you? Again, I don't want this to continue if eventually I won't be enough. I don't want to go through that again. I *can't* go through that again. It was a rough road I don't want to travel again."

"Well, the good thing about grandchildren is you can spend time with them and get your baby fix, but you always give them back. You can spoil them and—" Her head jerked and her brain glitched. "What the fuck? How did we get here? Why are you making me think about being a grandmother? I'm only twenty-eight years old!"

His lips twitched. "You're not ready to be called Grandma?"

"No!" she shouted.

"Grammy?"

"Crew..."

"How about Nanna?"

"Fuck you."

He chuckled. "You'd be one hot GILF."

She shoved his arm. "Gross."

He grabbed her hand and pulled her into him. "C'mon, Granny, give me some."

"Ew!" She broke free and jumped out of bed. "Shut up!"

He popped out of bed and stalked toward her. "Yank out your dentures and give me some head."

"Crew!"

As he went to tackle her, she spun and hit a wall of hair, tripping over Murphy as the poor dog tried to scoot out of her way. She crash landed on the floor. Hard.

"Did you break a hip? Should I grab your walker, Grandma?" he asked, dropping to his knees at her side, then moving to straddle her waist. He clamped his hands around her wrists, pulled them over her head and pinned them to the floor. He went nose to nose with her, his gray eyes full of mischief. "Now I have you where I want you."

"On the floor?"

"I'll take you wherever I can get you." His gravelly tone shot a shiver down her spine.

"You sound desperate."

"Desperately in love with you."

Her lungs seized and his gray eyes went wide.

She bit her bottom lip and he straightened, releasing her wrists.

Was he panicking? He looked as if he was panicking.

"Crew," she whispered. "Are you... Is it true?"

"That's not something I would joke about, Cami. It's why I brought the whole vasectomy thing up."

"I thought it was because you wanted us to be exclusive, not because you loved me."

"Why would I want to be exclusive if I didn't love you?"

She rolled her eyes. "But how is loving me tied directly to your vas deferens?"

"Very funny. And I explained that already."

"Fine. You're worried that I'll change my mind down the road. That I'll feel I'm missing out. And then I'll leave you, leaving you broken-hearted and devastated. You will walk the Earth flagellating yourself as you mourn my loss for the rest of your life."

"Jesus Christ. Let's not go overboard," he muttered. "The truth is, I don't want to hold you back. Not ever."

She reached up and stroked his bearded jawline. Since they were lobbing truth bombs... "And I love you for that."

His nostrils flared at her admission. But he didn't look happy about it, he looked even more worried. "I don't want to ruin this."

"You won't."

"I don't want you to have regrets."

"Life is full of regrets," she countered.

"I don't want you to ever leave me."

"I knew it!" she exclaimed. "You need someone young enough to push your wheelchair, wipe the drool from your lips and change your diapers."

He closed his eyes and shook his head. "If someone has to, I want it to be you stuck doing it."

She laughed. "Well, if I don't get to change baby diapers, I might as well change adult ones. Right?"

"That's the spirit."

"Well, you know... I *am* a team player."

"Cami, I need an answer."

"Whether I want to break up with you now or later?"

He closed his eyes and sighed. When he opened them again, he said, "Basically, yes. But it wouldn't be a break up since we aren't officially a couple yet."

"Oh, I think that ship has sailed already. When's the last time we haven't woken up in the same bed, other than the weekends you get your kids?"

"Does sharing a bed almost every night automatically turn it into a relationship?"

"It's more than sharing a bed. I've never fucked anyone as much as I have fucked you. That has to count for something."

"For fuck's sake," he muttered.

"Well, we *were* doing it for the sake of fucking but now—"

"Cami," he growled.

She pressed her lips together for a few seconds. Once she could keep from giggling, she said, "Fine. But if I tell you I don't want kids, am I going to be stuck with you forever?"

"Yes."

"That seems like a long time."

"That's the point."

"The good part about you being *so much* older is your forever will be shorter than mine. I can shop for a newer model once you're gone."

He inhaled deeply, then on the exhale muttered, "I need to rethink this."

"Give it five minutes. You'll forget this whole conversation."

"Someone needs a spanking."

She grinned. "Is that someone me?"

"It certainly isn't me."

"*Huh.* Your brothers told me you do a lot of spanking when you're by yourself."

"Can we get serious here?"

"I guess so."

"Then?" he prodded.

Was he holding his breath while waiting for her answer? *Damn*, he *really* wanted this. Wanted her. For forever. *Holy shit.*

Forever was a long time but she couldn't imagine spending one minute without him. "Crew..." When she cupped his cheek, suspicion filled his eyes. He expected her to make another smart-ass comment instead of being serious. But this *was* serious. She was serious. About him. "Crew..."

His jaw tightened. "Jesus fucking Christ, Cami..."

"I choose you."

His expression relaxed. "You'll have to accept my kids."

"I'm aware of that."

"And deal with my ex being a..."

"Pain?"

"That wasn't how I was going to describe her."

"I know. But are you trying to talk me out of it?"

"Fuck no," he answered. "You said you choose me, but I wanted to remind you that I come along with baggage."

"Again, I'm aware. If I can deal with those Demons, I can deal with your ex. And your kids will come around. I've met them a few times now. They're good kids at heart, they're just being steered in the wrong direction. If they're anything like you, they'll figure out what's been in front of their face the whole time." She lifted an eyebrow to emphasize the double meaning of that last sentence.

He dropped his weight down, pressing her harder into the floor, and swept the hair away from her face. "Do you promise to love me forever? 'Til death do us part?"

"Or until a major diaper blow out. Then I'll have real regrets."

"In turn, I'll promise to hold off on shitting my pants as long as possible."

She grinned. "Can't ask for more than that."

His gray eyes met hers and held. "I never thought I'd be in this position again."

"On the floor? Will you need help getting up?"

"I need no help getting it up."

"Don't jinx yourself. I can live without having kids, I'm not sure I can live without your cock."

"Since it's attached to me, I come along with it."

"If you must... Now, can you kiss me to seal this deal?"

"If I must..."

She lifted her head as he lowered his and when their mouths met and their tongues touched, there was something in that kiss that made her believe he would do everything in his power to make her happy for the rest of her life.

She planned on doing the same.

She came to Pittsburgh for her job, never in her wildest dreams thinking she'd fall in love. But here she was... Here they were...

Kissing on a floor in the bedroom of a house owned by his MC brother and fellow task force member.

In all these weeks she had never once been to Crew's place. That would soon change. Though, she might need to find a place of her own until his kids accepted her in their father's life. She was okay with not living together until her footing was solid with them. Because she had no doubt that Sasha would make a big deal when it came to Crew moving on and would use their age difference to try to cause problems.

However, they'd deal with it. Together.

They continued to kiss until they were both breathless, he was rock hard and she was wet.

But being naked on the floor meant condoms weren't in reach, so they'd have to consummate the next step in their relationship once some were nearby. She made a mental note to schedule tests for both of them so they could have no barriers between them.

She had found her "forever man" when she hadn't even been looking. She was going to take that as this was meant to be.

Once he broke the seal on their lip lock, he pressed a soft kiss on her forehead, before lifting his head. "By the way, I was right."

"About?"

"You being a handful."

"Why are women who take charge of their own life considered a handful? My parents raised us to be independent free thinkers and to stand up for ourselves."

"I wouldn't want you any other way. Honestly, I hope my kids grow up to be the same."

"I know you'll do your best to make sure they do."

He sighed softly. "Sometimes my best isn't good enough when other factors are involved."

"You're pretty damn stubborn. You'll never give up. Especially when it comes to your kids."

"And you," he added.

"I can't ask for anything more."

"You can ask for a lot more."

"Then I'll make a list."

"I'm not Santa."

She plucked at his hair. "You keep graying like you are, you'll look like him soon. But, hell, you'd be the hottest damn Santa I've ever seen. Especially when you're eating my cookies by the Christmas tree."

He slid down her naked body. "I don't think I can wait until Christmas to taste test those cookies."

She lifted her head as he dropped his between her thighs, asking, "What's your favorite flavor?"

"It's a spicy cookie called Camila."

"Oh good. I have a fresh batch of those."

"And they smell fucking delicious." He dragged his tongue through her pussy. "Taste delicious, too."

Chapter Thirty-Three

"You CAN GO IN NOW, SIR," Williams' executive assistant told him.

Crew got up from the uncomfortable chair where he'd had his ass planted for longer than he liked and, without knocking, opened the door to the supervising special agent's office.

He had been summoned.

He figured it had to do with the task force and how they were going to wrap up the investigation. But as soon as he stepped through the doorway, Williams rose from his desk and jerked his chin toward one of the two chairs in front of it. "Have a seat. I'll be right back." Then he stepped through the door Crew just came through and closed it behind him.

What the hell? He already waited over forty minutes. Now he had to wait even longer?

His time was just as valuable as Williams'.

He ground his teeth after sitting alone in the office for five more minutes.

After ten, his knee began to bounce.

At the fifteen-minute mark, the office door finally opened.

Thank fuck.

As he turned in his seat to give Williams a rash of shit, he quickly choked those words back down.

Oh shit.

It wasn't Williams returning to his office.

Crew surged to his feet and scrubbed his suddenly damp palms down the sides of his jeans before spinning around to face the person he least expected.

"Well, there's a man I haven't seen in about eighteen years." Luis Cabrera extended his hand.

Crew took it and gave it a firm shake, hoping his palm wasn't sopping wet. "I can't say the same. Because of your position, I see your picture everywhere." *Including on your daughter's goddamn nightstand.*

"Williams has nothing but praise for you when it comes to the task force you're heading. He's not the only one."

Crew braced. Was Cabrera building him up only to turn around and knock him down? "My team is top-notch."

"I'm a little biased about one of them."

"Which one?" he joked.

Cabrera didn't find that funny. "I trust you're looking out for her."

"She doesn't need it. She's perfectly capable of doing that on her own."

"As a father yourself, you know that you never stop worrying. No matter how old they get. No matter how capable they prove themselves to be. She's still my child. She's still a part of me. And always will be."

Crew pulled in a breath at the underlying warning. "I definitely understand that. I have protected my own from the moment they were born and will continue until the moment I stop breathing."

"As a good father should. And that's why I'm here. I heard some rumors recently."

Oh fuck.

"So, I figured I'd come to Pittsburgh to either confirm or dispel them."

Oh fuck!

"Since neither of the involved parties came to me directly."

Wait. Was Crew supposed to call Cabrera up and tell the man that he'd been sleeping with his daughter?

Hello, sir? I just wanted to give you the heads up I've been banging your daughter.

He assumed Cami would tell her parents about their relationship when she was ready.

Apparently, the gossip grapevine was waiting for no one.

And that fucking grapevine might be strangling Crew soon.

Like in the next few minutes.

Should he stay? Run? Drop to his knees and beg forgiveness?

Pretend he was having a heart attack so the EMTs could help him make his escape?

Or should he just call the coroner and have them on standby?

No, he wasn't a goddamn coward. He needed to face Cami's father like a fucking man and take full responsibility.

"Your record as an agent is a stellar one, Crew. You also impressed me when we worked together eighteen years ago."

Crew pulled his shoulders back and straightened his spine, looking directly in the man's eyes. "I remember."

"When C.C. was only ten and... you were not."

Maybe the whole heart attack thing *was* a better plan. "I remember that, too."

"She has her whole career ahead of her."

"She'll do well with the agency."

"She has her whole life ahead of her, too. In my eyes, she'll always be my baby."

For fuck's sake, he respected the man but not this bullshit guilt trip. Time to end it. "She's not a baby in mine. She's a very strong, capable woman."

"From what I heard, you didn't believe that at first. You thought she was too young and too green for the task force."

"She proved me wrong."

"But despite your belief she was inexperienced, she wasn't too young for *you*."

Shots fired.

"What are you now, forty-three?" Cami's father asked.

The man knew exactly how old he was. He came prepared for this ambush. "I am."

"Divorced. Two kids."

Luis Cabrera had already known that, too. "Yes." Where was he going with this?

"I'd like to have grandchildren someday."

There it was. "I'm sure at least one of your five children will be providing you with that gift."

"It would be nice if all of them did. My wife and I love having a big family. We love having a full house filled with the sound of children laughing and playing..."

Jesus fucking Christ, was the man laying it on thick. "I'm sure my house will sound like that, too, if my children decide to have their own."

"But you're done having any more."

Crew's eyes narrowed. That wasn't a question, that was a

fucking statement. "I'm not sure what this has to do with my position as a senior special agent."

"It has to do with your position with my daughter."

"She's capable of making her own decisions."

"Children always need guidance."

Crew's jaw shifted. "She's not a child."

Cabrera stared at him for a little too long for Crew's liking. "It's difficult not to still think of her as one."

"How about when you attended her graduation from the academy *after* she served her country in the Navy? Did you think of her as a child then, or were you proud of her for following in your footsteps?"

Crew caught the slight flare of the man's nostrils. "I've been proud of everything she's accomplished. I just don't see what a forty-three-year-old man sees in a twenty-eight-year-old besides being able to brag about having an attractive young woman hanging on his arm."

Crew had to remind himself that he *liked* Cabrera, he *respected* him. And he'd get fired if he broke the man's nose with his fist. He also had to tell himself that he might act the same way when it came to his own daughter. "First of all, I don't need to brag about shit. I wasn't looking for eye candy to hang on my arm like an accessory, whether in her twenties, thirties or in her eighties. Second, I see past her age to the woman Cami is. It's a shame you are reducing her to her age."

Pot meet kettle.

"She has her whole life ahead of her and by being with you, she's limiting that life."

"That's for her to decide and she made that decision. I gave her an out. She didn't take it."

"What out was that? Your vasectomy?"

For fuck's sake, how fucking deep did the man dig?

"All my shortcomings you already listed." The inability to

give her children, Sasha and his kids. Luckily, none of those scared her away. He was done with this line of discussion. "Does she know you're in town?" Because if Cami did, she didn't warn him.

"I didn't tell her. I wanted it to be a surprise."

It certainly would be that. "She'll be happy to see you. I can make reservations for dinner somewhere if you plan on staying in the area overnight."

"I plan on staying with C.C. at her place for a few nights to get caught up. I'm sure she won't mind."

That meant Crew would have to sleep at his own place. Alone.

Annoyed, he drew a hand down his beard.

"Is there a problem with that?"

There sure as fuck was. "Not at all. I'll make dinner reservations for the three of us for tonight. Six-thirty work?"

"Perfect."

"Great. But let me say this... I'm letting you get your cuts in now but once we walk out of this office," Crew jabbed his finger toward the closed door, "this conversation doesn't go past that door. Do not bring it with you to dinner. This discussion ends here." He pointed to the floor. That was a warning, not a request. "You don't have to like our relationship, but it's *our* relationship, not yours. You have no say in it, only we do."

"I want what's best for my daughter."

"That makes two of us."

"And you think that's you?"

"No, I don't, but she does. And that's all that matters."

Cabrera tipped his head and studied Crew. He did not avoid the man's gaze but met it head-on.

"You'd fight for her, wouldn't you?"

Did he mean physically? Or metaphorically? Either

way... "I would. And I'd do everything in my power to protect her, too, whether she likes it or not."

"She's a challenge."

And that was news? "I'm aware."

"I want grandchildren."

"Step-grandkids will have to suffice. And even if it doesn't, it's her choice whether to have children or not, not yours."

"You've made that decision for her."

"You raised her to be independent. Do you really think she'd allow me to make that decision for her? I was completely open and honest with her about both my vasectomy and what stage I'm at in my life."

Once more, Luis Cabrera stared at him for far longer than was comfortable. And because of that, Crew wasn't expecting the next statement out of the man's mouth. "You love her."

"I wouldn't still be standing here dealing with the shit you've been shoveling at me if I didn't."

"While you're a good man and a great agent, Crew, I'm not sure you're good for my daughter."

"I guess time will tell."

"And I'll be watching."

"Like any good father would," Crew responded. "I only ask you don't interfere."

"That's a lot to ask."

"Then I won't ask. I'll outright tell you not to interfere. It's a quick and sure way to alienate your daughter if you do."

"You act like you know my daughter better than I do."

"We know her in two different ways. To you, as a child. To me, as a partner. I thank you for everything you've done for her as her father, by raising her and giving her a solid start, but I'll take it from here."

Again, Cami's father didn't say shit for the longest time and only stared at Crew.

After a few more moments, Cabrera said, "I look forward to us reconnecting over dinner. I'm sure we both have eighteen years' worth of stories to tell about our time in the DEA."

What just happened?

Even if it was only a temporary reprieve, it made Crew's chest loosen enough for him to breathe a little easier.

He nodded. "Should be an interesting conversation. I'll let Cami know you're in town. I'm sure you'll hear from her once I do. Now... Am I dismissed or does Williams need me for something else?"

"He doesn't and you are."

Thank fuck.

Crew blinked in surprise when the man extended his hand again. Could this be a truce? Was Cabrera done trying to flay Crew open?

He took it and gave it a firm shake. "See you tonight," Crew said as he stepped around Cami's father so he could get the fuck out of there while the getting was good.

As he did, Cabrera stopped him with, "One more thing... Don't ever call me Dad," and slapped him hard on the back.

Epilogue

"Is that normal?" Cami whispered in Crew's ear.

"What?"

"That the man rides behind the woman. I never saw that before. Not with your MC or with the Demons."

"It is definitely not normal," Crew assured her, glancing over at where Monty straddled her Harley and her boyfriend Clark sat behind her as her backpack. Clueless to the fucking world. And the judgment from the rest of Monty's "brothers."

"Why do I get the feeling you guys bust on him for it?"

"Now why would you think that?" he asked innocently.

"You can't see my eyes rolling," she said, "but you can probably hear them."

"We were told to leave Clark alone."

"And do you?"

"We do our best," he answered.

Cami snorted. "I think it's cute that he rides on her bike instead of his own."

Crew kept his thoughts about that to himself.

"Don't you?"

"*Mmm hmm.*"

"I've never seen a man look at a woman like he does her. He's so enamored with her."

"*Mmm hmm.*"

Cami whacked his arm. "Don't be a jerk."

"Look," he finally said, "the man is so far gone over Monty, I'm sure he doesn't give a fuck what we think." *Or say.*

"He probably doesn't and I'm sure that drives all of you crazy. The man is just living his life and loving his woman. He's obviously content simply spending time with her."

He squeezed her denim-clad knee. "Like I am with mine."

"You don't look at me like that."

"Sure I do. You just don't pay attention."

"Can you go grab my eyeballs? They rolled right out of my head this time."

"Where'd they go?"

"If I could see them, I'd tell you."

"Probably the same place Clark's balls went."

"Crew!"

He shrugged.

"Anyway, now that I know I'm going to be staying in the area and will soon have a permanent place to live, I think I'll go Harley shopping."

They were currently both staying in Fletch's house for two reasons. The first being the pool so Cami could swim daily. The second was Murphy. Fletch's house was bigger than Crew's condo, plus it had a fenced yard.

Getting Cami a permanent place to live was something Crew needed to work on. Because as soon as he pulled Fletch and Wilder from their undercover assignment—which could be any day now—Fletch would want to sleep in his own bed.

He'd want to share that bed with Wilder, not with Crew and Cami.

It was past time to start looking for a bigger place for the both of them. One with a backyard and maybe even a pool. Between their two salaries, they shouldn't have a problem finding the right place.

"Or... You can continue to ride with me," he suggested.

"Or I can get my own."

"Or you can just ride with me," he insisted. "How about we compromise? You can ride with me until you get your own. You'll also need to take a course first. Get your permit. Practice. You don't just buy a bike, hop on it and go." Did he sound discouraging? Because he was doing his damnedest to do so.

"I'm aware of that."

"The truth is, I like having you on the back of my bike. I like having your arms wrapped around me. Is that so bad?"

"*Aw.* Look at you being sweet and everything. Did that hurt? How's this for a compromise? I ride with you on club runs. But having my own Harley will also give me the option to ride by myself. Riding isn't only for pleasure, it's also a form of transportation."

"I'm aware of that," he echoed. "If you buy anything, you really should get a vehicle that will cut it in the snow. The Audi won't. A Harley definitely will not. One good snowstorm and you're stranded."

"Good point."

"I occasionally have one or two of those."

Finn approached where they waited in formation, interrupting the conversation he'd had with her several times already. "Hey, we're going to need that investment from you tomorrow."

"I'll get it to you."

Finn pointed a crooked grin at Cami. "Looking good, Cam-Shaft."

"You're looking mighty fine yourself, Prince Harry."

The woman now had a variety of nicknames like the rest of them. Despite not being an official member of the Blue Avengers.

Yet.

Regardless of the numerous times he'd expressed his displeasure of her getting her own ride, she was determined.

He would lose that battle but, truthfully, it was a loss he could live with. With the two of them having their own bikes, they could take his kids out on long runs as a family.

He was surprised by how fast Dylan and Chloé accepted Cami. Despite the garbage Sasha fed them about their age difference. She continually pressed the fact that Cami was closer in age to Chloé than Crew.

Luis Cabrera took note of that, too. Only he mentioned it once and then let it go. Unlike the Wicked Witch of Western Pennsylvania. She jumped on anything to make his life miserable or make him look bad. While he bit his fucking tongue until it was shredded and bloody.

He was pretty damn sure his kids liked Cami better than their own father.

Maybe she was much cooler than him.

Actually, she was.

But having her in his life was actually helping him reforge his relationship with his children. A result he hadn't expected. Maybe it was fact the kids could relate to Cami easier than their old man. She was a good bridge between the two generations.

"So, what investment is Finn talking about?" Cami asked as Finn wandered back to his bike and his woman.

"I told you... In Mel's new club, The Pink Pearl."

"Oh, you were serious about that?"

"Yeah. It's a good investment. You don't mind me becoming a silent partner, right?"

"I'd tell you if I did."

That was for damn sure. If the woman had an opinion, she did not hold it back.

"If we're lucky, it'll put The Peach Pit out of business," he continued. Even though the Demons were doing that perfectly fine on their own. The Pink Pearl might be the final death blow, if the feds didn't strike first.

"Indictments and arrests should put that club out of business. Both of them. The feds will probably seize all the businesses they've used for selling and distributing meth or laundering money."

"We can only hope. But we need to get this investigation to the finish line first."

"The wheels of justice move so fucking slow," she muttered.

"No shit. We only need those wheels to roll faster than the Russos." Because Crew expected shit to go sideways any day now. They were trying to tie all the loose ends as fast as possible.

The president of the Blue Avengers jogged over to them. "Hey, where's Nox?"

Good fucking question. Crew glanced around. "I don't know."

"You don't have him on any kind of special assignment for the task force, do you?" Axel Jamison's face was a mask of concern.

Crew's frown mirrored Jamison's. "No."

"Wasn't he supposed to be here?"

"I thought he was. Did you ask Pippi?" Crew asked him.

"Yeah, Finn hasn't heard from him."

What the actual fuck? "He lives on this fucking property. Did anyone check to see if his truck and bike are here?"

"I'll check," Jamison said.

Just as the BAMC prez was heading toward the side lot where Nox parked his vehicles, the rumble of another Harley coming through the open gate had them all turning their heads.

It was Nox.

And he was not alone.

———

Sign up for Jeanne's newsletter to learn about her upcoming releases, sales and more! http:// www.jeannestjames.com/newslettersignup

———

Beyond the Badge: Nox

This ride with the Blue Avengers MC ends with Bradley Lennox aka "Nox."

Nox is:
* Member of the Blue Avengers MC
* Police officer with the Shadow Valley PD
* Member of the Tri-State Federal Drug Task Force
* Widower
* Army Veteran

Heroine is:
* Single mother and widow
* Daughter of a member of an outlaw MC

Description coming soon!

Note: Beyond the Badge: Nox is the sixth and final book in the Blue Avengers MC series. It's HIGHLY recommended to read this six-book action/adventure series in order due to the continuing story arcs (subplots). However, each book focuses on a different couple who gets their HEA. This series has no cheating or relationship cliffhangers.

The adventures with the Blue Avengers MC and the Tri-State Drug Task Force continue in Beyond the Badge: Nox (Blue Avengers MC, book 6) Turn the page to read the prologue

Beyond the Badge: Nox
(Unedited)
Prologue

A POUNDING on his apartment door had Nox cursing under his breath.

"Nox," he heard yelled through it.

It sounded like Cross.

What the hell did he want?

Nox pulled in a breath and tamped down his annoyance. He loved his brothers, he'd do anything for them, so he wished he didn't get so fucking irritated when they tried to include him in shit.

Some days were worse than others. There was no rhyme or reason for it, but today was one of those days.

He'd even struggled with being up on the third floor with the task force and had headed down to his apartment earlier than he should have. If Crew had a problem with it, the task force leader knew where to find him.

Normally, Crew left him alone because Nox spent more than a normal amount of time upstairs working. Usually late at night when he couldn't sleep.

Or when he didn't want to sleep.

When he knew closing his eyes would be more difficult than trying to keep them open.

More pounding. "Nox! You in there?"

"For fuck's sake," he muttered, put down the biography he was reading, then forced himself to his feet and over to the door.

With his hand on the knob, he took a few seconds to brace himself before flipping the deadbolt and yanking open the door.

Aiden Cross, the Blue Avengers MC secretary and a Southern Allegheny Regional PD officer, stood before him with concern not very well hidden on his face. But that wasn't all...

He was nervous about something.

"Need you downstairs."

Dread filled Nox's chest. "Who does?"

"Jamison asked me to come get you for a quick meeting."

It had to be Blue Avenger business since the prez wasn't on the task force. But their club's meetings took time and effort to schedule since it was difficult to get all of them together with of their various work schedules. So, *yeah*, something was off with this whole thing. "About?"

Cross shifted from one foot to the other. "He didn't say. He just asked me to get you."

This was starting to smell like bullshit. "Everybody else here already?"

"Everybody who can be. We're just waiting on you."

"I must've missed the original memo," he said dryly since they did not schedule BAMC meetings on the fly. "You could've just texted me."

"I needed the exercise." Cross's Adam's apple jumped.

Nox wasn't liking this.

Not at fucking all.

Cross tipped his head and turned. "C'mon. Let's go before we're late."

"Cross," Nox started with a warning in his voice, but the man was already jogging down the steps.

Setting his jaw, he stepped out and locked the door behind him.

He paused on the second floor landing and stared down at Cross now waiting at the bottom. Sucking on his teeth, Nox slowly followed.

Every step he took down the stairs felt weighted. As if he were wearing cement blocks instead of boots.

When he got to the bottom, Cross opened the door and waved him inside.

He met the man's eyes for a moment, took a breath and then walked through the BAMC's meeting room. The only way to get into their church besides the rear entrance.

Two ways in.

Two ways to escape.

With Cross close on his heels, Nox stepped out of the room where the executive committee met and into the clubhouse's common area.

There he stopped short and took all of them in.

Grim expressions. Nervous gestures. Perched stiffly on the three couches and some chairs set around that sitting area.

All eyes turned toward him.

This was not a goddamn BAMC meeting. "What the fuck is this?"

Cross was suddenly crowding him and pressing a firm hand to his back, urging, "Go have a seat."

Nox's nostrils flared and his jaw flexed. "No. We had no meeting scheduled so I don't know what the fuck this is."

When he turned, Cross quickly blocked him from going out the same way they came in.

He spun on his heels and was about to head toward the back door when, just quickly, Decker was there, blocking his path.

"Get out of my way, brother," Nox warned just loud enough for Decker to hear. "Don't fucking do this."

Decker lips pressed together so tightly they were nothing but a slash.

Nox's heartbeat thumped in his ears. "Deck..."

"Have a seat," Jamison called out.

With a glance over his shoulder, Nox saw the club president pointing to the only empty spot on the center couch. The middle cushion, of course, so he'd be flanked by two of his brothers.

"Is this task force business?" he asked Crew, not bothering to mask the betrayal in his voice. He already knew it wasn't because only BAMC members were in the room, but he was looking for any way to stall what was about to come next.

The task force leader answered, "No, but you still answer to me."

"Not off the clock," Nox reminded him.

Before Crew could respond, Jamison rose from his seat. "If you want to be that way, you do answer to me. I'm not only your sergeant at SVPD, I'm your prez." He jabbed a finger toward the couch. "Now sit the fuck down."

Nox's spine snapped straight and his chin lifted with defiance. "You can't force me to do shit." He turned again only to find himself toe-to-toe with Cross. "Get the fuck out of my way." His fingers curled into fists, an automatic reaction to the flight or flight instinct and no one was letting him leave.

Cross shook his head. "No, brother, I'm not going to do that."

"Nox," Jamison called out. "Do us a favor and give us a few minutes of your times. That's all we're asking."

"You're not asking. You're telling. I don't like being ambushed."

"And we don't like having to ambush you," Crew insisted.

"But you did it anyway."

Finn threw his hands up. "Because we had no choice! C'mon, man, just sit so we can get this over with."

"You're family and we all love you like a brother, and you have us all worried," North said next.

Nox pulled at his chin and let his gaze circle the group. "What's this about?"

He knew. He fucking *knew*.

"Sit and we'll explain," Jamison urged. "If you want to keep your job at SVPD and also stay on the task force," Nox did not miss him and Crew exchanging glances, "you need to sit."

"What are you going to do, fire me?"

"I'll put you on administrative leave," Jamison threatened, "and if you're on that, you'll be automatically removed from the task force."

Jesus fucking Christ. If he lost his job and was also removed from the task force, he'd have nothing left to keep his mind busy.

His own brothers were hobbling him. "For my own good, right?"

Did he sound bitter? *Yeah well*, he was fucking more than bitter.

"Yes, Nox, for your own good," Jamison answered. "Now, don't make me do shit I don't want to do."

"Then, don't."

Pinching his nose, Crew dropped his head. Without warning, the man surged to his feet and yelled, "You're off the task force!" The room went dead silent at that outburst. He glared at Nox as he spat out, "You made your choice, now you have to live with it. You can go back to SVPD and working patrol."

"No, he won't." Jamison shook his head. "Like I said, with the way he is right now, I'll be talking to the Captain. He won't be on patrol, either."

Nox's gaze bounced from Crew to Jamison, before it dropped to his boots. He pulled in a deep breath, held it and after a few moments, finally released it.

He needed to go.

He needed to get the fuck out of that room.

He masked his expression when he lifted his head and considered them all.

Everyone in that room loved him like family. They cared about him. They were worried about him.

That was cemented when Rez said softly, "We love you, brother. If you love us, then you'll hear us out."

Fuck.

His heart knew they cared about him, but his brain was still screaming at him to escape.

His heart and mind warred with each other.

The bottom line was, he needed his job, he needed the task force, and he needed his brotherhood.

The last being the most important.

He'd be nowhere right now without them.

With a single nod, Nox went over and sat in the spot where Jamison had pointed.

Avoiding everyone's eyes, he stared straight ahead at the wall. "Let's get this over with."

"You've fallen down that deep, dark well again," Jamison started.

Nox's brow furrowed. "I'm fine."

"You were getting to that point," Rez agreed. "Until we found Sadie. Something triggered you when we did."

A switch flipped inside him when he saw Sloane's sister was nothing but a cold, defiled corpse on that bed. Even though he knew the woman had been dead long before her last breath.

She had given up. She had let her addiction rule her life.

No differently than Nox giving up and letting his grief rule his.

It smothered him like a weighted blanket he couldn't shake free.

"We can guess what," Decker added, "so we don't need to discuss those details, but we do need to discuss you."

He definitely didn't want to relive the moment when he stared into that motel room in Ohio.

"I'm fine," Nox repeated, trying to stay focused on the blank screen of the TV, instead.

"I wish that was true."

When he heard Crew's agonized whisper behind him, Nox yanked his baseball cap even lower to hide any reaction.

Cross spoke next. "We're here for you. No matter how bad it gets. But none of us have the skill or experience needed to truly help you."

"I'm fine."

"Christ almighty!" Crew barked, making Nox jolt in his seat. "You're not. Did you forget we knew you before..." The man blew out a breath and continued, "We knew you when you *were* fine. You are far from that now, brother. You can keep saying that, but it's all bullshit."

The view of the TV disappeared when someone stepped in front of him.

A hand appeared before his face. In Jamison's hand was a business card and a pamphlet. "Take them."

Nox wouldn't take them because he wanted the info, he would take them simply to get this shit over with.

He quickly scanned them both.

One was a business card to a cognitive behavioral therapist, the other for a grief support group. Not the same group he had attended right after Jackie's death.

Thank fuck. He had hated that group and he was never going back.

The group leader had constantly urged Nox to "get in touch with his feelings."

That was impossible because, at the time, Nox didn't have any. He'd been nothing but a hollow shell.

This pamphlet was for a group specifically for spouses and loved ones of law enforcement and military, whether lost in the line of duty or not.

Nox asked, "I get to pick?"

"No," Jamison answered. "You're going to do both."

He squeezed his eyes shut, fighting the urge to argue. They weren't doing this to hurt him. They were doing this to help.

As he stared at the back of his closed eyelids, he relived something that had stuck with him.

A conversation that took place on the day of Sadie Parrish's funeral.

Right after the graveside service, Nox had picked up Val, Decker's four-year-old, and set her on his hip to carry her back to the line-up of parked vehicles.

Valee Girl had wrapped her arms tightly around his neck

and pressed her forehead against the side of his head. "Uncle Nox?"

Her soft, cautious whisper got him right in the chest. "Yeah, baby?"

"Why are you so sad?"

"Today's a sad day."

"But... you're always sad."

Jesus.

"Daddy says it's 'cause of Aunt Jackie."

Your Daddy isn't wrong. "Do you remember her?"

"A little bit."

"What do you remember?"

"I remember her sneakin' me a lollipop after Daddy said I couldn't have one."

At the time, Nox had closed his eyes and swallowed down the uncomfortable lump wedged in his throat.

That lump had returned and no amount of swallowing could get rid of it.

When he finally opened his eyes, he looked directly at Jamison.

He gave the man a single nod and an, "Okay."

Get it here: Beyond the Badge: Nox (Blue Avengers MC, book 6)

If You Enjoyed This Book

Thank you for reading Beyond the Badge: Rez. If you enjoyed Rez and Sapphire's story, please consider leaving a review at your favorite retailer and/or Goodreads to let other readers know. Reviews are always appreciated and just a few words can help an independent author like me tremendously!

Want to read a sample of my work? Download a sampler book here: BookHip.com/MTQQKK

Also by Jeanne St. James

Find my complete reading order here:

https://www.jeannestjames.com/reading-order

Standalone Books:

Made Maleen: A Modern Twist on a Fairy Tale

Damaged

Rip Cord: The Complete Trilogy

Everything About You (A Second Chance Gay Romance)

Reigniting Chase (An M/M Standalone)

Brothers in Blue Series

A four-book series based around three brothers who are small-town cops and former Marines

The Dare Ménage Series

A six-book MMF, interracial ménage series

The Obsessed Novellas

A collection of five standalone BDSM novellas

Down & Dirty: Dirty Angels MC®

A ten-book motorcycle club series

Guts & Glory: In the Shadows Security

A six-book former special forces series

(A spin-off of the Dirty Angels MC)

Blood & Bones: Blood Fury MC®

A twelve-book motorcycle club series

Motorcycle Club Crossovers:

Crossing the Line: A DAMC/Blue Avengers MC Crossover

Magnum: A Dark Knights MC/Dirty Angels MC Crossover

Crash: A Dirty Angels MC/Blood Fury MC Crossover

Beyond the Badge: Blue Avengers MC™

A six-book law enforcement/motorcycle club series

COMING SOON!

Double D Ranch (An MMF Ménage Series)

Dirty Angels MC®: The Next Generation

WRITING AS J.J. MASTERS:

The Royal Alpha Series

A five-book gay mpreg shifter series

About the Author

JEANNE ST. JAMES is a USA Today, Amazon and international bestselling romance author who loves writing about strong women and alpha males. She was only thirteen when she first started writing. Her first published piece was an erotic short story in Playgirl magazine. She then went on to publish her first romance novel in 2009. She is now an author of over sixty contemporary romances. She writes M/F, M/M, and M/M/F ménages, including interracial romance. She also writes M/M paranormal romance under the name: J.J. Masters.

Want to read a sample of her work? Download a sampler book here: BookHip.com/MTQQKK

To keep up with her busy release schedule check her website at www.jeannestjames.com or sign up for her newsletter: http://www.jeannestjames.com/newslettersignup

www.jeannestjames.com
jeanne@jeannestjames.com

Newsletter: http://www.jeannestjames.com/newslettersignup
Jeanne's Down & Dirty Book Crew: https://www.facebook.com/groups/JeannesReviewCrew/

TikTok: https://www.tiktok.com/@jeannestjames

f facebook.com/JeanneStJamesAuthor

instagram.com/JeanneStJames

BB bookbub.com/authors/jeanne-st-james

g goodreads.com/JeanneStJames

pinterest.com/JeanneStJames

Get a FREE Sampler Book

This book contains the first chapter of a variety of my books. This will give you a taste of the type of books I write and if you enjoy the first chapter, I hope you'll be interested in reading the rest of the book.

Each book I list in the sampler will include the description of the book, the genre, and the first chapter, along with links to find out more. I hope you find a book you will enjoy curling up with!

Get it here: BookHip.com/MTQQKK

Printed in Great Britain
by Amazon

32670724R10249